Modern Literature of the Gulf

Studies in Oriental Culture and Literature

Edited by Barbara Michalak-Pikulska

Volume 2

Barbara Michalak-Pikulska

Modern Literature of the Gulf

PL ACADEMIC RESEARCH

Bibliographic Information published by the Deutsche Nationalbibliothek
The Deutsche Nationalbibliothek lists this publication in
the Deutsche Nationalbibliografie; detailed bibliographic
data is available in the internet at http://dnb.d-nb.de.

This publication has been financially supported
by the Institute of Oriental Studies
of the Jagiellonian University in Kraków.

Library of Congress Cataloging-in-Publication Data
Names: Michalak-Pikulska, Barbara, editor.
Title: Modern literature of the Gulf / [edited by] Barbara Michalak-Pikulska.
Description: Frankfurt ; New York : Peter Lang, 2016. | In Arabic with
  introduction in English.
Identifiers: LCCN 2015049146 | ISBN 9783631665640
Subjects: LCSH: Short stories, Arabic--Arabian Peninsula. | Arabic
  fiction--21st century.
Classification: LCC PJ8000.8 .M74 2016 | DDC 892.7/30108953--dc23 LC record
available at http://lccn.loc.gov/2015049146

ISSN 2191-3269
ISBN 978-3-631-66564-0 (Print)
E-ISBN 978-3-653-05961-8 (E-Book)
DOI 10.3726/978-3-653-05961-8
© Peter Lang GmbH
Internationaler Verlag der Wissenschaften
Frankfurt am Main 2016
All rights reserved.
PL Academic Research is an Imprint of Peter Lang GmbH.

Peter Lang – Frankfurt am Main · Bern · Bruxelles · New York ·
Oxford · Warszawa · Wien

This publication has been peer reviewed.

www.peterlang.com

Contents

Foreword

The present book has appeared as a response of the interest in the contemporary Works of the writers of the Gulf countries: The Kingdom of Saudi Arabia, The Kingdom of Bahrain, The United Arab Emirates, Sultanate of Oman, State of Kuwait and State of Qatar.

In the study preceding the selection of texts I described the beginnings of the development of the press which played an important and influential role in the creation of short story writing. I tried to present as well the range of problems that appear in the literature of the region together with examples of short stories.

In the presented outline of this young and unknown literature reference is however made to history as well as the rate of the social, political and cultural changes taking place in these countries since without this knowledge a full understanding of the significance of their works would be impossible. The aim is simple to present an outline of Contemporary short story writing in the region of the Gulf.

The selection of Authors and short stories has been extremely problematic. The writers presented are individuals who I have come to know personally along with their literary output during many years spent in Kuwait and the possibilities this afforded me to travel to other countries of the Gulf.

In the countries of the Gulf writers expressed to a greater or lesser degree an interest in the promotion of their works in the world. They have given me their book and interviews which explains the more numerous and broader works in the present book.

The book contains a selection of texts available neither in Europe nor in the majority of Arab countries. This is a result of the fact that the publishing market in the Gulf countries differs from that of the remaining Arab countries in as far as the writers themselves publish their own books which in accordance with popularity appear in the book shops of the given country. As a result of the relatively limited quantity of published works these writers are not as known as widely read Egyptian or Syrian authors. Therefore in a lot of cases there is a need to make direct contact with the writers themselves which is no simple matter for an orientalist considering the difficulties associated with travel in these countries. Therefore the assembled material presented in the book is unique and innovatory.

The selected works have intentionally not been translated or annotated to allow each reader the chance for independent analysis and interpretation. My work is an attempt to assemble in a single book texts and information on the subject of Modern short story writing in the Gulf countries.

Krakow, January 2016   Barbara Michalak-Pikulska

Introduction

A new, modern literature is being created in the countries of the Gulf: Saudi Arabia, Kuwait, Bahrain, slightly later in the United Arab Emirates, Oman and Qatar, under the clear influence of contacts with Arab countries like Egypt, the Lebanon or Syria, together with contacts with Europe. Its origins go back more or less to the 1930s, when the Arabs in those countries were trying to gain independence.[1] Despite the fact that the cultural and literary revival in particular countries did not take the same route, it did have common elements such as the sense of unity of old culture and language.[2]

An extremely important factor in influencing the development of contemporary Arab literature in the countries of the Gulf was to be the numerous contacts with Europe. The manifestations of these contacts were varied: the sending of Arabs to Europe to acquaint them with modern civilisation, or religious mission activities, which set up their educational and scientific centres. Besides, the countries also started to organise primary and higher education.

In Saudi Arabia education was already in the process of development under King ʿAbd Al-Azīz Al Saʿūd. On the tenth of November 1957 the first university was founded in Riyadh.[3]

In Bahrain the school system had already started to develop by 1919.[4] In Kuwait the first school Al-Mubārakiyya was founded in 1912, and the university only in 1965.[5]

---

1 Saudi Arabia gained independence in 1932, Kuwait in 1961, Bahrain, Qatar, Oman and the United Arab Emirates in 1971.

2 Muḥammad Ṭālib Ad-Dwīk, *Al-qiṣṣa al-qaṣīra fī Qaṭar* (The Short Story in Qatar) in: ***Al-Adab***, Beirut 1989, nos. 2–3, p. 147,

3 compare *"**This is our country**"* a prospectus issued by the Ministry of Information, Kingdom of Saudi Arabia, Riyadh, N.D., pp. 48–49,

4 Manṣūr Muḥammad Sarḥān, ***Wāqʿ al-ḥaraka al-fikriyya fī Al-Baḥrayn 1940–1990*** (The Realism of the Intellectual Movement in Bahrain 1940–1990), Manama 1993 p. 114,

5 Dr Muḥammad Ḥasan ʿAbd Allah, ***Al-ḥaraka al-adabiyya wa al-fikriyya fī Al-Kuwayt*** (The Literary and Intellectual Movement in Kuwait), Kuwait 1973, p. 134,

As far as the United Arab Emirates are concerned at the moment independence was gained there were in the region of 60 schools. The Al-ʿAyn University campus was founded in 1977.[6]

In Qatar the Ministry of Education was set up in 1956 before the country gained independence. Qatar University was founded in 1973.[7] And finally the Sultan Qaboos University in Muscat was founded in 1986.

The alumni and the graduates from those newly organised schools and universities constituted the seeds of the first intelligentsia in this area. Young people gathered at Literary Clubs and wrote for the arising and developing newspapers and magazines. It should be stressed that it was journalism that played a particularly important role in the development of short narrational forms - which were, and still are the literary lifeblood of the Gulf region. The editors of these newspapers and magazines were very often authors themselves, and so propagated the short story, which in concentrating on one event seemed to be the most proper means of addressing specific social problems. Equally the writers themselves felt more comfortable following directly through them the quick changes occurring in the country and society, without loosing currentness.

The first newspaper to appear in 1908 on the market in Hijaz was the weekly *Al-Ḥijāz* published in two languages: Arabic and Turkish. The newspaper *Al-Qiblah*, the first edition of which appeared in 1916, played an important role in literary life there. From 1924 the newspaper *Umm al-qurā* was published, which fulfilled the function of an official state paper in Saudi Arabia. Articles devoted to literature were also published in it. Subsequently other titles started to appear: from 1931 *Ṣawt Al-Ḥijāz*, on whose pages the works of debut writers were published. In 1936 there arose the first literary journal *Al-Manhal*, and *Jarīda al-Madīna* which was founded in 1936 also published short stories. It was right on the pages of *Ṣawt Al-Ḥijāz* that the short story *Al-ibn al-ʿaq* (The Disobedient Son) written by ʿAzīz Ḍiyāʾ was published in 1938. This is a depressing tale of a son who decides to leave his poisonous and invasive mother.

During the course of the Second World War the Saudi press stopped publishing. Its activities were renewed after the end of hostilities. On the market during the 1960s, besides the old titles there appeared the new ones: *Akhbār Aẓ-Ẓahrān*, *Al-Fajr al-jadīd*, *Al-Aḍwāʾ*, *Al-Khalīj al-ʿArabī* and *Quraysh*. It is worth emphasising that the period from 1945 to 1964 was unusually profitable

---

6   *The United Arab Emirates 1993*, prospectus published by the Ministry of Information and Culture, Abu Dhabi 1993, p. 100,

7   *Qatar Year Book 1994–1995*, prospectus issued by The Ministry of Information and Culture, Doha 1996, p. 69

for the development of literature in Saudi Arabia. After 1964 on the pages of the press literary cultural subjects gave way to information from the world of politics and economics.[8]

As far as Kuwait is concerned the first journal appeared on the 20th November 1928 and was called *Al-Kuwayt*. It was printed in Iraq and its publisher was the writer and historian 'Abd Al-Azīz Ar-Rashīd. The journal was a monthly of a religious, literary and historical character. It was on its pages in 1929 that Khālid Al-Faraj published the first Kuwaiti short story entitled *Munīra* (Munira). In the short story the heroine on her family's advice marries her cousin. She is, however, unhappy because she can not have children. This results in her personal value crisis as a woman and a member of Arab society. Tragedy is furthered by her husband's constant complaints about the absence of an heir. Munira driven to despair resorts to various methods, consulting with magicians and giving into their spells. These people use her however and psychologically and physically ruined she commits suicide.

The next journal *Al-Kāẓima* came into being in 1948 and was printed in Kuwait. It had an already mature literary, scientific and social profile confronting as things happened with the activities of Kuwaiti writers. Next to appear were journals like: the weekly *Al-Fukāha* founded by the writer Farḥān Rāshid Farḥān in 1950 and the monthly *Ar-Rā'id* in 1952. Currently literary subjects are discussed within the pages of *Al-Bayān*, the organ of the Kuwait Writers' Union.[9]

In Bahrain, as in other countries of the Gulf, the press has played an important role in the development of prose. Among the titles worthy of mention are to be found: the newspaper *Al-Baḥrayn*, where next to the political and economic news are published poetry and literary articles. It was on its pages that Muḥammad Yūsuf published the first Bahraini short stories e.g.: *Ḥā'ira* (The Distressed One), *Ash-shā'ir* (The Poet) or *Bayna sāriq wa bakhīl* (Between a Miser and a Thief). Later appeared the subsequent titles: *Al-Qāfila*, *Al-Waṭan* and *Ṣawt Al-Baḥrayn*. An important stage in the development of Bahraini literature was the creation in the 1960s of the literary journal *Al-Aḍwā'*.[10]

---

8   compare Saḥmī Mājid Al-Hājirī, *Al-qiṣṣa al-qaṣīra fī Al-Mamlakat Al-'Arabiyya As-Sa'ūdiyya*, (The Short Story in Saudi Arabia), Riyadh 1987, pp. 51–66,

9   compare Dr Muḥammad Ḥasan 'Abd Allah, op., cit. pp. 181–250,

10 compare 'Abd Al-Qādir 'Aqīl, *Lamḥa mūjaza 'an al- qiṣṣa al-qaṣīra fī Al-Baḥrayn* (A short Outline of the History of the Short Story in Bahrain), in: *Al-Adāb*, Beirut 1989, nos. 2–3, pp. 154–157,

In Qatar the first short narrational forms were to be found in the magazines: *Ad-Dūḥa*, *Al-'Ahd* and *Al-'Urūba*.[11] In Oman there are such titles as: daily *'Umān*, *Ash-Shabība* or the cultural-literary journal *Nizwā*.

The first literary attempts by the young generation of United Arab Emirates writers were published within the pages of the journals: *An-Naṣr*, *Az-Zamālik*, *Ash-Shabāb* and *Al-Ahlī*. In the 1980s appeared the daily *Al-Ittiḥād*, the weekly *Akhbār Dubaī* and the monthly *Al-Majma'*. The author of the first short story entitled *Qulūb lā tarḥam* (Merciless Hearts), which appeared at the end of the 1960s was 'Abd Allah Ṣaqr Aḥmad.[12]

The first attempts at prose met in time a rising level of social consciousness. Thus, short stories were able to certify social injustice, they also were able to show the author's attitude towards reality, as his voice represented the hidden drama of the members of Arab society, particularly that of women. Those initial short stories concentrated round the dramatic conflict-ridden social reality. The development of action was clearly foreseeable from the outset, because of the fossilised structure and unchanging mechanisms of Arab society depicted. The realistic presentation of the world was accompanied by the underdeveloped form of the story. The authors tried to show some social tragedy, which was the effect of the backwardness, miscomprehension or underdevelopment of the Arab world. Short stories depicted chiefly mere facts and events. Slowly, however, many writers, as a consequence of widened horizons and reading introduced new techniques of depicting the world portrayed, and enriched their adroitness in writing with new means of expression. Besides the dry, meaningless storytelling, there appears regressiveness to the past as a means of portraying contemporary problems. The differences between the time of action and the age, as well as the social position of the characters deepen, which is used to show social and personal view differences resulting from the changes brought about by the times.

An important moment in the cultural life of the Gulf was the establishment of Literary Clubs - it was here that discussions on cultural and literary problems were conducted. In Saudi Arabia it being **Al-Jama'iyya al-'arabiyya as-sa'ūdiyya li-l-thaqāfa wa al-funūn**, in Kuwait **Ar-Rābiṭa al-Udabā'**, in Bahrain **Usra Al-Udabā' wa Al-Kuttāb**, in the United Arab Emirates **Ittiḥād Kuttāb wa Udabā' Al-Imārāt, an-Nādī ath-Thaqāfī** in Muscat.

---

11   compare Muḥammad Ṭālib Ad-Dwīk, op.cit., p. 149,

12   compare *Multaqā al-awwal lilkitābāt al-qaṣṣaṣiyya wa ar-riwāiyya fī dawla al-imārāt al-muttaḥida* (Proceedings from the First Meeting of Writers of Short Stories and Novels in the United Arab Emirates), Sharjah 1989, pp. 11–22,

The mission of the contemporary Arab writer was stated by Dhū-Nūn Ayyūb in the introduction to the first collection of short stories from 1937, entitled ***Rusūl ath-thaqāfa*** (The Messengers of Culture): „The most important duty for writers is to present pictures that are faithful to what they see: the events, characters, social systems, national laws and folk traditions, which are not written down but obeyed by society. They should criticize, not fearing the consequences, the backward systems, cruel traditions and customs, and at the same time uncover and analyse their reasons and basis."

The short story developed in the new Arab literature of the Gulf after poetry. As far as the problems are concerned those traditional topics depicting the amazing past of these countries, society and family relations were joined by new ones characteristic for the Gulf. The main ones being the discovery of the crude oil and the subsequent economic boom, political, social and cultural changes, the inflow of a large number of immigrants, the place of man from the Gulf Region in contemporary Arab and world society, or freeing from old alliances: the sea and the desert.

The most graceful subject of the stories is love: often filled with the aroma of folklore and enshrouded with mystery. The younger generation of authors frequently consciously relates in their works to the tradition of the desert. In the new form the motif of romantic love of the Udhra tribe from the Hijaz desert, is constantly repeated. At present this subject is often related to the strict norms of traditional social divisions, concerning both equally men and women. At the beginnings the dramas of alienation and cruelty were never talked about, but later they started to awaken social attention and interest.

The female problem in Saudi prose takes up a lot of room. The writers presented portraits of mother, mother-in-law, wife, sister, divorcee or widow. They wrote about her problems connected not solely with a good marriage, but also her limited educational possibilities. Interesting works devoted to this problem include Muḥammad Amīn Yaḥyā's short stories: *I'tirāf* (Confession) or *Al-'Īd* (Holiday).[13] The case of egoism relating to the marriage of daughters is well illustrated by the short story *Al-Mutarahhiba* (The Nun) by Muḥammad 'Alī Maghribī.[14] In another story entitled *Al-muṭallaqa* (The Divorcee) Sa'd Al-Bawārdī shows a woman hurt

---

13 Muḥammad Amīn Yaḥyā was born in 1342 h (1923/24). He gained his legal papers at the 'Ayn Shams University in Cairo. His literary work has been published in Saudi newspapers and journals. (from: Saḥmī Mājid Al-Hājirī, op.cit., pp. 159–184),

14 Muḥammad 'Alī Maghribī born in Jadda in 1332 h (1913/14). He finished the Al-Falāḥ school in Jaddah. He worked for press organs in Mecca. He has printed poetry, short stories and critical-literary articles within the pages of literary journals and newspapers. (from: Saḥmī Mājid Al-Hājirī, op.cit., pp. 184–209),

by fate, and forced into a marriage with a man whose only attribute is money. In the works by Halīl Al-Fazī' entitled: **Az-zawja ath-thāniyya** (The Second Wife) and **Al-jidār al-khashabī** (Wooden Walls) the women represent different psychological types, and have originated from different social backgrounds. They are sensitive women, with broad imaginations and a sensitive reception of the surrounding world. In contemporary Saudi literature women also spoke out on the subjects directly concerning them. Here should be mentioned, among others, Jamīla Fatānī and her collection of short stories entitled **Al-intiṣār 'alā al-mustaḥīl** (Victory), Ruqayya Ash-Shabīb and her collection **Hilm** (The Dream) and Fāṭima Al-'Utaybī and her interesting collection entitled **Iḥtifāl bi 'anni imra'a** (I Celebrate for I am a Woman). In many families there still took place the old way of treating a woman like an object; women who were barely able to lead their own lives as they had no way out of the trap. This is why they revolted so often, and were even able to kill to get freedom and dignity back as is shown in the story of the Kuwaiti writer Laylā Al-'Uthmān[15] entitled *Min milaff imra'a* (From the Diary of a Woman).

Laylā Al-'Uthmān devotes many of her works to women.[16] Her heroines are not only young imprisoned by their families or forced to share intimate relations with men despised chosen by their families. There appears also in her works women-mothers presented here in a surprisingly negative way, who mercilessly invade their daughters' private lives and are the pillars of the opportunism there present, e.g. in the short story *Al-qalb wa rā'iḥat al-khubz al-maḥrūq* (Heart and the Smell of Fresh Bread). In Thurayyā Al-Baqṣamī short stories[17] from the collection **As-Sidra** (Lotus) the heroines do not agree with the fate allotted them, and do not obey the dogma of a woman's total dependence on man. They often rebel, each in her own way, according to her temperament and existential dignity. The short story *Yā al-mashmūm* (Musk) shows the tragedy of the right to a free choice of partner which deepens consciousness of the unavoidable character of the relationship forced by contracts and financial relations, as a result of which daughters were simply sold by their families. An important place in Kuwaiti women's literature is

---

15 Laylā Al-'Uthmān born in Kuwait in 1945.

16 collections of short stories **Imra'a fī ina'** (The Trapped Woman) Kuwait 1977, **Ar-Raḥīl** (Departure) Beirut 1979, **Al-ḥubb lahu ṣuwar** (Images of Love) Kuwait 1982, **Fathiyya takhtār mawtahā** (Fathiyya Chooses her Death) Cairo 1987; novels: **Wasmiyya takhruj min al-baḥr** (Wasmiyya Comes Out of the Sea) Kuwait 1987, **Al-mar'a wa al-qiṭṭa** (The Woman and the Cat) Beirut 1985,

17 Thurayyā Al-Baqṣamī born in Kuwait in 1952 is a well-known contemporary writer and painter. She studied at the Collage of Fine Art in Cairo, and then graduated from the Surikov Institute of Art in Moscow.

14

occupied by Laylā Muḥammad Ṣāliḥ's collection of short stories entitled *Jirāḥ fī al-'uyūn* (Wounds in the Eyes). It tells of the internal experience of a contemporary Arab woman and her possibilities in society. Her second collection entitled *Liqā' fī mawsim al-ward* (Meeting in a Season of Flowers) expresses the painful recollections from the period of Iraqi occupation. The short stories undertake the subject of war and love in war conditions and their participation in the resistance movement.

In Bahrain female topics have been dealt with by, among others: Muḥammad Al-Mājid in the short story *Jarīma fī ḥayy majhūl* (Crime in an Unknown District), Hidāya Sulṭān As-Sālim in the short story *Lan takrah al-fajr* (You Are Not Going to Hate the Morn) as well as Fawziyya Rashīd in the collection *Marāyā aẓ-ẓull wa al-faraḥ* (Reflections of Sadness and Joy) and Munīra Al-Fāḍil in the collection *Ar-Rīmūrā* (Rimura).

The heroines of the short stories *Bidāya aṭ-ṭarīq* (The Beginning of the Road) or *Khawāṭir fatāt ṣaghīra* (Danger Threatens the Young Girl) written by Qatari authors Maryam Muḥammad 'Abd Allah and Amīna Ismā'īl Al-Anṣārī respectively, are never indifferent or bored although almost always torn by conflicting feelings and unease. Their drama chiefly results from personal entanglement in the conflicts with the dogmatism of the traditional structures of Arab society.

Equally young Emirate literature adds its output to the subject matter of unwanted marriages which are to be found in the short stories entitled: *Bushrā fī as-sittīn* (Bushra is Sixty) written by 'Abd Ar-Riḍā As-Sajwānī and *Al-'Urs* (Weddings) by Salmā Maṭar Yūsuf. Salmā Yūsuf's work deals mainly with woman and their daily problems. She tries to show in her works that a woman does not selflessly follow the will of others. The woman is forced to act so by fear or necessity as can be seen in the short story *'Ushba* (Herb), which is the story of a neglected orphan brought up by an uncle in order to receive in the future a good dowry.

Omani writers: Fāṭima Sha'bān, Khawla aẓ-Ẓāhirī, Ṭāhira bint 'Abd al-Khāliq al-Lawātī, Bushrā Khalfān al-Wahaybī tackle a great variety of themes in their output, and the central characters are mainly women and children. They discuss the problem of equal rights for men and women, both in the general social sphere as well as referring to their own love life.

The prose works of writers, both male and female, of the countries of the Gulf bring the world of Arab women closer to us, as well as directly the surroundings presenting before one's eyes the rich panorama of genre custom scenes. All of them try to grasp a fragment of the passing reality and that just arriving. In their works one can see generally two bases in relation to the past: the basis which demands changes in the name of essential progress as well as the basis of reflection, melancholy and sometimes remorse for the former, simple way of life.

The Saudi writer Ibrāhīm An-Nāṣir in the collection *Al-Arḍ bilā maṭar* (The Land without Rain) sketches interesting pictures from the lives of the inhabitants of Saudi Arabia, particularly his native Najd. He devotes his works to the conflicts between traditional customs and the reality of present time and the desire for happiness for the younger generation, which extends beyond the borders of the desert villages. The young men manage to reach the oil regions, work and earn there, since the moment of oil's discovery became a real turning point not only in the field of economics but equally in the field of culture. The authors of the short stories became witnesses to the social and cultural changes.

The discovery of oil caused a sudden influx of foreign capital and traders, the intensified construction of new districts and exchange of information. The newly created social classes brought about an undermining of many traditional concepts. The mature generation of grandfathers and fathers still held on tightly to traditions and religion, but the generation of educated sons were open to progress and civilisation.[18] Besides, the discovery of oil caused huge changes in the traditional social structure. Citizens were faced with a fiscal-social conflict. Besides which there took place a conflict between the values which were in force prior to the discovery of oil and those associated with the new era.

In the literary output of Gulf writers short stories slowly stopped being a passive relation of events illustrating traditional social life and gradually and consciously started to examine the problems of man and his place in the contemporary world. This only deepens the range of the short story as well as equally varying the time of action, the social and individual roles of the heroes' attitudes to all the changes that are being brought in with the times. Accompanying the development of the quickly erected rich new districts there is a mixture of feelings among the older inhabitants. This is illustrated by the short story *Al-hājis wa al-ḥuṭām* (Phantoms and Ruins) by the Kuwaiti writer Sulaymān Ash-Shaṭṭī,[19] in which the hero - an old bricklayer observes the demolition of old houses which he himself once built. In their place new buildings are being put up which reflect by their size and abundance society's new wealth. This builder observing this feels sadness and pain. At the same time there develop in him strange feelings that together with the destruction of the last house so too his life will end. Another short story by the same author entitled *Wajhān fī 'atma* (Two Faces in the Darkness) shows another valued profession in Gulf countries - that of a trader. The hero is the representative

---

18 compare Barbara Michalak, Innovatory trends in the Modern Kuwaiti short story, Warszawa: *Majalla ad-dirāsāt al-'arabiyya wa al-islāmiyya*, No 2, 1994, pp. 23–28,

19 Sulaymān Ash-Shaṭṭī, born in Kuwait in 1943. He is a writer, literary critic and doctor at Kuwait University,

of a backward form of trade without agreements. He is connected to his job not only economically but also emotionally. However, the climate of the old bazaar and trade is disappearing in these countries day by day.

The problems of people who have come from the country to the town together with the problems brought connected with this are shown in Muḥammad Al-Yaḥyā'ī's collection entitled *Kharzat al-mashī* (Talisman). He clearly shows the difficulty the inhabitants of the country encounter in trying to adapt to life in the town. Often the price was too high and the weaker individuals were forced to return. His stories are filled with sad irony and compassion for simple people who are unable to find their place in the new reality.

At the basis of the literature of the Gulf lies respect for one's past, a desire to continue tradition, but after its application to new contents and functions. Hence contemporariness is characterised by a fierce conflict between riches and the access to luxuries and possibilities of world travel associated with it, and traditional culture, which is constantly the basic factor that causes inhabitants of the Gulf to feel a degree of dissimilarity in relation to other Arab countries. The story *'Āshiq al-baḥr* (The Sea's Lover) by Ibrāhīm Mubārak from the United Arab Emirates, is filled with an enormous yearning for the past. It tells of the life of a diver who has to give up his beloved sea. The romanticism of the story awakens in the reader a longing for former traditions and the climate of the Orient: the sea, tents, narrow streets, little cafes, traditional bazaars and earthen clay buildings. The present as understood by Emirate writers is a period of social, political and economic changes that have yet to take on a final form. The Emirate writer Sa'īd Al-Ḥankī in the short story *Humūm al-muwaṭin S* (The Worries of Citizen S) shows us the unhealthy state of relations between people: falseness, superficiality and hypocrisy which has taken over the newly rich society of the Gulf. "The author in this story has included a message for the old and young generation. He considers that a lot of time will be needed for the generations to come closer to each other and to understand each other mutually as long as they are divided by a ravine."[20] Muḥammad Amīn Yaḥyyā in the short story *Al-Wafā'* (Faithfulness) touches on the problem of friendship and shows its consequences. The writer in his work accentuates some noble features such as friendship and faithfulness which serve

---

20 Dr. Diyā' Aṣ-Ṣadīqī, Al-bī'a al-maḥalliya fī al-qiṣṣa al-qaṣīra fī Al-Imārāt (The Local Environment in the Emirate Short Story), in: *Abḥāth al-multaqā ath-thanī lilkitābāt al-qaṣaṣiyya wa ar-riwā'iyya fī dawla Al-Imārāt Al-'Arabiyya Al-Muttaḥida* (Proceedings from the Second Meeting of Short Story and Novel Writers in the United Arab Emirates), part I, Sharjah 1989, pp. 191–192,

to bring closer the features of the society of the town of Jaddah, thanks to which he gained the nickname Al-Jaddī (inhabitant of Jaddah).

Finally the discovery of oil changed and divided society in the Gulf countries, which had lived until then through fishing and the pearl trade. The generation of fathers and grandfathers based on the traditional model of living took pride in the customs and traditions prior to the economic boom. The young generation of sons and grandsons, brought up in the prosperity is set for the quickest possible profit and ease. The most important for it is the achievement of a high material standard. The Emirate writer Amīna ʿAbd Allah Būshhān considers such behaviour as a disease which day by day infects an increasing number of people. She describes this in the short story entitled *Ẓahīra ḥāmīya* (High Noon). Omani writer Suʿūd al-Muẓaffar in his first collection od short stories **Yawm qabla shurūq ash-shams** (The day before the sunrise) talks about social relations and general situation in Oman prior to the government of Sultan Qaboos. This is conveyed by the very title of the collection. The brief short story *Ḥayāt rubbamā ḥadītha* (Modern Life Can?) touches upon important problems for Omani society. Here is the element of emigration, as well as the ongoing westernization, which the author perceives in the way young people feed themselves on hamburgers, steaks and spaghetti. Equally certain generational conflicts are revealed; the lack of understanding between young generation derived from mass culture and the generation of the fathers who are attached to their Arab roots.

The inhabitants of the Gulf understand that they have to introduce certain changes in social and family relations, while at the same time they are consistent in many areas, like in dressing habits. They are afraid of the loss of their own identity as well as the rupture of existing social relations that would lead to a situation where connections were solely based on business and money. "The authors of the short stories (…) have tried to look at the past from the angle of linking it to the present, while at the same time taking all that is the best from the past and supplementing the present with it."[21]

The newly rich society of the Gulf came across equally the problem of the influx of large numbers of foreigners who came to work bringing with them other languages, cultures and religions. "Following the discovery of oil the Arabian Peninsula became a region to which people came from all over the world in order to find work. They came to build new states. They brought with themselves their customs, ways of thinking, ways of dress and many other strange things unknown

---

21 Walīd Abū Bakr, *Aṣ-ṣawt ath-thānī fī al-qiṣṣa al-kuwaytiyya* (A Second Voice in the Kuwaiti Short Story), Kuwait 1985, p. 27,

before in the countries of the Gulf. Arab society was enriched by new experiences, while at the same time causing many political and social problems. There started to appear class differences between employer and employee."[22]

The short story *Ṭufūla wa ḥulm al-qabīla* (Childhood and Tribal Dreams) by the Emirate writer Su'ad Al-'Arīmī is a protest against the throwing off of tradition. It shows the life of a man in the new social reality together with the daily choices he must make connected with it. The hero moves from the country to the town where he finds work in one of the government institutions. His new surroundings mean that he has to change his previous life, habits, way of dressing and utterance. He has to also get use to total subordinance in relation to superiors, accepting their niggling and cynical comments and orders. He was even forced to shave off his beard, which in his traditional surroundings was a symbol of masculinity. The acceptance of a new style and new reality turned out to be beyond his resilience and led to his committing suicide. This act is an expression of the condemnation of this new reality as well as the casting off of the new social relations and principles based on material gain and hypocrisy. The arbitrariness of the relations between employee and employer is shown by the short story *Wisām sharaf* (The Order of honour) by the Emirate writer Muḥammad Ḥasan Al-Ḥarbī. He presents the nature of the new work relations where greed and using the other person hold sway. The hero spent the best years of his life in a factory where he was given the sack when he started to sicken. This sad story ends with the death of the hero at the plant in full view of his work colleagues.

The literary output of the Gulf that concerns immigrants is small when one considers that they make up the majority of the Gulf's population. The indigenous inhabitants try to isolate themselves from the new comers, especially from Asian countries. One example could be the Kuwaiti writer Walīd Ar-Rujayyib's short story entitled *Ta'luq nuqṭa tasquṭ... ṭaq* (The Drop Rises and Falls...Drip, Drip) in which the hero arriving illegally to his dreamt of Kuwait - the place full of dreams of fortunes. However after a few weeks he undergoes a psychological crisis for he realises the impossibility of achieving his desires. Finally he accepts his fate as somebody condemned to menial work which will bring neither money nor guarantee a quick return home. In other stories Walīd Ar-Rujayyib describes „normal" citizens who lose the sense in life as a result of the injustice of relations between employers and employees - who on the whole are exploited

---

22 Nūriyya Ar-Rūmī, Al-qiṣṣa al-qaṣīra fī al-khalīj al-'arabī wa al-jazīra al-'arabiyya (Short Stories in Countries of the Arabian Gulf and Arabian Peninsula), **Al-Fuṣūl** (Cairo) No 4, July-August-September 1982, pp. 252–253,

and preoccupied by work which barely guarantees them a vegetating existence.[23]
The problem of disillusioned and disappointed immigrants is continued by the
Kuwaiti writer Fahd Ad-Duwayrī in the short story *Rajul al-fundūq* (The Man
from the Hotel) in which the hero breaks down because of lack of work and
takes to stealing in order to survive. Laylā Al-ʿUthmān's story entitled *Nashāṭ
tajassusī* (Spy Acts) also deals with this subject matter telling of the bitter fate
of those lonely, weak and exploited immigrants, whose share becomes finally a
premature - often by unknown hands - death. The above mentioned short stories
deal with the always actual problem of credulous immigrants, who believe in the
possibility of becoming rich quickly, and what often leads to a destruction of
health and financial ruin for them and their families.

Short stories devoted to servants are to be found only in the output of writers
of Gulf countries. Their heroes are ordinary Indian or Asian servants. This subject
was the outcome of the huge influx of labour force from poor Asian countries
with the aim of making money. The writers in their works showed the problems
connected with their presence in Arab houses. The greatest writers' concern was
immense and long term influence on the up-bringing of children. Servants were
usually of a different faith, spoke in a different and poor language as well as represented different traditions. Besides which the servants knew the secrets of their
masters and mistresses or were intertwined in personal relations with their employers. It is worth remembering here the works of Kuwaiti authors: the short
story *Munā 13* (Muna 13) by Ismāʿil Fahd Ismāʿil or *Ṭufūlatī al-ukhrā* (My Second
Childhood) by Laylā Al-ʿUthmān. In the story *Munā 13*, a poor girl servant is
used by the rich master. The employer's wife starts to be jealous and accuses her
of being late home because of flirting with traders. This was put the husband off
the girl, but the effect is the reverse and the husband all the more is fascinated.
As a result of her severe protest because of fear of the wife the servant rejects the
master's advances, who in an act of revenge cuts off her long hair - the symbol of
femininity. Sulaymān Al-Khulayfī's short story entitled *Yaʾkulūna ʿalā sufra sākhina*
(They Eat at a Warm Table) concerns the touchy subject of romances with servants.
This subject becomes especially painful when the witnesses to such situations are
innocent children.

The young generation of Arabs from the Gulf tries to free itself of two elements:
the sea and the desert - being their time immemorial natural life environments.

---

23 Walīd Ar-Rujayyib - short stories: *Al-furṣa al-ūlā... akhīra* (The Only Occasion), *Wa
al-insān lā yasman* (And the Man still Doesn't Get Fat), *Man afragh qāʿ al-jasad al-
marʿuq min al-milḥ?* (Who sucked out the Salt from that Wasted Body).

20

The sea was, is and will be a great might for them. Extremely many references to the sea as to everyday reality can be found particularly in works of literature in which the subject of old Kuwait is voiced. The sea then was the main motor of life providing food, employment, recreation, freedom, hope and a subject for a story. In the short stories the sea does not appear purely in a descriptive form, but appears as the all present backcloth for the life of fishermen, pearl divers, smugglers, travellers or women doing their housework, playing with children and those they love. From this period come the colourful stories about fantastic phantoms and unusual phenomena accompanying the element, which are recorded in the short stories.[24]

In the short stories of the Kuwaiti writer Laylā Al-'Uthmān, the sea is the fundamental element of dependence, identification and love for the fatherland. In the short story *Zahra tadkhul al-ḥayy* (Zahra Conquers the Village) the heroine adds to the suffering and alienation of the resident, autonomous population the subject of whose envious feelings becomes the sea - the constant companion and partners of the inhabitants loves and lives. The sea fulfils an important function in her novel *Wasmiyya takhruj min al-baḥr* (Wasmiya Comes out of the Sea) where the drama of unrequited love is collaborated by the heroine's suicide in the sea. In turn in Thurayyā Al-Baqṣamī's short story *Ad-dumya* (The Doll) the sea and its scenery are places of everyday women's work.

The sea for the inhabitants of the Gulf plays a fundamental role in the direct context, for not only do they love it but equally have total faith in it. Daily contact means that their experiences are directed towards it, the generous provider and uncompromising opponent. All human matters of life and death were saturated with its presence. Such an image of the sea is emphasised by the Bahrainian writers: 'Alī Sayyār in the stories: *As-Sayyid* (Master) or *Al-maʿraka* (The Fight), and 'Isā Rāshid Al-Khalīfa in the short story *An-Nawkhidha Aḥmad* (Captain Ahmad).

Equally Emirate writers have not neglected the subject of the sea. 'Abd Al-Azīz Ash-Sharhān in the story *Ash-Shaqā* (Pains) shows a student studying abroad and his yearning for the sea. The work of fishermen and their daily painful labour of the haul are presented in 'Ali Muḥammad Rāshid's short story entitled *Rijāl fī miḥna* (Men in Unhappiness). Saʿīd Sālim Al-Ḥankī's short story *Ilā 'Abd Allah Aṣ-Ṣaghīr... waṣīya* (Advice for Little 'Abd Allah) is filled with descriptions of children's games at the seaside as well as the customs of the inhabitants. In the novel entitled **As-sayf wa az-zahra** (Sword and Flower) by 'Ali Abū Ar-Rīsh

---

24 compare Barbara Michalak-Pikulska, *The Contemporary Kuwaiti Short Story in Peace Time and War 1929–1995*, Kraków 1998, pp. 69–74,

the sea is depicted in the context of the influx of illegal immigrants. The author opened a broad discussion on the difficult subject of the influx of illegal labour to the Emirates.

The desert is not a favourite literary subject even though it is after all the natural environment for the life of the Arabs of the Gulf. The Bedouins and their attempts to find their place in contemporary, modern society is described in the short story entitled *Abū 'Arab* (Abu 'Arab) or *'Araq wa ṭīn* (Sweat and Clay) by the Saudi writer 'Abd Ar-Raḥman Ash-Shā'ir.

An important theme that appears on the pages of literature is the problem of the so-called *bidūn* or people without citizenship. The most numerous being the Bedouin who free for centuries did not want register, and at the same time belonged to a definite state from the very beginning. At present the young generation accuses the government of not informing their uneducated fathers of the need to register, to possess identity cards and the consequences that result from not fulfilling these conditions. By the end of the 1980s the United Arab Emirates and Saudi Arabia had dealt with these problems.[25] In Kuwait the problem continues to remain unsolved.[26] Many writers belong to the so-called *bidūn*, even though they were born in Kuwait. Today they are refused citizenship for various reasons even though they are involved in raising the culture of their country. Among them one should mention Ṭālib Ar-Rifā'ī, Laylā Muḥammad Ṣāliḥ, Sa'diyya Mifraḥ, Nāṣir Az-Ẓafirī, 'Alī Al-Mas'ūdī, Jāsim Muḥammad Ash-Shamrī. Despite their lack of Kuwaiti citizenship they feel themselves Kuwaiti, and have no intention of leaving the land of their fathers. This problem - unique on a world scale - has found its reflection in the literature of the countries of the Gulf, as equally among writers without citizenship as those with. And so, for example, Jāsim Muḥammad Ash-Shamrī in the short story *Al-alam…al-amal wa antunna* (Pain…Hope and You) condoles with the minimal chances for the *bidūns* in the new order that exists in Kuwait post Iraqi invasion. A painful admission also shows itself in another of his short stories *Isa'idtum bi-ish'āl al-'ilm* (The Nipping of Education in the Bud), in which the festivities associated with

---

25 Andzej Kapiszewski, **Native Arab Population and Foreign Workers in the Gulf States**, Kraków 1999, pp. 67–77,

26 Official sources do not give the present figures for the number of people without citizenship in Kuwait. The last time there were taken into consideration was in the 1975 census with the figure being a mere 168. It is difficult therefore to understand where the present figure of 116,694. Before the Iraqi invasion of the 2nd August 1990 there were 219,942 of them (from: Khālid Ar-Rāshid, **Qabas** newspaper, Kuwait, 24 April 1993, edition 7134, p. 1),

the start of the school year following liberation are described. Children lacking citizenship are not admitted to the jollity. The author demands universal access to education. In turn the Kuwaiti writer Munā Ash-Shāfaʿī joins the struggle of women without citizenship in the short story *Usṭūra* (Legend) where the heroine not possessing citizenship opposes her mother who is persuading her to marry a Kuwaiti in order solely to secure citizenship. The heroine yearns to have her own because she loves the fatherland in which she was born and brought up, and is unable to understand why the land doesn't want her.

This problem area has equally found its reflection in the short story *Al-Baydār* (The Threshing Floor) by the Emirate writer ʿAbd Al-Ḥamīd Aḥmad. The hero is here an Omani, who came to the Emirates in his youth. He worked on the date palm plantations, but with the changes he lost his job. In the course of these thirty years he did not think of sorting out an identity card, and when he wanted to return home he was not allowed in. Driven to extremes he commits suicide.

In connection with the existence of a new economic and political situation the authors of short stories adopted a penetration of the social relationships in force within the family. They demanded a reduction in paternal authority in favour of all members of the family and analysed the reasons for women's subservience to men. "One could say that the writers (…) took upon themselves the burden of responsibility for the changes which came into society (…), and which were caused by sudden and quick material changes."[27]

The works of the pioneers in short story writing dealt, chiefly, with the realistic portrayal of the social state of things, in part still traditionally understanding life's sense as well as the status of individual family members along with individual and collective attitudes concerning the existing problems. For strength, wealth, good social position and an influential family is expected of men. While from women; total servitude, the conscientious fulfilment of domestic duties as well as the possibility of numerous offspring. In other words to support an image of a wife and mother as was confirmed by the words of the Prophet Mohammed "(she) should delight in his eyes when he looks at her, be obedient when he orders and never challenge her husband when he decides for her and for himself."[28] If one of those elements disappoints then society uncompromisingly and brutally reacts throwing such a unit to the margins of social life, often pushing towards

---

27 Walīd Abū Bakr, op.cit., pp. 5–6,
28 from: Wiebke Walther, **Kobieta w Islamie** (The Woman in Islam), Warsaw 1982, pp. 35–36,

death, as is the case in the first Kuwaiti short story *Munīra* (Munira) by Khālid Al-Faraj.[29]

Much has been written about paternal authority which was indisputable. Immediately behind it came the authority of the oldest son and then only the mother, who introduced into the family chaos as well as being the reason for argument and many personal problems particularly in relation to daughters. In Saudi literature this subject is realised in the short story *Hayba amal* (Disillusionment) by Ibrāhīm An-Nāṣir, as well as in short stories: *Al-ḥubb lā yakfī* (Love is Not Enough) and *Al-ukht al-Wasṭā* (Sister Wasta) by Muḥammad 'Isā Al-Mashhadī. In Bahrain 'Alī Sayyār has written on this subject in the work *Shams lā tushriq kulla yawm* (The Sun Doesn't Rise Every Day). The subject matter of a mother's authority appears in the short stories of the Kuwaiti woman writer Laylā Al-'Uthmān with unusual frequency. The mothers mercilessly interfere in the private life of their daughters, pulling them by the hair, beating, causing scenes and going through their things in order to find proof of forbidden rendezvous, e.g. in the short stories *Al-qalb wa rā'iḥat al-hubz al-maḥrūq* (Heart and the Smell of Baked Bread) or *Al-awrām* (The Swelling). In Qatar the greatest room for the subjects of authority has been devoted by Khalīl Al-Fazī'. In his story *Al-Kalimāt al-'āriya* (Naked Words) author describes the grasping and toxic love of a mother for her son and the attempt to take control of him and impose her will on him. Another of his short stories entitled *Al-hudū' aṣ-ṣākhib* (The Lord's Silence) presents the opposition of the son to his father's will. Finally the authority and place of the oldest son finds expression in the short story *Al-fash adh-dharī'* (The Great Defeat). The matter of authority became one of the most important subjects in the countries of the Gulf. The authors tried to depict this problem in a civilized way presenting in their short stories heroes not only negative but also positive who can be met daily on the street.[30]

The authors of the short stories demand equal access to culture and education, as equally for men as women. Internal family structures change and with them the reduction in authority: paternal, of the eldest brother and maternal. Social differences of course still exist, but slowly the heroes and heroines of the short stories

---

29 The short story entitled *Munīra* by Khālid Al-Faraj is the first to be written not only in Kuwait but in the entire Arabian Gulf. It was published in the journal **Al-Kuwayt**, in edition 6–7, November December 1929 (from: Khālid Sa'ud Az-Zayd, **Qiṣaṣ yatīma fī al-majallāt al-kuwaytiyya 1929–1955** (Orphaned Short Stories in Kuwaiti Journals 1929–1955), Kuwait 1982, p. 33),

30 compare: Nūriyya Ar-Rūmī, **Al-qiṣṣa al-qaṣīra fī al:khalij al-'arabī wa al-jazīra al-'arabiyya** (The Short Story in Countries of the Arabian Gulf and Arabian Peninsula) op.cit., pp. 246–247,

gain consciousness of the new situation and either revolt or search for possibilities of fulfilling many of their dreams and expectations. In many works appear the problems of emancipated consciousness, which starts to triumph over the barriers of sex. This subject can be found e.g. in the short story entitled *Khawṭāir fatāt ṣaghīra* (Danger Threatening a Young Girl) by the Qatari writer Amīna Ismāʿīl Al-Anṣārī, or in the work of the Kuwaiti Laylā Al-ʿUthmān entitled *Imraʾa fī ināʾ* (The Trapped Woman).

The authors of the short stories start to ask about the place and social role of a woman, who all the more often is taking up professional employment. In the short story by the Kuwaiti writer Thurayyā Al-Baqṣamī entitled *Buqʿa lawn* (The Coloured Stain) the heroine is a woman - an artist freed from the traditional roles of wife and mother, she stands facing the new problem which is the artist's calling and consciousness. Often it is a dangerous partner as is emphasized by Laylā Al-ʿUthmān's short story entitled *At-timthāl* (The Sculpture), which offers the reflection that even a calling is unable to bring an Arab woman happiness. For the sculptress achieves her mastery at the price of her health, and finally life. The crowning of this theme could be the work by the Kuwaiti Munā Ash-Shāfaʿī entitled *Ḥālat haṣṣa* (Special State), in which the emancipated consciousness of the heroine is presented overcoming the barriers of sex. The appearance of this new type of female-artist heroine, an educated partner loving and understanding her husband is an usually revolutionary angle of the approaching modern times. Love equally is slowly not prohibited, since the partners equally value it. Thurayyā Al-Baqṣamī from Kuwait as pronounced as follows on the subject: "Now everything depends on people. Each lives as he feels fit, while society has now no right to interfere, as once it did when ever it felt like it.'[31]

Descent and inheritance played an important role in social relations. A superb illustration of which is the short story entitled *ʿAwdat Saʿīd* (Saʿid's Return) from the pen of Muḥammad ʿĀlim Al-Afghānī,[32] who as an immigrant in Saudi Arabia had the particular right to broach such subject matter.

The drama of social differences was felt by children as we can observe in the short stories entitled: *Ad-dumya* (The Doll) and *Tawāṣul* (Continuity) by the Kuwaiti writers: Thurayyā Al-Baqṣamī and Walīd Ar-Rujayyib respectively. In

---

31 interview conducted by Barbara Michalak-Pikulska with Thurayyā Al-Baqṣamī, Kuwait 28th October 1994,

32 Muḥammad ʿĀlim Al-Afghānī - born in Pakistan. He was employed in Medina. He wrote short stories for the journal **Al-Manhal, Ṣawt Al-Hijāz**. He worked in education and diplomacy. He stopped writing after 1950 (from: Saḥmī Mājid Al-Hājirī, op.cit., pp. 146–147),

another work of Walīd Ar-Rujayyib entitled *Nujūm aqal... nujūm akthar* (The Star the Lesser ... the Star the Greater) the author compares social relations current in the armed forces where the holding of office expands not only one's administrative competency, but allows disturbance of one's private life. The writer emphasizes the fact that the post occupied is often abused and used in social relations. Wamḍa Amal's short story *Al-fā'iḍ* (Excess) presents the class conflict between the rich and the poor, which is an obstacle in the union of two lovers: a rich young girl and her impoverished cousin.

In the United Arab Emirates the woman writer Amīna ʿAbd Allah Būshhān described the force of money in the work *Mahra* (The Mare), in which the inhabitants of a small, poor village sanction and agree to the conditions of a rich sheikh Sulaymān who marries their daughters in turn only to discard them after a few months.

The short stories from the Gulf loyally accompany the changes in social relations. Their authors in presenting concrete examples from the reality, which surrounds them, desire to inform and teach society subtly. This is clear in the marriage ceremonies: resounding from the selection of sweetheart through the engagement to the very day of the wedding. Before, however, marriage vows are taken the whole process is accompanied by numerous frauds brought about by the means of matchmakers. The matchmakers often in their mission were frauds in their exaggeration of facts about the future spouses, which resulted in many family conflicts. This has its reflection in Thurayyā Al-Baqṣamī's short story entitled *ʿArūs al-qamar* (A Fiancée like the Moon), where the matchmaker heavily exaggerates in his description of the wealth and possessions of the groom arousing with this the fears of the bride who is in awe of such a perfect husband.

In the story *at-Taqālīd* (Tradition) ʿAlī al-Kalbānī concentrates upon the dependence of Arab women upon men and traditional forms of life. For a European reader the action of the story seems to be comical. It begins on Friday evening when Muhammad recalls his sweetheart of long ago. As a result of a series of coincidences he happened to meet the next day the child of his former beloved Zaynab and recognizing the child he takes it to its desperate mother. During the time that she is thanking him her husband returns and accuses her of betrayal and the whole matter finishes up in court. Forced by her husband, Zaynab accuses her benefactor, who is sentenced to several months' imprisonment. He sits out his sentence until the day when the repentant woman admits to lying in court. The heroine, with unexpected bravery, blames the tradition and customs to which she was brought up and which led to her personal tragedy and to which, as one can easily imagine, many other women are partly.

The imposition of marriage traditions is still one of the greatest problems in countries of the Arabian Gulf. Young people have to marry to strengthen blood ties and for purely material motives. Besides which it remains one of the only ways of impressing with one's wealth. The short story by the Kuwaiti writer Sulaymān Al-Khulayfī entitled *Zawāj* (Marriage) presents money as the purchasing force in the fiancée stakes. A rich merchant marries a girl chosen also by his nephew for himself, whose love was unable to surmount his uncle's riches. Writers covered also the subject of the possibilities of mixed marriages as is shown by the short story entitled *Lā khabar lā…* (No, no there's no news) by the Kuwaiti writer Laylā Al-ʿUthmān or by the other entitled *Bushrā fī sittīn* (Bushra is Sixty) by the Emirate writer ʿAbd Ar-Riḍā As-Sajwānī.

The writers did not avoid embarrassing subjects like marital betrayal. In traditional Arab society this problem belonged to the range of taboo subjects and could not see the light of day. In Gulf society of present day, short stories described betrayals or their attempts, and their authors attempted to analyse their causes as equally on the part of men as women. Female betrayal was something new. Up until then it was only the man who did the betraying. Betrayal on the part of women was the means of blaming tradition for unfair treatment. The authors discovered therefore the reasons that pushed one to betrayal as well as the void which surrounded and in which one was forced to live. We can find an unusual form of betrayal in Sulaymān Al-Khulayfī's short story entitled *Ya'kulūna 'alā sufra sākhina* (They Eat at a Warm Table), where the husband and wife mutually betray each other for each of them feels the void. They have affairs with the staff. The author follows the romances of the master of the house with an Indian serving girl and his wife with the chauffeur. Eventually matters come to a head with the discovery of the affairs by the young daughter who is a witness to her parents' doings. In turn the Saudi writer Ḥamīd Ad-Damanhīrī in the novel **Thaman at-taḍhiya** (The Victim's Price) presents the story of a young Saudi married to his cousin who is sent to study in Cairo. There he strikes up a close acquaintance with an Egyptian girl though ultimately despite emotional involvement he splits up with her and returns to his wife. This self same subject matter is to be found in the Qatari short story entitled *Safā't ar-rūḥ* (Purity of Soul) by Nāṣir Ṣāliḥ Al-Faḍāl. The hero of this story leaves for Europe to study and there falls in love with a European girl yet when he finds out that she has had other relationship returns to his beloved from Qatar.

One of the most recent problems that have occurred together with the economic development of the countries of the Gulf was the taking up of employment by women. This was a completely new situation and initially unacceptable. However with the passing of time an increasing number of women decided on employment outside of the home. Many of them started to educate themselves and fight for social position. This subject is effectively dealt with in Kuwait by Laylā Al-'Uthmān for example in the title story from the collection *Imra'a fī ināʾ* (The Trapped Woman), where a young university graduate seeking her independence is portrayed. Equally the heroine of the short story *At-timthāl* (Sculpture) is totally independent and emancipated. In Saudi Arabia this subject has been dealt with by Muḥammad Al-Mirbātī in the short story *Al-'Āmila* (The Employee) as well as by 'Abd As-Salām Hāshim Ḥāfiẓ in the story *Lahā māḍin* (The Woman with a Past). In the latter erotic scenes dominate. In Qatar the woman writer Maryam Muḥammad 'Abd Allah is noted for this subject matter, especially with the short story *Bidāya aṭ-ṭarīq* (The Beginning of the Way). The heroine decisively refuses to marry her cousin simply because tradition deems it so. The author is clearly on the side of the girl emphasising how many families have split up due to the unsuitability of the spouses. A day in the life of a young female Qatari student is described in the short story *Al-huwa* (The Abyss) by Nūra Muḥammad As-Sa'd and Salmā Maṭar Yūsuf from the United Arab Emirates in the short story *Az-Zahra* (Flower) shows how important a role a woman plays in the life of a man. The hero of the work on the basis of a relationship with a woman discovers a new, different world, which was earlier unknown to him. The life of his partner intrigued him to the point whereby he attempts to think in her categories, to get to know more deeper her life situation, as well as all the social conditioning which limits her freedom. This author presents equally a woman discarded by society in the short story *An-Nashīd* (Hymn). The heroine is here a beautiful woman, who through her appearance, behaviour and personal charm attempts to capture men's hearts. She uses her body as bait to take her revenge on men for treating women as objects.

In the literature of the Gulf we can equally observe the commitment of writers to the problems of struggles for self-determination as well as Arab unity. An important and often undertaken theme is that of the Palestinians. In Saudi Arabia Sa'd Al-Bawāridī has written the collection *Shabaḥ al-Filasṭīn* (The Spectre of Palestine). Equally the heroes of the short story *Ummuhātunā wa an-niḍāl* (Our Mothers and Struggle) by Ibrāhīm An-Naṣīr sign up as volunteers in order to defend Egypt during the Anglo-French-Israeli aggression. *Al-baṭal Ibrāhīm* (Ibrahim the Hero) by Ḥasan 'Abd Allah Al-Quraysh is the story of a pupil planning to study medicine. Fate has it, however, differently planned, for the hero joins the army to die defending Palestine.

The struggle of the Omanis against Portuguese rule is illustrated by the short story *'Azzān* by Ḥamad Rashīd bin Rāshid. The story begins with a description of nature that is characteristic for Ḥamad's work. In this landscape we are shown a march of armed people going to meet the enemy. They are proudly bade farewell by women and other man. The author has endowed his young hero with courage, loyalty to himself, and the fatherland, God and the determination necessary to realize the task. Finally, his young life is cut short by death. At the time of his death his mother gives birth to his brother. The death of the main hero is therethore changed into new life. So the continuity of generations is preserved in order for there to be someone to defend the beloved fatherland.

In Kuwait, long before the Iraqi aggression in 1990, subjects concerned with aggression and conspiracy had been embarked upon by Laylā Al-ʿUthmān. One should here mention the symbolic short story *An-naml al-ashqar* (Red Ants), which was as if a prophetic vision of the invasion which was to come. Another of Laylā Al-ʿUthmān's short stories entitled *Al-ḥasharāt* (Bugs) is a timeless and universal tale of patriotism. The author's attitude is unequivocal. She believes that all Arab countries are one body and the creation of any divisions is criminal, so all forms of aggression and family separation with the actual view of the perspective of the dependent peace of humanity from its dawn.

The Palestinian subject often appears in Emirate literature too, for example in the short story *Hadhā al-wajh laysa lī* (That Face is not Mine) by Suʿād Al-ʿArīmī. The writer also examines the theme of the Iran-Iraq war in the short story *Baqāyā damm* (The Remains of the Blood). The Palestinian problem is presented in an extremely interesting way against the backcloth of the conflicts of the Arab world in the short story *Safar al-asfār* (The Journey's Journey). The main hero travels from one Arab country to another in search of work. Eventually he achieves his aim and is employed as a night watchman in a twenty two-storey building. It is no coincidence that the building is twenty-two stories high. The same number as there are Arab countries. The author also deals with their problems and conflicts in order to eventually charge the Arab world with guilt for the tragedy of the Palestinian nation.

The dramatic events of the 2nd of August 1990 in Kuwait: the course of the war as well as its results became the basis for rich short story output. The majority of already active writers decided to give expression to the topic. Among them one should mention: Ismāʿīl Fahd Ismāʿīl,[33] Thurayyā Al-Baqṣamī,[34] Ḥamad

---

33 Ismāʿīl Fahd Ismāʿīl - author of the collection **Iḥdāthiyyāt zaman al-ʿazla** (Events from the Troubled Time), Kuwait 1996,

34 Thurayyā Al-Baqṣamī - author of the collections: **Shumūʿ as-sarādīb** (Cellar Candles), Kuwait 1992, **Raḥīl an-nawāfidh** (The Windows' Flight), Kuwait 1994,

Al-Ḥamad,[35] Walīd Ar-Rujayyib,[36] Munā Ash-Shāfaʿī[37] Laylā Muḥammad Ṣāliḥ[38] or Laylā Al-ʿUthmān.[39]

The first of the problems presented by the Kuwaiti writers, as an aim was the creation of wide war documentation. Looking at the literary output, which resulted as the reply to the war drama, we are able to compile almost chronologically the whole picture of the war with its beginning, course and joyful ending. The points and figures in the centre of attention differ. In the fates of the heroes' of the short stories we can see the whole cross section of social attitudes and behaviour whose personal story belongs to that general story of war.

Women devote the most space to the subject of beliefs, superstition and magic. This was connected with the frequent presence of women at home and their participation in acts of magic, palm reading or fortune telling from coffee grounds. The Kuwaiti Thurayyā Al-Baqṣamī's short stories from the collection *Al-ʿaraq al-aswad* (The Black Sweat) in portraying attitudes are rooted in the belief fully superstitious in demons, genies, evil spirits who disrupt life and are the cause of the unfortunate incidences. In one of the short stories from this collection, entitled *Umm Adam* (Umm Adam), the author presents people who believe in good and evil spirits. The heroine seems to be versed in the art of magic to the point where everyone starts to fear her, considering her at the same time to be a witch and finally killing her. Later it turns out that she was a useful and good old woman. We can equally find this sort of depiction in Ḥamad Al-Ḥamad's work in short stories such as: *Shabaḥ al-layl* (Night Spirit), *Manzyl al-jadīd* (The New House) or *Marzūq … marratan ukhrā*, (Marzuq Again). Among Laylā Al-ʿUthmān's short stories are several that refer to the fantastic area of the imagination including *Al-Jinniya* (Genie), which is an oneiric tale of a fantastic phantom which activates imagination and consciousness.

The current of symbolism all the more often appears in the prose of writers of the Gulf. The most numerous constitutes symbols as the carriers of meanings

---

35 Ḥamad Al-Ḥamad - author of the collection *Layālī al-jamr* (Sweltering Nights), Kuwait 1991,

36 Walīd Ar-Rujayyib - author of the collection *Ṭalqa fī ṣadr ash-shimāl* (A Shot in the Breast of the North), Beirut 1992,

37 Munā Ash-Shāfaʿī - author of the collection *Drāmā al-ḥawās* (The Drama of Senses), Kuwait 1995,

38 Laylā Muḥammad Ṣāliḥ - author of the collection *Liqāʾ fī mawsim al-ward* (Meeting in the Season of Flowers), Kuwait 1994,

39 Laylā Al-ʿUthmān - author of the collection *Al-ḥawājiz as-sawdāʾ* (Black Control Points), Kuwait 1994,

known from life, surroundings or one's own experiences, and particularly those resulting from a close relationship with nature. Manfred Lurker writes: "When we talk today about the literary symbol we get stuck constantly with Goethe (…), who notices a real symbol where it particularly represents the whole shape not as a dream or shadow but as life and the momentary manifestation of what is not banal."[40] In the next part of the argument he writes that: "the designatons of a symbol can be: the carrier of the meaning, a visual concept, comparison, personification, paradigm, pattern, type or even archetype, metaphor and allegory"[41]

The Saudi 'Abd Al-Quddūs Al-Anṣārī in the short story *Marham at-tanāsī* (The Forgetting Ointment) attempts to present his thoughts through the help of symbols e.g. the suitcase of worries is an inseparable part of the heart, while the forgetting ointment can be bought in the Hope Chemist's. The short story of the Qatari Nūra Muḥammad As-Sa'd entitled *Al-huwa* (The Abyss) is equally full of symbols, which require explanation and serve to express the fear of opposing social reality. In the Arab Emirates Laylā Aḥmad and her collection of short stories **Al-khayma, al-mahrajān, al-waṭan** (Tent, Festival, Fatherland) is considered to be a representative of the symbolic current. In the short story *Kanāra* (Canary) woman is a symbol of the fatherland. The Kuwaiti writers Thurayyā Al-Baqṣamī and Laylā Al-'Uthmān's work is also full of symbolism. In Thurayyā's prose symbols appear in the most varied of functions: obstruction, exposure, concentrating attention, constructing the correct mood, the attainment of the expression of truth. For example in the short story *Ṣurṣūr* (Cockroach) the insect appears in two roles: of a directly hideous impression as well as of oppressive fate. In turn in the short story *Buqa't lawn* (The Coloured Stain) the title stain means defeat and creative languor. In the title story from the collection **As-Sidra** (Lotus) the main symbol is a lotus tree, which for Muslims is the symbol of prosperity. They believe the lotus was the Prophet Mohammed's favourite tree. The often-repeating symbols in Laylā Al-'Uthmān's short stories are the sea or a cat. The cat means the appearance of something significant and changing e.g. in the short stories *Muḥākamatān* (Two Hearings), *'Ajūzān… lawḥa wa qiṭṭa* (Two Old People … a Picture and Cat…) and *Al-mawā'* (Miaowing). The symbolism concerning the sea and its element needs to be considered as a special group. The daily contact of the inhabitants of the Gulf with the sea meant that they directed in its direction the experiences of everyday. Laylā Al-'Uthmān portrays this in her short stories: *Riḥla as-sawā'id as-samrā'*

---

40 Manfred Lurker, **Przeslanie symboli w mitach, kulturach i religiach**, (The Transference of Symbols in Myths, Cultures and Religions) Kraków 1994, p. 103,

41 ibid., p. 27,

(The Wandering of the Dark Shoulders), *Zahra tadkhul al-ḥayy* (Zahra Conquers the Village) or *Fatḥiyya takhtār mawtahā* (Fathiyya Chooses her Death).

In summing up one needs to emphasise that the short story of countries of the Gulf is created in the classic literary language which has survived almost one and a half thousand years. Hence contemporary Arabic literature always maintains a tradition going back to the sixth century even when dealing with matters of the modern world. The common denominator in Gulf literature became the criticism of former traditions, the abuse of authority and paternal power against women and children. Besides which the writers record the quick social, economic, cultural and political changes taking place in Gulf countries.

An important factor in forging the unity of contemporary Arab Gulf literature are the close contacts and cultural exchange linking the creators of all countries. They have adopted the custom of organising cultural festivals, which give them the possibility of meeting and exchanging views. For these writers are envoys, mediators and translators of reality, spokesmen of creative thought and literary culture, regardless of the level of their works. They have brought and are bringing influence to bear on the attitude of postulating for the loosening of unconditional rights limiting man's freedom regardless of sex. The century old attitude of the poet - the defender of his tribe has been reborn in the figure of the contemporary writer involved in problems of nation and society.

إبراهيم مبارك ـ الامارات العربية المتحدة

شتاء

حرث البحر .. قبض على الماء .. حملته أمه في بطنها وبعد تسعة أشهر خرج كالسمكة ، فسبح في البحر .. احتضنته أصابع متشققة تبرز منها نتوءات الصخور الكبريتية من أثر حبال الشباك وخيوط الصيد ، عمدوه بقطرات مالحة من ماء المحيط ، فانفتح القلب كبوابة السماء الواسعة ، برق البحر في عينيه منذ اليوم الأول .. مرسوم طريقك ....

أيها الخارج من ظهر البؤس والفقر .. الماء أمامك وخلفك ، فاحرق العمر حتى يخرج من رماده الآخرون وتمتد الحياة ، ولتشعل أيامك شمعة حتى يهتدي للطريق من يسير .... بصقه المحيط في الخليج لتمتد صداقته مع البحر .

حقيبة صغيرة أعدتها زوجته .. وضعت بها بعض المأكولات الهندية وصورة صغيرة . وفي المساء حادثها بشكل جنوني ، كأن رغبة العمر كله تأتي في ليلة واحدة .

لم يشاهد في الخليج إلا طريقاً واحداً من المطار حتى كوخ خشبي بجوار ميناء صغير للصيادين . الشباك تمتد في كل مكان ورائحة الأسماك والبحر تنعش أنوف البحارة .. قوارب الصيد تحتل الميناء الصغير واليابسة ، وظهور الرجال أقواس نبال ، والأيادي أسهم تعالج الشباك المهترئة والممزقة .. فتح رئتيه واستنشق الهواء المحمل برائحة السمك .

– أبو بكر ، محيي الدين ، بابو رفاق عمل . على ظهر القارب ، قال ذلك خلفان صاحب قارب الصيد لكومار .. فابتسم .

الميناء حذوة حصان عجوز أفناه الدهر ، تطرزه القوارب ، وتسبح بقايا الأخشاب في أرجائه ، وتتناثر بقايا الأسماك الفاسدة على شواطئه وتختلط رائحة الزيت ، وعفونة الأسماك والطبخ المنبعث من أكواخ الصيادين والتبغ فيه .. وتدوي صرخات العائدين من أعماق البحر والراحلين إليه ، وهي تسحب القارب .. (يا الله .. يا حيل الله) .

تُنشر الشباك على الرمال الملتهبة ، لتشرب الماء ، بينما تحتل طيور البحر الصخور وكذلك السرطانات .

يعود منهكاً ، مكدوداً وتظل كالمنار تشعل الاحتراق بداخله .. عندما تأوي إلى ذاتك يوقظك صدى الذاكرة ، تتجسد في اللاشعور الرغبة والاشتياق لحضن امرأة ، تغسل غربتك وتروض جموحك .. أمام ناظريه وقفت قريته وامرأة .. كرجع الصدى يأتي صوتها من كهف أعماق :

– انتظر عودتك كالمطر ، واتنسم أخبارك كالهواء ..

يشعل المصباح ، ثم يكتب إليها رسالة طويلة .. افتقدتك ، بداخلي اشتعال حريق ، رأيت عينيك بالأمس تخرج من الشباك ، راقبت سمكة تسبح في الماء فخلتك تسبحين في دمي ، وعندما هبت نسمة عليلة أحسستك تغزين جسدي ثم تدمرينه وتلقين به كالرماد في محرقة الشوق .. أشتهي كرزات رائعة نبتت فوق ثغرك .. ما زال طعم جوز الهند ينساب في فمي ورائحة المانجا .. يا ثمرة جوز في قلبي .. الآن أسمع قطرات المطر تعانق سقف الكوخ ، أكاد أعد القطرات ، هذه بعضها ، تسقط بجوار سريري الخشبي من ثقب في سقف الكوخ ، ثم تقفز لتبلل أطراف دفتري ، ثم تتبعها قطرات أخرى .. هذه القطرات تشكل حفرة صغيرة في الأرض ، هكذا تحفرين قلبي الملتاع .

إنه الشتاء .. أتعلمين يا حبيبتي ما يفعله الشتاء بالرجال ؟!

أتذكرين يوماً كنت أطوقك بذراعي ثم ننظر لأسراب الطيور المهاجرة في السماء ؟

عندها قلت لك إنها تبحث عن الدفء .. هكذا الرجل أيضاً عندما يأتي الشتاء يكون أكثر شوقاً إلى الدفء .. انك تحتلين قلبي ، بينما أربض في الصقيع وتحتلني الصحراء .

هذا الخليج يبعث في قلبي الخوف والرعب ، بعد أن كان ينبوع عطاء فبالأمس لم يعد أعز أصدقائي بعد أن خرج للصيد ، واليوم أعلنت تمردي . فأنا أحبك وأخاف أن تلتهمني وحوش البحر والألغام .

يا قيثارة حبي .. سأعود إليك .

1988/02/29

اسماء الزرعوني ـ الامارات العربية المتحدة

عندما يموت الفرح

وقفت أمام خزانة ملابسها حائرة ، هل تلبس البدلة الرمادية أم فستان السهرة الوردي ؟ نسيت من فرحتها أن الوقت متأخر ، الواحدة بعد منتصف الليل .

هو أكد ذلك عندما اتصل بها بالأمس ، مكياج بسيط وقميص النوم الذي اشترته بالأمس جميل أسود ومطرز بالأحمر ، ألقت نظرة على صورته ، لا يزال الوقت طويلا ، نحن لا نزال في بداية النهار أخذت الصورة أمطرتها قبلات احتضنتها بقوة .. أتعرف أنك تسكن شواطئ قلبي ومجرى عروقي ؟ أتعرف أننا بالأمس أكملنا عامنا السابع من زواجنا ؟ لأوّل مرة تكون بعيدا عني .. لا أعرف كيف وافقتك على فكرة السفر بدوني ؟ كيف استطعت أن تبتعد عنا طوال شهر مرّ عليّ وكأنه دهر ، إنني اشتاق إليك وإلى أنفاسك ، كنت واثقة بأنني أحبك ، ولكن لم أتوقع إنني أسيرة هواك إلى درجة الجنون ! لا ألوم عبلة ولا ليلى عندما أحرقتهما لوعة الفراق .

نظرت إلى صورته بشوق ومحبة .. أتتذكر يا كل روحي ولهفة أيامي عندما جئت لخطبتي ؟ رفضت في البداية ، لأنني كنت أحلم بالدراسة ، ولم أخطط للزواج ، بعد ولكن عندما وقعت عيناي على عينيك غرقت ، ولم استطع أن أنتشل نفسي من هذا الغرق الجميل ، عشت كملكة فوق عرش قلبك .. اتجهت عيناها نحو الساعة ، تذمرت ، لماذا أنت بطيئة هذا اليوم ؟ لماذا تأبى عقاربك أن تجري لكي أكحّل عيني وأرسم بسمتي ، ويدق قلبي طرباً وعناقا بمن يسكن دنياي .

ها هو اليوم سيرجع أيضا ، قالتها وهي تقلّب صورته ، وتبعده عن وجهها .. ليتك تفعلها وتبقى هناك فأنت الآن لا تعنيني ، لقد مات الحب في عروقي وذاب الكحل في جفوني ، قتلت روحي المرحة في ذلك اليوم التعس عندما رفعت هاتفك النقال ، أجل لقد توقفت حروفي يومها وثبتت في ذاكرتي إعلان موت الفرح .

يومها كنت أتابع مسلسلا في التلفاز ،كانت الساعة تشير إلى الثانية عشرة بعد منتصف الليل جلست وحدي في الصالون بعد أن نام الأولاد ، ونام خالد ، سمعت صوت الهاتف يصرخ ، بحثت عن مصدر الصوت ، لا أعرف من أين يأتي هذا الصوت المزعج في سكون الليل ، الرنين يصر ويصرخ ، تسللت خارج الصالون ، اكتشفت أن الهاتف بداخل سيارة خالد وقد نسي زجاج السيارة الآمامي مفتوحاً لذا كان الصوت يصلني .. ترددت في الرد عليه ، لا فائدة ، الرنين لا يسكت ، اعتراني الخوف ، لعل شيئا خطيرا قد حدث ويدعو إلى الاتصال في هذا الوقت تلاحقت الأفكار السوداء في رأسي ، يجب أن أرد قلت بصوت يغلبه الخوف .

ـ آلو من المتصل ؟

داهمني صوت امرأة فكررت : من المتحدث ؟

ـ أليس هذا هاتف خالد ؟

ـ نعم نعم إنه هو ..

ـ اذن من أنت ؟

ـ أنا أنا أخته .. لا أعرف ، كيف نطقتها

- لو سمحت قدّمي التهاني له وأخبريه بأن ولده يشبهه تماماً .. أقفلت الخط وكأنها أقفلت الدنيا في وجهي ، نزعت قلبي من مكانه ارتجف جسدي ، لم أتحمل الوقوف ، ثقل الجبل وقع على جسدي ، لم أستطع أن أحرك رجلي ، كأنهما شلّتا .. حرّكت أطرافي بصعوبة وجسمي يسبح في العرق كمن يأخذ حماما ساخنا فقدت كل حواسي ، دخان أسود كثيف أمام ناظري ، ثقلت عينايّ من التحريك ، ألقيت نفسي فوق الكرسي ، وأنا أحاول الصراخ بكل جوارحي ، لم أستطع ، كانت أسناني تصطك ، وفجأة أصبحت بحالة لا أعرف كيف أصفها ، كل الذي أذكره إنني صفقت وغنيت بأعلى صوتي ، وأنا أناجي خالداً حتى استيقظ من نومه .

- ما بك هل جننت ؟ هل الفيلم كان مؤثرا إلى هذه الدرجة حتى أفقدك صوابك ؟!

- بشارة يا حبي ، اكتملت فرحتك ، جاءك الولد الرابع !!

- ماذا بك هل أنت طبيعية ؟ رفعت رأسي وأنا أحاول أن أحبس الدموع في عينيّ ، وهل تظن أنني تجرعت كأسا ؟ صفعني على وجهي ، ما هذا الكلام ؟ توقفي عن جنونك ؟ تكلّمي بوضوح عن أي شيء تتحدثين ؟؟

- أريد أن أعرف ألست جميلة ؟ ألم أنجب لك الولد والبنت ؟ هل قصرت معك في شيء ، لقد أعطيتك كل شيء وكانت ثقتي بك أكثر من نفسي ..

لم يهتم لكلامي بل أسرع إلى الهاتف كالمجنون يدير أرقامه ، سمعته يطلب منى ، ويتحدث إليها وكأني غير موجودة ، كانت كلماته كالسكاكين تقطع أحشائي ، حبست أنفاسي ، ولم أنم ليلتها ، النار كانت تأكل كبدي ، عقلي توقف عن التفكير في مصيبتي ، و بلا شعور وجدت نفسي أقف أمام خزانة ملابسي ملأت الحقيبة بالملابس ، أخذت جواز سفري وفي الطريق فكرت في السفر ، إلى أين ؟ لا أعرف .. أبعدت الفكرة عن رأسي ضللت الطريق إلى بيت والدي ، حتى عجلات سيارتي كانت مثقلة بالهم الذي أحمله ، أخيراً وصلت وأنا أجر حقيبة ملابسي ، رأيت الدهشة في عيون الجميع ، قاطعتهم :

- جئتكم بخبر سعيد لقد تزوج خالد ، تركت له البيت وخرجت .

- أمجنونة أنت كيف تتركين البيت ؟ وأولادك ؟!

- وكرامتي يا أبي ؟

- حرام يا ابنتي أن تتركي أولادك ، فهم بحاجة إليك ، ولا أحد يعوضهم حنان الأم ، فكري جيدا وارجعي لبيتك وأولادك . لم أتحمل أن أسمع المزيد من والدي ، حملت نفسي ورجعت ، ومنذ ذلك اليوم وأنا أعيش لأولادي ، وقد مات العشب الأخضر في قلبي ، الغبار تراكم على فساتيني ، أعيش وجرحي يكبر يوما بعد يوم ، ماتت الفرحة في عينيّ ، لا أهتم لوجوده ، ولا أشعر بأي شعور تجاهه ، أصبح كالضيف الثقيل ، لقد عافته النفس وأصبحت ظلا لنفسي بعد أن مات كل شيء فيها .

د. سعاد العريمي ـ الامارات العربية المتحدة

تاج السمان

إلى الطيب صالح

في مواسم الهجرة إلى الشمال تتجمع طيور السمان في برزخ المقرن ، حيث يلتقي النيلان ، الأبيض والأزرق . تاج السر ، الولد الرابع للقاضي عثمان طه ، تستهويه هذه الرحلة المنظمة فيتسرب من المدرسة لملاحقة الطيور ومناوشتها ، تارة بالنشابة المطاطية وتارة أخرى بالحجارة .

عسس المدارس في مدينة أم درمان ، رصدوا حركة تاج السر وأبلغوا القاضي :

" ابنكم يتسرب من المدرسة يا مولانا " . ضمر القاضي لتاج السر واستل له العصماء[42] فأدماه وكسر فؤاد أمه . ولم يعاود تاج السر فعلته تلك حتى انقضاء الموسم الدراسي . قالت له أمه : ستأتي مواسم أخرى ، وتكون قد كبرت ... وستكون حر نفسك بعيداً عن عيون العسس وعصا أبيك .

تكررت المواسم وشغف تاج السر لم يعد أبداً ، بل تحولت المناوشات الموسمية إلى حب ثم إلى اهتمام بالغ . بدّل تاج السر النشابة المطاطية بكاميرا لها منظار موصول بمكبرّ (زوم) يرصد من خلاله حركة الطيور ، أشكالها وحتى طريقة تزاوجها . فيبث الأخبار في المدرسة مما أثار شبق المراهقين ، فتحولت مدرسة أم درمان الثانوية برمتها إلى صوب المقرن .

الشيخ المعتصم بالله ، إمام المسجد ، ندد بفعلة تاج السر غير المحتشمة ووجد فيها أمراً يفسد الأخلاق ويشيع الفتنة بين اليافعين . أثار تنديد شيخ المسجد حفيظة القاضي عثمان طه فساط[43] ابنه في باحة الجامع الكبير بعد صلاة الجمعة ، جلدهُ حتى تورم منه الوجه وُفقئت منه العين . لملمت فاطمة بنت عمران جراح ابنها وهرعت به إلى المستشفى .

كثر لغط الرجال وثرثرة النساء حول دار القاضي وما حل بها ، إذ قيل بأن عثمان طه رمى على فاطمة بنت عمران يمين الطلاق إن هي زارت تاج السر في المستشفى ، فلم تأبه له . قالت زوجة الإمام بأن فاطمة تعتبر في عداد المطلقات ولكنها لازالت تسكن دار القاضي .

عجز أطباء أم درمان عن ترميم عين تاج السر ، فطلبوا العون من الخرطوم مما أخر شفاء الصبي وأعاق خروجه من المشفى حتى نهاية الصيف ، فرط تاج السر ولم يكمل عامه الدراسي . قالت فاطمة يكفي شفاءه والقراءة آتية .

لم يعد تاج السر إلى بيت القاضي ، بل أرسلته أمه إلى دار أخيها في الخرطوم ... كي يبعد عن المقرن وعن لغط نساء أم درمان . أما القاضي فكان خجلاً من فعلته ، ولكنه لم يظهر ندماً لفاطمة . هاجر تاج السر شمالاً ، تاركاً السمان والبرزخ وفتية المدرسة الثانوية .

فالتاً أصبح بعد أن غادر منزله ، خاله الذي أكرم مثواه لم يضيّق عليه الخناق كما كان يفعل والده ، بل اقتنى له منظاراً وكاميرا جديدة بدلاً من تلك التي أتلفها القاضي ، وقال له بأنه حر فيما يفعل مع الطيور بشرط ألا يهمل القراءة . امتثل تاج السر فرحاً لهذا الأمر الجديد .

---

42 **العصماء** : نوع من العصيّ .
43 أي ضربه بالسوط / **العصا** .

في فيافي وبحيرات الخرطوم وأزقتها المائية وجد تاج السر ضالته ، فلم تعد الطيور المهاجرة وحدها المرتكز الأساسي لاهتماماته ، بل أيضاً وجد في الطيور الداجنة ما يستحق المراقبة بالمنظار ، إلا أنه بين الحين و الآخر يحن للمقرن وطيوره النادرة .

قيل بأن صبية أم درمان لازالوا يلتقون (بتاج السمان) ، هكذا يلقبه أصحابه ، في منطقة البرزخ في فصل التزاوج ، وبأن فاطمة بنت عمران هي الأخرى تلتقي بابنها في المكان ذاته . تناهت الحكاية إلى أسماع القاضي عثمان طه فلم ينزعج ، بل أخذ يتسلل إلى منطقة الفيافي عله يلمح طرفة من تاج السر .

نبغ تاج السر في مدارس الخرطوم وأصبح محط أنظار أهل العلم فيها . كتب في دورياتها عن هجرة المواسم ، وفند أصول الطيور ومنابتها ، فحُملت الأخبار إلى أبيه الذي لم يغتبط فرحاً عندما رأى اسم ابنه مذيلاً بالسمان . قال أهل اللغط بأن تاج السر تبرأ من أبيه .

ضاقت آفاق المواسم على تاج السر وأصبح يبحث عن شمال آخر ، عن هجرة أخرى بعيدة تماماً عن أرخبيلات الخرطوم . قال لأمه سأذهب لدراسة الدكتوراه ... أريد أن أكون متخصصاً في على الأحياء . فرح القاضي بقرار ابنه وقال لزوجته دعيه يتبحر في علمه يا فاطمة .

في ولاية Michigan في الولايات المتحدة ، شعر تاج السر بأن للنهار لوناً أخضر وأن القمر يملأ السماء بشعاع لا زوردي وبأن البحيرات الخمس لها شكل آخر مختلف تماماً عن برازخ المقرن . التهم تاج السر فضاءات العالم الجديد كلها وشرب مياه شلالاته بأكملها ولم ترو ظمأه إذ تجاوزت أحلامه آفاق العالم بأسره .

قال الشيخ المعتصم بأن تاج السر أصبح متبحراً في علوم الدنيا والأحياء ويحضّر خلايا منبّتة لمخلوقات الله في مختبرات أمريكا وهو بذلك يحلل ما حرمه الله . بكت فاطمة بنت عمران عند سماعها لهذه الأنباء وخرج القاضي مدافعاً عن ابنه الذي تنحني له الهامات تبجيلاً وإجلالاً .

ضاقت المسافات بفاطمة ، فلم يهنأ لها مهجع ولا يطيب لها منزل إلا منطقة المقرن :

"يفرح فؤادي يا مولانا عندما أرى طيور السمان تتزاحم في منطقة الفيافي وأحزن إذا رأيتها ترفرف مغادرة ، قلبي يحدثني قلقا على تاج السر " .

انتقل الفزع إلى محيا القاضي وأذعن لشكوك زوجته : لماذا لم يعد يتصل ... ولم يعد يكاتب أخاه من خلال البريد الإلكتروني أتظنين أنه مشغول ؟

رقرقت عينا فاطمة عند سماعها لكلمة مشغول ، فحدسها صور لها غير ذلك ، فابتسمت :

" هل تتذكر عندما كان يتصل بعد منتصف الليل فتقفز أنت من فراشك فرحاً كالطفل ، قلبي يناهدني عليه يا عثمان أشعر بأنني طليقة ولكنني مقيدة ، أحس بطعم الماء ولكنني لا أتذوقه" . فقد القاضي نقطة الارتكاز ولم يبق لديه منفذ واحد لتبرير انقطاع الابن فبكى . ولأول مرة ترى فاطمة دموع زوجها .

كانا جالسين في منطقة الفيافي ميممين وجهيهما للمقرن ، يراقبان طيور السمان وهي تنفض أرياشها استعداداً لموسم الهجرة إلى الشمال كانت هنيهات الشفق توشك على الأفول ، عندما أتى من يخبرهما بأن تاج السر في معتقل غوانتانامو .

عبد الحميد احمد ـ الامارات العربية المتحدة

البيدار

- 1 -

حول الخيمة المشيدة فوق تلة رمل جنوب المساكن الشعبية تجمهر كثيرون : رجال . نساء . أطفال . ثمة رجال ملثمون . أطفال مذعورون . نساء يولولن ويصطخبن .

صوت :

– الباب مغلق .

صوت آخر :

– الرائحة كريهة لا تطاق .

صوت ثالث :

– كأنها عفونة فئران ميتة .

الشمس حارقة . الرمل ساخن كالرماد تحته الجمر . العرق ينضح من الوجوه . مزيد من الناس يقبل تجاه الخيمة . الضوضاء تعلو والصخب يتزايد .

تتشابك الأنفاس الحارة بروائح العرق . تتكاثف الرطوبة . ورغم ذلك يظل للرائحة المنبعثة من الخيمة صراخ حاد وجارح .

صوت :

– هذه خيمة"مريش" ... أليس كذاك ؟

صوت آخر :

– لكن"مريش"تركها ورحل .

صوت نسائي :

– أخبرني بنفسه انه راجع إلى عمان .

صوت ... :

– لمن ترك الخيمة إذن ؟

صوت ... :

– لعله الحمار . حماره .

صوت ... :

– الأمر لا يخلو من غرابة .

الصوت الأول :

– "مريش" لن يترك حماره . حتماً سيأخذه معه .

الرجال الملثمون يشددون اللثام على أنوفهم . همهمات . تأفف :

– أمف ... ما هذه الرائحة ؟

وسط الضجيج وأمواج الصخب والرطوبة سأل طفل أمه ببراءة :

– من هو "مريش" يا أمي ؟

... لكن أمه لم نسمعه .

- 2 -

حين تسلق النخلة " القحال " ووصل إلى قمتها فتح " الغيظ " . شم رائحة شبيهة برائحة المني . داعبت مخيلته وازداد شوقه إلى المرأة التي يراها دائماً وبسهولة ، ولكنه لا يلمسها ... لم يلمسها في حياته أبداً . حمل " النبات " تحت إبطه . رجع إلى خيمته في وقت الظهيرة . تناول حبات من التمر وشرب القهوة . اشعل " المدواخ " وراح ينتشي بطعم التبغ العماني في فمه . استلقى على ظهره فوق حصيرة . باعد بين الجريد ليسمح للهواء بالدخول . حاول أن يغفو .

الحمار يحمل المتاع ويمشي أمامهما . يهشه بين فترة وأخرى بالعصا . قطعا الجبال والأودية الصخرية والصحارى الرملية . كم استغرقت الرحلة ؟ "مريش" لا يستطيع أن يتذكر ، لكنها كانت رحلة طويلة وشاقة . قال له أخوه :

– "الباطنة" صارت بعيدة الآن .
– علينا أن نصل الساحل .
– سوف أشتاق إليها يا "مريش" .
– المهم أن نعمل . أن نكسب . أن نعيش .
– ومتى سنرجع ؟
– علم ذلك عند ربك .

أخوه صار "محلوي" بارعاً ذاع صيته في دبي كلها . "مريش" استقر به المقام في الجميرة . تذكر ذلك . دمعت عيناه . حاول أن يغفو مرة أخرى لكنه تذكر أن "بوجاسم" كان قد طلبه ليأتي إلى بيته ليذبح له خروفين لمناسبة ختان ولديه . حمل السكين وخرج قاصداً بيت "بوجاسم" .

- 3 -

صوت أول :

– الحرارة تزداد والرائحة تخنقنا .

صوت ثان :

– يجب اقتحام الخيمة .

صوت ثالث لشاب على عينيه نظارة طبية :

– علينا أن نستدعي الشرطة ورجال الصحة كذلك .

صوت :

– لماذا ؟ هل نحن عاجزون ؟

صوت الشاب :

– قد تسبب الرائحة وباء.

صوت ... لرجل انبرى فجأة وسط الزحام :

– من قال إن "مريش" رحل إلى عمان ؟

صوت نسائي :

– أخبرني بذلك .

صوت الرجل ذاته :

– لكنني رأيته قبل أربعة أيام يجلس في ظل نخلة . كان مهموماً.

الصخب يختلط . الأجساد المتزاحمة ترفع حرارة الجو . الضوضاء تتكاثف . الأصوات ترن في الفضاء . عاد الطفل يسأل أمه :

– من هو "مريش" يا أمي ؟

... لكن صوته ضاع في اللجة .

- 4 -

حزين . وحيد . دخن التبغ كثيراً . مر به صديقه سالم البعير الذي لم يره منذ فترة طويلة . دخّنا معاً . فكّرا معاً .

قال له صديقه بدهشة :

– ولكن لماذا تريد العودة ؟

هصره الألم ... قال بأسى :

– كيف أعيش هنا ؟ لا أحد يلتفت لي .

وبعد صمت . ارتعشت عيناه . همست شفتاه :

– النسيان لا أحتمله !
– ولكن ...

قاطعه وقد شارف حافة البكاء :

– لم يعد أحد مهتماً بالنخيل ، والخرفان تذبح في مسالخ السوق .

- ولكن ... بإمكانك العمل . ناطور . مزارع للبلدية . فراش . كما عملت أنا ناطوراً . أو لماذا لا تعمل مع أخيك في محله ؟

حدجه بعينين مطفأتين . قال :

- مات أخي منذ عامين .

- يرحمه الله .

صب له فنجاناً من القهوة . قال وهو يحك أنفه بقوة :

- العمل يحتاج إلى هوية . جنسية . جواز . لا أحد سيقبلني .

صمت . نهشه الحزن واليأس :

- أولاد الحلال ماتوا ... تفرقوا ... ولا أحد يذكرني الآن .

صمتا ... تبادلا نظرات حائرة قلقة :

- أترحل بعد 30 سنة يا "مريش" وكأنك لم تأتِ إلى هذه البلاد ؟

- أعود ... كما جئت . سأعمر مزرعة في "الباطنة" .

لملم "مريش" حاجاته . نهضا معاً . وقبل أن يغادرا الخيمة قال :

- خذ الحمار يا سالم . لعله يفيدك .

أوصله إلى حيث أقعى "مريش" في "الوانيت" الذاهب إلى عمان . عانقه طويلاً . امتزجت أنفاسهما واندلحت قطرات من عيني "مريش" وهو يلوح لصديقه مودعاً .

- 5 -

كنت في الثامنة . ذات يوم سمعت أن "مريش" سيأتي لمساعدة أبي في تلقيح النخلة في بيتنا . فرحت لأنني سأرى "مريش" كنت سمعت عنه كثيراً ولم أره .
سألت أبي ونحن جالسان في ظل الجدار :

- ماذا يعمل "مريش" ؟
- "بيدار" يا ولدي .
- وهل عنده أولاد ؟
- يعيش وحيداً في خيمته . لا زوجة . لا أهل .
- لماذا لا يتزوج ؟
- إنه من عمان ، وفقير . من سيزوجه ؟

... "أوي ها ... أوي ها ... هود هل الدار" . ثم سمعت نحنحة ورأيت رجلاً أقبل يعرج . في يده "داس" لحيته سوداء . رأسه ملفوفة بغترة مصفرة . عيناه ضيقتان . فتحة أنفه اليمنى متآكلة محمرة . إزاره مخطط بالأزرق والأخضر . قميصه أبيض مبقع بالعرق والتراب .
داعبني :

- هاه ... أنت "ولد مخبوق رأسه" .

وضعت يدي فوق رأسي أتحسس إن كان هناك "خبق". أبي أخذ يبتسم وقال لـ"مريش" الذي أصدر ضحكة لم أسمع مثلها من قبل .

– ألا تترك "سوالفك" يا "مرشان" ؟

ثم شرعا يعملان وأنا أراقب "مريش".

بعد أن انتهيا ، قدمت لهما أمي تمراً و "بلاليط" وقهوة. قالت تخاطب "مريش" في دعابة :

– سنزوجك "حنتومة" . ما رأيك ؟

أعرفها . امرأة سوداء مرحة . تجلب الماء من "الحليو" فوق حمار .
قالت لي مرة في خبث :

– انته يا "بوسمبول" دائماً متعلق في ذيل أمك ؟

أجاب "مريش" ضاحكاً ضحكته الخاصة :

– لا أريدها ... أخ ... أخ .

... وأحببت "مريش" . صار أمراً نادراً ألا أراه في كل مكان . في الحي . في النخل. في البيوت . مع الرجال والنساء . في الأعياد . في حفلات المولد والختان والأعراس . فوق بئر الماء وفوق سيف البحر . يداعب الجميع وصدى ضحكاته المميزة تتردد في الأزقة والأسماع .
ومرت السنون . سافرت للدراسة . حين رجعت لم أسمع أحداً يذكره أو يتحدث عنه .

- 6 -

الخيمة تكاد تختفي خلف الأجساد المتزاحمة حولها . الشمس تلعن المكان بضربات حامية . الأصوات تتصاعد خليطاً من التساؤلات والهمهمات والثرثرة . مساحة الذعر والدهشة تتسع في وجوه الأطفال . الرائحة الكريهة ممزوجة بالعرق الآدمي تستفحل في الجو .
صوت :

– يا جماعة ... يجب أن نفعل شيئاً .

صوت آخر :

– ماذا ؟ هل نستدعي الشرطة ؟

صوت أول :

– كلا ... نكسر الباب لينكشف السر.

صوت ... :

– الحر قاتل . لنكسر الباب . ليس أمامنا إلا هذا .

أصوات :

– هيا إذن .

اشرأبت الأعناق . اندفع ثلاثة رجال بقوة صوب الباب . سمع الآخرون قرقعة ودوياً . ساد صراخ وهرج . امتلأ المكان ببكاء نساء وحشرجات أطفال . تدفقت الرائحة قوية كانها شلال . صفعت الوجوه . أزكمت الأنوف ثم أخذت تتصاعد في الهواء الساخن . علا بكاء النساء . بعضهن تأفف :

– تفوه ... أية رائحة هذه ؟

تصايح الرجال :

– لا حول ولا قوة إلا بالله .

- 7 -

في اليوم التالي جلسَت أم عبد الله مع جارتها أم حسين تتحادثان . قالت الأولى وفي عينيها دمعتان :

– واحسرتي عليه ... مات مثلما يموت الحمار .
– يقولون انهم وجدوه منتفخاً مثل القربة . وأقسم أبو حسين أنهم لم يستطيعوا معرفته . فقد كان وجهه متورماً وعيناه مطموستين تحت اللحم . ويقول أبو حسين انه رأى ديداناً تخرج من فتحة أنفه وفمه .

بصقت أم عبد الله . دفنت بصقتها . قالت :

– أهكذا يموت بني آدم ؟ ... تفوه .
– هذا زمان الأخ فيه ينسى أخاه .

بعد أن حوقلت أم عند الله قالت :

– يقول بو عبد الله ان أبا ناصر رآه قبل خمسة أيام . سأله : "لماذا لم تذهب إلى عمان؟" فأجابه بأنهم منعوه من الدخول على الحدود . سألوه عن جواز سفره . فأخبرهم أنه عماني لكنه يعيش في الامارات . لم يصدقوه فرجع .

قالت أم حسين متأثرة :

– حرموه من رؤية أهله وبلاده .

واصلت أم عبد الله :

– ويقول بو عبد الله انهم لم يعطوه جواز الامارات كذلك .
– الله يغفر له ويرحمه .

ساد صمت ثقيل كسرته أم حسين :

– أتعلمين يا أم عبد الله أن "مريش" لم يمت .

اتسعت حدقتا المرأة دهشة . تساءلت :

– ماذا ؟ لقد دفنوه البارحة .
– أعلم ... لكن الذين دخلوا عليه الخيمة ، قالوا انهم وجدوا جروحاً كثيرة في بدنه ، ورأوا في رقبته جرحاً عميقا والدماء السوداء الجافة كانت تغطي الأرض تحته ، وعلى مقربة وجدوا "الداس" .
– هل نحر نفسه ؟

تساءلت في وجل غير مصدقة . وضعت يدها فوق خدها . سكبت القهوة من فتحة فمها اليمنى . اغرورقت عيناها . تمتمت :

– واحسرتي عليك يا "مريش" . قتلك القهر فمت وحيداً لا أهل ولازوجة .

... ثم انشغلت الحارة لشهر كامل في رواية ما جرى ل "مريش" .
جرت قصته على ألسنة النساء والرجال ممزوجة بالدمع والرثاء و ... الأسف .
وقبل أن تهدأ عاصفة الحكاية التي أثارت الجميع جاء إلى أم عبد الله طفلها الأصغر . سألها :

– من هو "مريش" يا أمي ؟

إضاءات :

1. "الفحال" : النخلة المذكر .
2. "الغيظ" : الطلع .
3. "النبات" : حبوب اللقاح .
4. "المدواخ" : مبسم أو أنبوب التدخين القليدي (البايب حديثاً) .
5. "الباطنة" : منطقة تقع في عمان . اقليم .
6. "محلوي" : صانع حلوى عمانية .
7. "داس" : منجل له أسنان كالمنشار .
8. "حنتومة" : اسم امرأة .
9. "الوانيت" : سيارة النقل الكبيرة .
10. "بوسمبول" السمبول قضيب الطفل الصغير . مداعبة .
11. "مخبوق" : منقوب و "الخبق" هو الثقب .
12. "الحليو" : بئر الماء العذبة كان الأهالي يجلبون منها الماء .
13. "بلاليط" : الشعيرية .
14. "الجميرة" : منطقة ساحلية في دبي .

عبد العزيز الشرهان ـ الامارات العربية المتحدة

حفرة دون قاع

الهدوء يسيطر على الحي الذي اعتاد السكوت الميت ، عدا صيحات الأطفال ، وهمسات الرجال مع زوجاتهم ، نباح تلك الكلاب التي تبدو وكأنها قد أوكل اليها أن تجوب الآزقة بحثا عن الطعام او جرياً خلف القطط .

قبل ان يعلن المؤذن نداء الصلاة .. استيقظت ايعازاً من جسمي الذي مل تلك الانبطاحة الثقيلة على تلك الحصيرة المصنوعة من سعف النخيل والتي طالما تتركت علامات محفورة على ظهري ، نهضت متثاقلا ، يسود الخيمة العتيقة ظلام مميت .. تحسست المصباح بحذر .. اشعلة .. خطوت نحو موضع الماء .. اغتسلت وأديت واجبي تجاه الرب حيث أديت صلاة الفجر .. تفحصت تلك الادوات التي أعددتها قبل نومي .. الاعشاب البحرية .. بعض الحبال .. سلة السمك . غادرت الخيمة وبريق الأمل يوحي بأن البحر سيكون هادىء الموج . خطوت متثاقلاً بتأثير ذلك النوم المتعب .. بدأت بذلك الزقاق الذي يربط هذه الخيمة البائسة بالبحر ، والذي تعوّد مثل هذه الخطوات في مثل هذه الساعات . اثناءها يرافقني فوج من القطط و الكلاب الجائعة ، التي طالما حصلت على غذائها من صاحب هذه الخطوات . انتابني تفكبر حول تلك المرأة التي تعودت المجيء إليّ لأخذ ما أحضرت من سمك . إن ما يشغلني أنها فاتنة الجمال ذات جاذبية غريبة .. ولكن .. إيه .. ما الفائدة ؟ لمثل سني البائس .. إنها تريد من يملك عضلات مفتولة .. وماذا في ذلك .. ألست رجلا ؟! وأذكر بالأمس انني احتضنتها بذراعي عندما ذكرت لها بأنني قد احضرت كمية بسيطة من السمك .. وبطرف عينها التي تحمل حيويتها المرحة أجابت بأن ذلك لا يهم .. يكفي أنه يوجد ما فيه الكفاية .. ونحن لبعض .

كلمات جعلتني أقتنع بأنها تجد فيّ الانسان المطلوب لهاء وخاصة انها فقدت زوجها و هناك ما يدهشني حقا .. أليس ارتباطها بي هو بدافع حاجتها المستمرة للسمك الذي يتوفر لها دون مقابل ؟!

لا .. لا .. انها تحبني .. إنها لا تستطيع أن تعتبر السمك بمثابة ثمن لمتعتي معها .. وما دام الأمر كذلك فسوف أبحر بعيداً .. بعيداً حتى احضر أجمل أنواع السمك من أجلها .

اقتربت من القارب ـ الهوري ـ المنتظر فوق الرمال بصمت ، وبكل قوتي دفعته إلى المياه البعيدة وأنا أتطلع إلى السماء الصافية والنجوم التي تزينها ، وتبعث ببريقها البارد وكأنها تبشر بصيد وافر . توسطت القارب .. تحركت المجاذيف .. والقارب يمخر البحر الهادىء بفخر واعتزاز ، بقوتي التي تدفع المجاذيف بتناسق مع ألحان متناسقة تصدر من الأوتاد ، بعد سير مسافة استغرقت الساعتين ، قذفت بالمرسى وبدأت في الغطس ، أخرجت الشبك الأول ـ الكركور ـ ولشدة ثقله عانيت من دفعه إلى باطن القارب .. اليوم .. اليوم ستفرح .. إذاً سأحتضنها .. سأستمتع بحضنها الدافىء وأنفاسها الحارة الممزوجة ببقايا عطور الهند وهمساتها التي تشجعني فيها لآكثر من احتضانها . بسرعة لا إرادية قفزت إلى الماء ، بدأت في إخراج الشباك الثاني والثالث وقررت عدم العودة الا والقارب ممتلىء بالأسماك .. اللحظة تلك أتوسط عمق البحر .. إنه يقترب .. يلاحقني .. عليّ ان أحذر .. لكنه يقترب .. سمك القرش .. يقترب، دفعت بالشبك الذي أحمله .. أتجهت الى القارب .. وإذا بي أشعر بأسنانه تطبق على كف رجلي .. أمسكت بالقارب .. أصدرت صراخاً حاداً .. لم استطع التحرك حتى لا أفقد القارب .. ظل القرش ممسكا برجلي .. بعد صراع عنيف وسط الألم العميق والصراخ قرر الوحش افتراس رجلي .. وبألم كاد أن ينزع قلبي من موضعه .. فصل كف رجلي اليمنى وترك المياه المحيطة بالقارب بلون أحمر داكن .. فقدت قواي وبضعف بالغ رفعت المرسى .. جذفت بعد أن ضمدت تلك الرجل بقميصي المتسخ .. وصلت الشاطىء بعد رحلة من اللألم جعلتني أفقد قوتي .. قررت أن أصل الخيمة .. تركت القارب وما يحويه من أسماك ومع الألم الحاد

أضطجعت على تلك الحصيرة .. سيطر عليّ الاغماء وفقدت شعوري ، صحوت في اليوم التالي .. تحيط بي مجموعة من النساء .. الرجال .. الأطفال .. وفي محيط الأحاديث المتنوعة : مسكين ، لعنة الله على سمك القرش .. التهنئة بالسلامة .. طفت بنظري . لم أجدها . لم تأت . ماذا تريد ؟! ماذا تريد من إنسان فقد رجله وفوق ذلك في الستين من عمره .. إنه السمك .. السمك . حقا السمك الذي يشدها إلى هذه الخيمة البائسة ، وهذا الجسم الهزيل ، عصرني الألم .. بقيت أتخبط على الفراش ، والأيدي تمتد اليّ بالماء .. انصرفوا .. مرت الأيام .. ولم يطرق الباب .. أحسست بالنهاية تقترب .. بينما اعيش آلامي .. يتردد على مسمعي حوار خارجي .. انه يمتلك ثروة ؟ ومن سيرثه ؟ لا أحد .. إذاً أين خبأها ؟ غريبة هذه البشرية .. يريدون موتي طمعا في المال .. إن حقيقة مرة ستضرب وجوههم الطامعة عندما يجدون أن الذي يحتضر لا يملك إلا قاربه الخشبي وأدوات صيده ، وحصيرته التي يفترشها تحته .. اقتربت الساعة وسيطر علي نوم عميق .. عميق .. وداعا أيتها الحياة .. إنك حفرة دون قاع .. دون قاع .. دون ق .. ا .. ع ..

محمد المرّ ـ الامارات العربية المتحدة

الأب

- 1 -

مرحلة الطفولة والصبا مرحلة عجيبة من حياة الإنسان ، وكثير من الناس يظرون دائماً ـ خصوصاً إذا تقدموا في السن ـ إلى تلك المرحلة بشوق وحنين ورومانسية ويتحدثون عن لهوهم ولعبهم وشقاوتهم وسعادتهم في تلك الطفولة بكثير من الافتتان والحب .

" عيسى بن ماجد "ليس من أولئك الناس ، فطفولته كانت فاجعة ، شقية ، مبهمة . لايذكر لهوه أو سعادته بتلك الفترة بل إن معظم أحداث طفولته نسيها ما عدا القليل من الصور التي رسخت في ذهنه رسوخ قضبان الحديد على جانبي خور دبي . الصورة الأولى عندما كان في الثامنة من عمره بدأ والده يصطحبه معه عندما كان يذهب من حي " الشندغة " حيث كان يعمل مؤذناً وإماماً لأحد المساجد إلى " ديرة " لكي يجلس مع الناس المتواجدين في مجالس تجار اللؤلؤ والوجهاء فيراقب البيع والشراء للؤلؤ الذي بدأت أسعره بالانخفاض ، وحل محل التفاؤل السابق تشاؤم جديد ، ولم يعد للؤلؤ القديم سحره حتى الحاج والوجيه والتاجر " محمد بن خالد " فارقه أدبه وهيبته وبدأ يجادل في الأسعار ويرفع صوته مع الذين يحضرون له صرّات اللؤلؤ . عالم رخاء نسبي كان ينهار تدريجياً ، ورائحة الفاجعة التي خنقت كثيراً من الأرواح الإنسانية في بداية الأربعينات في مختلف أنحاء العالم وخصوصاً في جبهات القتال الأوروبية والآسيوية بدأت بالتسرب إلى " دبي " . في صباح يوم شتائي مشمس في زاوية منعزلة بالقرب من سوق السمك المجفف كان عيسى يراقب الده وهو يحتجم عند أحد الحجامين . وكان شكل والده طريفاً وقرن الحجامة مركب على الجزء المحلوق من رأسه ، تذكر إحدى حكايات والدته عن الشيطان ذي القرنين ، والده كان يبدو كشيطان له قرن واحد ، بعد أن نزع القرن ، ظهرت ورمة صغيرة في رأس والده . أخذ الحجام الموسى وجعل يضرب تلك الورمة ضربات سريعة مسبباً جروحاً خفيفة ، ثم أرجع الحجام القرن على الورمة وأخذ يشفط ويمص طرفها المفتوح ، احمرّت عيناه ، تقلص خداه ، كان شكله طريفاً وعجيباً . نزع القرن مرة ثانية ، كانت الورمة مغطاة بدم أسود ، مسحه الحجام ثم أعاد وضع القرن على الورمة ، كرر تلك العملية ثلاث أو أربع مرات .

عندما انتهت عملية الحجامة ، وقف " ماجد " ووقف عيسى وجاء إلى جانب والده الذي وضع طاقيته وغترته على رأسه ووضع عباءته على كتفه ورمى أجرة الحجامة في حضن الحجام الذي عندما نظر إليها صرخ غاضباً وأعلن عدم رضاه . غضب والد عيسى وسحب الأجرة منه وأمسك بيد عيسى واستدار لينصرف . وقف الحجام وأمسك بطرف عباءته ، أفلت ماجد يد ابنه من يده وتلاحم مع الحجام . كان ضعيفاً بفعل الحجامة ونزيف الدم منه ، ولكنه استطاع أن يطيل أمد المعركة ، أمسك الحجام بسكين كانت لديه وطعن بها ماجد ، نفذت السكين إلى القلب . وقع ماجد . تلفت الحجام حوله ثم هرب في أحد الأزقة تاركاً الجثة وأدوات الحجامة وعيسى . حدث الأمر بسرعة ، نظر عيسى إلى والده ، كان مستلقياً على ظهره والدم يلون ثوبه الأبيض وعباءته البيضاء ، كان يئن وقد وضع يده على قلبه ، بعد فترة وجيزة همدت حركته ، بدأ الذباب بالتجمع على الدم المتسرب من رأسه وطرفي شفتيه وفمه وعلى عينيه ، لم يعرف عيسى كنه الموت بعد ولكنه عرف أن شيئاً خطيراً حدث لوالده ولم يتصور أنها النهاية . كيف ينتهي والده العملاق ، القوي ، الإمام ؟ إنه يقرأ القرآن ، لا يمكن أن يموت وينتهي من يقرأ القرآن ، جلس بجانب رأسه وجعل يطرد الذباب عن وجهه ورأسه ، لا يدري ما حدث بعد ، لكنه يتذكر أنه في صباح اليوم التالي شاهد الحجام مربوطاً بالقرب من أحد الأبراج الطينية ونظراته زائغة وشاهد أعمامه الثلاثة بعماماتهم مع بعض

الحرس . لم يكن يدري من أحضره ليكون من الجمهور المتجمع ليشاهد حكم الإعدام على قاتل والده الذي أصرت السلطات على أن يكون قتله بنفس أداة القتل التي قتل بها والده . وفي لحظات خاطفة شاهد أعمامه وهم يغمدون خناجرهم في بطن وصدر ووجه الحجام الذي زعق زعقتين وسقط .

- 2 -

الصورة الثانية عندما كان في الخامسة عشرة من عمره ، أصابته حمى رهيبة ألهبت ظهره وخنقت صوته وجعلته لا يقدر على الكلام ، كان ينتفض ويهذي ، ظنت أمه في البداية أنها حمى عادية ، سقته شراب الزعتر الحار ، تقيّاً .

بعد أربعة أيام بدأت بثور صغيرة بالظهور على جسده ، عرفت أمه أنه مصاب بالجدري . حضر أحد أعمامه وحمله إلى الحجرات الصغيرة التي بناها أحد فاعلي الخير على خور دبي في طرف "ديرة" لكي يعزل فيها المجدورون . في الأيام الأولى لوجوده في إحدى تلك الحجرات الشبيهة بالأقبية كان يسمع أنات المجدورين وتنهداتهم ، كان بعضهم يهذي وآخرون يتلون ما يحفظون من آيات قرآنية متقطعة وأدعية ، بأصوات ضعيفة ضارعة ، وأحدهم كان يبكي ليل نهار خوفا من الموت الذي كان كثيرا ما يزور تلك الحجرات . في اليوم الرابع لوجوده هناك أحضروا "سليمان" أحد أصدقاء طفولته ، اندهش حينما شاهد وجهه ، التشويه الذي أحدثه الجدري في وجهه كان مخيفاً ، "سليمان" بعكس كثير من الصبية في حي الشندغة لم يكن أسمر ، بل كان أبيض أشقر وعيناه خضراوان لأن أمه كانت من منطقة رؤوس الجبال ، وكان الصبية يلقبونه "بالانجليزي" و " عيون القطة " عندما يمزحون معه ، كان جميلا ولكن الجدري شوّه وجهه وجسمه بشكل عنيف . قدم له سالم المشرف على المرضى بعض الرز فلم يستطع أكله ، مات في نفس الليلة التي أحضروه فيها . في صباح اليوم التالي نظر عيسى بهلع الى سالم وهو يجر جثة "سليمان" من الحجرة المجاورة . في كل يوم كانت أمه ترسل له أقراصاً من السكر بسبب الاعتقاد الشائع أن الأطعمة الحلوة تساعد في نضج بثور الجدري . أكل في ذلك اليوم أربعة أقراص سكر مرة واحدة . في ليلة اليوم الخامس عشر اشتدت عليه الحمى ، كانت البثور متضخمة وكأنها جلد آخر يلبسه على جلده . في تلك الليلة أحس بوجود ثقيل في الغرفة ، عرف أنه الموت . كان حضوراً رهيباً ، جف حلقه ، أحس ببرودة أطرافه ، قلبه بعكس العادة لم تزد دقّاته بل أخذ يدق بشكل بطيء . أغمض عينيه وأعلن الاستسلام الكامل . في صباح اليوم التالي بدأت بثور الجدري بالتمزّق . عرف أن الجدري لن يقتله . بعد خمسة وأربعين يوماً انتهت مدة الحجر ، أخذه سالم الى الخور لكي يغسل جسمه ووجهه في مياهه ، كانت مياه الخور هادئة جداً ، شاهد " عيسى" صورته منعكسة على مياه الخور وجهاً جديداً مليئاً بالثقوب . فرح بالسمك الذي كان يتقافز بالقرب منه .

- 3 -

في تلك الأيام ، شيئان متلازمان كان الحي يتوقعهما من كل شاب إذا بلغ العشرين من عمره . الشيء الأول أن يتزوج والثاني أن ينجب . وعندما بلغ " عيسى " سن العشرين تزوج بنت أحد أعمامه . ولمدة ثلاث سنوات لم ينجب .

فكر في أن يتزوج مرة ثانية ولكنه يحب ابنة عمه و لا يقدر مادياً على الزواج مرة أخرى ، دخله من صغره كان متواضعاً ، عندما كان صغيراً كان يساعد السماكين في دهن قوارب الصيد بالزيت وفي نشر الشباك وفي دفع القوارب إلى البحر ، فكانوا يعطونه بضع أسماك يبيع معظمها في السوق ويحضر النقود ويحمل الباقي من الأسماك الهزيلة لوالدته . عندما تزوج كان سمّاكاً يذهب للصيد مع مجموعة من السماكين ، شكا لأحد زملائه من عدم إنجاب زوجته فنصحه بأن يذهب لسدر السيد هاشم . في أحد الأيام

أرسلوه ليشتري بعض الحبال من عمارة " خليفة الصوري " والعمارة عبارة عن دكان مبني من سعف النخيل ، يبيع فيه صاحبه لوازم الصيد من حبال وشباك وزيوت وغيرها . سأل عيسى " خليفة " عن بركات سدر السيد هاشم ، فأجابه خليفة بينما كان يلف طيات الحبل على يديه قائلا :

‑ لا تصدق هذه الخرافات ، اعتقاد باطل ، متى كان الشجر ينفع أو يضر . سيدكم لو يقدر لأنقذ نفسه ، قتله عبده ولم يقدر عليه .

لم يقتنع " عيسى " بإجابة " خليفة " فهو إنسان حقود ولا يترك العمارة حتى للصلاة ، همه البيع والشراء والنقود .

سأل عيسى " الشيخ " محمد أحد أصدقاء والده عن السيد " هاشم " فأجابه بصوت يتخلله الأسى والشجن :

‑ كنت من مريدي السيد ، كان ولياً عظيماً وعابداً صلحاً ، كان يحيي في بيته الطاهر ليالي الذكر ، ولقد عاينّا كراماته ، سقاني من قدر واحدة كانت بين يديه كأس عصير بارد ، وكأس ماء عذب وكأس لبن له حلاوة العسل ، من ذاق تلك الكؤوس لم يحسب أنها من نتاج هذه الأرض بل من خيرات الجنة ونعيمها ولكننا لم نكن محظوظين فلم يطل مقامه عندنا .

سأل عيسى :

‑ كيف ؟

قال الشيخ محمد مذهولاً :

‑ ذهب إلى حيث كتبت له الشهادة في مدينة " لنجة " ، وهناك بدأت خطواته إلى لقاء ربه ، لقاء طالما تشوّق إليه وأنشد الأناشيد رغبة فيه .

قال عيسى بحذر :

‑ يقال إن عبده قتله .

قال الشيخ محمد بصوت عميق :

‑ بلال لم يكن ليقتله ، كان ابنه وعبده وصديقه وتلميذه وخادمه . ما كان ليجرؤ أو ليقدر أن يفعل ذلك ولكن جاءه الأمر ، هو الذي أعطاه خنجره " الأصفهاني " ، بلال نفذ الرغبة العليا ، بعد أن نفذت الرغبة كان وجهه كما يقول الرواة يشع بالنور ، في تلك الأثناء غلف الكون الحبور " يتنهد " لم نكن محظوظين ، لم نكن محظوظين ، لم يبق لدينا إلا هذه الأشجار المباركة التي أظلت ذلك السيد العظيم .

في ذلك المساء ذهب " عيسى " مع زوجته لزيارة سدر السيد هاشم ، كان منظر الشجرات الثلاث في وقت الغروب مهيباً وعجيباً ، أشعل البخور وصلى مع زوجته ركعتين احتراما لمقام السيد . بعد عدة شهور من الزيارة أنجبت زوجته ابنه الوحيد " راشد " .

الابن

‑ 4 ‑

راشد الابن الذي حصل عليه عيسى ببركة أشجار السيد ، عاش أيضا بالبركة ، ففي طفولته تعرض لكل أمراض الطفولة من حصبة وسعال ديكي وحميات مختلفة الأنواع . كان معظمها شديد الوطأة . كان كل

مرض من تلك الأمراض وكل حمى من تلك الحميات كفيلة بأن تقضي عليه لولا الحظ أو البركة أو الطبيب الهندي الذي كان من الأطباء القلائل في دبي في ذلك الوقت ، ولصعوبة نطق اسمه فقد اصطلح السكان على تسميته بالدكتور "الأسود" لأنه كان شديد السمرة وكان عيسى كثيراً ما يحضر راشد حتى في ليالي الشتاء البارد للدكتور "الأسود" الذي يقيم ويمارس مهنته في نفس المسكن . وعندما تشتد الحمى على "راشد" وينقل عيسى مخاوفه حول ابنه وهل سيتمكن من مواصلة العيش للدكتور "الأسود" كان هذا الأخير يبتسم ويعلمه أنه يجب أن لا يخاف لأن راشد لن يموت في دبي .

درس "راشد" في المدرسة المتوسطة حيث كان مشاغباً من الطراز الأول ، وبالرغم من الضرب المبرح الذي كان يتلقاه من والده ومن المدرسين استمر في سلوكه المنحرف . كان يحضر دائماً متأخراً عن الطابور اليومي وإذا حضر يوماً في الطابور فإنه لا يحيي العلم وعندما يردد زملاؤه الهتاف اليومي (وطننا ــ من المحيط إلى الخليج ، أمتنا ــ أمة عربية واحدة ، نموت لتحيا القومية العربية) فإنه يسخر من ذلك الهتاف ويخرج صوتاً ناشزاً . كان قد جعل من تسلق أسوار المدرسة والهرب اليومي من الدروس عادة مستديمة ، حتى أن وكيل المدرسة الفلسطيني بكل حماسه القومي وشدته يئس من تأديبه . ولعل أغرب منظر شهدته تلك المدرسة كان عندما أتت قوادة إيرانية معروفة ، بجسمها الضخم وعباءتها المميزة وبرقعها اللامع وعينيها الواسعتين الجاحظتين لكي تشتكي من "راشد" وبعض زملائه الذين سرقوا دجاجها وبطها من بيتها القريب من المدرسة وباعوه في السوق . بعد تلك الحادث تغيب "راشد" أسبوعاً عن المدرسة وعندما أحضره "عيسى" إلى الوكيل وهو يعتذر عن الحادثة ، أوشك الوكيل أن يطرده كلياً لولا ترجي وتذلل "عيسى" وحماس الوكيل القومي . عندما واصل راشد سقوطه في كل صف ، مرات عدة ، لدرجة أنه عندما وصل الى الصف الرابع الابتدائي ، كان عمره قد أصبح سبعة عشر عاماً ، يئس أبوه منه فأخرجه من المدرسة . كان الأب قد أصبح صاحب قارب صيد متوسط الحجم وعنده ثلاثة بحارة يعملون معه ، عمل "راشد" جابياً في البلدية ، يمر على باعة السمك والقصابين وغيرهم لكي يأخذ منهم رسوم البلدية التي كان يضع معظمها في جيبه . بعد استقلال الامارات ، أسس "راشد" ثلاث شركات وهمية وذلك ليحصل على رخصة جماعية ويتاجر بالفيز ، اسم الأولى "شركة القطط السوداء" ، والثانية "شركة الامارات المشعة" والثالثة "شركة الخمسة الكبار" . كان يبيع الفيزا الواحدة بخمسة آلاف درهم . حصل على ثروة صغيرة ، اشترى لوالده لنشأ كبير الحجم وأكبر بكثير من قاربه السابق وأصر على تسميته "الفيزا" . ذهب إلى مصر وتزوج فلاحة مصرية اسمها "فاطمة" ، وبعد شهرين ذهب الى الهند وتزوج فتاة أخرى اسمها "خديجة" ، دون أن يكترث لعدم رضى والده عنه . بعد الاستقلال ترك كثيرون من زملاء عيسى البحر . البعض منهم عاشوا مع أبنائهم والبعض الآخر عملوا كفراشين وسعاة في الوزارات والمدارس وآخرون يعيشون على رواتب الشؤون الاجتماعية ولكن "عيسى" استمر في عمله وكان متشككاً في أمر الثروة البترولية لأنه عاش معظم حياته في كدح وتعب وشقاء حيث كان ينتزع لقمة العيش انتزاعاً من فم البحر الشرس لذلك فإنه لم يطمئن لثروة البترول التي جاءت بدون تعب أو جهد كبيرين فكان كثيراً ما يكرر :

ــ المال الذي يأتي بدون تعب ، لا يبقى .

شيء غير معقول ، حتى الخدم والسمّاكين والبحارة أصبح عندهم الآن سيارات وخدم هنود في منازلهم . شيء عجيب ! ناس كسالى ، لا يعملون ويحصلون على كثير من المال ، حتى البدو أصبحوا ينفقون ويبذرون الآلاف في زيجات أبنائهم .

في الصيف الماضي ذهب "راشد" مع بعض أصدقائه إلى بانكوك عاصمة تايلاند . وفي صباح يوم ضبابي وبينما كان " عيسى " ينزل أكياس السمك مع مساعديه بالقرب من سوق السمك في دبي ، جاءه أحد الضباط وكان صديقا لراشد وأخبره أن ابنه قد قتل في مشاجرة في أحد الملاهي في بانكوك .

صدمه الخبر ، جلس مذهولاً وعيناه متجهتان إلى مياه الخور . كان الضباب يخفي معالم الضفة الأخرى للخور . تذكر جثة أبيه وأعمامه وهم يطعنون الحجام . تذكر سدر السيد هاشم والدكتور "الأسود". مسح وجهه وقال لسانه بشكل خافت وميت : إنّا لله وإنّا إليه راجعون .

عبدالله خليفة ـ البحرين

الدرب

إلى أين يسير هذا الطابور الدامي الأقدام ؟

لا أثر للقرية أو القصر أو البحر أو الحدائق أو النسمات الشمالية ، تلال من الرمل وحقل من النخيل الشيطاني ومرتفعات صخرية ومنخفضات كأفواه جائعة ، والشمس هذا البركان المتنقل المتفجر يرسل قذائفه في الوجوه وهذا الطابور يزحف بمعاوله ورفوشه وجراراته وخيامه وعرقه وأرقه وصرخاته وسياطه مجتاحاً الرمال والأعشاب والصخور والتلال والنخيل، خيوطاً من الدخان تعلو فوقه ، يشق طريقه مخلفاً خطاً أسود ودماً وعظاماً وبقايا الطعام ..

واجهنا حقل من النخل ، جذوع منتصبة بانحناءات مكسورة ، مجموعة من الشيوخ الشحّاذين على أبواب الصحراء .. تمد أيديها للماء ولكن البلدوزر الأصفر يمد لها أسنانة .. تجتاح الأعشاب والفسائل الصغيرة تقطعها جدة وقوة ، ننظر إلى الشمس الصاعدة نحو قلب السماء ونخفض رؤوسنا بسرعة ، انها تعصر القلب وتشرب الدم ، يطعن البلدوزر النخلة الشامخة ، تلك التي تتصب في عمق الطريق ، يجأر بالغضب وهي تقاوم بصلابة ، يتناثر "الكرب "فوق الأرض وتنتزع الأسنان تلك القشرة السوداء لتصل إلى البياض الجميل ، تتحني النخلة قليلاً ، تغوص الأسنان ، يرهف السمع إلى الأرض اللامبالية ، أقطع بذور ، اجمع الحجارة اصطدم بعامل آخر .. جوزيف ينحني لي بابتسامة جميلة ، كوجهه الوسيم .. اكتسى سمرة الهند الجنوبية نتعاون على قطع نخلة صغيرة ، نضربها بحدة وغضب ، لكنها لا تتأثر .. أرى البلدوزر يتراجع عن النخلة العملاقة ، ويفاجئها من الخلف بضربة حادة ، تهتز ، ضربة أخرى ، لكنها لا تسقط ، العامل الانكليزي الذي يقود البلدوزر يصرخ بهياج ، نسمعه فنحفر لنخلتنا ونقطعها من الأسفل ، يتراجع الانكليزي ويطلب من العمال الانتباه .. يهجم بضراوة ، تقطع السكين الضخمة النخلة فتتهاوى جثتها بصخب ننطلق إليها ، نرفعها بسرعة وخفة ونلقيها حيث تجمعت الجذوع في مقبرة هائلة ..

تحتشد السواعد ، تتقارب أجساد كثيرة لمئات الرجال العرق ينضح ويغسل الخرق الكاكية اللون ، الجذوع تقذف بعيداً ، الحصى ينزع ، الجذور تقلع بعنف أو تقطع أو تحرق ، بقايا البركة تهدم وتسوى بالأرض انصت إلى صيحات الأطفال الذين كانوا يغوصون ويتسابقون من أجل حبة لوز ، يتذكر جوزيف مدينته الكبيرة التي قدم منها ، انها باتساع هذا الرمل وذاك البحر ، والبشر أنهار تصب في كل مجرى ، والغابات الساكتة قرب الجبال ، الخضرة بامتداد النظر ، الورقة الخضراء صفحة من كتاب مقدس ، والمطر والانهار والمعابد والقلاع القديمة ومصنعه الذي غادره ، واصدقاؤه وزوجته وطفلتاه ، يضرب الأحجار بعنف ويرملها ، يتوقف يدخن ، يميل قبعة القش نحو عينيه ، يقول :

ـ يا للشمس ؟؟ نحن لدينا شمس مؤذية ولكن ليست مثل هذه ؟

ذهبت مراراً إلى غرفته الواسعة ، حيث عسكر جيش صغير من زملائه ، اصطفت الأسرة قرب بعض ، فتحت النوافذ على مصراعيها ، وانهالت موسيقى الرقص والغابات والجبال والثلوج .. يحدق في السقف طويلاً أو يرمق صورة العائلة المشتركة .. ما أجمل وجه زوجته ؟؟ تنطق العينان والقسمات والفم الصغير والأنف الجميل"تعال ! "يتأوه بحدة ، ويسحب علبة البيرة وينفث الدخان .. قطار صغير يمضي في البحر أو الرمال وهو يلوح من بعيد النافذة ، تضيع حقيبته في المطار ، يقرأ نص العقد فيفاجىء بالغرفة الجماعية ، ينتظر دوره للحمام وهو يئن من الألم .. يلوح لزوجته وتضيع ملامحها في النهر البشري المتدفق ، يتذكر أنه نسي أن يقبل ابنته الكبرى لآخر مرة ، يرفع يده ، يصرخ ، وينطلق القطار ، تضيع صيحاته

55

في الأجواء والزحام والمطارات والتأشيرات والتفتيش والحجر الصحي وعقد العمل الغريب واللغات والوجوه المكفهرة ، ينهار على فراشه مفرغاً العلب والنقود والسجائر ..

يقترب رئيس الملاحظين الانكليزي "ديفيد" يخزنا باحدى عينيه ويهز العصا في يده .. اكتسى بالعرق :

– لا أريد أية أحاديث أثناء العمل ؟؟

طالما ردّد هذه الملاحظة ، أمس تشاجر مع عامل وضربه بالعصا ، توقف العمال لحظة وهم يسمعون شجاره مع الرجل ، تصاعدت صرخاته ، هجم بحدة ، تحاوط الملاحظون العمال ، دفعوهم نحو العمل ، مهدنا الأرض بصمت ، سمعنا عويل الرجل ثم رأيناه ينهض وينفض التراب ويندس في الجموع ..

استوت الأرض تماماً ، اختفت البركة والأوراق والجذور ، فرغت الشاحنات حمولتها من الأسفلت .. اقتربنا منه فلسعتنا أنفاسه الحارة ، غرفنا برفوشنا ونثرناه .. أيدٍ كثيرة ، تلال سوداء عديدة ، نجار حار يتصاعد ، أحس بوجهي يشوى ببطء وبلا توقف .. كم بحثت في المكاتب عن عمل ؟؟

زاحمتني الأكتاف والرسائل ودخلت مكاتب باردة كالثلاجات ، رمقتني السكرتيرات بلا مبالاة ، سرت على الأرصفة ، قرأت اعلانات الصحف ، ثم فتحت الشمس ذراعيها الطويلتين وضمتني ، تمدد الأسفلت على الطريق النامي ..

بدأت الصحراء تستقبلنا ، الرمل الأصفر لا نهاية له ، ثمة تلال وحفر وأتربة ، الطابور يغادر مكانه ويمضي ، ثمة حفر واسعة علينا أن نردمها .. الآلات والرجال تنطلق حيث تكوم الرمل .. جوزيف أيضاً معي يبدو أن تعباً عنيفاً قد تسلل إلى هيكله الصغير .. يملأ الشاحنة بالرمل ببطء .. اغرفوا ، اغرفوا ، املأوا هذه الحفر بالرمل ، الطريق لا يعرف أحد إلى أين تقود ، بعضهم يقول إلى قصر فخم ، البعض الآخر يؤكد انه إلى جسر ، اغرفوا ، اضربوا هذه التلال ، يتطاير الغبار ، اسمعه يتألم من عينيه .. روى لي جوزيف انه كان مدمناً على القراءة، في المصنع الذي عمل فيه اكتشف أشياء كثيرة ، الحروف وأسرار الكلمات ، الأصدقاء السواعد التي تقف معاً ، الابتسامات الطالعة من القلب ، جلسات الغناء والاكتشاف والرحلات ، كان المطر والشمس الهادئة ، كان الشتاء والمعاطف والجمر ، الطفلتان والأم والسمر ، هناك غرفتاه الصغير تان ، اكتمل كل شيء .. كيف جاء ؟ كيف اندفع وألقى كل شيء وراءه ؟ كيف وجد نفسه فجأة في صحراء يشتعل رملها وتقذف سماؤهم الحمم ؟

عيناه ، كأنه لا يرى ، يقذف الرمل بعيداً عن الشاحنة ، يملأ وجه أحد العمال ، يشتمه الآخر ، يقترب ديفيد منه ، يهزه بعنف :

– ألا ترى جيداً أيها الغبي ؟
– امتلأت عيناي بالغبار ..
– أهذه خدعة للراحة ؟

من جديد يغرف ، الحفر عميقة كالآمال الخائبة ، الشمس استوت فوق السماء ، اندفع اللهب من الرمل والقار .. الأعماق الخائبة لا ترتوي بالرمل ، لم تعد لديه كتب هنا ، في النهار تحت الشمس ، في الليل يقدم المشروبات في البار ، الدخان والسهر والاهانات والتعب والرغبة في النوم والرحيل ، ومرة أسقط كأس البيرة المليء في حضن رجل فلكمه بقوة ، سقط تحت الطاولة ، كانت الأشياء كلها تدور حوله ، الكؤوس والوجوه والمصابيح الصفراء والكوفيات البيضاء والطاولات ، أحس بنفسه يرتفع ويحلق في الأعالي ، كأنه يجثم على مقعده في الطائرة ، كأنه يمد يده من القطار ويتذكر أنه لم يقبل ابنته الكبرى المريضة ، لم يودع اصدقاءه في المصنع ، أخذت الأضواء الخافتة تدور كالزنابير ، الوجوه تدور ، كانت اللكمة موجعة وحد الطاولة موجع ، الندل يغسلون ثوب الرجل الذي راح يدور ، أبصر نفسه يغرق في بحر عميق من البشر والأحجار والزجاجات الفارغة ..

اقتربت سيارة فخمة منا .. أزيحت ستائر داخلية وأطل وجه رجل عجوز .. طالع ما انجزناه بغضب و اضح .. ثم اندفعت العجلات الأربع وأطلقت سحابة غبار عارمة ..

نصف ساعة الغداء ابتدأت .. تجمعنا في الخيام الكبيرة المنصوبة .. تزاحمنا في بقعة ضيقة وظهرت أكلات من الجنوب والشرق والغرب .. تصاعدت الشكاوى والضحكات والآمال ، قال أحدهم : إن رجلين أصيبا بضربة شمس ونقلا إلى المستشفى .. كم تمنى جوزيف أن يصاب بضربة شمس ويرتاح عدة أيام ! أمس حطم ديفيد وجه رجل رفض أن يعمل ، سمعنا صيحاته ، نظرنا إليه ، كانت الأيدي تمسك الرفوش والمعاول وتقود العربات والآلات ، ثمة لحظة خاطفة توقف فيها كل صوت ، تلك اللحظة الغريبة التي لم يسمع فيها سوى الضرب ، وقفت الأيدي لحظة حداد على شيء مبهم ، انصتنا إلى الرجل وهو يبكي ، الرجل ذي اللحية الكثة وأسمال الجبال ، بدا أن النشيج قد انبعث من الشمس والأرض والتلال والخيام ، ملأ الصوت الفضاء .. استحالت اللحظة الخاطفة إلى وقت طويل لا يريد أن يفضي إلى نهاية .. نظرنا إلى بعضنا البعض ، رجال سود وصفر وبيض ، أنبتتنا جبال وأنهار ومدن وصحاري ثم ألقانا التيار الصاخب في جدول ضيق .. النظرات تقترب ، تكون شيئاً غامضاً ، كأن الأيدي تمتد وتتجمع .. لكن البكاء توقف ، واستعادت الضجة مكانها المفقود ..

انتهت نصف ساعة الغداء الخاطفة ، فترة لذيذة رغم التكديس في الخيام .. غفوة صغيرة منعشة .. لم تزل الشمس مرابطة فوق العيون ، لا نسمات ، لا طيور ، لا نخيل ، أسربة وأتربة وأفاعون أسود يزحف إلى جهة مجهولة .. قالوا إن الطريق يفضي إلى قصر عال في الصحراء ، وأنه ينتظر قدوم مالكه من رحلة شهر عسل . قالوا إن زفافاً مذهلاً سيبدأ فيه .. لم يعد يهمني شيء في هذه الحياة ، سرت وسرت وركضت في الطرق ، بحثت عن عمل حتى اهترأت أصابع قدمي ، انحنيت أمام تاجر سلع مهربة ، انتظرت أياماً أمام باب مقاول .. حتى خفت صوتي .. لا يبدوَ أي قصر في هذه الآفاق ، وعلينا أن نهرول في هذا الرمل المجهول .. حثتني زوجتي على أن أصمت دائهاً ، أمسكتني بحدة وهي تصرخ ، خرجت من المنزل لاعناً كل شيء ..

زحفنا ، جاءت الشاحنات وألقت الأسفلت .. الملاحظون انطلقوا يعنفوننا على الكسل والأحاديث ، ارتفعت عصيهم وأصواتهم .. اندفع الطابور الهائل إلى تلال القار المتكومة ، راحت الرفوش تأكل الوجبة السوداء بنهم ، تتصاعد الأبخرة وهو ينثر على الأرض ..

اقترب مني جوزيف وقال :

‫– لا أستطيع أن أحتمل أكثر ..

الكلمات التشجيعية تتبخر في هذه الجو . سقط عامل على الاسفلت . اندفعنا إليه ، غاص في القار وشوى ظهره . يتكلم بلغة رنانة كالعصافير . نزعنا قميصه ورأينا آثاراً حمراء و انتفاخات في كل جسده . يرتعش . أخذناه إلى احدى الخيام . الملاحظون يدعوننا إلى ترك الرجل فوراً .

يتقدم ديفيد بحنق :

‫– عندما يسقط رجل لا أريد أن أرى أحداً يقترب منه ..

يفض الصفوف بعصاه ويديه وبصاقه وشتائمه .. نعود . أنصت إلى طاشر متعب يرفرف في الساء ، يطلق نداءات من أعماقه إلى كائنات بعيدة ، إلى أين تريد أن تمضي في هذه البراري الموحشة ؟ يلتفت جوزيف ويصغي .. يقترب طائر آخر ، ظهر من لهيب النار الذائب في الهواء .. يمضيان معاً ، ويتغلغلان في الضوء ..

أي هدير لهذا الطابور ؟ اهتزت الأرض ، ترنحت التلال من المعاول وآلات الحفر ، حاولت الصخور أن تصد التوغل ، أطنان من الحصى تقذف بعيداً ، الطريق يبدأ خطوة ثم يتسع ، العرق والكره لكل شيء

والحقد على الناس والحجارة والشمس والقصر والأفراح .. ذات ليلة تضاء بقعة كبيرة في الصحراء ، تأتي قوافل من السيارات الفخمة ، عبر الطريق .. تنتشر النار تحت السفافيد والقدور الكبيرة السوداء ، رائحة السعف المحترق والشمبانيا والكافور تهفهف مع الريح ، دقات الطبول والدفوف وضجّة الجاز تسري في الصحراء الباردة .. هل سيرى المخمورون النائمون على مقاعد سياراتهم أية عظام على الطريق ؟

تتناثر الصخور بعيداً عن الطريق ، يريني جوزيف كائناً غريباً يزحف هارياً .. كان ضباً كبيراً مذعوراً . قالت لي زوجتي أصمت فصمت .. اندفعت في الشوارع وأرصفة الميناء ، دخلت المكتب الأنيق فقال لي الرجل اننا نريد أن نوظفك ولكن .. سرت بين الحديد الخردة ، واسترحت في الظل ، قرأت في الجريدة ، أبصرت ألسنة مقطوعة وأنفاقاً مهدمة ..

سقطت قبعة القش التي يلبسها .. يمسكها بصعوبة ، وجهه احقن بالدماء في حمرة النفط المشتعل ، أضواء الآبار تسحبه من زحمة البشر المتكدسين .. يلقي الكتاب جانباً وينطلق ، القطار ضجة مدوية في الآفاق الخضراء ، قالت زوجتي : أصمت ! تضيع الحقيبة والحقيقة ويشعر بأنه طفل ضاع في غابة ، قالت زوجته : تعال ! لم يرسل بطاقة العيد للأصدقاء ، ترنح على الأرض ترنح المعول والقبعة ، أمسك حجراً دخل في كيفه .. لم يتجمهر العمال حوله ، سرت نحوه ، الملاحظون تنبهوا ، سمعت نداءات خلفي خفتت الضجة قليلاً ، كان جوزيف بلا حراك ، كأن حربة سحرية تثبت رأسه ، رفعته ، نداءات وصرخات حولي ، توقف البلدوزر ورأيت النخلة تنحني ، قلت : سأحمله إلى الخيمة ثم أعود بسرعة ، دفعني أحدهم بقوة ، رأيت ديفيد فوق رأسي ، خفت .

– قلت لا تفعلوا ذلك .

ضربني بحدة على كتفي بعصاه . جاش صدري بماء حارق ، استكنت وأنا أمسك حجراً، النخيل المحتضر الدب الهارب ، البار الطاولة التي سقط تحتها جوزيف ، تدور ، الشمس التنور ، طابور العمال الصامت يدور ، اللافتات ، اعلانات الجرائد .

– لا يحق لك أن تضربني .
– اخرس ؟؟

حرك رأس جوزيف بحذائه . أمسكه من ياقته بعنف :

– انهض ؟؟

الرجل لا يقوى على الوقوف ، يضربه ، يصرخ به أن ينهض ، يضربه ، توقفت المحركات ، الرجل يسقط كخرقة ، تسكن الرفوش والمعاول . يتقدم عاملان نحو الخيام . صمت كل شيء . النظرات تلتقي . لغات عديدة تتكسر في النور الباهر . ثلاثة عمال يتقدمون أيضاً . الملاحظون ينتشرون . صرخات غاضبة تتردد في البرية الشايعة . لكن الصمت عاد يلف كل شيء .

58

علي سيار ـ البحرين

شمس لا تشرق كل يوم

رفع الكأس بيده وأفرغها في جوفه .. ومن جديد عاد يهذى .. ماذا يظنون ؟ لست غبيا مثلهم … الاخلاق .. يتحدثون عن الاخلاق … ! مالها اخلاقى ؟ لا تعجبهم .. ولكنهم لا يقولون مثلا أن هناك أشياء لا تعجبنى أنا .. لماذا يسكتون عندما يأتى الحديث عن نعيمة ؟ لماذا لا يقولون أنها لا تعجبهم أيضا ؟ لانها من صنع يدهم .. ومع ذلك فهم لايخجلون منى …

قلت لهم هذه المرأة بالذات لا أريدها .. انها قبيحة .. في قبح أم ابراهيم الخياطة .. فقلت لهم انها جاهلة .. أجهل من البقرة التى نشرب حليها كل يوم … وقلت لهم انها شرسة .. أشرس من كلب الجيران .. وقلت لهم .. وقلت لهم .. كل العيوب تتجمع فيها .. ورغم ذلك قالت لى أمى ذات صباح : "نعيمة أمرأة قل ان يجود الزمان بمثلها .. الجمال .. ؟ اسطورة .. العلم ؟ ان الاكابر لا يعلمون بناتهم .. ولم ابه بكلام امى .. فقد كنت فى حالة نفسية جعلتنى أتوهم أن الدنيا كلها تحاربنى .. وهذه ليست المرة الاولى التى تردد أمى على مسمعى هذه الاسطوانة .. ألف مرة سمعتها .. وكنت فى باديء الامر أتبرم واثور .. ولكننى ماعتمت أن ألفت سماعها كل يوم حتى بت أكره أن أمد يدى الى طعام في البيت .. وأصبح شيئا عاديا .. أن يتبلد احساسى وتتجمد مشاعرى ..

وذات يوم ـ والاسطوانة تدور ـ احسست باننى اضعف من أن أقاوم .. وأن عنادى أصبح اضحوكة بين أفراد العائلة .. فقلت لها : يا أمي .. الامر أمرك ..

وتلقفت أمى هذه الكلمة وتحولت فى فمها الى زغرودة منغمة .. وتوالت بعد ذلك الايام فى الاعداد والتجهيز .. وبعد أسبوع كنت أشد قامتى أمام المدعوين وأعلق على فمى ابتسامة بلهاء وأنا أنتظر اللحظة الرهيبة التى أزف فيها الى عروستى .. بنت الاكابر .. ووسط الزغاريد والاضواء ودق الطبول جيء بها الى .. ولم يفتنى فى تلك اللحظة أن ألمح العيون الماكرة وهى تتطلع الى فى رثاء واشفاق .. كما لو كانت تتطلع الى جندى يخوض معركة خاسرة ..

ولم أشأ أن أكون ضحية سهلة .. فقد انفجر فى نفسى بعدها احساس عاصف بأننى كنت ضحية مؤامرة خبيثة اشتركت فى وضعها أمى وأمها .. والظروف التى خلقتنى فقيرا وخلقتها ذات نعمة وجاه …. وكبر الاحساس فى نفسى ذات يوم .. كبر لدرجة أننى بت لا أنفر فقط من المخدع الذى يضمنى واياها .. ولكن من البيت كله .. من كل الوجوه الساخرة الهازئة التى تطالعنى كل مرة أدخل أو أخرج فيها الى البيت .. بل ما عدت أستطيع حتى النظر الى الشارع الذى يقع فيه البيت .. مسرح المأساة .. ووجدت أنه لم يكن هناك بد من وضع حد لهذه الحياة السخيفة ..

وما كان هناك أمامى غير طريق واحد .. طريق الطلاق …

وفى صباح بارد ثقيل خيل الى فيه أننى أكثر شجاعة من اللحظة التى أقدمت فيها على الزواج .. ألقيت اليها بيمين الطلاق .. يمينا انتزعته من بين ضلوعى .. كأنما كنت أنتزع رصاصة غائصة فيه ..

ومرت أيام عصيبة بعد ذلك كدت أفقد فيها هذا الشيء الصغير الذى يسمونه العقل .. فقد أعلنت على أمي الحرب .. وشننت على أمها هجوما ساحقا من الكلام البذيء الساخر .. وشعرت أن كل الجبهات قد فتحت على نيرانها .. ولم أستطع أن أواجه المعركة فقد كان ميزان القوى غير متكافيء .. وهربت من الميدان .. تركت البيت لهم .. ونزلت الى الشارع أضرب فيه .. انها أول مرة أخرج فيها على ارادتهم .. وأول مرة أخرج فيها من البيت وأنا أعتزم أن لا أعود .. واحتوانى الشارع الكبير .. وزاغت عينى هنا وهناك .. وحشرت نفسى بين الجموع الادمية التى يكتظ بها الشارع .. وأحسست لاول مرة أننى لم أعد

ذلك المسحوق الضائع المسلوب الارادة .. احسست بلذة الانعتاق وبلذة الانطلاق حيث أشاء .. ومررت فى طريقى بنساء كثيرات .. نساء بعضهن لا يفترقن كثيرا عن أم ابراهيم الخياطة ... وأخريات يمشين وكأنهن يرقصن .. وكنت أطل فى عيونهن .. وكان يخيل الى أننى أطل على عالم غامض سعيد .. ومع كل لفتة امرأة كانت تتثائب فى أعماقى رغبة مجنونة .. فقد كنت أشعر بكل ذرة فى جسمى تتواثب كفقاعات المياه الغازية .. وبدأ لى أن هناك شيئا ما يعبث فى رأسى .. شيئا كالذكرى .. ولم تجهد ذاكرتى كثيرا للتعرف على هذا الشىء .. انها هى بدون شك .. بدرية .. ومر فى ذهنى خاطر .. لماذا لا أذهب اليها ؟ انها أول وآخر امرأة خطت اليها قدماى فى طريق الرذيلة .. وهى لميست شرسة ككلب الجيران .. وفوق ذلك فهى تحبنى .. هكذا كانت تقول لى قبل ان تقع كارثة زواجى بنعيمة ..

ولكن كيف سأذهب اليها بعد أن تنكرت لها قبيل زواجى .. ؟ اننى ما أزال أذكر كيف واجهتها ذات يوم بقرارى الحازم .. هكذا كنت أتصور قرارى حينئذ .. وما أزال أذكر كيف لوت بوزها وهى تتلقى هذا القرار .. وكيف أشارت بأصبعها ناحية الباب وهى تطلب منى أن أغادر البيت حالا .. لقد خيل الى ساعتها – لسذاجتى – انها لم تفعل ذلك الا لتعلقها الشديد بى .. لم يدر بخلدى قط أنها تبيع جسدها لكل من يدفع .. واننى ما عدت بالنسبة لها – بعد القرار المشئوم – ذلك الذى يستطيع أن يواصل الدفع بعد أن انسحبت مسئولياتى والتزاماتى المادية على شخص آخر ..

وعبرت الطريق خفيفا رشيقا وفى رأسى خيالات برنامج براق .. ولكن كيف تراها ستقابلنى .. كيف أصبحت .. كيف .. كيف .. ؟ ولم ينقذنى من دوامة الاسئلة الحائرة الا وقوفى أمام الباب .. الباب الاخضر الصغير القابع فى أحد زوايا الشارع المثير.. هكذا كنت أسمى الشارع الذى يقع فيه بيتها ..

وخيل الى وأنا أطرق الباب بأننى أنسلخ عن شخصيتى الضائعة البلهاء .. وأعود كما كنت ذلك الشاب المرح الانيق الذى يقتطف من جنة الحياة أزهى زهورها وأحلاها .. وتناهى الى سمعى صوت ناعم أخاذ .. لابد وأن يكون صوتها .. فقد كنت أعرفه من بين الاف الاصوات ..

وفتحت الباب .. وكانت هى على الباب .. وللحظات فقدت نفسى .. فقدت القدرة على ان أتصرف .. وتحسست لسانى كمن يفتش عن شىء ضاع منه .. وانتشلتنى هى من دوامة الضياع .. كانت تبتسم فى وجهى ... كأنما كانت تريد أن تقول :

– وأخيرا ها أنت ذا تعود ..

وطأطأت رأسى فى خجل .. فقد كان الموقف مخجلا حقا .. ثم انطلقت الى الداخل وأنا أزيحها برفق من أمامى .. ورويدا رويدا – عندما استقربى المقام – أخذ لسانى ينطلق .. بل أخذت اثرثر وأهذى بكلام أعى بعضه ولا أعى أغلبه .. قلت لها كل شىء .. وقدمت لها كشفا مفصلا بالايام التى ابتعدت فيها عنها .. ورويت لها كيف وضعت للقصة .. وكيف فكرت فى أن أعود اليها ..

وشعرت بارتياح عميق وأنا أفتح لها نافذة واسعة على أفكارى .. وكانت هى – ولا أدرى كيف . فما كانت هذه عادتها – كانت تنصت باهتمام بالغ الى كل ثرثرتى وحكاياتى .. ونظرت الى عينيها فى شبه تساؤل عن هذا التحول فى طبيعتها .. فقد كنت أعرفها ثرثارة كثيرة الكلام .. بل كنت كثيرا ما أحذرها من أن تفتح فمها رهى تشرب الماء خشية أن تشرق به ...

وبنظرة فيها الكثير من الاعتداد .. والكثير من التحدى والصمود .. وجدتها تقوم من مكانها ثم تتجه صوب دولاب صغير فى أحد أركان الغرفة .. صامتة هادئة متزنة .. ومن فوق الدولاب تلتقط صورة رجل فى اطار أنيق .. وجاءت الى بالصورة .. وحدقت فيها .. شارب أنيق تنفر بعض شعيراته . ووجه بشوش هادىء .. وفى كلمات حادة ثقيلة انبعث صوتها كلسعة سوط مبلول :

– هذا زوجى ..

وفى لحظة تصورت كل شىء وكأنه يمشى بالمقلوب .. وفتحت فمى فى بلاهة أريد أن أتكلم .. أن أقول
شيئا .. ولكن الكلمات ماتت فى حلقى وهى تتلمس طريقها الى لسانى .. وبعدها لم أدر .. هل أضحك ..
هل اتجاهل كلماتها الحادة الثقيلة .. هل أخرج من دارها .. ؟ الموقف غريب .. امرأة متزوجة .. ورجل
سكران يهذى ويثرثر معها فى دارها .. وخيل الى أننى ماعدت أعنى شيئا بالنسبة لها .. هذه المرأة التى
كانت تموء جوعا وعطشا كلما غبت عنها يوما ... ونظرت الى الارض وأنا أدارى فى داخلى شعورا
بالذلة والانكسار ... ولم أقل شيئا .. فقد كانت الكلمات أعجز من أن تعنى شيئا .

وفى لحظة أحسست كأن شيئا ما يموت فى داخلى .. وأن شيئا ما – أيضا – يولد فى داخلى ..
هذه المرأة .. وجدت أخيرا نفسها .. اكتشفت أن سوق الخطيئة قد يكون براقا .. ولكنه أبدا يحز فى اللحم
ويطحن فى العظم .. وها هى ذى أخيرا تعرف لحياتها معنى غير معنى الضياع الذى كانت تستحم فيه قبل
أن تبدأ رحلتها الجديدة .. وعلى الوجه الاخر أحسست أننى أيضا أفقد نفسى .. أتوه فى سوق صنعته فى
أعماقى وزخرفته وجملته .. سوق الخطيئة الذى عرفته بدرية بعد سنوات الاثم والضياع .

ورويدا رويدا .. أشرقت فى أعماقى شمس جديدة .. شمس لاتشرق كل يوم ..

فريد رمضان – البحرين

البياض

أنا محتاج لأن ارسم وجهك بكل وضوح كى أجد الخيط الضائع في انارة هذا الوطن .
.... فريد

- 1 -

الدخان يخنق الجرة .. هذه العجوز التى زاد عمرها عن مائة سنة ، تضاجع حزنى .. شرعت أفتش بين الثنايا عن الفرشاة .. أتعبنى البحث ، كانت عالما من الشيخوخة والفوضى ، وحين وجدت الفرشاة , كانت خالية من الالوان ..

"كيف أكتب اسمها بهذه الالوان المتداولة ؟" .

أمسكت قاموس الكلمات وبدأت أبحث عن حروف متلونة بالفرح ، راقصتنى كل الحروف فوقفت عند احدها :

ف : عالم ينتظر الزوبعة .

أ : عالم تؤرجحه الرياح .

تساءلت :

– أين أدفن ثقل هذا اللون الحزين ؟

هذا الدخان كثيف ، والسيجارة تسابق الزمن في احتظارى ، وأنا أرسم شكل اللقاء .. فتشت في تربة هذه الحجرة عن اللون وعنها .

"أى امرأة تحسسنى بدفء أيامى ، وبالعشق المتواصل ، بالنجمة المقبلة ؟" .

أمسكت الفرشاة بكل قوة .. شىء ما يجول بخاطرى .. يدى ترتجف فأخاف تحريكها ، اللوحة البيضاء تدعونى للرسم .. أنظر اليها .. أدخن بعمق .. أنفث الدخان بكل صعوبة .. تتحرك يدى على مساحة اللوحة .

"حين تبدع الالوان ، تكونين أنت الالهة" .

أرسم شيئا قد يدعى العشق أو الاحتضار .. أجد تشابها كبيراً بينهما .. أحس بألم شديد يعصر أمعائى .. مفاصلى ويدي ترتجف .. أضغط بشدة على الفرشاة ، أدعوها لمواصلة الرسم ، لكن الحجرة المتهالكة لا تقوى على مساندتى فتلفضنى .. تسقط الفرشاة من يدى .. أسقط .. أضيع في فوضوية الحجرة .. تجول عيناى على :

* الالوان المتناثرة .

* الكتب المتبعثرة .

* اللوحات المنتصبة على الحائط .

أكتشف أن بينى وبين هذه المواد مسافة أميال من الشوق . أنظر الى اللوحة البيضاء ، أراها تبتسم في وجهى . [اللوحة بيضاء .. مساحة بيضاء ونقط من الالوان منتشرة بصمت .. قوس قزح يأخذ شكل كلمة واضحة بين البقع] .

– أهذا وجهها ، وجه التربة النخلة ، وجه العالم ؟

واجهتنى اللوحة .. قالت :

"تعال أريك اللحظة عمراً يمتد .

أريك الجبل يذوب .

أريك البحر يجف" .

أرعبنى حديث اللوحة .. جحظت عيناى مستغربة .. قلت لها :

ـ هذا لا يمكن ، أنت تنطقين حروف شفتيها ، أتعلمين ان هذا الحرف يدخلنى ، يمتد فى ويمارس الحلم .
  أتكونين أنت هى ؟

يدخل الصمت فجأة ، كان عاريا .. اخجلتنى اجزاء جسده البارزة ، فأشعلت سيجارة أخرى ، نفثت الدخان ..
نفذت كل السجائر ، فلففت قصاصة ورق وشرعت أدخنها .. ضُحكت .
"لاحراق القلب بكل الوسائل الحديثة أمر سهل" .
عادت نظراتى تقتحم اللوحة وتدخل فيها أكثر .. اشعر بنبض اللوحة داخلى .. أطرافها تتحرك ، قوس
قزح .. هذه الالوان لا تسعها مساحة اللوحة فتمتد .. ألوان الطيف تمتد .. تخترق الحيطان وتمتد .. تخترق
صدرى وتمتد .. تكبر .. تصبح بحجم قلب خال من الاسود .. ملىء بالابيض .. تتحرك داخل الحجرة
العجوز . الدهشة . الخوف . الفرح .

ـ تتزوجينى ؟

تستغرب الوان الطيف من هذه الدعوة ، تخاطبنى بلطف :

ـ ان ترسمنا ، سنكون امتدادا للمستقبل ، بسمة لكل حزين .
ـ ولكن ...

تطلب منى السكوت لتقول :

ـ دعنا نمتد الى كل العيون الخالية ونرسمها براءة طفل ، ونظرات عاشق وحنان أم .
ـ اذن ، سوف ارسم العالم بأحسن الصور .

ألملم الفرشاة والاصباغ . أقف على الكرسى وأرسم على حيطان المكتبة لغة جيدة ، ألتصق بحيطان
الحجرة العجوز ، أرسم عليها لحظة ابحار أحد فقراء الحارة الى عالم ملىء بالدانة والحلم .
تتوقف الفرشاة ، فيتحنط الرجل / البحر / الدانة .

- 2 -

ـ من أين أندأ ؟

رسمت على سيارتى وانطلقت مسرعا ، الثوب ملطخ ببقع من الالوان .
"هل أرسم وجهها على جلدى ؟" .
عند البحر قبلت المسافات البعيدة ودنوت لحظة غروب الشمس ..
خاطبتها :

ـ شىء في داخلى دعانى أقبل وجنتيك ، وارسم نقطة صغيرة من فرشاتى على خدك الشامخ ، فشع على
  هذا العالم الوانى .

قبلت البحر ، هذا الغول الذى أرهبني أبى بحكايات كثيرة عنه .. اننى أتذكر صور الرعب وهى تدخل قلوب الغواصين المتمردين داخل المراكب ، لا يواسيهم شىء غير صور اطفالهم والعباءات التى تنتظر على الشاطىء .

– أترعبنى أيها البحر كما فعلت مع أبى ؟

ابتسم البحر قائلا :

– أنت الان تحمل سلاحاً .

كان يشير الى الفرشاة .. ابتسمت كثيرا .. قبلته طويلا ، وحين تعبت ، تمددت داخل أحد القوارب المتناثرة على الشاطىء ، وحلمت بالشراع يمتد داخلى ويشرعنى للرياح الشمالية ، فابحر نحو قرار قلبها .

- 3 -

أتلفت ، ماذا يحدث ؟ .. الحلم يهرب ، واللون يضيع من وجنة الشمس ..
كانوا مدججين بالاسلحة .
كان عزلا .. ألوان وفرشاة .
كانوا لا يعرفون معنى الابيض في اللون .
كنا نعرف .
كانوا ...
كنا ...

- 4 -

في المبنى البعيد عن المدينة ، خاطبنى أحدهم باستهزاء ، قرأ لائحة قتلى :

1. تغيير العالم .
2. الرسم في الشوارع .
3. تحريض الالوان على ...
4. وشوشة الطبيعة .
5. ....

طلبوا منى ان اسجل توقيعى ، فرسمت وجه اللوحة البيضاء ، وشرعت أضحك ، أضحك بكل جنون .. يصابون بالغضب .. يركلونى .. لا أكف عن الضحك .. أشياء كثيرة داخلتنى وأنا أضحك ..

• صورتها .
• الفرشاة والالوان .
• الحجرة العجوز والفوضى .

يجرجرونى وأنا أرسم آخر الاسئلة :

– هل أجد الابيض بعد الآن ؟

1982/02/27 م

فوزيه رشيد – البحرين

من أرشيف الوحدة

- 1 -

كنت أدخل هدأة السكون على الشاطىء الرملي ووجع شبحي يلفّني ، تلهبني سياط الوحدة . " البحر خير رفيق الآن " . نسيمه يغري جسدي ويدعوني إليه . وددت لحظتها أن أسير هكذا دون حدود . فجأة تقف خلفي سيارة ، تصبح اثنتين ، ثم ثلاث ، ألتفت وأتذكر شيئاً " أنا امرأة ! حتى في التوحد .. ليس من حقي .. " ودون أن أستمر في حزني ركضت مسرعة وعدت أدراجي ألى جحيم البيت .

- 2 -

عرفته نجماً سحرياً يقطع ظلمة سمائي .. أحببته .
قال مرة إني ضالته الأبدية وإنه يحبني .
في ليلة هادئة لم يكن يقطع خلوتنا شيء ، انساب في حديث طويل ، عن حياته ، تجاربه قلقة وأحلامه . تدفق في قلبي نهر الذكريات وانسابت أحزاني ، تحدثت معه بالمقابل عن حياتي ، قلقي ، تجاربي وأحلامي .
لا أدري لم حدث ذلك بعد فترة . فقد انقطع عني تماماً .. ولم أعد أراه !

- 3 -

خلته الوحيد الذي أحبني ، اعتدته ، لم أستطع أن أعيش لحظة دونه . ضحكنا كثيراً وأجهشت بالبكاء مرات معه . رأيته الحلم والآتي والضوء في دروب الغد ونبتة الجنون الراحلة أبداً في عروقي تزيدني شوقاً إليه . كان يتحدث عن الفرح طويلاً .. قلت وجديه ! وفي أمسية منسابة كغدير الوجد تبادلنا معاً حديثاً طويلاً . شرعت أحدثه عن حلمي في الزواج . ارتبك قليلاً وأشاح بوجهه في البعيد ، لم أفهم . حدثته عن الحب ، عادت الفرحة إليه ثم قال :

- الحب شيء والزواج شيء آخر !

- 4 -

اعتدنا أن نتحاور في كل شيء . بدا لى أفقاً واسعاً لا حدود له . جمعنا الحلم ومنذ ذلك دخلنا في أتون الحرب الضاربة فينا . أخبرته مرة : أنا لا أحب اليأس والحزن رغم ارتحالي الطويل فيهما . قال : إفرحي ولكن معي ! (سجل حضوره !) ضاع فرحي .
أخبرته واليأس يطاردني : أني أحب أن أقرر لنفسي الأشياء (كان هو يفعل ذلك دون نقاش !) دار حوار طويل !!
وفي مرة اكتست ملامحه الكآبة وكان قد غضب طويلاً . سماني غروراً .. عجبت ، ظننته لغواً ثم تهنا في فجاجة المغالطات .
قال : لست طفلاً .

عجبت أيضاً .

حاولت مرة انتشال ما تبقى من فرحي بأن أعلنت غضبي .. صفعني !

تعاطيت جراحي طويلاً مع نفسي .. وغرقت بين حلمي وواقعه .

أدركت : أن حضوري حوار متطاير بيننا فقط .

أدركت أيضاً : أن الميعاد بين الحلم والواقع لا يزال بعيداً .

أدركت أخيراً : أني لا زلت بالنسبة إليه أنثى فقط .

نوفمبر 1979 م

محمد عبد الملك ـ البحرين

موت صاحب العربة

اشرقت الشمس وبسطت اجنحتها الذهبية على الحارة ، كان شعاع خفيف يزور بيته وكان يربط احزمته حول خصره بعد ان غطى جسمه بملابس ممزقة ومتباينة الأحجام . بدا السرور في محياه وهو يتمم الربطة الأخيرة . لبس حذاءه الممزق واطل من باب بيته فسقطت عيناه على العربة وتبادلا النظرات . كانت في انتظاره منذ ان تركها وحيدة في الخارج . اقترب منها بخطوات متحفزة ثم صافح يديها الطويلتين ورفعها ثم استدار وانطلق يسير وهو يدفعها بحنو عبر الشارع الطويل المتد أمامه . واصل سيره وهو يتطلع الى الشارع بعينين تحملان الطيبة والرضا الممزوج بالثقة .. ها هم الاطفال يجرون حقائبهم الصغيرة امامه وهاهي ابتسامة سعادة بريئة ساذجة ترتسم على وجوههم ، وها هم يهزأون منه ويقلدون مشيته . وبصوت مليء بالحسرة قال :

- يا لهم من اشقياء ينشرون السعادة في الأرض .. انهم يسخرون منك أيها القط العجوز ولكن لا يجب ان يضيرك عملهم هذا .. لو كنت محلهم لفعلت نفس ما يفعلون وهل هناك احد اجدى منك بالسخرية في الحارة .

وكان قد اجتاز الشارع الطويل مخلفاً أزقة الذباب وبيوت سعف النخيل التعسة وراءه . العربة تريد إسقاطه . أنيابها تجلجل تحت قدميه تنتظر سقوطه يوماً ما ، ولكنه لا يريد الاستسلام وعزيمته في ذلك كالحديد . فكر في العربة وهو يدخل سوق الحمالين :

- صراعي معها فوق ما يتصوره الجميع ... رافتها في سني شبابي ولكنها كانت سهلة الانقياد في الماضي ... هي تختلف الآن ... تختلف كثيراً .

واستمر في تفكيره بينما العربة تسمعه دقات اقدام الزمن الثقيلة حتى ضاع مع الزحام .

عند الظهيرة رجعع الى منزله الغائب في امعاء ازقة ضيقة ؛ كان التعب يمخر عظامه بينما مفاصله كانت عاجزة عن الحركة .

استرخى على الحصير ورفع رأسه وحدق في السقف رفيق وحدته في هذا البيت الصامت بلا نسوة ، بلا اطفال يلعبون في حوشه . لقد اختفى الآن ضجيج الناس والسيارات والعربات التي تشبه قطيعاً من الماعز في تزاحمها ، اختفى صراخ الحمالين في السوق الكبير ، وبعيون تشكو الضياع حدث السقف القديم :

- كم أنا في حاجة الآن إلى فراش يحشوه قطن كثير ... فراش من ماء الحرير لأغوص فيه واسبح ... لكن الغوص يحتاج إلى نفس طويل ... أنا لا املك هذا النفس الطويل ... جميع الحمالين لا يملكونه ... نحن لا نملك إلا العربات وانفاسنا تضيع في الحر والعرق !

وابتسم للسقف في سخرية فاستقبل بعض الغبار حتى ضاق نفسه ، طرد الغبار واخذ نفساً ارتفع له صدره ثم اغمض عينيه وشرع يحلم ، ويحلم ، ثم تمادى في حلمه فصنع قصوراً في الجنة وتجول فيها وشرب من خمرها فشعر بشوط كهربائي خفيف يسري في عروقه ، كمادة ثلجية تسير ها ايدي ناعمة ، لكنه انتبه الى صوت قد اعتاده في الخارج فتوقفت الايدي الناعمة الوهمية :

- لابد انهم الصبية عادوا لجر العربة .

اندفع الى الخارج فوجدهم قد ابتعدوا بها كثيراً فصاح فيهم :

– اتركوا العربة يا اولاد ... اتركوا العربة يا اولاد ...

حاول اللحاق بهم ولما رأوه قادماً تنافسوا في دفعها وركوبها ثم اخذوا يدفعونها ويركبونها بالتناوب ، ولما اقترب منها قفزوا من فوقها فارتطمت مقدمتها بالارض وتشتتوا في الأزقة وهم يشعرون بسعادة عظيمة .

عندما عاد بعربته كان أذان العصر ينساب في اذنه يعلن له انتهاء وقت الراحة . صلى العصر جماعة وعاد لدفع العربة من جديد وتمتم في طريقه بينما نظراته تعري كل شيء حوله في الشارع الطويل :

– لا راحة ها ... الراحة في القبر ... الراحة في القبر ... هكذا يقولون ... وقد صدقوا .. لأعود إلى السوق وانضم إلى القطيع !

مرت السنون وتلاحقت وغطى الشيب رأسه بخيوط بيضاء كبيرة تتخللها بقايا شعر اسود بينما نامت عيونه في زوايا وجهه تفترش شقاء سبعين عاماً .

كان عائداً من السوق وهو في حالة اعياء لم يدركه من قبل ، وكان هدير العجلات يصم آذانه بينما شمس اغسطس تحرق كل شيء من حوله . احس بشيء يشبه النهاية وشعر بدوار يتعاظم في اعلى رأسه وزحف جيش من النمل فوق وجهه فغرق في بحيرات العرق ، وضمرت الاشياء من أمامه ثم اختفت تماماً بينما اصبحت العربة في يده اثقل من همومه . تهالكت قدماه على الارض وافلتت العربة من يده فسجد بين يديها في استسلام .

وبعيداً عن حارته كان يحدث الناس بصمته . هذا الصمت الذي ليس له شبيه غير تصلب يده امامه تعترض طريق المصلين :

– اطلب الفائض يا سادة ... فائض سعادتكم ... بعض الهواء استعيش به ، لقد انقطع نفسي كما ترون وما عاد صالحاً لشيء ... بعض الهواء وتزاحمونا في ... الجنة ... اولستم تحملون بنصيب وافر منها ... رجاء ياسادة لا تنظروا إليَّ في عطف واستخفاف هكذا ... انني اراكم ... انني اراكم من خلف بصري الميت ... لقد دفعت العربة سنين طويلة وما عاد بوسعي عمل شيء الآن ... اعتقد انكم تعجزون عن دفعها وانتم في ريعان شبابكم ... هل حاولتم دفع عربة كبيرة يا سادة حاولوا ذلك فقد تكتشفون الحقيقة !

كانت ظهيرة صيف حارة بينما كانت العربة تستقبل زواراً كثيرين جاءوا حباً في استطلاع امر صاحبها ، ولما دخلوا حوش بيته توقفت عيونهم مكان الجثة . بعضهم حاول تفادي الرائحة بوضع يده فوق انفه والبعض الآخر اخذ يطرد الذباب بحركات من يده . كانت بعض الديدان الكبيرة تزحف صدره وبعض القيىء يخفى ملامح وجهه وقد ظهرت عظام فخذه . كان الذباب يحوم حول الجثة يشارك الدود عبثه .

قال احدهم وهو يشاهد دودة كبيرة تندفع فوق صدره :

– لقد مات المسكين موتة شنيعة .

ولما اجتازت الدودة مكانها أضاف :

– لن تكون له جنازة كالآخرين .

راع الصبية مشاهدة صاحب العربة في هذه الحال فانطلقوا من بيته يصيحون بالخبر لأهل الحارة . كان صوتهم يمزق شمس الظهيرة بينما كان اسمه يتجول معهم في الأزقة للمرات الأخيرة :

– لقد مات عبد الله ... لقد مات عبد الله .

وظلت العربة اياماً طوالاً لم يقترب منها احد لكن الصبية عادوا لجرها وتناوبوا دفعها وركوبها ثم ذهبوا بها بعيداً ، وبعيداً جداً حتى اختفوا معها في الأزقة ولكنهم ... لم يشعروا بسعادة .

منيرة الفاضل ـ البحرين

وِسان

لم يكن متعذرا علينا ونحن نجلس مبعثرين في المكان الذي أوصدناه بالمزلاج الحديدي القديم هذا ، كعادتنا كل شهر قمري ، أن يفوتنا قدومها الذي خبأته ، وأملت أن يضل مخزونا في محيطات طبطبت عليها بحنوٍّ في ذهابها الدائم . كانت ترنو لزهو المباغتة ، أو ربما لمجيء يتوارى محوِّطا نفسه بغلالة السكينة .

نجلس هكذا ، متمعنين في نتف الصدأ التي تعلق بأصابعنا كلما مستْ أيادينا صلابة الحديد البارد ، ونحن نسحبه بالتوالي لنتأكد من عزلة وقتية أربكتنا في أيامنا الأولى ونحن نشهد، في الترقيم الزمني الذي عُلِّق في منتصف المحيط المكاني هذا ، ما يشير إلى تشابهنا الزاخر بألفته الوديعة ، نحن الأربعة ، قبل ذهابها وارتيادنا بعد ذلك الفجوات والشروخ التي خلفها غيابها المنشطر عن أجسادنا .

هذا القدوم الذي تذرّعنا أن يحوّطنا بمعطف البنفسج المنسحب على مدار فصول طويلة عاتية ، وما يقال بشأنه من تفاصيل وردت إلينا عبر إيماءات خاطفة لعابرين غرباء كانوا يستريحون على الحد الفاصل بين هذه الجزيرة المرفأ والامتداد البحري الشاسع . يقبعون لدقائق في استراحة وقتية بعصيّهم الغليظة الطويلة ، متكأً ننحدر إليه ونستند بجذوعنا العارمة صوب ظله ، متقصين الحروف التي عادة ما تنثرها وِسان شغفنا هذا ، آملة كما تحدثنا دائما في حفنة الوقت النائم ، محصَّنة بشفافية الحلم ، أن نجد صيغة لهذا الرواح الخارج عن متناولنا .

قلوبنا تنزُّ بالريبة إزاء هذه المماهاة التي تأتي متلبسة شجنا آخر غير الذي عهدناه . نجلس منصتين لقدومها ، نتبين الخطو الحثيث في مسالك إسفلتية ، وباحات رخامية باردة تمتد فيها صفوف من الوجوه والمقاعد المخملية وإشارات وعلامات توضح للتائه توجهه الذي قد رُسم له مسبقا حال اجتيازه العتبة للباب الالكتروني الكبير .

توجهها إلينا وهي تقحمه في سديم رابض لا يتحرك ، يماطل كل ما نستبطنه من كشف في ضياعنا الزمني هذا ، ونحن في لهْثٍ صوب وجود يُكمل ويُردم بيد مستبصرة غيابها الذي لم نَطُل شأنه بعد .

نبادر برصد أقياس من القُنَّب التي خاطتها يد الخيالة مردودة بعناية فائقة آن طفولتنا البهيجة . ترتسم عليها حروفنا الأولى ، لئلا ننفلت في غيّنا ومشاكستنا لها ، حين يتلبَّس كل منا هوية الآخر ، تاركينها في الالتباس والحيرة .

في هذا المحيط المكاني نصون ونُرتِّب وننفض الغبار عن تاريخنا الذي اختلط على الآخرين ، وظل شفيفاً رقراقا في وضوحه أمام أحداقنا . نتصفح الأوراق التي غالبتها الصفرة وطبعت عليها الرطوبة متعرجاتها ، لنأنس لخطابات سُطِّرت عليها بعض الحروف في لحظات لم نألف فيها البعد الوقتي ، على حين ظلت صفحات عديدة أخرى تطالعنا باصفرارها الشاحب تنتظر أن يرأف بها حبر ما ليشكل بالكلمات هاجسا عائما في محيطها . نطالعها كلها ، داخلين في حكاية الحرف أو في ردهات فضاءات السطور التي لم تُسطَّر بعد ، لنعيد طيِّها بسلاسة الترتيب الذي ارتأته يد وِسان لحظة انتهائها أو عجزها عن البوح بما يستكين عميقا في جذورها .

لهفتنا لا تطاق ، ننقر بأناملنا على القلب ليستكين ويداري انفلاتاته ، صوبها نحن في ارتياد المسافات دائما . نُطهِّم جذوعنا بزاد الانتظار المضني ، نزنُ الدقائق في أكفّنا الست المدودة لتستقيم كالمسلات في عبء وقت هو ليس لنا ، كشرك مفتون بذاته ، يُندي عسله في مصب هو منه وإليه . تباعا تدور عقارب هذه الساعة ، تباعا ينسَّل النور من ثقب الباب ، لنقف في عريِّنا أمام قمر يداعب بضوئه الضامر رؤى تشرق وتنفتت لتكشف وجه فتاتنا المحمولة لنا على خيوط من البردي في هشاشة الظل لكل هذا الحضور .

في اللحظة التي ارتأينا وقوفنا على ما خُفي علينا ، فاجأتنا قدما وِسان وهما تتخطيان عتبة الباب الخارجي ، حاملة معها صدى لخطوات أخرى بدت ثقيلة ومترددة . كانت تمسك به من يده ، حاضنة ذراعه اليسرى إليها ، تقوده مشرقة إلى الباحة الصغيرة ، حيث النافورة التي تجمعت حولها دواجن الخالة مردودة في قأقأتها اليومية وانشغالها بالتعريف بأحوال الطقس والحياة . الباحة التي عمدنا تنظيفها كل يوم تحسباً ورجاء .

هناك في منتصف المسافة ، تقف المرأة التي انتظرناها طويلا ، تريه ما حولها بحركاتها الطفولية التي نالت منا ، فوقفنا نحن أيضا في خفية المكان مصعوقين لهذا المشهد . الرجل الداكن اللون باضطرابه المباغت وابتسامته العريضة تجاه كل ما تشير به الأنامل الصغيرة المعروفة ، يُنزل بجهد الحقيبة الجلدية ثم يفترش الأرض . لوهلة لم نكن قادرين على الجزم في ما إذا كان ذلك جلوسا أم أن الجسد تهاوى أمام أعيننا في لحظة . ثم انتبهنا للصمت الذي بدأ يتسلل ببطء لحظة انقطاع الحديث حتى غشينا بوطأته وكدنا مشاهدة عبئه في أنفاسنا .

كنا قابعين هناك ، الرجل المتغضن الجلد والصبية التي امتلكتنا ملامحها ، يُحدِّقان بسكون في فراغ الأشياء التي امتلأت بشفق أرجواني داكن . يمسُّنا العبق المتكشف على مبعدة ونخلد للهدوء مستسلمين لنوازع يقين في المهبّ ، ضارب بظله في حلكة ما يتداعى بيننا في المسافة القصيرة لوقوفنا في هذه الدار .

في الصباح ، كان الحشد قد ملأ الباحة الصغيرة . نساء يلتحفن السواد تتراصُّ أجسادهن بعضها على بعض ، أطفال رُضَّع وآخرون في استنفار خطاهم الأولى ، يطاردون الدواجن المذهولة ويتراشقون مياه النافورة الآسنة . فاجأنا اللغط وهسهسة الكلام الممطوط المتكرر ، والبسملة ومناداة الخالق للتدخل في شؤون أجساد عليلة وأخرى غير متوازنة هي في التحول والتنقل عبر عوالك غير مرئية . خالجنا شعور بالبلبلة ونحن نخطو خارج محيطنا المكاني متفقدين ما بدا لنا ادراكا متأخرا لحدث قد فاتنا جدوثه ، محاولين جمع نثار الحديث في صبغة نعي من خلالها ما وجدنا حالنا عليه ساعة يقظتنا في هذا اليوم من شهر هو الثالث في التقويم القمري الذي احتل وعينا منذ اعتلى حارس موج التربة التي ظلت تلفظه نحونا على الدوام .

في حيرتنا تلك لم ننتبه لقدومها إلينا إلى أن انتابتنا الرجفة ، ومسَّ الصقيع الحاد قلوبنا ، فتجمدنا في مكاننا ذاك ونحن نحتضن الوجه والجسد في أحداقنا ، قبل أن تمسَّ قدماها موطئ وجودنا وتشعل الدفء في شرخ هالنا وجعه .

كانت حدود أجسادنا قد عكَّرها هذا الانفصال المفرط في قسوته وبانت عليها شراهة التمزق الذي وصمنا بشوائبه ووشمنا بحالة من الهذيان تتآكل فيها أعضاؤنا ولا نجد منفذا لهوس الفراغ الذي يمخر أرواحنا إلا حين نستكين في محيطنا المكاني حيث كل ما يتعلق بنشأتنا الأولى وتجلياتها الرابضة بهدوء في هواء يزخر باتصالنا الأبدي كما أوضحته الملفات الطيّعة في تراكمها الهرمي وبما دُوِّن فيها من زُخرف حرف ورسم عَمِد عكس حياتنا البهية في مرآة الصفحات المطوية .

هي في القرب الآن ، نمد أذرعنا حولنا فتلتف وتكتمل دائرتنا في دورانها الأخاذ ، متحلقين فيما تسرَّب من وقت خارج هذا الزمن الصباحي المحمول إلينا بأحداثه المتناوبة . ينتشلنا رنين الجذل في صوت وِسان وهي تسحبنا صوب الغرفة الجنوبية التي ظلت موصدة منذ موت الجدَّة..

‒ تعالوا ...

تسبق الكلمة المتعثر خطونا في المساحات الضيقة بين ساق ممدودة وأخرى ، لتتمايل في آذاننا كالزئبق إلى أن وقفنا في عتبة الباب الموارب . لفحت وجوهنا نسمات طرية هي ما تبقى من شذى قديم لنفحات أنفاس الجدَّة ، وقد جعلنا ذلك أكثر اطمئنانا وهدوءا وليونة تجاه الغريب الذي جلس في منتصف الغرفة مغمض العينين واضعا يديه على بطن وصدر جسد المرأة الممدد في استسلام طوعي ، غيرعابئة بملابسات

الذكورة للأصابع الغليظة لرجل بدا مبحرا في تقصي سريان أمر غائر في الجلد بسطوة هي في الاصفرار والتشقق وانسحاب الدم عن جريانه .

انتظرنا حتى أفاق من تقصيه المُجهَد ، ولمس الجبهة التي كانت تندي عرقها في سيولة جارفة ، ثم همس بشيء بالقرب من صدغ المرأة الممدودة ، ورفع نظره الى وِسان التي اقتربت وهي تُشير :

–   هذا هو فوستر .

هززنا رؤوسنا نحوه ، ولحظتها عرفنا أننا لن نستطيع الاقتراب أكثر . كان غاطسا في بحر ماؤه يشعُّ أرجوانيا طاغيا فيما الضوء ينكسر عليه عاكسا وجهه في بلورات صغيرة متناثرة .

–   هو هنا في النقاهة ...

قالت وهي تحضنه إليها . ثم دخلت امرأة أخرى غير آبهة بوجودنا ، لتتسمر أمامه وهي تشير إلى مواضيع في جسدها وتحكي بلغتها عن أسر الألم وصعوبة الحمل وأرق ينفلت في الظلمة فيما كان هو يهزُّ رأسه منصتا كمن يعي رغم اختلاف الحروف المتداولة مصدرا واحدا يُغدق فيه الحنوُّ عطفه ورأفته .

انسحبنا في صمت موزعين أنظارنا على الوجوه المختلفة التي تغصُّ بها ساحتنا الصغيرة ، متفكرين في الزمن المنطفيء في ذاكرتنا بين وصولهما معا الذي عايناه جيدا في وقفتنا التي خلناها بالأمس وبين انتشار صيته وارتياد العامة صوب وجوده العامر .

في المساءات وحين تخلو باحة البيت من روادها ، كنا نسمع ضجيج الآلة التي تركتها يد الجدة في الزاوية ، رأسه محنيٌّ عليها ، يُطرِّز ويُرتق في كومة ثياب لا نعرف مصدرها . نسترق النظر لهفة منا لطيِّ البعد الذي تُرسيه وِسان وهي تجلس على مقربة منه محوطة بكومة كتب وأوراق في انشغالها بالتدوين ، منشغلة عنا ، نحن الذين بايعنا وقايضنا المسافات والوجل ، وكبحنا الاختلاجة تلو الأخرى حتى تبين أمامنا المرأة الصبية التي أربكت قلوبنا منذ كنا صغارا . نتطلع إليها ونعرف أن عودتها مازالت في القدوم ، وأن حضورها بيننا الآن مازال في التكشف . نهمس في كوة الباب وفي حصانة حصى الجدار :

–   أرجئي الغياب .. يا حلما نحن في سطوته .. ورمّمي إلى الأبد شرخ الروح .

ابراهيم الناصر ـ المملكة العربية السعودية

أرض بلامطر [44]

كانت كثبان الرمال تحيط بنا في أقصى الصحراء من كل جانب ، فتغدو في العتمة الحالكة كالمردة والاشباح التي تكثر من زيارتنا في ليالي الشتاء الدهماء .

بينما الرياح تصفع بعنف سقوف خيامنا المقامة هناك ، بصفوفها المتراصة بانتظام ، كتلة من الجند تستعد لاستقبال أمرها بالتحية ؛ فتهتز قوائم الخيام وسقوفها تفرقع باصوات مستغيثة وكأنما هي فرقعة سياط تلهب ظهور جياد هدها التعب والاعياء ، فلم تعد تشعر بسعير الألم فوق ظهورها .

كانت الخيام المحاطة بالأسيجة تدعى حي الشركة . لم تعد حيا مأهولا بالمعنى الحرفي انما هي أقرب الى المعسكر ، اقامته الشركة لسكان عمالها من العرب . في طرفه بوابة كبيرة محاطة بالأسلاك على كلا جانبيها ، اتخذها الحراس الذين يقومون بمهمة التفتيش مقرأ لهم ، يقيهم عاتية الاعاصير والأتربة النافرة دائماً ، بينما تفضي تلك البوابة الى باحة واسعة مترامية الاطراف يحتضنها البحر من أحد جوانبها القصية .

كان ذلك معسكر العمل في الشركة ومساكن موظفيها الاجانب حيث يقبع في وسطه بناء خشبي مستطيل اتخذه الخبراء والرؤساء في الشركة مكاتباً لهم ، كما تتناثر هنا وهناك ورش كثيرة للآلات وتصليح السيارات وغيرها . وفي اقصى الشمال تشاهد سفن نقل كبيرة تفرغ شحناتها من الأنابيب والمعدات والرافعات والمعبأة بصناديق هائلة وغيرها مما يحتاجه جيش لجب من الناس في بقعة منعزلة تماماً ، يعيشون على حفيف الرياح الزاحفة بالأتربة كالسيول ، سواد الليل وسحابة النهار ..

كان حي العمال يقع على يمين البوابة ، أما نهاية الجهة اليسرى منها حيث لسان البحر يمتد ليطلق باستمرار كثبان الرمال المحاذية له فتتناثر اكشاك خشبية تحت أقدام كثيب رملي هائل العلو يربض على كتف البحر كأبي الهول ، ويعلو مستواه بعدة فراسخ .

من تلك الاكشاك الخشبية التي هي في الواقع سوق القرية ، يتزود العمال والموظفون بحوائجهم الغذائية .. كان عدد الأكشاك يربو على الأربعمائة ، اقيمت فرق مساند من الرمال أو شدت الى قواعد من الحجارة ، لتزيد من تحمل هجمات الرياح الكاسحة .

لم تكن الحياة في تلك القرية الخشبية امرا طبيعياً معتاداً انما كانت بالعكس مريرة شاقة للغاية بل ومحفوفة بالمخاطر .. فهي قبل كل شيء معزولة في أقصى الصحراء ، عن معالم الحضارة ، تحاصرها الرمال من جميع جوانبها ، كما لم تكن آبار المياه منها قريبة أبداً . إذ كانت تجلب اليها من مسافة لا تقل عن ثلاثمائة كيلومتر ...

تلك كانت قرية (رأس مشعاب) منذ عشرة أعوام تقريباً . تزدهر بحركة العمال الصاخبة ، وتموج بحياتهم فيها ، عندما التحقت بالعمل في شركة مد الأنابيب ، مثقلاً بأحلام عريضة في الكسب ، وشق طريق لي بين أكداس المتاعب يلقاها اناسها ، لم أكن قد بلغت العشرين من عمري تماماً آنذاك تحدوني رغبة صادقة في أن احقق الاحلام التي سكبتها أمي في اذني وهي تودعني بنشيجها المختلط بدعواتها الحارة ، وكأنما أنا مقدم على خوض معركة حقيقية ...

---

44 موسوعة الأدب العربي السعودي الحديث ـ نصوص مختارة ودراسات ، الطبعة الأولى ، الرياض 2001 م، ص 179ـ185

ومضيت شاقا طريقي في ذلك المنحدر الوعر والابتسامة الشاحبة التي ودعتني بها عجوزي الحبيبة ، تشرق دوماً في ظلمة أحلامي الراعشة . ورسائلها تترى عليّ تحثني على مقارعة الأقدار ..

كانت تلك القرية مزرعاً خصباً للاعاصير والزوابع الرملية التي تحيل أصيلها الى عتمة غبراء فتندفع سيول الرمال صوب البحر ، وكأنها شلالات تنحدر من جبل عال . في حين اننا عند هبوب العواصف نتجمع داخل خيامنا ، التي تحاول الرياح اقتلاعها بعناد وقسوة وهي تعج بأنفاس الرياح يملأ القذى عيوننا المعصوبة ، ونوبات السعال تختنق في صدورنا ...

وحين تتجلى السماء عن صفحتها اللازوردية ، وقد رصعت بلآليء تومض في عليائها بتيه وخيلاء. ينطلق الزملاء خارج خيامهم وانفاس القمر المشرق تتفث فيهم حيوية دافقة جديدة ، فيتسامرون بحدة قد تنتهي بتبادل الشتائم . كنت أنصت إلى أحاديثهم الشيقة فإذا هي مزيج من المشاعر الخابية ، والآمال المتوثبة العنيدة . وكانت مشكلتهم الأبدية ، أنهم لا يعرفون اليأس ، إنما كانوا يكافحون بضراوة كافة ما يعترض سبيلهم من عراقيل . وفي سويعات استرخائهم تتبع آلام حياتهم دفعة واحدة وكأنما وخزها لهم جراح مفتوحة لم تندمل قط .

ولعل الزميل "رافع" كأن أشد المتحمسين لأفكاره . لذا فهو يردد دوماً : هناك شيء اقوى منا ، يشدنا أبداً إلى عجلة الحياة و طاحونتها التي لا ترحم . قد يكون الإيمان أو التشبث بوهم يومض بصيصه الواهن ، في غمرة الكآبة بالاحزان التي تعشعش على سماء حياتنا فندعوه أملاً وليس في الواقع سوى سراب .. مجرد سراب يدفع بأحلامنا إلى الإنبثاق من بين ركام التعاسات والفشل ، القابع أبداً في منعطفات طريقنا الطويل ليمتص ويزدرد ذلك الأمل الصفيق . والنتيجة أننا سوف نبقى هكذا نلهث كالبغال في البيدر ، يقتلها الجوع والخيرات من حولها ...

فيجيبه "ظافر" بسخريته المطلاة بالألم الناخر في جراحاته : "حقا ما تقول يا رافع .. ولتكن تجربتي خير مثال لكم أيها الزملاء فلقد أمضيت خمسة وعشرين عاماً في الخدمة فماذا تراني ربحت ؟؟ لا شيء سوى شهادة بالتوفق . شهادة العاهة المستديمة ، ساق مقطوعة ونمش الحريق يلون جسمي كالحرباء . انني الآن لم أعد سوى كلب أجرب .. يتحاشاني أولئك الحمر ويهربون من ملامستي ، فأعقب في سري أن لا جدوى من هذه الحياة العقيمة التي لا تنفث سوى الصديد في اجوافنا .. نعم لا فائدة . إلا أنني لا ألبث وأصحو على اشراقة البسمة الحانية والنشيج المختلط بالدعوات الصادقة : "روح ربي يحرسك ويوفقك يا حبة قلبي" وأحس بالدماء تتدفق في عروقي من جديد ... دماء تفرش أمامي أرضاً بالورد والرياحين . وعندما أهمس بذلك الى زملائي اقابل بعاصفة شنيعة من السخرية ، فأصمت على مضض لتبقى بعض الأفكار الشاحبة تهوم في أعماقي ، ان التفكير بالمستقبل ينمو مع انثيال المحن وتكالبها الناحب ، فنرى البصيص والعتمة يرنوان إلينا كالشبح في غمرة الديجور يفزعان الراعي وينتزعانه من لذة الأحلام التي تخدر على تدفقها اللذيذ .

هكذا كنا نعيش في قلب الصحراء والتجربة والألم .. وتلك كانت آمالنا عندما تتسابق السياط على جلد احلامنا الوضيئة .. كنا نجد لذتنا الأخيرة في الفيئة التي تتظللنا في الملاذ الذي يمكننا استعماله في أية لحظة من حياتنا .. أعني الحرية في الموت جوعاً ...!!

وفي الهزيع الأخير من الليل .. حين تغفو عيون الرياح ويموت وهمهمتها نحييها وهمهمتها تحت أسجاف العتمة الغامقة وفي المعسكر تهدأ الحركة إلا من أصوات الشخير المتعالي في زوايا الخيام الغافية . واجساد الرجال المتعبة محشورة كالألواح تحت الأسرة وفوق الكثبان تحلم بالغد المجهول بسفوده وجراحاته .. حينذاك يمتص سمعي همسات الموسيقى الصاخبة المنبثقة من داخل المعسكر الذي يقطنه الاجانب .. تمر بسمعي على ذبذبات الأثير وهمهمة الرياح . ناعمة رقيقة في مبدأ الأمر ثم ضاجة صاخبة في آخر الليل . والضحكات الناعمة المعربدة تتكسر على أنغامها كما تتكسر الأمواج على حافة الكثبان الرملية .. وهكذا ينتزعني النوم

لأصحو في الصباح على مطارق الصداع والغثيان ، فالتهم أقراصاً بعد اقراص .. ورغم ذلك يبقى الصخب وسخريات الآخرين يطن في رأسي سحابة النهار ، فأبكي وأهرب للسوق ، حيث أعيش في مشكلة أخرى كبيرة يقصها كل من يصادفني في الطريق .. وكانت المشكلة تتلخص : في ان الشركة ترغب في نقل أكشاك القرية عن كتف البحر ، وابعادها إلى ماوراء التلال . وكان الأهلون ساخطين على تلك الفكرة ، ويعارضونها بكل شدة وعناد ، محتجين بأن الطقس هناك جاف للغاية ، وهذا ما سوف يؤدي إلى محالة لا اتلاف الاطعمة والخضار التي تساعد تهوية البحر الرطبة على مقاومتها لحرارة الجو ، التي تلدغ الاجساد كالعقارب . ولم يكن الأمر يعنيني كثيراً في مبدأ الأمر ، فلست بقالاً أو مالكا لكشك هناك ، فألوي شفتي وأهز اكتافي باستخفاف ، في عد الأيام المتبقية من عامي المصلوب على تلك الرمال ..

وتصرم العام زاحفاً ، وكنت قد اكتنزت من مرتبي الضئيل ، مبلغاً لم يكن يزيد عن الفي ريال ، أودعتها لدى قريب لي في القرية الخشبية يملك حانوتاً هناك . وكنت فرحاً للغاية .. فرحاً لأنني سوف أحقق الحلم الذي يرف على شفتي أمي المتيبستين . وبدأت أستعد للسفر ، وكان علي أن أتزود ببعض الهدايا من مدينة ليست قريبة .

وذهبت إلى هناك . لم أغب في المدينة سوى ثلاثة أيام ، وفي غبش المساء عدت أدراجي الى القرية الخشبية وعندما شارفنا حدودها فوجئنا بأن خفر الحدود يمنعون الدخول الى القرية . وألحجنا في معرفة السبب ، فاذا الجواب يأتينا بأن القرية قد شب فيها حريق هائل ، لذا يحذر الدخول اليها ليلا . وأحزنني أنني سوف أضطر لارجاء شخوصي الى أهلي يوماً آخر . وفي الصباح دخلنا القرية فاذا نحن نصعق بما نرى غير مصدقين ما هو ماثل أمامنا ..

لقد شاهدنا النيران وقد التهمت جميع أكشاك القرية ، فلم يعد لها من أثر سوى ألواح سوداء نخرتها النيران ، تطوح بها الرياح ، وندف الحريق تتطاير شظاياها كالخفافيش راكضة نحو البحر . ولا شيء هنا سوى الوجوه الملطخة بسحنها المرقطة والأحداق ناتئة من محاجرها بسخط واهتياج ..

بحثت عن قريبي ، فاذا هو ملقى مع جماعة آخرين قرب برزخ البحر ، وآثار الحريق تنز الصديد من جراحاته الطافحة على وجهه وأطرافه . وبكيت من أجله وصرخت من أجل نفسي .. ودعوت من كل قلبي أن تمن السماء علينا بالمطر ، بيد أننا لم نكن في فصل الشتاء فدعواتي تلك ستخيب حتما .

وعدت الى أهلي مثقل القلب ، كسير الخاطر لضياع نقودي التي أدخرتها عاماً كاملا في التشرد والجوع والمتاعب .

وتلقاني الجميع فرحين بعودتي .. وقصصت عليهم مشكلتي والعبرات تخنق صوتي .

لم تعقِّب أمي بشيء ، ولكن لحظت دمعة كبيرة تتدحرج بالرغم منها . أما أبي فقد نظر إليَّ شزرا وبصق على الأرض بتأفف وهو يقول : "كنت أعلم أنك ولد غير نافع ... ".

أميمة الخميس ـ المملكة العربية السعودية

سلمى العمانية ⁽⁴⁵⁾

في الحكاية القديمة عندما يتجوف جذع نخلة ويطير فإن بداخله ساحرة فاتنة من عُمان .

عُمان تجازف فتمد رأسها لتطل على المحيط ، بحر الظلمات ، حيث القاع المرصوفة بقماقم المردة المختومة والمهجورة لقرون .

وعُمان يختلط السكر بالهيل ، فيكون حلوى ، تتدور باستدارة خد (سلمى) . جواري عُمان دافئات كالتمر المبيت للشتاء ، مضيئات كزخارف الفضة حول مرايا القصور ، مستكينات كلهب قنديل يقاوم الفجر .

لذا كان على تجار الرقيق أن يمدوا أيديهم إلى قاع صرة الدراهم ليبذلوا كل ما بها لأجل الخلخال حول ساق عُمانية .

(أبو دوستين) تخوف به الأمهات الفتيات الصغيرات ، يسكن الكهوف ، ومغاور الجبال ، نحيل كأفعى ، حذر كجربوع ، ينحدر في الليالي المظلمة من دروب الجبال ، ويختطف الصبايا ، ليحملهن إلى أماكن بعيدة ، أو لربما قد يلتهمهن ، فقد روى الكثير من الرعاة عن بقايا العظام البشرية في قمم الجبال والتي يتناثر حولها عقود وأساور من الخرز الملون .

هو موجود .. وقد لا ، كالعفريت أو البساط السحري ، لم يره أحد والجميع يهذر به ، ويحمله القوم بداخلهم ليتقوه تماماً كالشيطان .

في بداية هذا القرن ، كان ذكره كافياً للملمة الفتيات الصغيرات من مداخل البيوت في عُمان ، وإسقاطهن في رعب التوقع لأقدام ليلية متلصصة .

الجبال هناك مرمرية عظيمة ، صامتة بشهقة أزلية في حضرة البحر .

اختارت أم سلمى ذلك اللسان الرملي الضيق الذي يفصل الجبل عن البحر لتبني (عشتها) تحت شجرة (غاف) عظيمة ، وتنتشر حولها الماعز ، والدجاج . وابنتها سلمى وموزة . تطاردان الموج إلى أقصاه ، ثم تفران من المد بفرح صاخب عابث إلى صخور الجبال . ويلتمع فوق البحر بيارق مئات البحارة المغامرين الذين وهبوا أشرعة سفنهم لطموحات جامحة فدمرتها العواصف .

سلمى رشيقة ضامرة كماعز الجبال ، تحلم بمدن سحرية خلف الجبال ، تلقي بالدلو في غور البئر فتطير (وطاويط) كانت قد اختبأت في خفايا البئر ، تطل برأسها فترى وجهها بالأسفل بعيداً يرف فوقه قطع سحاب مندوفة ومتناثرة في السماء . ينق الدجاج حولها ، ويدخل في معارك يومية ، فتعجب سلمى من التحالفات الجديدة التي تبرم كل يوم .

تنشب الحليب برفق في أوان خزفية لغبوق المساء ، تألف الجبال وقع خطوها فتتأملها بحنو من شاهق .

الحدود فضفاضة ، والقبائل تتوجس المدن ، وتخشاها ، وتعلم أن البدوي عندما يلج المدينة سيفقد الصحراء ومن ثم سيفقد نفسه .

في بدايات القرن الحدود مضطربة والمكان قلق متردد بين عرف القبيلة ودستور الدولة.

---

45 موسوعة الأدب العربي السعودي الحديث ــ نصوص مختارة ودراسات ، الطبعة الأولى ، الرياض 2001 م، ص 350–355

وخد سلمى يكمل استدارته كحلوى من سكر وهيل . إلى الآن لا يُدرى من الذي وشى بسلمى عند (أبي دوستين) هل هو الجبل ؟ أم طيور الهند الموسمسية ، أم هي محض صدفة بلورت الآمور في شكلها النهائي .

كان مساء ثلاثاء ، والبحر يلهث أنفاسه الحارة اللزجة على الشاطئ فتنزلق قواقع الشاطئ تحت الأقدام بينما تحدق النجوم بشدة إلى اضطرابات الموج .

يرتعد صدر (أم سلمى) بحكاية الفتاة (البلوشية) التي اختفت منذ أيام ، القرية تلهج بأخبارها ، تنتقل الروايات تتشكل لتختلف ، لكنها تعود وتستقر حول (أبي دوستين) .

جو (العشة) رطب وخانق ، أخرجت النسوة الثلاث مراقدهن إلى الخارج ، محتميات بالجبال وكلاب القرية ، أحكمن الرتاج حول سور الغنم ، أطفئت قناديل القرية ، سلمى تغرس يدها في رمل الشاطئ"دافئ وندي" ، فتكومه في تلال صغيرة وترصفها بالحصى .

من درب الجبل الغربي انحدر ، طقطقت القواقع البحرية بألم تحت حذائه الجلدي ، قبل أن يصل كان أن يتعثر ، تمسك بشجرة (سمر) جبلية ضئيلة ، خدشت يديه لكن سلمى كانت مستغرقة في نوم عميق .

اقترب وهمهم خلفه ظله ، الجسد الكبير للأم ، إذا فأحد الأجساد الصغيرة ، حين أصبح فوق رأس سلمى تماماً ، انحنى منقضاً ، ووضع يده حول فمها انتزع شماغه بسرعة ، وحشا به فمها ، أما عقاله فقد قيدها به كذبيحة ، وقبل أن تقبل الموجة الثانية وترتد ، كان قد وضعها في (زنبيل) وأمّ بها درب الجبل الغربي .

في الصباح وجدت الأم أحد الكلاب صريعاً ، موزة تنتفض تحت تأثير كابوس مرعب ، وسلمى قد اختفت ، عندها علمت أن النساء العمانيات الفاتنات ، لا يختفين فقط بداخل جذع نخل مجوف ، بل أيضاً بزنبيل يحملهن إلى درب الجبل الغربي .

في الطريق إلى نجد ، وعندما اختفت رائحة البحر ، وأشرعت الصحراء ودروبها العميقة ابتدأت بالزعيق ، أخذت تصرخ بالتياع بصوت يبدأ قوياً ثم يذوي شيئاً فشيئاً كطلقة ، ثم يفز فجأة ليسترد زخمه الأول .

لم تصمت إلا حين اكتشفت فضة في زنبيل آخر ، أخذت تضمها لأنها تشبه موزة أعطتها بعض التمر ، فهمست لها فضة عن كوكبة من الفرسان ستنطلق فجأة من البحر وتقدم اليهما لتخلصهما ، فتعودان لعمان ، صمتت عندها سلمى ، وأخذت فقط ترهف السمع ، وليس سوى وقع أخفاف الجمال ولغط رجال أبي دوستين والحجارة تبهت والأشجار تقل إلى أن وصلت مشارف الهضبة النجدية .

هناك أصبحت سلمى قطعاً ذهبية ، استقرت في جيب خفي في حزام أبي دوستين نامت ليلتها الأولى في القصر ، بداخل غرفة جارية زنجية ضخمة ، ذات صدر كبير متهدل ، كانت هي المرضعة الأم لكثير من نجباء القصر ، فتميزت بمكانة خاصة فيه .

عاودت سلمى الزعيق ، عندما قالوا لها إن هذه هي أمك الجديدة ، وطلبوا منها بمناداتها (أمي لويلوة) شرسة ومضنية هي ، وترفض أن تنصاع للأوامر .

لم تلمح البحر بعد ذلك إطلاقاً ، كانت تحلم به ولكنه كان يفر بموجة لاترد إطلاقاً ، تخيلت قلب أمها والحزن يدقه كحبة البن في (نجر) ، وودت أن تخبرها بأنها حية لم تمت وأن العظام البشرية وبقايا الخرز في الكهوف لا تمت لها بصلة .

ظلتَّ شرسة ومتوحشة حتى بات سكان القصر جميعهم ينادونها ب (سلمى عقرب الماء)!! .
تداولتها الأيدي والسنون ، بينما كان أطفالها يموتون بعد ولادتهم بأيام ، مما دعا النسوة بنصحها بالتمائم والتعاويذ لحمايتها من مختطفي الأطفال لكن يبدو أن مرض الصرع الذي أخذت تكثر نوباته عليها ، جعل الكثير من سكان القصر يتطيرون منها ، ويتناقلون بأنها ممسوسة .

لم يخطئ الهرم طريقه إليها ، فاسودت خواتم الفضة في يديها الناحلتين مما دعا سيدتها لترقب الفرص لعتقها .

ووفاء لنذر السيدة بعتق رقبة إن عاد ابنها الغائب في العراق ، أصبحت سلمى حرة من جديد .

توفيت أمها (لويلوة) منذ أمد طويل ، وتوالت نوبات الصرع بشكل مخيف ، كان الجميع ينظر لها بتوجس ، فلا يجرؤ أحد على الاقتراب منها لمسح الزبد الأبيض حول فمها عندما تباغتها النوبة .

وقبل أن تشارف الخمسين ، وبعد أن ظلت ثلاثة أيام في غرفتها لا يجرؤ أحد من الخدم على الاقتراب منها ، نقلها (مبارك) السائق هي ومعظم أغراضها لدار للعجزة .

وهناك كان سيف العماني ، حارس الدار ، احتكم إلى سنين طويلة من الترحال واستقرت به شيخوخته حارساً للدار .

تترقب وقع حذائه البلاستيكي في الباحة الخارجية كل صباح وفي أحاديثه استعادت بحر عمان قطرة فقطرة . عُمان بهجة الشواطئ بالبحر ، والتماع مرمر الجبال ببريق أقمار متتالية ، الماعز الضامرة كالغزلان ، وجنيات النخل الفاتنات .

ولأن أحاديثها ، ووقوفها بالباب طال ، فقد قرر أهل الدار أن يتزوج سيف بسلمى . أبهجت سيف التدابير وشارك بها بحماس .. بكت سلمى طويلاً على كتف سيف المتهالك ، وأخبرته أن اسم أمها سعيدة وأختها موزة .

غنى لها سيف ذات ليلة ، رنة الطار تسابق خطو الوتر ، فتغرف العقل في عتمة الليل بآنية من زجاج مزخرف ، وتنقله إلى الأرض المرصودة الموشاة بالبخور والحناء .

يهزج سيف أمامها ، ويقفز برقصات نشيطة مرحة (قمرى شِلْ بنتنا) .

فكانت سلمى تصفق له بيدها المعروقة والتي اسودت بها خواتم الفضة وتردد وإياه (شلها وراح .. شلها وراح) .

أمين سالم رويحي ـ المملكة العربية السعودية

الضحية(46)

(شقحا) فتاة بدوية سمراء ذات جمال طبيعي رائع ، فارعة القوام متناسقة الأعضاء ناهدة الصدر صلبة العود . في العقد الثاني من عمرها ذات عينين دعجاوين لا يكاد المرء يراهما من ثقب خمارها حتى يصاب بالدوار ، وكانت مخطوبة (لحمدان) صديق الطفولة وزميل المرعى ، والحق أن حمدان كان زينة الفتيان ، وهو أهل لها . فحمدان شاب فارع الطول عريض المنكبين ، وسيم التقاطيع ، حديدي البنية يتفجر قوة ونشاطاً ، هذا بالإضافة إلى أخلاق عالية وكرم وشجاعة .

وكانا على وشك اتمام عقد قرانهما لولا أن انتدب حمدان لإحضار بعض الأغذية لقبيلته. فذهب لقضاء تلك المهمة بعد أن ودع خطيبته وداعاً حاراً ، شهدته الصحراء الساحرة المترامية الأطراف .

فلما طالت غيبته اشتد الحنين (بشقحا) . فأخذت تنطلق كل صباح ومساء إلى أحد الجبال التي تبعد عن مضارب القبيلة بضعة كيلومترات لعلها ترى القافلة الحبيبة ، وذات صباح كوفئت على صبرها ، حينما رأت القافلة تبدو في الأفق كنقطة سوداء ، فاشتد وجيب قلبها وارتفعت الدماء الحمراء الى وجنتيها ، واشتد بها حبها وحنينها إلى حمدان . فلم تستطع صبراً فانحدرت من الجبل ، وانطلقت تركض كالظبي في خفته ورشاقته وسرعته ، وقد شمرت عن ردائها الطويل كي لا يعوق انطلاقها . فلما اقتربت من القافلة رآها حمدان فقفز من على ظهر بعيره ، وتقدم إليها فقابلها في منتصف الطريق ، فرفعت خمارها فتبدى وجهها الفاتن ، وقد تجمعت عليه بعض حبات العرق فبدا كاللؤلؤ الصافي فنظرت إليه برهة ثم ألقت بنفسها عليه لاهثة متهدجة الأنفاس ، وهي تقول بصوت مرتعش :" الحمد لله على سلامتك يا حمدان" .

فاحتضنها وهو يجيب : لم أجهدت نفسك يا حبيبتي ؟ قالت وهي تنتفض كالمقرورة :" واحرَّ قلباه يا حمدان ، لقد طال بعادك ، واشتد شوقي إليك . فلم أكد أرى القافلة حتى انطلقت إليك كي أكون أول من تكتحل عيناه برؤياك "فأجابها بصوت يفيض بالعاطفة الكريمة النقية : قسماً بالله يا شقحا : إن عيني لم تذق طعم المنام إلاَّ لماماً منذ أن غادرتك ، وإن طيفك لم يغب عن بالي . فكنت أستعجل العودة لأمتع عيني برؤياك ، وقد أحضرت إليك بعض الهدايا ، وكل مناي أن تحوز رضاك . فقالت بوله : إني أعلم صدق ما تقول ، أما الهدايا فأنت وحدك يا حمدان هديتي. وأخرجهما من ذلك الحوار العذب ابتعاد القافلة عنهما . فقال لها : هيا بنا .

ثم أردفها خلفه على البعير ، وانطلق بها وهي تتشبث به في قوة وكأنها تخشى أن يهرب منها . أما هو فقد كان سعيدا بذلك الضغط الحبيب . لم يكد حمدان يفرغ من تسليم كل ذي حق حقه حتى أقام حفلة زفافه فرقصت الفتيات بالسيوف ، وأطلقت العيارات النارية ابتهاجاً . فتم الزفاف بين فرح الجميع ، وظفر كل منهما بأمنية العمر .

فغدت (شقحا) وحمدان أسعد زوجين ، وازدادت سعادتهما حينما ظهرت بوادر الحمل على (شقحا) .

فلما انتهت المدة وضعت طفلاً جميلاً ، كان يشبه أباه إلى حد بعيد ، فأسميا الطفل (سطام) . فأنشآه كما ينشئ العرب أبناءهم . فنشا نشأة قوية صالحة . رجولة كاملة وشجاعة وبأس وأنفة وعزة .

<hr>

46 موسوعة الأدب العربي السعودي الحديث ـ نصوص مختارة ودراسات ، الطبعة الأولى ، الرياض 2001 م، ص 186–189

فلما بلغ الرابعة عشرة من عمره ، تحدث الوالد مع زوجته عن ضرورة ختان سطام . شعرت شقحا بالانقباض إزاء طلب زوجها لعلمها بقسوة الطريقة التي تتبعها بعض القبائل . ومنها قبيلتهما في عملية الختان هذا علاوة على أنها سمعت كثيراً عن سهولة تلك العملية في (الحضر) وخلوها من الألم وأخرجها من تفكيرها صوت زوجها وهو يقول : مالي أراك لا تجيبين على سؤالي ، ولم ارتسم على وجهك هذا الحزن والانقباض ؟ إن يوم طهور ابننا لهو يوم من أيام العمر ، وكان الأجدر بك أن تقابلي هذا النبأ بالسرور . فتمالكت نفسها وأجابت : صدقت ، ولكني أريد منك تأجيل هذا الأمر إلى فرصة أخرى . فقال بدهشة ولكن لم ؟

فشعرت شقحا أن الأمر سوف يخرج من يدها . فقد عزمت في نفسها على إقناع زوجها بأن يجري الختان لسطام على طريقة (أهل الحضر) ولم يتم لها ذلك إن لم تجعل زوجها يصرف النظر عن تلك الفكرة ، كي يتسنى لها الفرصة المناسبة لإقناعه . فاستجمعت شجاعتها واستعانت بكل ما تملكه المرأة من سلاح ، وقالت بصوت يفيض بالأنوثة : أستحلفك بحبي أن تصرف النظر عن هذا الأمر في الوقت الحاضر . فلبى طلبها ، ولكن لم تمض سنة واحدة حتى عاود الحديث مرة ثانية بصورة جدية . فظنت شقحا أن الوقت بات مناسباً فقالت : إني أخشى على ابننا من عاقبة ذلك الختان ، فإذا كنت غالية عليك حقاً ، فألتمس منك أن تدعنا نذهب إلى المدينة ليتم ختانه ، دون أن يقاسي ألماً ما . فلم تكد تتم حديثها حتى أخذت (حمدان) العزة بالإثم ، فقفز من مقعده وقد تغيرت ملامح وجهه من الغضب ، فصفعها صفعة قوية ، ألقت بها جانباً وقال وهو يهدر . ماذا تقولين أيتها الجبانة ؟ تالله لولا خوفي من الله لما تركتك تعيشين ، وأقسم أني سوف (أطهر) سطام هذا المساء . ثم انطلق وهو يلعنها بصوت صاخب .

وحل المساء ، وبدأت العملية الوحشية ، والأم المسكينة تسمع عويل ابنها وهو يهتف بأسماء جدوده على التوالي ، وبصوت مرتفع . إذ لم يكن في استطاعته أن يشكو ما يقاسيه من ألم بالغ ، خوفاً من أن يوصم بالجبن فتمتنع عنه نساء قبيلته ويغدو ذليلاً مهاناً . فلما تمت العملية وضع له بعض أدعياء الطب بعض العقاقير على جراحه البليغة ثم تركوه . فانطلقت الوالدة الحنون إليه ، وقلبها يتمزق ألما لما أصابه ، فوجدته مشدوداً على الأرض كالحيوان كي لا يتحرك ، وقد تلطخت بالدماء ملابسه وهو مصفر الوجه مرتعش الأطراف زائغ النظرات . فلم يكد يرى والدته حتى سألها بصوت متهافت : أرجو يا أماه أن أكون قد (بيضت) وجهكم ؟ فقالت وهي تحبس دمعها : لقد كنت مثال الشجاعة يا بني . فاطمأن ، فأشاح بوجهه محاولاً إخفاء دموعه .. لم يقدر لجراح الفتى أن تلتئم فامتلأت صديداً فتسممت دماء الفتى ففقد النطق والادراك .

وفي الليلة الرابعة دخل الفتى في دور النزع ، فلم تكد تشرق الشمس حتى أمسى سطام ، وكأنه لم يكن شيئاً مذكوراً فدفن ؛ وذهب ذلك الشاب الغض ضحية الجهل والتقاليد العمياء .

أما والدته فقد أفقدتها الصدمة صوابها فاختل شعورها ، فانطلقت تتجول بين مضارب القبيلة وهي تبكي وتضحك وتزغرد في آن واحد وتصرخ بصوت يقطع نياط القلوب : (واسطاماه) .

خيرية ابراهيم السقاف ـ المملكة العربية السعودية

واختلفت الخطوة [47]

عندما يبزغ الفجر ، وتلقي الشمس بجدائلها النورانية على صدر الأرض الخصيب ، وينفض العصفور المبلل بالندى جناحيه ، ويحرك جفنيه في استعداد ليوم حافل بالسفر والتجواب، ويأتي صوت الديكة تتنبئ بالفجر والصحو .

تعودت هي أن تكون من أول المستيقظين ، تصلي .. ثم تضع قهوتها على النار ، تشعل معها جذوة الحب الذي لا ينتهي .. تتمدد أضواؤها إلى اللامدى ، تحملها على هلاميتها كأنها الخيال أو الطيف ، لتستقر في جوفه "هكذا أرى .. انني المقيمة أبدا تحت جلده ، والسارية دوما في أوردته ، والممتزجة بلا منازع بدمه" .

وتعد كسرة الخبز وقطعة الجبن ثم تقترب منه .. بالقهوة .. والخبز .. والجبن .. بعدها تعوّد أن يبدأ يوما حافلا بالكفاح .. هذا الذي تعتقد انه محك رجولته ..

صلابته .. وثقته .. ووفائه !

"رجل يكافح .. هو ذلك الوفي في دمي"

فيما هو لم يكن أحسن حالا ممن يعيش حوله من أبناء الحي الشعبي المتواضع في إحدى ضواحي مدينة جدة .

هذه النائمة في حضن البحر .. الدافنة معها أسرار قلبيهما عن نظرات أبناء الحي الشرهة .. "كلهم يتحدثون عنا" كانت تتحدث إلى نفسها بذلك ، وما تلبث أن تنفل على جانبها الأيسر وتتمتم : أعوذ بالله من الشيطان" !

أما "سعيد" فكان يمضي جل يومه وساعة أو بضع ساعة من المساء في عمل متواصل .

لا تكاد تراه عائدا حتى تنسى أن تساله عما خطر لها في أثناء النهار إذ كانت تعقد العزم أن يحدثها عن يوم كامل من أيام عمله ، ماذا يفعل ؟ إلى من يتحدث ؟ كيف يمارس عمله وما هي طبيعته ؟ .. كم تتمنى أن تعيش معه ولو بالكلمات .. أن تتخلل ثنايا لحظاته ولو بالوصف .. أن تجد نفسها معه في كل مسامة من مسامات جلده ويومه .. وما أن تراه عائدا حتى تنسى ما عزمت عليه إلى يوم ثان فثالث فرابع .. وإلى ما لا نهاية "وجهه . ينسيني تساؤلاتي .. وجهه لحظاتي وأمسياتي وليلي وصباحاتي" !!.

أما هو فكان يأتيها بالتعب .. فهو لا يملك أكثر من درهم أو درهمين حصيلة فائض كل شهر .. وهي لم تكن لتطلب منه شيئا من أجل نفسها ، يكفي أن تعيش يومها تستعد له .. وتنسى همومها بمجرد أن تراه .. حتى عندما يمزق ثوبها ، فهي تعيد حياكته ورتقه دون أن تجعله يلمس ذلك وكثيرا ما كانت ترخي جلبابها وتمشي حافية القدمين . حتى تستعيد حذاءها من ذلك " العتيق" الذي يرابط غير بعيد عند مدخل الحي .

سألها ذات يوم بعد أن لمحها تمشي حافية عن سر حفاها : ضحكت وقالت له : سمعت من في المدينة يقولون أن القدم تحتاج إلى هواء وإلى ملامسة التراب .. وأيقنت أن أجدادنا الحفاة كانوا يدركون هذه الحكمة .

يومها : هز رأسه ، قال لها : فيك ذكاء .. لا أملك ربعه !

---

47 موسوعة الأدب العربي السعودي الحديث ــ نصوص مختارة ودراسات ، الطبعة الأولى ، الرياض 2001 م ، ص 417ـ423

كثيرا ما كانت تسهر الليل إلى جانبه .. عندما يئن في المساء ، وغالبا ما يعبر عن تعبه في المساء بصوت فاضح كانت تفزع من أن تتلمس رأسه ، تضع رأسها على صدره" اسمع دقات قلبه ، تتصل دقاته بعقلي وقلبي وأعصابي ، ليتني أدرك قراءة الدقات .. ليتني أستطيع فهم لغة القلب" .

ويحدث في لحظات أن يضحك .. والناس كلهم يضحكون ، شيء طبيعي أن يضحك الإنسان أما هي فكان عندما يضحك فهو يوم إعلان الفرح يزف إلى أعماقها .. لأنه كان لها الدنيا كلها وما عداه فهو شيء عادي لا يسترعي التفاتة من انتباهها .. بكل البساطة والعفوية والعادية والإنفعالية كانت تعبر عنه .

هو الأمل يملؤها كما لم تستشعر الشبع قبله ، وهو الثقة تثبتها كما لو أنها ريشة طارت واستقرت بين شقوق الجبال .

في رحلتها معه باعت كل شيء ثمين لها .. فقطعتا الذهب اللتان أهداهما إليها والدها عند الزفاف .. وذلك "الخلخال" الفضة الذي وهبتها إياه أمها .. وأشياء متناثرة .. تراب .. تراب كل مادي ماعداه تراب !!! .

كبرت ثقتها .. وحملته هذه الثقة إلى حواف الغيوم ، تسلقت به قمم الجبال ، داست تحته كل الذلة والضعف والخور ، ارتفع في كل شيء .. علمه .. فتحول إلى إنسان متعلم !! منصبه فغدا موظفاً مرموقاً تخرج بعد عمر سهرت فيه معه ، تقدم له القهوة في صمت ، والتمر والحب، ترضعه بعينيها اللتين تحولتا إلى حلمتين تدران كل العواطف التي يحتاجها إنسان في رحلة قاسية .

واصبح "سعيد" صاحب الشهادة الأولى في حيه الشعبي ! جلست ذات يوم تمارس الحلم وهي تراه يغرق في كتاب : "أرى الحرف بعينيه .. أتسلق صفحات الكتاب فوق أهدابه .. أغرق في عمق عميق من الإدراك وأنا : أتموّج مع تفكيره .. آه ما أروعك يا سعيد وقد حولت ضوء الفانوس في بيتنا إلى كهرباء والدرهم والدرهمين إلى عشرات فمئات .. فشيء كثير" .

وفي الصباح ودعته كما تعودت : "سيعود في الظهيرة .. وقت إيابه في البيت تحول .. اختصرنا الزمن معا .. لم يعد يأتي في المساء .. اختصرنا الزمن .. عمرنا أصبح وردة جميلة فواحة تعتلي غصنا أخضر ثريا .."!

سيعود في الظهيرة .. وستكون في استقباله .. اللحظة والأخرى ساعات قليلة والزمن المختصر .. تكوم عند وقع أقدامه :

‒ عائدة .. عائدة ..

‒ أهلا سعيد .. أراك تبتسم ..

هل من حدث سعيد ؟

‒ ربما لن يسعدك مثلي ..

‒ "إذن فما قالته بنات الحي صحيح .. سينتقل إلى المدينة الكبيرة .. حيث قد منح منزلا وعربة وسائقا" : ولماذا؟

‒ لأنك لن تفهمي ؟!

‒ أفهم ماذا ؟

‒ ان انتقل إلى المدينة ؟

‒ أو ستنتقل إلى المدينة ؟

‒ وبمفردي ..

‒ و .. عمرنا و .. رفقتنا .. ولماذا لا أكون معك ؟

‒ لأنك لن تستطيعي التعايش مع حياة المدينة .

أيام فقط قبل أن يغادرها :

غرقت في دموعها : "تيار عميق يجرفنا ، كنت أجدف ضد نفسي ما كنت أعلم ان للنهر روافد حتى تشعبت أمامي ، تيار عميق يحيطنا بذراته وشلالاته ويطوينا .. كنت أجدف ضد نفسي".
وحين كان يغادرها .. مدت إليه يدها تودعه .. قال لها :"عليك أن تذهبي إلى دار أهلك".
بكت عند أهلها .. تشقق ظاهر يدها من حرارة الدمع تجرح باطن قلبها .. بل عقلها .. بل وجنتاها ..
وحين كانت تجلس في انتظار شيء عنه .. مد أبوها إليها يده بخطاب ، ضحكت وبكت:

– لا أحسن القراءة يا أبي .

– ليتك تحسنينها .. ليتك علّمت نفسك وأبحرت نحوها فلقد جذّفتِ ضد نفسك .

– ما هي أخباره .. أيود رؤيتي .. وهل أعد لي بيتا .. أفينتظرني .. ؟

أقفل الأب راجعا من حيث جاءها .. على ظهره كانت تقرأ الفشل وأدركت بأن النهر قد نضب .
النضوب .. هذا الذي ما كانت تدري انها تحفر له قاعا ليلتهم كل المياه التي وفرتها للنهر !!
لم يتركها أبوها تغرق من جديد داخل هوة من عمق النهر الناضب .. حام حولها كثيرا .. مرة بالحسنى وأخرى بالعنف .. عار .. أن تظل شابة تحلم برجل مر في حياتها وانتهى !! عيب أن تحلم برجل لا يملكها ..
معاناة عنيفة تتجاذب آخر شريان نابض في جسد عائدة .. وعلى الجهة الأخرى كان سعيد يتعايش مع حياة المدينة وتكوّن الناس والصراعات الرهيبة الصفراء .. والخضراء والبيضاء والسوداء ..
ومرت الأيام
دخل الأب مستعجلا : عائدة .. غدا ستزفين إلى "عواد" !
وأضيئت الأنوار ..
ضحك الناس ، حركوا الطبول ..
تصايح الأطفال فرحاً .. حمل بعضهم السمط إلى خارج الدار الشعبي .. ونظف آخرون التراب .. ورش بعضهم الأرض بالماء .
امتزج زخم التراب المبلل .. بزخم الدموع تخضب وجنتيها وبعد ليلة حافلة .
أمسك بيدها عواد .. ولم يمسك بقلبها .. كانت تدعس على آخر جزء نابض فيه وهي تدير ظهرها عن بيت أبيها ..
الرياح تحمل بقايا رائحة تراب عربتهما .. تزخم بها أنف أبيها .. كانت تتلفت إلى الوراء .. تغرس نظراتها في زجاج العربة ..
خيل إليها أنها تراه ..
تراءى لها جسده ينتصب واقفا بجوار أبيها .. ليتها تدري ماذا يقولان .. حمل إليها الهواء من نافذة العربة ذبذبات صوته التوى عنقها إلى الوراء .. كانت السيارة تنهب بها الأرض تقطع الصوت .. غاب الخيال ..
أصبح طيفا ..
ولم تعلم سر عودته .

عبد الرحمن الشاعر ـ المملكة العربية السعودية

عرق وطين(48)

" ... وبسمة مشرقة تطفح بآماله على صفحة وجهه .. بسمة الاعرابي الذي لا يلين لسخر الحياة . ولا يستسلم للياس حينما تعاديه الحياة ... "

بف .. بف .. بف .. أطلقها عواد (أخو غزوى) من بين شفتيه ، وقد مط شفتيه السفلى فوق الشفة العليا ، التي انكمشت إلى اسفل ، وجرت معها أرنبة أنفه ، تاركة للشفة السفلى حرية الامتطاط إلى فوق والنفخ ، محاولاً بذلك طرد ذبابة حطت على أرنبة انفه تعرك جناحيها بقوائمها .. وهو ينظر إليها بحول من طرف عينيه .. ومرة أخرى .. بف .. بف .. مع ضيق في صدره لكن دون أن يحرك ساكناً من جسده المتراخي مع يديه المتشابكتين ، خلف رأسه ، وهو يرصهما إلى جذع شجرة عجوز واهية كنفسه وخواطره . بف .. بف ... مرة ثالثة للذبابة ، وللذبابة تتراقص بمرح وطرب على أرنبة انفه وتفرك رأسها وتنفضه ، بعد أن احست به يحاول تعكير صفوها وقطع ـ المزاج ـ عليها ، فنفضت هيكلها الصغير بغيظ وحنق ، واقصعرت على قوائمها تتأهب للافلات من دفقات انفاسه ، وانطلقت كالسهم على شكل نصف دائرة ، وانقضت لتخزه في جوف عينه ، وصرخ متألماً ـ آخ ـ وصفق براحتيه الهواء على الذبابة التي راحت اربا واشلاء بين راحتيه . وتحركت نفسه اشمئزازاً لذلك الخليط المنساح بين راحتيه ، ثم بصق بقشعريرة على وجه الأرض ، ولوى رأسه (متقريفا) قائلاً : " أمحق " من ذلك الخليط القيىء وراح يمسح راحتيه بتراب اليابسة ، ثم مرة أخرى جمع كل ما في فيه من لعاب نفسه وارسله رذاذا إلى وجه الهواء الذي رده إليه على شكل ذرات صغيرة انتثرت على صفحة وجهه ، فاستشاطت نفسه .. ومسح بكف يده أرنبة انفه ووجنتيه ، وضغط بطرف اصبعه على أحد منخريه وأطلق زفرة من انفه ـ انحدر على اثرها إلى شاربه (...) مسحه بكف يده قبل أن يصل إلى شفتيه . وطقت نفسه وتحركت أمعاؤه وارتجفت شفتاه وكاد (يعملها) ويتقياً لو لم يسارع إلى جذب نفس من الهواء البارد .. وتمتم وهو يغالب ضحكة"ما بقي إلا (...) ؟ "ولعله صدق ما طرأ على خاطره إذ أخذ ينظر إلى مقعده ويتحسس أعلى فخذيه ، ولكنها "جت سليمة" فتمتم مرة أخرى" اشوا فكنا الله " .. وبعد ... بعد كل هذه الزوبعة الطارئة التي لا تفتح النفس عاد الهدوء إليه ، وعاد بجسده يستند إلى جذع الشجرة .. عاد يلم شتات ما تقطع من خواطره ، ويصفها في ذاكرته ، وبدأ يجتر الذكريات من جديد .. (وعسى ما هنا ذبابة أخرى ... ؟ !) .

(ايه .. ايه .. يا الله حسن تدابيرك) قال ذلك بنفس موجعة ومن ضيق يدك ويعصر عليه ذهنه حينما بدأت شاشة الذكريات تعرض جزءأ من حياته الماضية .. تذكر كيف أنه كان (راعياً) وانه كان اجيراً وبأجر زهيد إلا أنه يغبط نفسه على ما كان ينعم به من حياة هانئة كلها الاستقرار والطمأنينة والنشوة لاسيما حينما كان يعتلي ظهر الناقة " الوضحا " .. يحتضن سنامها سكران بنشوة القصيد ما قاله العرب عن الكرم والشجاعة والوفاء ، أو حينما يرفع عقيرته لسكون البيداء وصمت ليلها البهيم وهو يصف ناقته بقول الشاعر النبطي :

رعي نهود كنها زمة العاج

ركن على صدر الحبيّب مقاعيد

---

48 موسوعة الأدب العربي السعودي الحديث ـ نصوص مختارة ودراسات ، الطبعة الأولى ، الرياض 2001 م، ص 258ـ267

ما هزعهن ولا لهجهن لهاج

ما زينهن في لبنة قلعة الجيد

راعي ثنايا كنهن حب علاج

ولا البرد في مرز من الرعاديد

أو حينما يكتنفه السكون الشامل ويداعب نسيم الصحراء شغاف قلبه وتطرأ عليه محبوبته ويحاول وصفها بقول الشاعر .

يا راكب أكوار هجن عراميس

هجن براه السير بري اليراعي

هجن من المسيار دقاق كوانيس

من كثر ما يرعن قفر المراعي

لا شيم اثرهن بالخلا ديب يا نس

عود وطنب بالعواء .. ثم اراعي

حياة ما حسب فيها قط أن تصاريف القدر قد خطت لها المنتكسات ، وان الشيء ابداً لن يدوم إلا لوجه الله .. فانقبضت نفسه واحتبست عواطفه ، وشاشة الذكريات تعرض ذلك المنظر الرهيب ، الذي طرأ على حياته وقلب رأسها على عقب ، وكان النصيب والسماء هما العاملان في نكسته ، فالسماء قد صامت بمائها عن الأرض وانتحت سحبها تسير مغربة ، كما يغرى السراب ، وأرسلت أشعة شمسها تحرق اليابس مع الأخضر ، فتحطم الحياة وتنثر الفناء في الأرض وفي زوايا النفوس ، فأجدبت الأرض وصامت " هي الأخرى "بمكنوناتها ، وغضبت السماء فاكفهرت بوجهها ونثرت عليه صفرة الموت ، فقذفت بالشجيرة مع الكبيرة إلى الهواء يدحرجها ويعبث بها بغشم ومجون ، وانشقت للرمال تتقيأ أمواجها لتتلاطم وتدفن في اثر سيرها كل أثر للحياة .. وبات العرب في فزع من أمرهم وعلى خوف من حياتهم ، وتضارب بينهم الرأي ، وأخذ شملهم يتشتت ، والموت من حولهم يفتح فاه يلتهم المواشي على الخيل والابل والشياه ، وكل ما على الأرض من دابة ، لا تطيق الجوع والظمأ ولا تصبر على وهج الشمس وكي الرمضاء .. فانتثر العربان يهربون إلى المدن يدرؤون الموت من الضياع وغائلة الجوع تاركين وراءهم المضارب ، وما بقي من ذكريات شواهد لنكبة الظمأ والصراع ، الذي انهزمت به الأرض على حسب شقاء الانسان .

وكان عواد فرداً من أولئك المنكوبين ، ومن القلة الذين أصروا على ملازمة البادية ، لما في نفوسهم من حنين وحب للبادية و "الديرة "وحياتها الحرة الكريمة ، فطفق يلتمس لنفسه عذراً بالبقاء ، ولكن البادية "والديرة "ضاقتا به .. والموت ، والضياع ، والألم ، والفقر كلها أشباح تتراءى له بين كل آونة وأخرى فيحس في قرارة ذاته ما يكذب عذره ويفل عزم بقائه .. ورغبة مترددة إلى الفرار والنجاة .. ويقول لنفسه ويقنعها (ماني بخير من مطلق وعقاب ودريهم وفلاح) . كل أولئك مشايخ القوم وكبارهم اقروا الواقع وهربوا للنجاة . وهو قد جلس أكثر يومه هذا إلى جذع الشجرة ، ليقنع نفسه ويقطع هذا التردد ما بين لا ونعم .. ولعل أخته (غزوى) أبصر منه وأبعد نظراً حينما أشارت عليه بالرحيل و "دوارة الشغل" فأخذ بنفسه المترددة وقلب لها الأمر على أوجهه وكان الواقع ... واقع حياته اللاشيء أبلغ مقنع له بالرحيل .. فاقتنع بحقيقة الواقع وبنصيحة أخته وقام .. قام يزم شفتيه وينقل الخبر إلى أخته . وعندما انتصب واقفا تمطى بجسده وتلوى كما تفعل الشاة عندما تهب من مربطها وطقطق أصابع يديه وسلسلة ظهره . ثم نفض عباءته مما علق بها من تراب وسوى عمامته (الشماغ) على رأسه حتى غاصت طاقيته إلى اذنيه . وتخلل لحيته الكثة بأصابعه .. ثم انحدر إلى الوادي تسبقه ساقاه يرثع ، فإذا به يفاجأ ب (غزوى) مقبلة اليه تدعوه بعد أن استبطأت مقامه هناك . فابتدرها يقول :

- يا غزوى .. يا بنت ابوي ... الله أعلم أني أبي اروح الرياض ! .

فافتر ثغرها اليابس ترد :

إني قلت لك مالك غير تنصا الرياض ..

وسكت وهو مكتف بهذه المقدمة وما بقي من الحديث والأخذ والرد سيطول شرحه في الليل .

وفي الليل كان حديثهما لا يتعدى عن الرياض وما بها من رزق . وأمل واحلام نفشتها أخته في رأسه مستشهدة على ذلك بوصف (شايع .. إبن خالها) من ان هناك عملاً ودراهم كثيرة .. وكلام كثير جداً امتلأ به رأسه الكبير حتى أنها لم تنس أن توصيه قائلة :

- وأنا بنت أبوك اذا طبيت الرياض فانص . (كمب .. بن لادن) .

بينما هو سايح في لجة افكاره الشاردة بما ينتظره من مجهول في البلد التي لم تطأها قدمه .. ! .

كان يحس بنوع من الرهبة ، وخوف لا يعرف كنهه . ولعله احساس وغريزة ألم الفراق . وشيء مجهول كعلم الغيب يتلقاه ..

وفي الغد كان يقف إلى اخته وهي تكرر عليه (وانا اختك لا تنس تطرش لي خط تخبرني عنك) فيرد وهو يخنق عبرة تحشرج في بلعومه (ودّعى ألله يا بنت ابوي ما والله انساك وأنا حي) ويربت على كتفها بينما رأسه يمسح ما انزلق من عينيه من دموع على كتفيها .. وأدبر عنها يتصوب خط السيارات الذي يبعد عن (الديرة) عدة أميال . فسار متنكباً بندقيته (أم أصبع) و (المزوده) تتأرجح على كتفه . وطال به المسير يدفن قدميه في الرمال وينزعهما ليواصل المسير حتى قرب على الخط . فوقف يرقب سيارة آتية يسبقها حنينها فاعترض الخط يومىء بردن ثوبه :

- هيه .. هيه .. يا ولد .. يا سواق .. اوقف .

فاوقف السائق السيارة وتساوم معه على أجرة الركوب ، ثم تسلق حوض السيارة فالفى بها شلة من الاعراب قد أغرقهم الغبار فكسا وجوههم فبدوا بنظراتهم الصارمة الجامدة كأنهم زبانية الشر فانحنى لهم يحييهم .

- بالخير ياعيال .

ومنهم من اكتفى بهز رأسه . وبالطبع لم يسألهم عن الصحة والحال (فالحال من بعضه) انما طرح بجسده بينهم وتعانق رأسه مع رؤوسهم يتمايل ويهتز . ولم يفته أن يودع (الديرة) بآخر نظرة . وهو يرى تلالها ورؤوس الجبال تتلاشى وتضمحل . فاحس بغصة من عبرة وزفرة انطلقت منه بغير قصد ، فالتفت اليه أحد الأعراب يسأله :

- من اين انت يا ولد ؟ من اي عرب ؟ ومن اي ديرة ؟

فتنهد عواد وزفر . وتردد في الجواب ماذا يقول ؟ قول انه من ديرة الهلاك ... من ديرة الموت .. وخطر على لسانه قول الشاعر الذي هجا وطنه و (الديرة) فرد عواد : وبصوت مرتفع .

– أنا من الديرة التي قال عنها الشاعر :

عسى مطرها البانزين وصافي الغاز
وابليس بالكبريت يشخط باثرها
فراح من حوله العرب يضحكون على هذا الهجاء الساخر ..
وانبرى أحدهم يؤنبه قائلاً :

- اعقب يا ذا ... ديرتك وأبوك للنار !

فاستدرك عواد .

‒ استغفر الله .. والله انها ديرتي غير أن الشيطان سبقني وقلتها !

ومن قوله هذا استخف القوم ظله واستروحوا لطراوة منطقه وسرعة بديهته فكان لهم خير رفيق يقطع عليهم طول الطريق بالشعر ، وما يتناقله العرب من نكات ، وسخر : واستطاع بلباقته أن يقشع ماجثم على صدورهم من يأس وقنوط وملل . حتى أشرفت بهم السيارة إلى الرياض ، وكان الوقت عصراً ، فانتثر شملهم عند مركز (الغرابي) وانسل هو من بينهم بعد أن تقلد (المزودة) وتنكب البندقية وسار متصوباً نحو الشمال من المدينة لا يدري أين هو وإلى أي جهة يسير ، فالمرئيات وتخاطف السيارات والحركة الصاخبة والاجناس المختلفة المتعاقبة حوله ، كل هذه اذهلته فجمدت شجاعته وارتبك ، وأضحى كالشاة المسبوعة حينما ترى السبع يتلحظ لافتراسها ، فظل جسده جامداً مشدوداً إلى الأرض .. وحاول أن ينتزع قدميه من شللهما ويسير .. وعلى حين غرة زعقت بجواره سيارة وهي تمرق كالبرق فهب وقفز كالصيد تسبقه (المزودة) التي انقطع حبلها وفرت هي الأخرى فزعة في الهواء ولطمت ظهر أحد المارة .. وكذلك البندقية دكت ركبته فشهق من شدة الوجع وانكب يعركها بيديه (آخ .. أمحق من قراده) .. و .. و .. واحس بشيء ثقيل يلطم هامة رأسه ، واحتولت عيناه وبعد جهد ولأي استقر نظره على المزودة تغطي أكثر رأسه ووجهه وبرجل أمامه يشتم .

‒ شوباك . العمى في عيونك .. ما تشوف .. قطعت قلبي بخيشتك ها يدي ؟!

فحرك عواد رأسه يمنة ويسرة لا يفهم "لغوة" الرجل . انما استسلم للواقع وصمت باعتبار ما حدث نموذجاً مما يرقبه من غرائب ومصائب .. وقام يواصل سيره ويسأل كل من صادفه :

‒ ما تدري وين "كمب أبو لادن" ؟

وتكرر سؤاله دون ما جواب مقنع ، فأحدهم يقول شمالاً ، وآخر يقول جنوباً ، وثالثاً يقول (ما ادري والله) .. وهو لم يزل يواصل خطواته حتى انتهى به ذلك الشارع الطويل إلى شارع آخر . شارع (القطار) . فبان له مصنع (البيبسي كولا) بواجهته الزجاجية فوقف عندها يحلق بعينيه في القوارير وهي تدور فارغة وتعود ممتلئة .. وتعاقب الآلات و .. واشياء لم يدركها ذهنه ، انما اكتفى بان علق عليها قائلاً :

‒ أهيب . يا والله الحرفة القشرا .. بسم الله الرحمن الرحيم !!

ثم أحس بيد تربت على كنفه ، فاستدار على عقبه فإذا هو برجل طويل القامة يحييه قائلاً:

‒ أمسيت بالخير يا ولد .

فانشرحت نفس عواد "بالعربي الذي يحكي مثله" ورد عليه :

‒ الله يمسيك بالخير يا أخوي ، ما تدري وين "كمب ابو لادن" ؟

فابتسم الرجل اذ أدرك ان صاحبه غريب عن المدينة ، وليس ثمة شك أن ما مر به "هو" حينما وطأت قدماه أرض الرياض قد مر بصاحبه الآن .. وكان الرجل كعادة العرب كريماً مضيافاً ولو من عسر وقلة ، فالزم على عواد ضيافته ، وأنه "وصل على خير "حيث أن الرجل من عمال "بن لادن" .

أيام وليالٍ مرت على عواد عند ضيفه كان خلالها يتهيأ للعمل ، بعد أن طاف بالمدينة مع صاحبه وباع بندقيته وعرف أكثر معالم المدينة ومجاهلها وتعود على حركتها وصخبها .. وجاء اليوم الذي يرقبه بفارغ الصبر "يوم العمل" عندما سلمه مدير العمل "النمرة" وعين له موقع العمل مع شلة وخليط من اجناس العرب .

فاسرع إلى الفأس يحمله على كتفه ، وسار مع الآخرين تلتهب في صدره نشوة ، وأمل عارم بحياته الجديدة وللمائة والخمسين ريالاً التي تنتظره آخر كل شهر . اضف إلى ذلك أن رئيس العمال " التنديل " من قومه ، فشمر عن ساعديه وحزم وسطه ، ولف عمامته على رأسه ، ورفع الفأس في الهواء وهوى به بقوة وعزم يشق الأرض ويهيل التراب .

كان يعمل بقوة .. بقوة المحتاج . وبصبر الأعرابي الذي ينشد الكرامة وحياة الأنفة والاباء ولو من شرف الغبار و " العرق والطين " .. كان يضرب الارض بالفأس بجد ويجلد كأنما هو يبحث بين طياتها عن ماضيه الذي خنقه الظمأ .. وابتلعته الأرض .. والأرض من فأسه تصرخ وتنشق لتبصق في جوفها مما علق بفيه من غبار وعرق وبسمة مشرقة تطفح بآماله على صفحة وجهه .. بسمة الأعرابي الذي لا يلين لسخر الحياة . ولا يستسلم للياس حينما تعاديه الحياة !! .

فوزية الجار الله ـ المملكة العربية السعودية

الواحدة صباحاً [49]

إنه حبك .. لا شيء آخر ..

حبك الذي يرفعني ويضعني .. يسحقني .. يشغلني .. يطفئني .. يذروني كذرات الغبار فوق قمم مسحورة .. يطرحني منذ أيام مريضاً معلولاً مسجّى الذاكرة لا يدرك سر علته ولا مصدر قوته ولا سبيلاً لخلاصه !

لا شيء يخمد تلك النار التي تدبُّ وتسري في أحشائي .. لا أدري منذ أيام وتلك الفكرة الساخنة المجنونة تسكنني .. تؤرقني .. تعذبني .. لا أدري كيف يكون الخلاص .. كيف أخلع عن رأسي هذا الطنين .. كي أهدأ .. كي أستكين وأطمئن .. سيجارة أخرى أيضاً !

أهو الشيطان الذي يذكره أبي دائماً لي .. كلمة تتكرر .. تتضخم في سمعي .. حين يقول لي :

الشيطان يضيرك .. يمنعك من الإستقاظ حالما تصافح خيوط الفجر الأولى أذرع الأشجار .. تسبح المخلوقات كلها للواحد .. إلا أنت .. الشيطان يزحف تحت جلدك .. يعرقل قدميك ... يقف بينك وبين عتبة المحاريب والمساجد .. الشيطان ينتصب تحت أظافرك .. تحت أجفانك ولكن أين هو الآن لقد هرب ... !

هجرنا وهجر الشيطان ولم أعد أسمع من يحذرني من الشيطان فهل أخذ أبي الشيطان معه ؟!!

ولقد اخترت الطريق ولاحاجة بي إلى تلك العبارات الغبية حين يطلقونها تحت مسمى النصيحة لا أريد أن أكون رهناً لأي شيء إلا نفسي .. إرادتي ... رغبتي !!

لقد اخترت الطريق بقناعتي أنا فمن أنا ؟!

***

يسكنني الملل والإحساس بلا جدوى الأشياء وتفاهة الحياة .. أقلّب خزنة الثياب ... أنفضها جميعها .. أقلب المجلات القديمة .. أمزقها .. أحرقها .. أفعل مثلما يفعل الآخرون ... آكل بنهم لكنني لا اشعر سوى بمزيد من التخمة والجوع معاً ومزيد من الإندفاع نحو فكرتي المجنونة ... بل الجميلة !!

إنني تائه لا أجد موضعاً لرأسي ولا لقدمي .. ولا لقلبي !

أبحث عن أنا .. منذ أن أطلقت هذه الفتاة رصاصتها القاتلة إلى ذاكرتي .. منذ قالت لا .. !!

كيف استطاعت ؟ ! كيف خلعت وجهها القديم .. كيف لم أشعر يوماً بأننا نسير في اتجاهين متعاكسين ؟ !

الحقيرة .. لكنني أحبها ولو كانت حقيرة .. نعم أحببتها بل إنني أحبها بجنون ولأني أحبها فذلك يعني أن أياماً أخرى تضاف إلى عمري . وأنني أمتلك حياة أخرى أضيفها إلى ممتلكاتي .. أغلق عليها في صندوق .. أتأملها .. أخشى عليها ..

نعم ليس للآخرين أدنى حق في التطفل أو الدخول عبر أبوابنا المحظورة .. ! وليغضب العالم أجمع ولتنفجر نيرانهم وصرخاتهم .. ليقولوا ما شاؤوا أما أنا فلا أحد يناز عني في أيام عمري ولا مساحات حياتي !

أيهما كان الأكثر ظلماً وأيهما ألاحق بالنهاية والتنحي عن طريقي ؟ ! أمها .. أبوها .. والداها معاً .. ايهما الأكثر جدارة بسحقه وقذفه في بئر النهايات ؟ . خطيبها أي جريرة أقترفها .. لا لقد جاء متأخراً !!

---

49 موسوعة الأدب العربي السعودي الحديث ـ نصوص مختارة ودراسات ، الطبعة الأولى ، الرياض 2001 م، ص 510–517

يزحف هذا الليل وصدى مدافع المساء الرمضانية لا تزال ترنّ في أذني .. ينادونني وأرفض الإندماج أو الإستجابة .. كرهت عصا أبي وهي توقظني للصلاة ، توقضني للمدرسة وتوقضني للحياة .. تقودني كالحمار إلى الدكان للوقوف فيه واستعطاف الزبائن للشراء ولا يظفر بي غالباً لأني لست حماراً .. كنت أشفق عليه أحياناً لقد أرهق نفسه بلا فائدة .. ليته يعلم! في أي أرض هو الآن .. هل يعقل أن يكون حياً .. أتأمل وجهي في المرآة وأود لو أحطمها .. لماذا أتنفس؟ لماذا أسير؟ لماذا خطواتي؟ لماذا أنتظر؟ لماذا أندفع؟ لماذا عيني .. لماذا أنفي؟!

لماذا المرايا هل وجدت لتعذيبنا .. أصب الشتائم على المرايا والزجاج والمصانع والشوارع .. على الأراضي والأرصفة .. أصب اللعنات على أولاد الحارة الذين لا يكفون عن الهذيان والصراخ طوال الليل وبشكل أكبر منذ حل شهر رمضان .. تغيب عيونهم نهاراً خلف الجدران ويستيقظون كالعفاريت ليلاً تارة يضحكون وتارة يتبادلون قذف الحجارة .. لم استطع النوم ، وهي بعد أيام ستكون له وأسمعهم يتحدثون .. يتهامسون .. كنت أشعر بتفاهتي .. لماذا هو وليس أنا؟!

قلت إني أحبك منذ كنت طفلة .. منذ كنت إراك صغيرة نلعب معاً .. تبهرينني بعينين هادئتين .. ببشرة سمراء .. بضفيرتين قد طالتا الآن !

ذات يوم رأيتك .. لمحت تأود قامتك أكثر من مرة .. حننت .. حدثت أمي برغبتي .. أريدها .. لا أريد سواها .. يصفعني رفضك .

تدور الليالي وأتفاءل ربما يحدث شيء ما .. ربما يتغير مجرى الأنهار . ربما كثرة ألحاحي ومطاردتي .. ربما كثرة خفقاتي المجنونة على هذا الباب المغلق .. تجعلك تعودين مرة أخرى إليّ منذ زمن بعيد .. عرفت وأعرف أنك ستكونين لي ولن تكوني لسواي !!

***

لم أصدق !! لكنه لا يفوقني بشيء .. أنا أجدر وأقرب وأحق .. أخشى عليك .. أود سعادتك .. لن تفرحي أبداً بعيداً عن شواطئي .. لن تتذوقي رحيق السعادة بعيداً عن إرادتي .. أنا أفضل ! .

أشعر بدوار في رأسي .. إنني لا أنام .. وكيف أنام؟! وأنت ذلك الجزء مني ستكونين هناك بعيداً وأنت ألمي الذي يتمرد على نفسه التي هي أنا .. تنطفئ جذوة مباهجي وتنتهي الأفراح ، وتخمد آخر ذرة من أنفاس وجودي . حين تضرب الدفوف شاهدة بامتزاج حياتين معاً حين تشهد تلك الوجوه الغبية بأنك له !

لا .. أصرخ بها .. أقف .. أقذف بقدح الماء من يدي .. أضربه بالحائط ويتطاير شظايا من نار تحرق كل يد تجرؤ على احتوائك .. لا يعلمون أنك محرمة عليهم جميعاً .. لا يعلمون أنني قد ضربت بقضبان أسطورية من الحب حول قلبك فأنت لي إذن .. !

صوت أمي يناديني مرة أخرى ، ويلتحم بصوت في ذاكرتي لنداءات بعيدة هجرتني منذ زمن .. لا لا سبيل إلى شيء آخر ! إنني متعب ولا وقت لأي شيء سوى مزيد من التفكير لإيجاد مخرج من هذا النفق الذي يسحقني !

الخامس من شوال ..

هكذا تقول بطاقة الجريمة بين يدي .. بطاقة الدعوة إلى عرسها .. إنهم يعدون لذبحي ونهايتي .. مددت يدي أمزق الورقة وأمزق معها كل عثرة تقف أمامي .. لا يستطيعون اقرار ذبحي بورقة فقط !

ذلك الموعد ينثقب نظراتي ويحزّ عنقي كالسيف .. زفافك .. كيف استطعت ولم تدركي بأنه لا فرح بعيداً عن شواطئي .. لا هي تحبني ..

***

ربما أجبرت على ذلك .

لكنني لمحتها ترتدي الدبلة في أصبعها فهل يعقل أن تغلق الأبواب دونك .. كيف يحدث بسهولة ؟ من يجرؤ على الوقوف أمامك ؟! لست رجلاً إن لم تفعل إن لم تقل للجميع بأنك وحدك الرجل وحدك الجدير بالحب .. بالاهتمام وحدك الجدير بالهيبة ..

سيجارة أخرى !

تشتعل النار في رأسي وأنا أتخيل ابتسامتها له .. كفها بين يديه .. لا .. ياللشيطان يدور في رأسي ... يطاردني مائة شيطان .. أدور في الحارات الضيقة هذه حارتنا التي شهدت يوماً ركضاً وضجيجاً .. حارتنا التي شهدت حجارتها ورمالها حفيف ثوبها وصرختها حيث تعثرت يوماً لازلت أذكر سقوطها وركضي إليها هلعاً .

أضغط باصبعي وأعالج الجرح حتى توقف نزيف الدم من جبينها .. أرقب المنزل إنها وحدها .. ذلك أمر مؤكد لقد رأيت أمها وأباها يتجهان إلى المسجد .. من المؤكد أيضاً أنهما سيطيلان البقاء هناك لصلاة التهجد .. الوقت مناسب جداً .. تضج المساجد بالتكبير ويضج رأسي بصرخات محمومة .. بضحكات تسخر من ضعفي .. من حقارتي ولكن لا .. لست رجلاً إن لم أخضع الجميع حتى الشياطين لسطوتي .. تشتعل النار في رأسي أقذف بالسيجارة ..

الواحدة صباحاً تبينت ذلك حين امعنت النظر في زجاج ساعتي .. الضوء خافت ، والإضاءة التي تضيء عتبة الباب مكسورة منذ أيام كسرها أحد الصبية !

خفقة .. اثنتان .. ثلاث .. مَنْ .. صوتها كان مرتعشاً ونائماً شعرت بأن الكلمات تتعثر .. تلوب داخل حنجرتي .

– أن .. ل . م .. إف .. افتحي ..

– افتحي ..

– مَنْ ؟! عاد الصوت قلقاً

– حسن .. جاركم .. !

– لا أحد هنا .. لك أن تعود فيما بعد ! تدافعت كلماتها ،، تناثرت كلماتي ..

صوتها يرتطم بذلك العطش الذي لا زال يحفر خندقاً في صدري ..

– خذي ما بيدي .. وسوف أنصرف فوراً .. لن أتمكن من العودة مرة أخرى !

لم تكن تريد .. كان صوتها خائفاً مرتبكاً ..

لم أشعر بساقي حين تجاوزت العتبة بسرعة رهيبة .. كانت الصورة تغوص وتطفو أمام عيني .. في أعماقي .. كانت الأصوات تطاردني .. تصفعني .. أشعر بأني أتحول الى كائن يوشك أن يولد من جديد .. يعانق الفرح ويرفع رايات النصر الأخير .. النصر الذي لا هزيمة بعده ..

بعد أن يقضي على كل شيء يقف أمامه .. وينهي كل صوت سوف يتنفس بحرية وانطلاق .. حين يُخمد كل الأصوات المضادة له .. ويحطم كل الأبواب المغلقة .. خطواتها .. عثراتها .. تأود قامتها .. نسيتها .. نسيتها .. أذكر الآن بوضوح .. لهفي غيرتي ، جنوني ، لوعتي انتظاري .. ذلك الجرح النازف في القلب ..

كانت تود إغلاق الباب بسرعة .. خُيل إليّ بأنها تؤكد أمامي (لا .. !!) تُعيد صفعي ألف مرة وتحقيري ..

***

لم يكن لدي ثمة وقت أضيعه بالسؤال أو العتاب .. عقارب الساعة تزحف قليلاً فوق الواحدة والشارع هادئ وليس ثمة سوانا أنا وهي ..بسرعة رهيبة اندفعت كانت تقاوم شدتها من شعرها .. أرادت أن تصرخ خُيل إليّ ذلك من نظرات عينيها الخائفة ..

97

لم أكن أفكر .. كنت أتحرك فقط .. الدهليز كان ضيقاً والاضاءة كانت تأتي خافتة من الداخل ولا صوت .. سوى أنفاس .. أنفاس .. أصابعي تتلمس الطريق إلى عنقها شعرت بالدفء يلامس راحة يدي .. عروقها كانت نابضة .. خائفة .. أنفاسها متهدجة .. تطفو الصور وتغوص أمام عينيّ .. ليس ثمة وقت .. تلسعني الأسئلة .. كالسياط ولا مجال للخلاص إلا في ذلك الضغط والإزاحة لتلك المضادات ..

نظراتها كانت تستعطف .. تستغيث .. اتجاهلها .. أحاصرها .. تمد يدها تحاول دفع يدي تشدني من كتفي .. من غترتي التي أحكمت تثبيتها على أنفي وفمي ..

تبينت مرأى بريق الدبلة في أصابعها تثقب عيني ... ازددت عنفاً لم أكن أرى شيئاً .. أحكمت قبضتي أكثر .. عروقها .. نابضة .. حارة .. تدفعني .. تشد كتفي . تنظر إليّ بهلع .. بقوة ... تخترقني عيناها .. لا وقت للسؤال أو العتاب .. لم أعد أشعر بشيء .. لم أعد أتبين نظراتها لقد انطفأ شيء ما ..

ارتخت أصابعها من كتفي .. تحسست يدها أبحث عن ذلك التحديد .. عن ذلك الدفء الحميم الذي كان يسحقني .. كانت مثلجة .. لم تتحرك .. لم تقاوم !

تتصاعد الأصوات وترتطم داخل رأسي .. كل الأشياء كانت تغيب .. تنتهي .. تذوب في قلبي .. أمام عيني .. آه كيف استطعت .. كيف فعلت .. بكل ذلك الحب الجارف .. بين الأضلاع أنهيت ذلك العذاب .. آه لقد فعلت نعم فعلت .. ق .. ت .. ل .. ت .. ها !

حمد بن رشيد بن راشد ـ عمان

"القصة الفائزة بالجائزة الأولى على مستوى سلطنة عُمان لعام 1984 في مسابقة شئون الشباب للقصة والشعر"

عزّان

رذاذ المطر اخذ شكل على هيئة سراب .. حبّات البرد تتساقط هنا وهناك على احدى مناطق الجبل الاخضر .. شتاء لافح .. شجيرات الرمان تتكمش على بعضها ، تتدفأ بأنفاس المارة .. يوم قارس فريد من نوعه .

الَمارة لم يكونوا بعض الفلاحين المتوجهين الى حقولهم كالمعتاد ، انما رجال مسلحون يتتطاير من اعينهم الشرر .. يمشون وفق خطوات كأنها منتظمة .

"عزان" في مؤخرة ذلك الركب لصغر سنّه .. ودّع امه بشعور حزن وفرح .. حزن فراقها وفرح الذهاب لقتال الاعداء .

يافع في طور ريعان الشباب .. قسماته توحي بأنه من رجال الجبل .. غلب على طبعه الهدوء والحزن بعد استشهاد ابيه في احدى المعارك مع الغزاة البرتغاليين .. تعدى مرحلة الطفولة لاتقانه ربط ازاره .

يمضي بخطوات شامخة مع الركب الزاحف نحو الساحل .. امه ترقبه مستبشرة .. شعور الامومة يطغى على كيانها .. تسارع الى مسح ما انحدر فوق وجنتيها من دمع .. دمع في حرارة الجمر وحرقة الالم .. يدها لم تسعفها ان تمتد لتجفف ذلك الانهمار .

صهيل النسوة يودّع الركب الزاحف .. الاطفال يرقبون ذلك بفضول ، يتجمعون كأنهم يشاهدون اهازيج "الرزحة" .

بين المجاميع برز خوة "عزان" يلقون نظرة فرح وزهو على اخيهم .. عزّان يتحسس زناد بندقيته .. بنادق اخرى اخذت بدورها صفين متقابلين تتبادل حوار مبهم .. وقع خطوات المجاهدين يتقمص نغما متصاعدا يتوافق مع صهيل النساء وهرج الاطفال .

على بعد خطوات عجوز تودّع وليدها الوحيد ، "ام عزّان" تتحسس بطنها المتكور .. آخر ذكرى من زوجها الشهيد .

***

بدأت البنادق بالعزف .. رصاص يتطاير هنا وهناك .. ارض طيبة تراود تقبيل شهداء خّروا صرعى .. دماء دافئة تسيل معانقة الثرى .. "عزّان" يصول ويجول ، رصاص يتهاوى في لحن شجي .. أنّات القتلى تتلاشى في خضم زخم النقع .. بندقية عزّان تواصل العزف طربا .. صرخات تكبير تتعالى .. لفظ الشهادة يختتم فصول حياة المجاهدين .. النخيل تتيه شموخا وكبرياء .

***

نسائم الفجر تداعب برقة اغصان الليمون .. الطيور تستقر في اوكارها .. قرى الجبل تتلهف لسماع آخر الانباء .. النسوة يتحدثن عن عزّان وصغر سنه .

زغاريد الرصاص تتواصل .. الموت يصبح غاية .. رصاصة غادرة تستقر في جبهة عزّان الناصعة .. قرص الشمس يرتفع عاليا .. عزّان يعاني سكرات الموت بينما امه في الجبل تعاني من آلام المخاض .

سَعُود بن سعد المُظَفَّر ـ عمان

حياة ربما حديثة

كانت تختلف عن كل النساء ، لها ابتسامتها الخاصة ، لها ضحكاتها الخاصة ، ولها الوانها الخاصة ، رآها في مكان عام مع شخص يبدو انه نصفها الاخر . كانت هي وكان هو في ومن عالمين مختلفين .. هي تعرف الحياة ومن هم فيها .. وهو ربما ظن انه الحياة . كانت هي تكبره ، ربما ، بخمسة اعوام ، كان هو في العشرين .. إلهى كم في الخمس سنوات من حياة ؟ كانت هي ذات شعر طويل ناعم مسدول يشبه الليل .. وكان هو ذا شعر مجعد يميل الى الحمرة . كانت هي طويلة ممتلئة .. وكان هو قصيرا نحيلا . كانت هي ذات بشرة بيضاء تكسوها الحمرة .. وكان هو أسمرا . كان يظن أنه يستطيع ان يفعل شيئا .. كان يظن ايضا انه اجمل منه واطول . كان يظن انه يستطيع ان ينال منها ولو بلمسة يد . كان وكانا هما في مطعم الحمراء في روى ، المكان يعج بالاجناس المختلفة الجذابة والتي ترى في نفسها أنها الكشف الجديد بدلا من الشكل الأسمر الهزيل الذي بدونهم والقدر كانوا لن يستطيعوا أن يصلوا أو يعرفوا ما معنى الحياة الجديدة .

من هي ؟ .. بالتأكيد من العاصمة . مسقط ذات القلاع التاريخية .. ذات الأزقة الضيقة وذات الابنية القديمة . مسقط ذات الحدائق المقفلة والشوراع الضعيفة النور . مسقط وربما شاركك وانت تسير في شوارعها شيء تائه .. مسقط ذات النكهة الترابية .

كانت الساعة العاشرة ليلا من مساء الجمعة . ماذا في مسقط تلك الليلة ؟ رب منتم ليس له منتمى .. ولكن ربما في هروب . رب نفس ليس لها نفوس .. ولكن ربما في سهرة حب يتيمة . ورب نفس ليس لها في هذا وذاك .. ولكن ربما في سبات عميق مضطرب طويل .

كانت هي تلبس اللون الاخضر .. وكان هو يلبس اللون الاسود والابيض .

كان الشاي الصنف الاخير على المائدة . كانا يتضاحكان .. كانا يتهامسان . كانت لحظة من الصعب وصفها عندما قال له"الجرسون":

‑ نعم يا حضرة ماذا تريد ؟

كان سمينا اسمرَ ومترهلا . كان ينطق الحاء هاء . كان عربيا . نظر اليه نظرة عميقة . كان المفروض ان يقول (سيدي) . انها لحظة جوع ينسى كل شيء فيها . قال ضاحكا وبراحة :

‑ اريد لحما طازجا .. لحما ابيض .

‑ ماذا تعنى ؟!

‑ ما تعلمت أو ظننت ان من ينطق بالضاد ولو جزافا يسال مرتين .. لابأس .. ماذا تعرف عن ذات الفستان الاخضر والشاب القصير ؟

قال الجرسون وبحاجب يرتفع تارة واخرى ينخفض وبصوت مبحوح :

‑ ياتيان في كل اسبوع مرة .. واحيانا مرتين .

‑ كيف عرفت ذلك ؟!

‑ منه هو .. هي من هنا وهو ..

قاطعه بنظرة من عينين جاحظتين مملوءتين بالأسف المقيد قائلا :

- من اين !؟

- من العرب .

- وماذا عن عرب هذه التربة ؟!

قال " الجرسون " وهو يضع يديه على حافة الطاولة وهامسا :

- سيدي عربكم لا يحفظون السر .. لا يحفظون اسم الاب والعائلة .... هن يطلبن الستر في كل شيء .

قال وهو مكفهر باسم :

- انها ضريبة الحياة الحديثة .. ماذا لديكم تقدمونه ؟

- دجاج وستيك وهمبرجر .

- سحقاً لكم .. انها صحونكم الدائمة .

- لا .. وهناك المكرونة ايضا .

- مكرونة مع الصلصة اظنها اخف على المعدة قبل النوم .

سار " الجرسون " وكأن كل المعلومات التي ارادها سارت معه . انه نصف المكان .. بل هو المكان . اتى الصحن الأول والثاني والثالث .. وذهب الصحن الاول والثاني والثالث ..
كانا يدخنان ويبتسمان معا . اين هو منهما في تلك اللحظة التائهة ؟! من الصعب ان يكتفي الانسان باللذة الثنائية المقدسة .
قال " الجرسون " مباغتا :

- هل تريد الشاي بعد الأكل ياسيدي ؟

نظر اليه متفحصا ، وتذكر ان من يحضر الى هذا البلد في مدة قصيرة يعرف ما طوته السنون واكثر .
قال والحزن يكسو وجهه :

- لا .. بل اريد ان اعرف وقت انصرافهما .

قال " الجرسون " وهو ينظر اليه بغرابة :

- يؤسفني ان اقول لك يا سيدي انك لم تتحضر بعد .

- كيف !؟

- انك تراقب الناس .. الناس الذين هم من بني جلدتك .

لقد شعر في تلك اللحظة بان القبور مهما اتسعت وعمقت لن تحوي جثته ومأساته الجديدة .
كان الوقت منتصف الليل .. وكان هو الواقف الوحيد بجانب سيارته الزرقاء منتظرا .
هل ردع كبرياءه المهدور كان ينتظر ؟ هل كبح العاطفة المبعثرة كان قصده الثبوت لها ؟ أو كان قصده الوقوف امام نفسه في شحص آخر تجاهله ؟[50]
رآهما يخرجان واليدان متعانقتان معا .
ماذا يقول لهما ؟ .. ماذا يقول لها ؟
تقدم منهما ببطء وغباء . جاحظ العينين محمر الوجنتين . قال :

---

50 نشرت في جريدة عُمان العدد 89 عام 1984 م .

- هل أوصلكما الى أي مكان ؟

نظر اليه القصير القامة الاسود الشعر المختار قائلا :

- لا لدينا سيارة .. تصبح على خير .

وقف مشدود الاعصاب متجمد الدم حائر الفكر .
قال مخاطبا نفسه :

- الهي ما هذه الحياة ؟ الحياة التي تنهش في ابداننا ونحن لها صاغرون .

كانت سيارته هى آخر السيارات التى تنعطف بعيدا متجهة الى الشارع العام .

على بن عبد الله الكلباني – عمان

التقاليد

كان الوقت صبيحة يوم الجمعة ، عندما اوقف محمد سيارته بين مجموعة من الأشجار وترجّل منها وأخذ يمشي بخطوات بطيئة ، يجول ببصره هنا وهناك وكأنه يبحث عن شيء فقده .. هو نفسه لا يدري أو لعلّه يتجاهل السبب الذي أتى به الى هذا المكان .. وما الذي دعاه للاستيقاظ اليوم مبكرا وهو يوم عطلة .. أخذ يرقب الشمس وهي تتوغّل في السماء رويدا ، رويدا تبخّر حبيبات النّدى التي كانت تتلألأ على أوراق الشجر .. وفجأة تسمّرت عيناه على منظر جميل .. منظر أشاع في جسمه رعشة سرت كتيّار كهربائي في دمه .. كانت حبيبات من النّدى وقد استقرت متراصة على ورقة شجر يخالها الناظر أسناناً ناصعة تضحك .. وقف يتأمل ملياً وأخذت تلك البسمة تتلاشى بتبخر حبيبات الندى وتنهّد تنهيدة تنم عن الألم والحسرة فحوّل بصره عن المنظر وسرح به بعيدا ، يالله ما أسرع مرور الأيام !! .. إن منظرها ماثل أمام عيني الآن .. هاهي تعدو وتضحك .. هذه شجرة (السّمر) التي طالما جلسنا تحتها نستريح .. نتّقي بظلها حرقة الشمس ونتقاسم بشوق قطرات من الماء كجنديّين في معركة انقطعت عنها المؤن ..هنا في هذا المكان كنا نغمس الخبز باللبن نراقب الشياه بكل سرور وهي تروح وتغدو في هذه البريّة .. كل شيء كما هو لم يتغيّر .. شيء واحد فقط غاب من هذا المكان انه العشب الأخضر .. فأين ذهب ؟ ماكان أسعدنا ونحن صغيران نرعى أغنام أسرتنا ونعتبر ذلك قمة في السعادة ، ما أسعدنا ونحن لا نفقه من أمر الحب شيئا .. ولا نعرف أن هناك قلوباً سوداء تملّكها الغل والحسد فجعلها كالحجارة أو هي أشد قسوة .. لم نكن نعرف ونحن أطفال أبرياء اننا سنفترق يوما .. ألم يتعهد (الحاج راشد) أمام أبي ان زينب لي وأنا لها؟ ألم يكرر ذلك مراراً ؟ .. آه يازمن يالك من غادر ؟ .. لكن الله يسعدك طول حياتك يازينب .. فأنت انسانة طيبة .. وانّ ما حصل كان خارجا عن ارادتي وارادتك .. وماذا كنت تستطيعين فعله ايتها المسكينة أمام رأي أبيك المتصلب .. تلك العادات التي لا ترحم ، والتقاليد التي لا تجعل للفتاة أية قيمة .. وانما هي في نظرهم سلعة تباع لمن يدفع أكثر .. بل هي في نظرهم كالحيوان الأعجم الذي لا يفقه شيئاً .. كل ما عليها أن تمتثل لأمر أبيها .. مهما كان هذا الأمر .. حتى لو أنه يتعلّق بمصير حياتها .. مسكينة أنت يازينب! .. ومسكينات من هُنّ أمثالك ..

وعندما أفاق محمد من تفكيره وتخيلاته كانت الساعة تقارب الحادية عشرة صباحا .. وكان عليه أن يسارع في العودة الى المنزل ليستعد لحضور صلاة الجمعة في المسجد .

وفي اليوم التالي وبينما هو عائد من مقر عمله شاهد طفلاً صغيرا ينشج بالبكاء وهو يسير في الشارع على غير هدى ، فعرفه محمد على الفور وأوقف سيارته وأخذ الطفل بين ذراعيه وهو يعاتبه : ماالذي أتى بك الى هنا (ياسيف)؟ أين امك؟

كيف تركتك تخرج من البيت تتخبط هكذا في الشوارع ألا تخاف عليك من حوادث السيارات؟ ألا تخاف أن يصيبك مكروه؟ .. هيّا تعال معي يابني لأوصلك الى البيت .

وحمل الطفل معه بسيارته .. وفي تلك الأثناء كانت الأم قد جُن جنونها عندما لم تعثر على طفلها داخل المنزل .. وبينما هي تهم بالخروج للبحث عنه سمعت جرس الباب يُقرع فخفق قلبها خشية أن يكون بالباب عبد الرحمن (زوجها) ماذا ستقول له عندما يسألها أين الطفل؟! .. كيف ستفهمه أنه خرج من المنزل دون أن تحس به؟ .. وتقدمت نحو الباب لتفتحه بخطى ثقيلة وهي ترتعد خوفاً .. وعندما فتحت الباب فوجئت بمحمد يحمل الطفل وهو يصيح بصوت ملهوف : أمي .. أمي فانفرجت أسارير وجهها وتهلل فرحاً .. وشكرت محمداً على فعلته الطيبة .. وأخذ محمد يحذرها من أخطار ترك الأطفال يخرجون من البيت ويلهون بالشوارع ، وما يسببه ذلك من كوارث لا تحمد عقباها .

105

ويصل فجأة زوجها عبد الرحمن ويراها واقفة أمام الباب تحادث محمدا .. وهو يعلم ماكان بينهما من حب ومودة .. وما أن اقترب منها حتى صاح مزمجرا ماذا تفعلين هنا يازينب؟ وحاولت زينب أن تجيبه لكنه لم يترك لها الفرصة لتقول شيئاً حيث انهال عليها سباً ولطماً واتَّهمها بخيانته مع ابن خالها .. وهدَّدها بالويل والثبور .. وانه سيخبر أباها أنه رآها مع محمد .. واخذت هي تبكي وتتوسل إليه أن يتركها تتكلم لتقص عليه ما حدث .. وحاولت جادة أن تفهمه الموقف .. بل أخذ يبيِّت في نفسه نيّة خبيثة .. ولم تُجِد معه محاولات محمد لتوضيح الموقف له على حقيقته .. بل أكثر من ذلك طرده وكاد يهوي عليه بقبضته لولا أنه قدّر العواقب ..

وأمام المحكمة وقفت زينب لتقول : نعم إن محمداً تهجّم علي في منزلي محاولاً الاعتداء علي .. قالت ذلك وولّت خارجة تمسح دموعها بكفيها .. بينما وقف محمد كالأبله لا يعي شيئاً مما حوله .. زائغ البصر .. يفكر فيما قالته زينب .. كيف تقول إنني حاولت الاعتداء عليها ؟ .. كيف استطاعت أن توجّه لي هذه التهمة الخطيرة وهي تعلم علم اليقين أنني برئ ، وتعلم جسامة النتائج .. واني ما فعلت إلاّ خيرا ؟! مالّذي دفعها إلى هذا الموقف المتجني ؟ .. مالّذي بدّلها؟ أنا لم أرتكب أي خطأ في حقها أبدا .. حتى عندما رفض أبوها تزويجها لى لم استغل حبها لي واغرر بها .. فهى أولا وقبل كل شيء ابنة عمتي .. ويجب أن احافظ عليها واصون عفافها وكرامتها كما كنت افعل طوال حياتي .. اعتبرتها كأختي عندما لم يحصل نصيب .. وكيف أُجازِيَ بشر على خير ؟! ، ولم يفق إلا والوالي يأمر أحد العسكر باخذه إلى السجن قائلا : خذه الى السجن ياعسكري فهو وأمثاله من المستهترين الذين ينتهكون أعراض وحرمات الآخرين ليس لهم جزاء إلا السجن .. خذه إلى السجن ، واظن ان الاشهر التي سيقضيها فيه كفيلة بأن تجعل منه انسانا يحترم الآخرين ويصون حرماتهم ..

ياللمصيبة !! كيف يقابل أهله ؟ ، ماذا سيقول عنه الناس ؟؟ .. كان يتمنى لو يعرف الوالي الحقيقة .. ولكن كيف ؟! ، وقد ادّعت زينب خلاف ذلك ولا سبيل إلى دفع حجة إمرأة على نفسها .. وسِيق محمد إلى السجن .

مرت أيام وليال وهو في سجنه مجرم في نظر الجميع ، والمرارة تعتصر قلبه .. أن كل ما يشغل تفكيره هو موقف زينب التي حكمت عليه بالشقاء بدلاً من أن تسعده مدى الحياة ، يالها من لعبة للاقدار .. وياله من تناقض .. غريبة هذه الحياة .. !!

وفي أحد الأيام وعلى غير العادة يفتح باب السجن ويحضر العسكري ويأخذه إلى الوالي .. وهناك رأى منظراً لم تصدقّه عيناه في البداية ففركهما ليتأكد أنه لم يكن يحلم .. وانه فعلا في كامل وعيه .

زينب تقف أمام الوالي .. والدموع تنهمر من عينيها .. تبلل خديها .. وهي تقول الحقيقة :

سعادة الوالي .. أرجو المعذرة .. أنا مذنبة .. أنا استحق الجزاء .. استحق أن تضعوا القيد في رجلي ويدي ، استحق أن تحبسوني بدلا منه .. لقد حكمت عليه بالسجن مع أنه بريء .. بريء والله .

واخذت في البكاء .. فحاول الوالي تهدئتها وراحت زينب تتحدث بصوت متهدّج والعبرات تخنق دموعها : قولي ، تكلمي يازينب .

فعادت إلى الكلام من جديد محاولة ضبط أعصابها : في اليوم الذي اعترفت فيه أمامكم هنا بأن محمدا مجرم وانه تهجّم علي .. كان ذلك بدافع من تهديد زوجي لي أنه سينتقم مني اذا لم أقل ماقلت .. والحقيقة أن محمداً عندما رآه زوجي كان واقفاً أمام الباب يحدثني وقد جلب طفلي من الشارع ، حيث خرج من البيت دون علم مني بينما كنت منشغلة في بعض أمور المنزل ، وعندما رآه محمد عرفه فأتى به إلى البيت وكان ينصحني بعدم تركه يخرج من البيت نظرا لما سيسببه ذلك من خطر على حياته وصدف أن حضر زوجي فانهال عليَّ ضربا وشتما .. واجبرني على الإعتراف الكاذب لينتقم من محمد الذي كان خطيبي قبل أن اتزوجه .. والذي يظنه زوجي أنه مازال عشيقي .. محمد ياسعادة الوالي أطهر من أن تُدنِّس سمعته .. ويكفي ان الظروف حكمت علينا بالفراق ولم تكن معاملته لي بعد زواجي الا معاملة الأخ لأخته .. إن قصة الحقد الذي يكنه زوجي لمحمد يرجع إلى سنوات عديدة مضت .. يوم كنا صغاراً .. وكان عبد الرحمن يحاول

استمالتي إلى جانبه هو واخته حيث كانا يكرهان محمداً نظر الخلافات بين اسرتيهما وكان يتشاجر مع محمد ، الذي كان طيب القلب ، هادئ الطباع .. وعندما تقدّم عبد الرحمن لخطبتي أول مرة رفضه أبي حيث أنني كنت مخطوبة لمحمد أو بالأحرى كان قد أعطى كلمة لوالد محمد على أن اكون أنا في المستقبل زوجة لمحمد .

استشاط هو غيظا .. وصار يحقد أكثر وأكثر عندما عرف بأن موعد زواجنا قد أزف .. ولم يدرِ ما يفعل حتى رآني في أحد الأيام أحادث محمداً ولم نكن وحدينا بل كانت أخته ، أقصد أخت محمد موجودة معنا .. فجرى مسرعا الى أبي .. واختلق قصصاً من خياله وادّعى أنه رآنا وحدنا بموقف مريب .. ولم يكن صادقاً فيما قال .. ونشر الخبر الكاذب في جميع أرجاء القرية واخيرا تحقق له ماأراد ، وحقّقت حيلته الماكرة هدفها فقد أقسم أبي ألاّ يزوجني لمحمد .. وان يزوجني من أول قادم يأتي لخطبتي وكان طبعا أول خاطب هو ، ولكنني حاولت رفضه فاجبرني والدي على قبوله بتهديد ووعيد صارم .. ومن يومها وهو لا يكن لمحمد إلا الكره والحقد ، بالرغم من أن محمداً لم يبد له أي نوع من العداء .. ولم يعاملني إلا كأخته .. زوجي ياسعادة الوالي شرّير .. وليس في قلبه ذرة من الشفقة أو الرحمة .. وحياتي معه تحولت إلى عذاب .. عذاب لا يطاق بالرغم مما أفعله من أجله .. وبالرغم من سكوتي وصبري على الإهانة والضرب والشتم .. فمغفرة يامحمد .. مغفرة يابن الخال وتأكّد انني لم أقل ماقلت إلا مُكرهة .. وها أنا اليوم أمام الوالي أطلب من زوجي الطلاق ، لا أريد أن أعيش مع شرّير .. لا أريده .. لا أريد أن أعيش مع إنسان يُلصق بي كل يوم تهمة باطلة ، إني لم أرَ منه طيلة السبع سنوات التي قضيتها معه تحت سقف واحد إلاّ الذل والهوان والمعاملة السيئة .. واسمحوا لي أن أقول : فلتذهب تقاليد القرية إلى الجحيم اذا كانت تنظر الى المرأة على أنها كالحيوان أو المتاع .. أو سلعة تُباع وتُشترى .. فالمرأة إنسانة .. إنسانة لها شعورها واحساسها .. تحب وتكره .. ويجب أن يكون لها الحق في اختيار شريك حياتها ، مدى العمر .. ويجب أن تختفي مثل هذه الخلافات والمشاكل الزوجية .. يجب أن تختفي وإلى الأبد ، ولن تختفي إلا باقناع الآباء أن أمر اختيار شريك الحياة ليس من اختصاصهم بالدرجة الأولى وانما هو من اختصاص صاحب الأمر وهما الشاب والفتاة وأن إكراه الفتيات على قبول من يختاره الآباء أمرا ليس في صالح أحد .. ويجب أن يعلم الآباء كذلك أن العادات والتقاليد المتوارثة ليست جميعها صالحة .. انا لا أطالب بالتخلي عن عاداتنا وتقاليدنا ومُثُلنا وقيمنا .. على العكس يجب أن نتمسك بها .. ولكن ما نراه سيئا أو سلبياً منها يجب أن نبتعد عنه ، وعلى الآباء أن يعلموا أن الحياة تتغير .. وأن الزواج لم يعد صفقة تجارية فيها الربح والخسارة ولن يكون كذلك أبدا .. بل هو رباط مقدس بين شخصين مدى الحياة ، وشركة مبنية على الحب والتفاهم الصادق بين الزوجين .. وأن ما حدث لي ولمحمد يجب ألاّيتكرر أنا لا أطالب بأن تترك الحرية الكاملة للفتاة من غير قيد أو رقيب وانما يجب منحها الحق والحرية وفق ما حدده ديننا الاسلامي الحنيف في الإعراب عن رأيها في مجال اختيار الإنسان الذي سيشاركها حياتها .

كان الوالي مأخوذا بكلامها مُعجبا بجرأتها الممزوجة بالحياء والتحفّظ مكبرا فيها شجاعتها .

فما أن أنهت كلامها حتى رفع رأسه اليها وقال : معك حق يابنتي يجب أن تختفي فعلا تلك العادات التي تتنافى مع ديننا الحنيف ، ومع عاداتنا واخلاقنا العربية الكريمة ...

نمير بن سالم آل سعيد – عمان

دعوة حضور

نحن الثلاثة ولدنا في نفس المكان والزمان ، عشنا وكبرنا معًا ، ولكن إذا دُعينا لمناسبة نذهب منفردين .

أولا : الكاتب

عادة ما يذهب بدعوة وأحياناً بدون دعوة يرتمي على أقرب كرسي في آخر القاعة أو يتقدم قليلا إلى الأمام من أجل وضوح الرؤية والإنصات ، يدفعه حب الاطلاع والمعرفة للاستفادة مما يقدَّم من دراسات وبحوث وأطروحات فكرية في كافة المجالات . لديه اهتمام بالثقافة كطريق يحقق للإنسان إنسانيته الراقية بعيدًا عن شوائب الماديات الدنيوية ، والصراعات البشرية ، والمتع الرخيصة . تغريه الفكرة باصطيادها ترفرف حوله أينما يذهب ، عصية أحيانًا ممتنعة أحيانًا وأحيانًا تسلم نفسها طوع يديه بدون عناء ، يؤمن بأن الإنسان خُلق ليعمر الكون بالعمل وعليه واجبات حياتية لا بد أن يقوم بها تجاه مجتمعه ، دون أن ينتظر مكسبًا ماديًا أو معنويًا ، أو إطراء أو إشادة من أحد . يكره المتقاعسين والاتكاليين والضعفاء ممن لا يعمل ولا يترك غيره يعمل ، يعتقد بأنه كمثقف لديه الكثير من الإمكانيات الفكرية المفيدة وبحاجة إلى مزيد من الاهتمام لتحقيق دوره كما يجب .

ثانيًا : المدير

تأتيه بطاقة الدعوة معنونة باسمه ووظيفته ، يحدد الوقت ويضبط المواعيد بالساعة والدقيقة ، يذهب إلى المناسبة قبل الموعد بنصف ساعة ، ينتظر خارج القاعة ينظر إلى القادمين ، يسلم على المديرين والوكلاء بابتسامة عريضة تعلو محياه ، يدخل القاعة ويجلس في الدور الثالث أو الرابع لا يتقدم أكثر من ذلك حتى لا يتهم بالتجاوز فتحاك ضده الضغائن والدسائس لإيقافه عند حده ، يحسب لكل شيء حسابه ، يحرص على الابتعاد عن الأحقاد الوظيفية أو إثارة العداوة مع الآخرين .

إذا رأى كاميرا التصوير قادمة نحوه يرفع رأسه قليلا ليظهر في الصورة .

ويسأل أصدقاءه فيما بعد إذا ما رأوه في أخبار السادسة أو على صفحات الجريدة ، فيردون بأنهم لم ينتبهوا له أو أنه لم يكن واضحًا بما فيه الكفاية .

يعمل بصبر وإخلاص ، مرن في تقبل التوجيه والإرشاد ، ملتزم في وظيفته بالقوانين والتعليمات ، لديه قدرة على المبادرة والابتكار لتطوير نظم وأساليب العمل ، وقدرة على اتخاذ القرارات ، يعتقد بأنه أتقن عمله الحالي وتؤهله قدراته لتحمل مسئوليات أعلى .

ثالثًا : صاحب الجاه

مهما كان ، فالمجتمع قبلي من الدرجة الأولى والاحترام لم يستطع أحد فك طلاسمه إلى الآن ، فعلى الرغم من أنه لا يشغل منصبًا حكوميًا كصديقة المدير وليس مشهورًا كصديقة الكاتب ، إلا أنه من أعيان المجتمع ، عريق الحسب والنسب ، مقدر من الناس تأتيه بطاقة الدعوة فيذهب ملبيًا ، يُستقبل بحفاوة وترحيب ، ويريد أن يجلس حيث يتأتى له فلا يدعه الآخرون ، يدفعونه إلى الصفوف الأمامية ، البعض يأتي من مكانه ليسلم

عليه ، البعض يترك مكانه ليجلس هو ، تأثير معنوي غارس جذوره في عمق التاريخ . متواضع في حياته ، تلقائي في تعامله ، يحب الخير للجميع يعامل الآخرين وكأنهم إخوة له ، عضو فعال في المجتمع .

يعتقد بأن صديقة الكاتب بأفكاره وثقافته وصديقة المدير بإدارته وإمكانياته ، وهو بتأثيراته المعنوية الإيجابية يستطيعون معًا أن يشكلوا فريقًا مقتدرًا فعالا معتمدًا .

وفي ذات يوم صحو اكتمل ضحاه جاءتهم معًا بطاقة دعوة لمناسبة عرض مهم ، وكعادتهم ذهبوا منفردين .

جاء صاحب الجاه وقدموه إلى الصف الأمامي ، جاء المدير فاصطحبوه ليجلس إلى جانبه ثم أتى الكاتب بهدوئه المعتاد ينظر حوله في أي مكان يجلس ، ولكنه رأى من يرحب به ويطلب منه أن يتقدم إلى الأمام فتردد أو لا ثم مالبث أن سار ليجلس في المقدمة ، ولأول مرة جلسوا جميعًا معًا في مكان واحد في مناسبة واحدة جنبًا إلى جنب .

وبنظرات متطلعة توجهت أعينهم إلى ستارة المسرح المغلقة ، لم يعرفوا في ذلك اليوم لماذا شعروا بأنهم شخص واحد حين أعطيت إشارة البدء .

محمد اليحيائي ــ عمان

خرزة المشي

أصدر الملكُ في الصباح الموالي لما حصل له من رؤيا وتَّرت منامه وفق ما حملته لنا دفاتر مدون الأحلام الملكية ، مرسوماً يوجب كلَّ من صادف ، من ناس المملكة ومن كان فيها ، عابراً أو مقيما ، من تجار وسائحين وبحرية ، خرزةً مدورةً في حجم حبة النبق ولونها ضارب في الزرقة تدرج في شوارع المملكة أن يسلمَها ديوان المملكة أو إلى أقرب مخفر .

وكل من قُدِّر له ذلك له عند الملك حظاً وحظوةً رفيعةً .

فلما شاع النبأ وذاع في الصحف المحلية وفي إذاعة وتلفزيون المملكة ازدحم الخلق في الشوارع وراء الخرزة الموصوفة ، طلبة عاهل البلاد وبغيته . وعطلّت الوزارات والمصالح والمدارس والجامعات وخلت الدور من ساكنيها وصار الناس راكضين في الشوارع ولسان حالهم خرزة الملك الدارجة في شوارع المملكة .

ولما انقضى اليوم الأول والأسبوع الأول والعام الأول وقد كنس الناس الشوارع ونفضوها ونخلوا رملها من حصاها ولم يبن لخرزة الملك بائنة ، عاد الناس وقد بلغ اليأس منهم مبلغا إلى دورهم مخلفين وراءهم مملكة نظيفة تلمع مثل عين الصقر .

كان الملك قد رأى في منامه خرزة في حجم حبة النبق ولونها ضارب في الزرقة نطت من ثقبه ودرجت على رخام الغرفة ثم هبطت الدرج الحلزوني وخرجت من باب القصر إلى شوارع المملكة . وكان الملك يركض وراء الخرزة عار في الشوارع والميادين والناس من حوله يكبرون الله وقد بهتوا أن رأوا ملكهم قد جُنَّ وهم لاينظرون الخرزة وينظرون الملك العاري وقد دوخه الركض يترامى بينهم مثل بقرة فارة خارت قواها .

وكانت الخرزة تشبه تماماً خرزة المشي التي فقدت برباطها الحرير من ساق الملك الطفل ، وريث عرش المملكة ، في حادث قامت على أثره المملكة ولم تقعد بحثاً عن خرزة مشي الملك الصغير والذي ، إن لم تعد الخرزة ، سيظل طريح مؤخرته إلى الأبد ، وسيكون ، حسب مرسوم الملك "نوح الزمان" والد الملك الحالي ، مستقبل المملكة ملكاً كسيحا .

ولم يظهر للخرزة ظاهر . ومات الملك نوح الزمان وقعد على عرش المملكة ملك مقعد يحلم في صحوه وفي منانه بخرزته المفقودة التي تشبه حبة النبق والتي لونها ضارب في الزرقة ، علها تدرج راكضة باتجاه القدمين اليابستين ويشفى من الكساح وتقويان على المشي فيمشي .

ولما تنبه الملك وهو خائر القوى وسط جموع شعبه التي تكُبر وتصيح مشى الملك فجنَّ .. عاد إلى قصره واغلق الأبواب وصعد الدرج الحلزوني الموصل إلى غرفة نومه وارتمى على سريره وشدَّ عليه اللحاف ونام ليرى خيط دم ناعم يغزل منديلاً موشاة حوافه بالحرفين من اسمه المقدس .. ورأى صبيةً تخفي تحت صرتها خرزة مدورة مربوطة برباط من حرير تشبه حبة النبق ولونها ضارب في الزرقة ، وكان في اللحظة ذاتها ، في الزمن الذائب والمتماهي في أوفاق الطوالع المنعكسة بصفاء كامل على فصوص الثريا المعلقة فوق رأسه على سقف الغرفة البعيد ، لشخصين تربطهما ، دون أن يجتمعا ، الحدوس والإرتعاشات . كان الملك يختّض ويرتعش بالقدر نفسه الذي تحدثه الصبية وهي تخفي خرزتها ، نزولاً وصعودا ، في مخمل السرير . كان كل منهما ، الملك والصبية ، يرى ملامح الآخر ساطعةً ، وكان لكل منهما وقته ليفكر في الآخر الذي لم يره والذي يراه بوضوح تام . كان الملك في حوض صابونه وسط الرغوة البيضاء والفقاعات التي يذكره تفتقها بما كان يحدثه في نسائه الجديدات ، يتنفس مكروباً وقد غامت في رأسه

واختلطت حدود المملكة بحواف الخرزة المدورة التي نطت قبل لحظات من ثقبه إلى شوارع المملكة والتي اعياه الركض وراءها وفضحه عريه وسط رعيته . وكانت أبخرة مقدسة تصّاعد من منخريه وهو يجتر صوراً مائلة إلى الرمل لحدود المملكة التي تذوي وتذوب في عين الخرزة .

وفي اليوم التالي استلقى الملك على ظهره تحت شجرة النبق العتيقة والتي تقف ، تكاد تكون الوحيدة إلى جواره في سنوات خريفه الباهتة ، على العشب البارد ، وأومأ مغمض العينين إلى الصبية التي تخفي تحت صرتها خرزة المشي التي تشبه خرزة المشي التي فقدت من على ساقه اليمنى في طفولته ، أن اجلسي عليّ . ففعلت .

ولما فتح عينيه بعد إغفاءة لا يعلم مداها إلا الله وجد على مثانته لطخاً من دم يابس فقشرها بأظافره وهو يحاسب ألايخدش اللحم المتغضن ، ووجد بين فخذيه خرزة المشي التي أضاعها في طفولته برباطها الحرير فربطها حول ساقه اليمنى عند الجوزة وقام وشلح إزاره وبال على جذع شجرة النبق ومشى .

وفي الصباح التالي أصدر مرسومه الآنف الذكر .

يونس الأخزمي ــ عمان

يوم صمت في مطرح

جفلتُ هذا الصباح على حلم غريب ، حيث وجدتُ جيوبي خاوية وملابسي رثة ممزقة وأنا أتسمرُ رصيف شارع "كورنيش مطرح" المزدحم بالمارة ، أمد يدي بذل عل يداً سخية تعطفُ علي ، وحين التفت يميناً وشمالاً وجدتُ الرصيف وقد تحول إلى صف متسول يمتد إلى اللانهاية . ضحكتُ وأنا أرتدي ملابسي هاماً بالخروج باتجاه سوق السمك التي أحبها . "متسول؟ !!!!"

الجمعة ، حيث تكتظ الممرات الضيقة في الأسواق وعلى ضفاف شاطء مطرح ، وأمام المحلات في الشوارع الرئيسية . كانت بوابة "المثاعيب" المرممة حديثاً المواجهة لبيتي أول ما يطالعني كل صباح . تقفُ هكذا منذ زمن بعيد ، وقد تحولت مع الأيام إلى بقايا ذكرى لطفلٍ مجنونٍ وسخ الملابس يحمل في حزامه الذي اشتراه له أبوه في العيد الماضي مسدساً بلاستيكياً صغيراً ، يتصيد به أصدقاءه الذين يصرخون بأعلى صوت "الله أكبر" بينما يحشر هو جسدُه الضئيل داخل صندوق القمامة العمومي الكائن أسفل البوابة حيث لا يخطر للأطفال النظاف الاقتراب منه ، ويبقى هو هناك حتى ينتهي رصاص المسدسات الأخرى ، فيخرج متوحشاً غادرا مبيداً الكل ، أو يختبئ في البرج الصغير الواقع أعلى البوابة حيث حذر الآباء أبناءهم منذ زمن من مغبة الولوج إلى داخله خشية الجن والسحرة التي تسكنه منذ الأزل ، حيث تجرأت شابة جميلة (يقال إنها كانت أجمل فتاة في مطرح) على الدخول هناك خوفاً من عقاب أبيها بعد أن رآها تحادث شاباً قدام باب البيت ، ولم تخرج من البرج منذ حينها ، وحيث أنه كان يلمح بقايا علب لأسماك التونة وزجاجات عطر كبيرة كلما أطل على البرج من خارج الباب فقد اعتقد أيامها بأن ما يراه هو طعام وشراب الجن المفضل . يبقى في البرج مرتعشاً خائفاً من شيء لم يظهر له بعد ، مسلحاً نفسه بشجاعة غريبة لم يربّ عليها حتى تنتهي ذخيرة الأطفال الآخرين .

الصبح شديد البرودة مع بداية شهر شباط ، والأرض رطبة . وما أن عبرت البوابة حتى لفت انتباهي حالة الصمت اللاطبيعية . كانت المحلات التي اعتادت فتح أبوابها مع صلاة الفجر مغلقة ، " المخبز اللبناني" لا تتبعث منه رائحة رغيف كالعادة ، ودكان الحاج علي بائع المرطبات وعصير البرتقال الطازج والخضروات بدا ساكناً هامداً . مصطبة العجوز ميّاء بائعة الحمص والفول خالية ، حيث اعتدت على شرب شاي الحليب الساخن وتناول رغيف مملوء بالفول تارة وبالجبن تارة أخرى قبل توجهي للعمل كل صباح ، وكانت العجوز كثيرا ما تستغل تلك الفترات في الحديث عن ابنتها التي ساعدتها في إعداد قدور الحمص والفول ، والتي تقوم عادة بغسل الأطباق والملابس وتنظيف البيت الصغير . كانت العجوز قلما تأخذ مني نقوداً مقابل ما أتناوله من الطعام ، حتى تلك المصطبة بدت جافة يابسة ، وحتى سيارات الأجرة التي يملكها خلفان وسالم وسعيد والتي عادة ما أسمع شخير محركاتها على امتداد الطرقات ، بقيت هي الأخرى صامتة .

وحين توقفت لبرهة من الوقت أمام بيت العجوز ميّاء الطيني المسقوف بسعف النخيل اليابس ، وطرقت الباب المتداعي ، لم تجب ، فأيقنت بأن ثمة سرّاً غريباً يشمل المكان ، وأنني ربما أخطأت حين لم أسمع للإذاعة ليلة أمس أو حتى هذا الصباح ، وشتمت نفسي على الوقت الطويل الذي أهدرته سدى في محاولة فاشلة لتهذيب قصيدة رثاء لوالد صديقي الذي مات في نزوى قبل ليال هاما بإرسالها للجريدة صبيحة الغد .

منذ يومين أو أكثر ، حيث بدأت إجازتي السنوية وحيث قررت السفر باتجاه الشرق القريب بعد أسبوع ، تسمرت قدام جهاز التلفزيون الذي يبث قنوات فضائية جميلة ، وكنت قد اعتدت مع صبيحة كل

جمعة على حلاقة لحيتي والتوغل في الأسواق حيث يروق لي كثيراً مشاهدة الباعة والتجار والزبائن ووجوه النساء المتزاحمات على المحلات قبل أن أصل إلى سوق السمك . هذا الصباح تبدو الأشياء غريبة جداً ، البيوت هادئة ، السكك صامتة ، المحلات جافة ميتة ، حتى صياح الديكة الذي كثيرا ما نرفزني مع كل فجر جديد ، اختفى اليوم تماماً . وترددت وأنا أهم بالعودة إلى بيتي في البداية ، لكنني ، وباعتقاد جازم ، شحذت همتي ومضيت ، فاليوم يأتي بعد ليلة خميس باردة جداً ، وربما فضل الجميع النوم . كانت الساعة قد تجاوزت السابعة بقليل ، وكنت كلما توغلت في السكك واستدرت ناحية المحلات المغلقة والطرقات الهادئة ، كبر الصمت واتسع السؤال . وحين اشتعلت أعماقي وغدت مثل لهيب يضطرم ، عدت أدراجي ناحية البيت . كنت خائفاً من شيء ما لا أعيه ، أدرت جهاز التلفزيون ، أدرت المذياع ، لكنني فوجئت بصمتٍ عميق جداً ، كل الأشياء تبدو صامتة ساكنة هذا الصباح ، عداي وجوفي .

لم أستطع المكوث في البيت لأكثر من ساعة . حالة الصمت الغريبة جداً لم تترك لي فرصة للبقاء أكثر ، إن في الأمر سراً ما ، سرّاً غريباً جداً . خرجت ثانية . الساعة تجاوزت الثامنة ، وليس ثمة حس . ولجت سوق مطرح القديمة ، كانت بوابات المحلات الخشبية مغلقة يتقاطر منها صمت عميق ، وكانت الممرات خاوية تماماً من المارة وعربات الحمالين الخشبية ، واختفت تماماً جلسات المتسولين وبائعي الساعات اليدوية والصرافين ورائحة الأجساد المكتظّة والمختلطة بالبخور وعطر النساء الحريف . وجزمت ساعتها أن أمراً ما غير طبيعي يحصل ، أو أن ما أراه مجرد حلم آخر وسأصحو منه بعد قليل .

انعطفت صوب سوق الظلام ، حيث اعتدت أن أمرّ بها في اتجاهي نحو سوق السمك ، وحيث كنت أشتم روائح البهارات المختلفة بروائح البخور الكثيرة وروائح الصندل ودهن العود وألمح عن قرب وجوه النساء المزدحمة أمام شرفات المحلات وأيدي الهنود والسيخ التي تتعمد ملامسة النساء في الأماكن الرخوة .

كانت السوق تبدو مظلمة هذه المرة مثل اسمها ، حتى تلك الحشرات الصغيرة التي كثيراً ما ألمحُها تُسحق تحت الأقدام وهي تتراكضُ بجموعٍ نحو قطع السكر الملقاة . اختفت هي الأخرى . وتساءلت حينها : هل هو يومُ صمتٍ عالمي تكاتف فيه سائرُ المخلوقاتِ الأرضية عداي ؟!!!

اتجهتُ بعد ذلك ناحيةً الكورنيش الموازي لسور اللواتيا القديم ، حيث تكتنز منازلهم ما بين السور الأبيض الأمامي والجبل الشاهق في الخلف وحيث اعتدتُ على رؤية بشرتهم البيضاء الناعمة أمام محلاتهم أو أمام بوابة السور ، وبدا كأنه هو الآخر يعيش حالة صمت حتى تخيلته وحشاً غابت عنه الحياة . حينها ارتعش قلبي ، وتوجست خيفة ، وجزمت بأن شيئاً ما ربما حدث أو سيحدث بعد قليل ، وأن الكل قد علم بالنبأ ، وأنني أنا الوحيد الأحمق ، الذي غفل عن سماع الإذاعة . وفاجأني وجه عجوز متغضن البشرة ، اندلق فجأة من بين ألواح النافذة ، كانت سيماؤه توحي بغضب ما . حدق إليّ بنظرته الحادة ، بزق ، ثم أغلق النافذة . كاد بزاقه يتوسط وجهي لولا أنني تنحيت عنه فسقط على نعلي . التهبت بعدها الأسئلة في رأسي ، كبرت وتعاظمت ، سخنت النفس وأوشكت على الانفجار .

ما الذي يجري هنا ؟

هيجني الصمتُ الجاثم مثل موت مطبق عميق ، فكدتُ أزعق في البيوت الهامدة ، وأصرخ بحدة حبالي الصوتية كي أعقل ما يحدث .

ما مردُ هذا الصمت غير العادي ؟!

ولماذا لا يوجد سواي في الشارع ؟!

في الفجر ، الفجر المملوء برطوبة البحر ورائحة الأسماك تستيقظ مطرح لزجة برطوبةٍ مالحة ، يتصاعد الأذان من الجهات الأربع وتبدأ مشاوير الأقدام .

أين مطرح تلك؟ ما الذي يجري حقاً؟!!!

إن الناس ، ناس العالم كله ، من الهند من السند ، من نيويورك المخيفة ، ومن لندن الواسعة كلهم يأتون إلى مطرح ليشمّوا لساعات بسيطة رائحة الهدوء الفريد ويتسكّعوا بحرية حلوة وأمان لن يجدوه أبداً في كوكب الأرض . إن أبي الذي زارني قبل ليلتين لم يفلح في محاولته الطويلة في إقناعي بالنكوص معه إلى نزوى . أخبرتهُ بأنني مسكون بمطرح ، وأن مطرح الحلوة في دمي . لكن مطرح تبدو غريبة عليَّ هذا اليوم .

صبيحة الجمعة لا تجد متسعاً تخطو عليه في سوق مطرح ولا فسحة تضع عليها جسدك . أنفاسك تختلط بأنفاس آخر أو أخرى ، وينطلق رجل مجنون بعصاه وابتسامته الدائمة ، يهش على المارة والسيارات . أين هو اليوم أيضاً؟!

ما سر هذا الصمت الغريب؟!

أين البشر؟!!!

أين تلك الجموع الشديدة التي تعودتها تملأ الشوارع خصوصاً أيام الجمع؟! حتى مسجد اللواتيا بقي مغلقاً بارداً على غير العادة .

والهنود !! أين كل أولئك الذين تعودت الاصطدام بأجسادهم الطافرة بروائح حادة ؟!!

حين وصلت إلى سوق السمك ، حيث تعوّدت على مزاحمة المشترين ، والتصبيح على وجوه الباعة والصيادين الذين حفظوا اسمي وحفظت أنا وجوههم وأسماءهم وأنواع الأسماك التي يصطادونها والأوقات التي يرمون فيها شباكهم وأنواع المراكب التي يملكونها ، لأصل في النهاية إلى وجه العم " ضحى " العجوز الذي اعتاد تخصيص سمكة طازجة لي . حين وصلت إليه ، ألفيته خالياً يابساً ، تنبعث منه روائح عفنة . كانت المصاطب بيضاء لامعة وخالية من بقايا الأسماك والدماء الكثيرة . حينها أدركت أنني أخطأت بخروجي هذا الصباح ، وأنني عما قليل ربما سأرتطم بموتٍ مفاجئٍ غير متوقع ، أو مصير مجهول ينحدر باتجاه جهنم .

وتذكرت أني صليت هذا الصباح ، والبارحة ، وأنني لم أفعل سوءاً سوى ملاحقة فتاة متزوجة تسكن في البناية المجاورة . وتذكرتُ الرسالة التي وجدتها قبل شهر أسفل الباب ، وكيف أني ضحكت ساخراً غير مصدق بأنه لم يتبق على القيامة سوى أربعين ليلة .

كان شعورٌ بالخوف قد طغى علي وشملني حتى هطل عرقي برغم برودة الجو . شعور حادٌ صاخب يغلي في الداخل فيحرق بقابا تماسكي الواهن . وتسمرتُ مكاني ذاعراً من شيء لا أفهمه ، شيء ربما سيحدث بعد لحظة أو ربما سينفجر الآن ، وربما اختارني ضحية دون كل البشر . وتأكدت من أنّ كل الذي أعددته للزواج في الشتاء القادم قد احترق ، وأنني الآن أخرج من ملابسي وأطير صوب البحر أو صوب الصحراء . سيحدث ذلك لي دون كل البشر ، فأنا الذي خالفت قانون الطبيعة وخرجت ، في حين بقي الكل في بيوتهم . حتى العجوز مياء لم تبرح دارها ولا استجابت لطرقاتي . أنا الوحيد إذن ، الذي خالف قانون اليوم والمكوث في المنازل ، وربما خالفت أشياء كثيرة لا أعقلها .

بقيت هكذا لفترة طويلة وأنا أحدق في زرقة السماء والبحر . حتى البحر بدا هادئاً وديعاً هذا الصباح . المراكب هادئة ، السفن الضخمة في البعيد هادئة ، إن ظاهرة غير طبيعية سوف تحدث عما قليل . وسردت على نفسي كل الاحتمالات الممكنة :

قلت : إن هدوء البحر هو الهدوء الذي يسبق العاصفة ، وربما أنه الطوفان ، وأن العالم استمع لتحذير الأرصاد الجوية فبقي الناس في بيوتهم ، وأنني المخبول الوحيد في مطرح الذي خرج ليستقبل حتفه بترحاب . وأمعنت النظر في السماء فكانت صافية .

قلت : إنها ربما حادثة مشابهة لتلك التي مكثنا فيها داخل حجرنا هلعاً من سماع تحذير عنيف اللهجة ، جازم بأن أشلاء من قمر صناعي ستسقط فوق أحد السطوح الهشة في مطرح ، وأنه محمل بأشعة مهلكة .

115

قلت : أو ربما أنه المذنب الهائل الذي قرأت عنه في كتب المدرسة منذ زمن بعيد ، والذي يتوقع سقوطه اليوم ، وربما هذا الصباح ، أو ربما هذه اللحظة ، وحينها سيصطدم بالأرض بجلبة عنيفة فتتدثر البيوت والجبال وينطمر الخلق أجمعين .

وتذكرت الأوزون والحكايات الغريبة التي لا أصدقها ، وتذكرت الإيدز ، بداية انتهاء البشرية كما انتهت قبل ذلك الديناصورات ، فربما اكتشفوا كما كنت ألحُ على زملائي في المكتب أن الأيدز ينتشر الآن في الهواء بكثرة .

بقيت هكذا لثوان ، قبل أن أقرر ، بسرعة ، العودة أدراجي من حيث أتيت قبل فواتِ الأوان . قلبي يرتجف بشدة داخل تجويفي الصدري ، وأنا أجتاز الشارع الرئيسي باتجاه الشارع السفلي المقابل لسور اللواتيا . وتساءلت : هل كان أبي على علم بما سيحدث ولذا كان إصراره قوياً هذه المرة ؟

كانت السيارات المصطفة في كل الاتجاهات ، صامتة ميتة ، والتفت ثانية ناحية البحر في محاولة أخيرة لرؤية حياة ما فكانت مناظر السفن والمراكب توحي بحزن دفين غامق ، ولا ثمة صوت لموجة يتيمة . حينها ، وعلى حين غرة ، داهم مسمعي صوت محرك سيارة ، فتوقفت فاغراً فاهي شاخصاً بعينين صامتتين ، اعتقدت جازماً في البداية بأن ما أسمعه هو من وحي داخلي الحالمة بهمسة صوت واحدة وسط غابة الصمت الهائلة حولي . أصغت السمع أكثر . أجل ، إنه صوت سيارة . أيقنتُ وقتها بأن الحياة قد بدأت تدب من جديد على الأرصفة وفي المحيط ، وأن الفوضى المعتادة والأصوات المتداخلة والروائح المختلفة ستحتدم في الساحة الفارغة بعد قليل ، وستكتظ الممرات والسكك والأسواق ثانية ، فابتسمت لذلك الشعور المريح أخيراً ، لا بد أن أحدهم كان قد عبث بساعتي فخرجت مبكراً جداً . إلا أن هذا الشعور الذي خامرني لثوانٍ معدودات لم يلبث أن تبخر فجأة وتلبسني شعورٌ بالخوف من جديد حين خشيت من أن يكون القادم واحداً مثلي ، مخبولاً آخر فاته الاستماع لإذاعة فخرج يلاقي حتفه هو الآخر .

مكثتُ محدقاً في السيارة التي بدأت تقترب حتى غدت في الجانب المواجه لي . حينها التفت ، إليّ الثلاثة الذين عجت بهم السيارة . فرمل سائقها ، فانبعث من تحت العجلات صوت غليظ ودخان ، ولمحت الثلاثة يترجلون ، يحملُ كل واحد منهم عصا غليظة مكورة الرأس ، فشملتني رجفة حادة من دقائق رأسي حتى أخمص القدمين ، ووقف الدم في عروقي .

ما الذي يجري ؟ !!

من هؤلاء ؟!؟!!

صاح بي أحدهم : أنت .. قف مكانك .

اعتقدت لبرهة بأنهم يلاحقون شخصاً ما يحقدون عليه ويريدون هصره بعصيهم المخيفة ، وأنهم ربما تخيلوني ذلك الشخص . لكن ، مع دنوّهم مني ، ولهاجس لم أتبين حقيقته ، أطلقت لساقيّ العنان . رفعت طرف دشداشتي وضغطت عليه بين أسناني ، وركضتُ . هبطتُ السلم القريب والثلاثة يتدافعون خلفي مثل طوفان . كانوا هائلين بعصيهم المرعبة الغامقة ، وكان صوت أحدهم حاداً فظيعاً : قف يا حمار ، قف يا بغل ، يا نذل ....

انحدرت ناحية سوق الظلام ، وهم يتراكضون خلفي ، ودقات قلبي خائفة ، ونفسي يختنق تدريجياً . كنت متأكداً من أنهم لن يتوقفوا عن ملاحقتي ، وأن تنفسي سيخور بعد لحظات .

برحت سوق الظلام ، وولجتُ سككا ضيقة ، واكتشفتُ ، وأصواتهم القميئة تبتعد تدريجيّاً أنني أملك ساقين سريعتين . وضحكتُ بهستيريا غريبة وأنا أستحضرُ ما يحصل . كأنني وسط كابوس مفزع . وأنها ليست مطرح هذه التي أراها اليوم والتي عشقتها منذ نعومة عقلي . وأن شيئاً ما عصيباً قد حصل دون أن أعلم به . كان نفسي قد بدأ في النضوب التام مع اقتراب خطواتهم وتزايد صراخهم وشتائمهم . وكنت على يقين بأنني لو وقعت بين أيديهم الآن ، حتى لو لم أكن من يريدون ، فإنهم لن يتركوني وشأني ،

116

بل سيمزقون جسدي كله . كانت الطرق جميعها تقودني نحو طرق جديدة ، حين لاح لي صندوق قمامة عمومي ، فشددت على ساقيَّ وقذفتُ بجسدي وسطه .

بقيتُ أشهق هواء عفناً متسارعاً قبل أن أسمع اقتراب أقدامهم من المكان ، فخفضت تنفسي . كادت الرائحة الخانقة تهلكني هي الأخرى ، وتساقطت بقايا أرزّ وعظام أسماك على ملابسي ، وانسكبَ سائل على وجهي . كان قلبي ملتهباً في الداخل ، ويسبح جسدي في ذعر وعرق كثيف لم أعرف مثله من قبل . وكان كلّما هدأ ركضهم ازدادت لعناتهم وشتائمهم ..

- أين هرب ابن الكلبة ؟
- سأحطم هذه العصا على رأسه .
- سأسوّد حياته النذل .
- جبان .. حقير .
- ....

ما الذي يجري اليوم ؟!!!
وما كل هذه الشتائم المقززة ؟!!
ومن هؤلاء ؟!!
ومن يلاحقون في الأصل ؟!!
وتذكرت أحداث اليوم ، والأسواق الصامتة ، والسكك الذابلة ، والبيوت الهامدة .
لا بد أن في الأمر سرّاً ما .
كانت الأسئلة الحارقة تتسارع نحو ذهني ، تتسابق وتتشابك في عقلي الذي يوشك على الانشطار . بقيت بعدها للحظات كاتماً على نفسي بين أكوام القمامة الكثيفة دون حراك . حينها ، ابعثت من اللاشيء خطوات جديدة راكضة في البعيد .
فصرخ أحدهم : ذاك هو .
وزعق الثاني : إنه آخر .
وركضوا خلفه وهم يصرخون : قف ، قف مكانك وإلا كسرنا عنقك ، قف يا غشيم ، يا قليل التربية ، يا زبالة .

- هناك ثالث .
- يا أولاد الحرام ، يا ......

بقيت مكاني لفترة بسيطة وأنا أصيخُ السمع للخطوات التي ابتعدت وانتشرت ، وبقيت الأسئلة العصيبة تحرق كل رأسي . كنت لا أزال مقتنعاً في الداخل بأن ما أراه هو مجرد كابوس لم ينتهِ بعد ، وأنني ما زلت نائماً ، لم أستيقظ بعد .

استقمت ، وقفزت من على الصندوق . بكمّ ثوبي مسحت السائل الذي انسكب على وجهي ورقبتي ، ونفضت ما على ملابسي من عظام وطعام . تنفست بعمق ، وتلفتُ في الاتجاهات ، كانت القمامة العمومية تقع وسط منازل قديمة متشابكة تفصل بينها سِكَكٌ ضيقة . حدقت في الوجوه الشاخصة من بين فتحات النوافذ والستائر ، ابتسمت وانطلقت صوب سوق السمك .

كارولينا الشمالية ، تموز 1994

امينة إسماعيل الأنصاري – قطر

خواطر فتاة صغيرة

(أمية إسماعيل الأنصاري)

عادات وتقاليد .. لقد سئمت هذه الكلمة ومللت من سماعها . تحاصرني التقاليد من كل جهة ولا أجد مفراً منها . ليتني ولدت في مكان آخر .. في بقعة من الأرض لا تعرف معنى للتقاليد وليس لها ماض موروث من الأجداد . تقاليد ورثوها منذ مئات الأجيال ومازالوا يحافظون عليها ويدعونها تتحكم في مصائرنا نحن .. لقد تزوج ابي من امي لانها ابنة عمه فقط ولان التقاليد تأمر بذلك وعاد وتزوج عليها بعد ذلك ولم تجد التقاليد حرجاً في ذلك . واختي الكبرى المسكينة بلغت الثلاثين دون زواج لان مهرها غال كما تنص التقاليد ولانه لا يجوز لها ان تتزوج ايا كان ولا احد يجرؤ على التقدم لها . وابنة عمتي العبقرية كما يسمونها حرمت من السفر إلى الخارج لاكمال دراستها . والتقاليد هي المسؤولة بالطبع . والكثير الكثير من الامثلة والمآسي ترتكب بسبب هذه التقاليد البالية .. اما من احد يتقدم ويعلن الثورة عليها .. ولكن اذا كانت التقاليد قد تحكمت في الجميع فلا يمكن ان تتحكم فيها هي .

هي قوية الارادة وذات ذكاء وطموح شديدين .. والأهم من ذلك أنها جميلة بل جميلة جداً ويسمونها جميلة العائلة . وهي في ريعان شبابها وان كان البعض ما يزال يعتبرها صغيرة رغم انها في الخامسة عشر من عمرها . هي لا يمكن ان تخضع للتقاليد كما فعلت اختها وامها و لا يمكن ان ترضى بمصير الجواري . هي تريد ان تكون شيئاً مهما .. بل يجب ذلك . انها تحب الاثارة والمغامرة .. وأكثر منهما الأضواء والشهرة .. أما الحياة البسيطة الروتينية فلا ترضيها أبدا .. ولا تريد أن تظل حبيسة البيت مثل امها وخالتها اللتان تعتقدان انهما تعيشان على سطح الأرض بينما هما في الحقيقة مغمورتان تحتها .. نعم هكذا هن النساء في بلادي .. التقاليد هذه .. اذا ما مل منها الرجل سرعان ما يتركها ويستبدلها بغيرها ويتركها مهجورة كسقط المتاع .. ولكن صبراً حتى تنهي دراستها وتصبح مستقلة . حينئذ ستعتمد على نفسها ولن يوقفها شيء عن هدفها لا تقاليد ولا عائلة . وستحقق هدفها .. " التمثيل " وستصبح مشهورة وتكتب عنها المجلات والجرائد العالمية وسيتسابق اليها الصحفيون والمعجبون ليحظوا بكلمة منها .. آه ما أجمل هذا الهدف !

أجل يجب ان تثور وتتخلص من بيئتها هذه التي تمنح للشباب الحرية في الخروج والدخول كما يشاء بينما الفتيات محبوسات في بيوتهن ولا يستطعن التصرف الا بعد الحصول على الاذن المقدس .

ها هي اختها الضحية قادمة .. وهي تحب ان تسميها كذلك رغم ان هذه الكلمة تسبب شجاراً بينهما . والضحية لا تعمل رغم حصولها على الشهادة الجامعية والسبب انها لا تحب التدريس والتقاليد لا تسمح بغير ذلك والا فالبيت أولى بها ريثما ياتي ابن الحلال الذي لم يظهر له أي أثر حتى الآن . وهي لا يمكن ان تتصور نفسها مكان اختها أبداً لانهما مختلفتان تماماً . وهي متفوقة على أختها في كل شيء وحتى والدها العابس دائماً يبتسم لها هي فقط ويدللها لانها آخر العنقود ولانها جميلة . وهي لا تتذكر أنه رفض لها طلباً أو نهرها منذ يوم ولادتها حتى يوم أمس المشؤوم عندما لمحت الى رغبتها في السفر إلى الخارج بعد ان تكمل دراستها وذلك لتدرس فن التمثيل ، فسرعان ما عبس وجهه وقد وصل به الأمر إلى محاولة صفعها على خدها لو لم تهرب من أمامه .

المهم ان تسافر وتبتعد عن هذه البيئة وتلتقي بالناس وتكون الصداقات كما تشاء وتتصرف دون حسيب أو رقيب كما تفعل فتيات أوروبا المحظوظات . ولكن آه .. ما باليد حيلة وهي مضطرة لكتم خواطرها عن الجميع وقد يشتد بها الكبت أحياناً فتصارح أختها الضحية التي تكتفي بالاصغاء وتقديم المواعظ والنصائح

كغيرها من عجائز العائلة . وقد تصارح "مريم" وهي صديقة أختها ولنها لا تحب مناقشاتها السخيفة . أما أخوها اللاهي كما تسميه – فلكل فرد في العائلة لقب عندها – فهي قلما تراه وهو أيضا نفس عقلية والدها وعمها وغيرهم من رجال العائلة الذين يسمحون لانفسهم بكل شيء ويحرمون النساء من كل شيء فقط لأنهن نساء . والنساء ناقصات كما يدعون .

وفي اليوم التالي – عادت نورة من المدرسة وبينما هي تتوجه إلى حجرتها .. رن جرس الهاتف فأسرعت بالتقاط السماعة .. كان المتكلم "علي "وهو شاب تعرفت عليه منذ حوالي شهرين عن طريق الهاتف .. وهي ترتاح لحديثه لانه لا يعارضها أبداً ويحب ان يستمع لها وهي تتكلم عن احلامها وطموحاتها ثم يشجعها على تحقيق هدفها . وهي تعرف انها لا تحبه ولكنها ترتاح لحديثه وتكلمه كنوع من التحدي للتقاليد والقيود التي يفرضها المجتمع عليها .. كما انها تعرف شاباً آخر اسمه "عبد العزيز "وهو شقيق صديقتها "سلمى "وهي تحس من حديثه أنه يحبها كثيراً وقد يطلبها للزواج ولكنها غير مستعجلة .. انها تكره الزواج أيضاً وتحس به كنوع من القيد لأنه يفترض قيام علاقة إلى الأبد وبالتالي تكون الحياة روتينية مملة . وهي تحب التجديد والانطلاق وحتى "علي "هذا بدأت تمله لانها تحس معه بأنها تتكلم أمام جهاز تسجيل يردد لها نفس كلماتها دون تغيير اقفلت السماعة ثم ذهبت إلى حجرتها لتخلع ملابسها .. أف لقد سئمت هذه الملابس أيضاً .. كل يوم نفس الزي ونفس الموديل الطويل .. وياللعجب فالتقاليد في هذه البلاد تتحكم في كل شيء حتى في الملابس وهي أخص خصوصيات الانسان ولا تكتفي بذلك بل لابد من لبس هذه الخرقة السوداء التي يسمونها العباءة أيضاً .. أف ضاق صدرها وأصبحت حياتها تعيسة بسبب هذه التقاليد تتمنى لو تجسدت هذه التقاليد في صورة شخص لاخذت سكينا ونزلت فيه طعنا الى ان ترتاح .

في المساء جاءت "مريم" لزيارة أختها . وهي متزوجة منذ حوالي سبع سنوات . وهي امرأة عاملة ولكنها تركت العمل حالياً لتتفرغ لتربية طفلها الصغير . انها تكره مريم هذه رغم انها لا تستطيع ان تمنع نفسها من احترامها لانها تحس انها امرأة مستقلة تماماً ولها شخصية يحسب حسابها . ولكنها تزعم انها سعيدة مع زوجها وهذا أشد ما تكرهه في مريم لانها موقنة من انها كاذبة – فهي ليست جميلة بل أن زوجها أجمل منها ويبدو كما لو كان أصغر منها سناً رغم أنها تؤكد العكس دائماً .. أف مالها ولهذه المرأة ستتحجج بأي عذر ولن تذهب لمقابلتها فهي قد ملتها . ملت اراءها المصبوغة بصبغة التقاليد .. بل ان رائحة الماضي تفوح منها بكل وضوح .. أف ها هما قادمتان إلى حجرتها ولا مفر من الجدال اليوم .. ربما يكون من الأفضل لو تتجاهلها .

كيف حال الفيلسوفة الصغيرة

أولا انا لست فيلسوفة ، وثانيا أنا لست صغيرة

حسناً .. لقد أخبرتني اختك انك سيئة المزاج اليوم

طبعاً .. بسبب والدك .. ولكن اخبريني .. هل حقاً تودين العمل كممثلة ؟

نعم .. وهل هذا عيب .. هل لديك اعتراض ؟

تعرفين ان تقاليدنا لا تسمح بذلك .. و ..

(تقاطعها) عدنا الى سيرة التقاليد ثانية .. أعرف ما تريدين قوله .. فلقد سمعته مئات المرات وسئمته نفسي .. ستقولين لا يجوز التقاليد .. فنحن تقاليدنا أصيلة وهي مستمدة من الدين

لا .. ليست كلها مستمدة من الدين .. وأنا أتفق معك في ان بعض التقاليد بالية ويجب التخلص منها مثل غلاء المهور مثلاً .

حسناً .. آسفة .. سأحفظ الأسطوانة بطريقة أفضل المرة القادمة . في هذه اللحظة ذهبت اختها لتعد الشاي .. بينما اقتربت منها مريم وحدثتها بصوت خافت :

نورة .. أريد أن استوضحك من أمر .. وأرجوك لا تزعلي مني هل صحيح انك انقطعت عن الصلاة .. لماذا لا تجيبين ؟

يبدو انها لم تترك أمراً يخصني الا واخبرتك به .. على كل هذه شؤوني الخاصة وقلت لك مراراً اني لا أحب القيود .

أستغفر الله العظيم .. وهل الصلاة قيد .. لماذا تقلبين الآية يا نورة ؟ .. المفروض ان الصلاة تحرر وانطلاق .. تحرر من قيود العام وماديته ، ورحلة الى عالم الروحانيات الى حيث الله يا نورة .. ما أجمل الخشوع والسكون الذي يشيع في النفس بعد اداء الصلاة والطمأنينة التي تنبت في القلب عند ذكر الله .. انك لست صغيرة فعلاً وأنا أعلم انك تستثقلين كلامي وربما تكرهينني لانني اتدخل في خصوصياتك كما تقولين دائما .. ولكنني احبك وأخاف عليك من افكارك الطائشة التي قد تسوقك إلى نهاية سيئة وحينئذ يحدث ما لاتحمد عقباه .

أنا لست غبية يا مريم واعرف كيف اتصرف .. لقد وضعت لي هدفاً نصب عيني وسأسعى لتحقيقه .. ولن يثنيني شيء عن عزمي .. ربما تجدين ارائي غريبة أو مستنكرة ولكنها هي الحقيقة وأنا ارائي هي طبيعية جداً وانا متأكدة ان معظم الفتيات يؤمنّ بها ولكنها ليست لديهن الجرأة والشجاعة ليصارحن الناس بها كما فعلت أنا .

انا آسفة حقاً من أجلك

وتركتها مريم وذهبت الى الصالة حيث اختها .. بينما جلست هي مع خواطرها .. آه ليتها ولدت في مكان آخر .. ليتها ولدت في الغرب المتقدم ، الغرب الراقي .. حيث يعيش كل على هواه أوليتها كانت فتاة وحيدة بلا عائلة ولا رقباء يحصون عليها انفاسها لكانت فعلت ما تشتهي وترغب ولكن آه ما باليد حيلة .

رأت أمها واقفة على عتبة الباب تنظر اليها في حنان .. فندمت على خواطرها السابقة وحمدت الله على ان لها أما .. انها الحنان بعينه وهي تستغرب كيف يحوي هذا الهيكل الشاحب النحيل كل هذا الحنان والحب والرحمة ؟

هل أنت متعبة يا عزيزتي

كلا يا امي . انا بأحسن حال

اتصلت بك صديقتك وأخبرتها انك نائمة

حسنا ، سأتصل بها الان

هي تحب أمها كثيراً رغم انها غير معجبة بها لانها من النساء الضعيفات المستكينات اللواتي يتقبلن القدر بحلوه ومره وهي تكره الصفه في امها .

الو منى .. ماذا تريدين ؟

اين انت يا كسولة ..؟ عندي لك خبر سار

لا شيء يسر هذه الأيام

لا تبالغي .. أما زلت حزينة بسبب ثورة والدك

سأثور يوماً على التقاليد هذه

أوه .. سمعتك ترددين هذه الاسطوانة الاف المرات

اسمعي .. عندي لك رسالة من أخي جاسم .. غداً الجمعة سيأخذني إلى البحر .. ما رأيك لو تأتين معنا ؟ وهل سيكون الحرس معكم ؟

تقصدين والديّ . لا .. سيذهبان لزيارة جدتي معهم اخواتي الصغار هذا جيد جداً .. بل ممتاز .. أنا موافقة

لاتنسي .. خذي الاذن أولاً

لاتكوني سخيفة .. بأي !

في مساء اليوم التالي .. وبعد أن رجعت نورة من البحر .. سألتها اختها : ها .. كيف كان يومك .. لا يبدو على وجهك انك قضيت يوماً سعيداً .

أوف .. حدث ما عكر مزاجي . وباختصار شديد .. لاحقنا بعض المراهقين على البحر .. غضب جاسم واشتبك معهم في مشادة وعرف ان احدهم ان له علاقة بأخته فغضب أكثر وتطور الامر .. ثم تدخلت الشرطة لفك النزاع .

ثم .. ماذا حدث ؟

سحب جاسم اخته من يدها إلى السيارة ومشيت أنا وراءهم كالبلهاء

عرفت .. لقد ذهبتم انتم الثلاثة فقط

يا للذكاء .. ياللعبقرية .. المهم انني عرفت شيئاً وهو ان الشباب هنا تافهون ومغرورون .. حضرته يسمح لنفسه بأن يقيم علاقة معي ثم يزعل اذا اكتشف ان لاخته علاقة باحدهم .. ماذا يعني هذا ياذكية .. وما يغيظني اكثر هو أنه كان دائما يتفاخر ويزعم أنه متحرّر وان افكاره تقدمية بينما هو لايختلف عن غيره من الرجال هنا .. هذا المنافق .

آه يانورة .. عندما اسمعك أكاد أجن .. كيف تفكرين ولماذا تتصرفين على هذا النحو .. آه لو عرف والدي بما يحدث .. لكان مات المسكين قهراً .

مسكين .. والدي مسكين .. انت المسكينة والله .. دعيني لوحدي الآن .. لقد أضعت هذا اليوم هدراً بكل أسف .. ليتني قضيته في كتابة رسائل لاصدقائي .

كنت أريد اخبارك بأمر قد يسرك ولكنك مشغولة بما هو أهم .

هاتي مالديك .. أولاً .. هل هو أمر يتعلق بي أنا ؟

لا .. بل بي أنا .. تعرفين ان والد مريم من أعز أصدقاء والدي وان والدي يحترمه كثيراً .

أعرف .. أعرف .. أكملي .

لقد زارنا أمس وجلس مع والدي في الصالون لمدة ساعتين .. هل تعريفن ماذا قال له .. لقد جلس ينصحه ويقنعه بأن يقبل عرض محمد ابن خالتي للزواج .

للزواج ... ممن ؟

مني أنا طبعاً ... ولقد وافق والدي اخيراً ... هل تتصورين ذلك وبمهر بسيط نسبياً .. آه كم أحب والدي .

هبت نورة واقفة على قدميها وصرخت : متى حدث كل هذا ... لماذا لم يخبرني به احد من قبل .

ما بالك يانورة ... لم أنت غاضبة هكذا ...كنت أريد اخبارك البارحة ولكنك دائما منشغلة بنفسك ولا تعيرين غيرك أهمية ... ما بالك ؟

دعيني لوحدي ... اخرجي ... اخرجي ...

أقفلت الباب بقوة وارتمت على السرير ثم قامت كالمجنونة واتجهت نحو المرآة وهي تنظر إلى نفسها وصرخت : لا لايمكن .. لماذا يطلبها هي بالذات ولا يطلبني أنا انه لا يصلح لأختي أبداً .. انها كبيرة في السن بل انها عجوز بالنسبة له .. ثم هي ليست جميلة ولا ذكية مثلها ... انها هي مثار إعجاب العائلة دائماً ... كيف يتجاهلها محمد ... محمد بالذات ... انها تحس انه يختلف عن غيره وهي معجبة به كثيراً ... رغم انه كان يتجاهلها دائماً ... وهي تتذكر كيف كانت تلمح نظرات الاعجاب من جميع شباب العائلة ما عدا محمد ابن خالتها .. انه شاب في الثلاثين من عمره وهو يعتبرها صغيرة طائشة كما قال لها ذلك في احدى مرات نقاشه معها .. وهي كانت دائماً تتحداه وتلقي بآرائها الجريئة في وجهه دون تحفظ بل كانت تحاول أن تثير غيرته أيضاً كان هو يقابل محاولتها بالضحك والاستهزاء ، وبالاشفاق أحياناً أخرى

122

ولكنه كان يتظاهر بذلك أجل انها متأكدة انه يحبها ولكنه يخاف أن ترفضه .. لابد ان هذه هي الحقيقة ... بل يجب ان تكون كذلك .

لقد سمعته مرة يردد بأنه لا يحب الممثلات ... لابد أنه عندما سمع آراءها خاف من جرأتها وأفكارها المتقدمة ... أجل ... ثم أن أختها لا تثير اعجاب أحد ولا تلفت الانظار أبداً .

آه ... أحست انها ستختنق .. فخرجت ... ودت لوتكلم احداً ... لديها الكثير من المعجبين ولايهم لو خسرت واحداً أو اثنين . ستكلم أحدهم في الهاتف . من ؟ من؟ ... آه .. لا يوجد غيره ... علي .

ألو .. علي موجود ؟ ردت عليها امرأة أجابت بصوت حاسم : لا ثم أغلقت السماعه ... ما هذه المرأة السخيفة ... كيف تسمح لنفسها أن تكلمها بهذه اللهجة .. لا يهم ... يجب أن تكلم علي وستواصل الاتصال .. لا يهمها أحد اتصلت .. ووجدت الخط مشغولاً .. لابد أن هذه اللعينة قد رفعت السماعة هه ... لابد انها تخاف على ولدها من الفتيات الطائشات .. ياللعجب عاودت الاتصال بعد ساعة فقد كانت مصممة على أن تكلم علي . وجاءها صوته على الطرف الثاني :

ألو .. علي .. أين أنت ؟

من نوره ؟ أهلاً

ما بك ... صوتك يبدو مضطربا ؟

أبداً ... كنت أريد الاتصال بك .. لديّ امر اريد اخبرك به وارجوك لا تقاطعينني . ستكون هذه المكالمة هي الأخيرة أنا آسف ولكني لا اريد أن اخدعك . أنا أحب احدى قريباتي وقد خطبتها من أسبوع .. ولا أحب أن اخدعها .

ماذا أيها الوقح ؟.. وهل تظن أنك تخونها عندما تكلمني .

أرجوك يانورة .. اهدأي .. كل ما في الأمر انني لا أجد داعيا لهذه المكالمة بيننا .

ها ... الآن تقول هذا الكلام .

أنا آسف .. ولكن كنت أنت البادئة ... ثم أننا قضينا وقتاً لا بأس به معا ولكن آن الأوان لألتفت لمستقبلي وأنصحك بذلك .

نحن لم نعد صغاراً .. وداعا وأرجو لك التوفيق . ثم أغلق السماعه .

وهذه خيبة أخرى .. ثلاث خيبات في يوم واحد ... ثم ماذا أيضاً .

وفجأة أحست بتفاهة الأمر كله .. وبفراغ رهيب يغمر كيانها .. أحست أنها أهينت وأنها فقدت احترامها وكبرياءها . وودت لو تفضي بهمومها لأحد ... ولكن من لديها ؟ ... وأين منها عالم الاضواء والشهرة الآن .

انه بعيد جداً .. جداً .. انها لؤلؤة مغمورة الآن .. وكم تود لو انتشلها أحد من قاع البحر ورفعها إلى السماء نجمه متألقة كما يجب أن تكون .

غداً ستذهب لزيارة محمد .. ابن خالتها وستوضح له كل شيء ولابد أنه سيغير رأيه بشأن خطبة أختها . قضت ليلتها مسهدة مؤرقة وهي تتساءل ماذا حدث لي ؟ .. كانت ماتزال مذهولة وتحس بالكرامة الجريحة والاهانة البالغة من جراء ما حدث أمس ... لقد سئمت كل شيء .. وسئمت دور الفراشة المتنقلة من زهرة إلى أخرى وتود لو تستقر على زهرة واحدة وهي تود أكثر لو كانت هي زهرة جميلة تحط عليها فراشة واحدة .

وفي الصباح لم تذهب للمدرسة وقضت فترة الظهر تخطط لزيارة بيت خالتها الذي كان على بعد خطوات من بيتها .

أعدت نفسها جيداً وقضت ساعة ونصف وهي تضع المكياج على وجهها وتصفف شعرها ثم ارتدت أجمل فستان لديها وذهبت لزيارة خالتها دون أن تخبر أحداً .

ولم تجد أحداً هناك سوى ابن خالتها الصغير فسألته عن محمد فأشار الصغير إلى حجرة أخيه وهو مندهش من وجودها .

دخلت الى حجرته بعد أن طرقت الباب ووجدته مستلقيا على سريره وبيده مجلة يقرأها باهتمام بالغ . اعتدل حينما رآها واقفة عند الباب وارتسمت على وجهه ملامح الدهشة .. فأسرعت تقول :

لاتندهش .. لقد جئت لزيارتك لامر هام جداً .

لابد انك جئت لتباركي لي .. هل يمكنك أن تنتظريني قليلاً في الصالون ريثما ألبس ملابسي.

لا داعي لذلك .. أفضل أن أكلمك على انفراد .. انه موضوع خاص .

هل هو متعلق باختك ؟

ردت في غيظ .. كلا .. انه خاص بي أنا .. وبك أنت . أرجوك لا تقاطعني ... أنت ربما لم تلاحظ شعوري نحوك من قبل .. كنت دائماً اتحداك بآرائي .. وكنت أنت دائماً تتجاهلني .. أما الآن فقد سئمت هذه اللعبة ويجب أن تنتهي عند هذا الحد لنبدأ مرحلة أخرى .

قالت هذه الكلمات بسرعة ثم توقفت فجأه .

فقام ووضع يده على كتفها وابتسم لها وقال : هل تدركين معنى ما تقولين ؟ هذا الكلام لا يصدر الا من فتاه صغيره مراهقه .. بينما انت دائماً تنكرين هذا الأمر أنا متأكد من أنك لا تدركين شعورك نحوي جيداً وأنا متأكد أنه ليس كما تظنين أنت .. أنت فقط تريدين أن تلفتي انتباهي اليك لانني لم أنبهر بجمالك وشبابك كما فعل الجميع . أنا لا أنكر انك فتاة جميلة وذكية ولكنني أعتبرك اختي الصغيره .. وقريباً سأصبح زوج اختك .. أي مثل أخيك بالضبط . وستدركين حينئذ أنك كنت مخطئة .

في الحقيقة أنك كنت دائماً تحيرينني وكنت أتساءل – لماذا تتصرف بهذه الطريقة .. ولماذا تصدر عنها هذه الآراء الجريئة .. ثم اكتشفت انك فتاة جريئة وتملكين شجاعة وصراحه تحسدين عليها . ولكن كل ما في الأمر أنك لم تستغليها الاستغلال المناسب . سأحاول في المستقبل القريب ان شاء الله أن أناقشك في هذا الموضوع وذلك عندما تزورين أختك في بيتها .. ما رأيك ؟

كان وجهها خالياً من أي تعبير رغم انها كانت تحس بحاجة ملحة للبكاء لكنها خجلت لاول مره من أن تبكي أمام رجل غريب . هكذا أحست به ولم تجرؤ على النظر إليه ... مشت بتثاقل نحو الباب وهي تحس مره أخرى انها تافهه سخيفه . وفي الطريق تذكرت زوج مريم الذي حدثها عن احدى رحلاته الكثيرة إلى أوروبا . وتذكرت ما قاله لها عن الحياة هناك : لا تنخدعي يانوره بما تشاهدينه من أفلام امريكية تبين لك حياة الرفاهية هناك . الشباب في أوروبا تائهون ضائعون وقد فقدوا كل شيء .. فاما أن تجدينهم منطرحين على الطرقات كالمتسولين يعيشون في عالم خاص بهم من جراء المخدرات . واما أن يلجأوا للسرقة والقتل وهناك آخرون لا يجدون خلاصهم الا في الانتحار . هل تصدقين أن أعلى نسبة انتحار موجودة عندهم لقد حدثتني احدى الفتيات هناك عن حياتها . هي فتاه شابة جميله وحره التصرف وتعمل لتكسب عيشها . كما تتمنين أن تكوني ولكن هل تظنين انها سعيده . كلا .. لقد كانت تشتكي لي من حياتها . قالت لي انها تركت منزل اسرتها مضطره وهي في الثامنة عشر من عمرها واضطرت أن تؤمن عيشها بنفسها . وأنها تحس بالوحده والخوف وتحس انها وحيده لا سند لها ولاملاذ واعترفت لي انها تخشى أن تموت دون أن يحس بها احد . لاأحد هناك يحترم النساء ويقدرهن كالحال هنا . هذه الفتاه"سوزان" تتمنى لو تتزوج أي شخص يحترمها لكي تحس بنفسها مرتبطة بشخص ما .

هي تريد شيئاً تعيش لأجله ...

تذكرت"نوره"كل هذا وتذكرت أنها سمعت هذا الكلام مراراً ولكنها أحست وكأنها تسمعه اليوم لأول مره . طبقة كثيفه من الدموع ملأت عينيها وحجبت عنها الرؤية فكادت تصطدم باحدى المقاعد في صالون بيت خالتها وأحست انها وحيدة وتود لو تركض بأقصى ما تستطيع إلى حضن أسرتها الدافئ .. إلى حيث

يجتمع أفراد الأسره في هذا الوقت . حنت لحضن أمها وقبلاتها الحنون . ولاخيها ومشاكاته ولاختها .. حتى اختها أحست أنها فرحه من أجلها ... ياللعجب لقد حنت لوالدها وقساوته وللخادمة السيلانيه البلهاء ... للجميع .. سمعت صوت محمد من خلفها :

نوره ... هل تأخرت عليك ... لقد كنت ارتدي ملابسي .. ما رأيك لوتأتين معي ... أريد أن اشتري هدية لاختك .. سأقدمها لها في المساء ... هل تساعدينني .. لك ذوق ممتاز كما ارى .

أحست انها تحترم هذا الرجل وتقدره كثيرا ..وأحست انها صغيرة أمامه وابتسمت له وركبت إلى جواره وقالت له وهي تغلق باب السياره بصوت متلهف حسناً ولكن أسرع أرجوك .. أخاف أن يغضب والدي لو تأخرت .. كما أنني لم استأذن أمي بعد .

(أمينة اسماعيل الأنصاري)

حسن رشيد ــ قطر

بعض الحقيقة

فوق صندوق خشبي متهالك كان جالساً .. ينظر إلى المارة .. يعلق على هذا وذاك .. يتطلع إلى الوجه .. عن أي شيء كان يبحث .. لا أدري .. دفعني الفضول إلى التأمل في سحنته .. لم أكن أعرفه مسبقاً .. ولم ألتق به من قبل .. ولكنه نموذج بشري من ملايين النماذج .. بعض هذه النماذج تترك أثراً في مخيلة الإنسان .

وكأنما أحس بإندهاشي وتأملي له فقال : من أنت ؟ .. هكذا بادرني .. قلت كي أقطع عليه طريق الفضول .. انسان .. قال أعرف .. ولكن ما اسمك .. في سري قلت .. بلا شك أنه فضولي أو مجنون .. وعلى أسوأ الاحتمالات شحاذ يريد صدقة ..

لم أكن في حقيقة الأمر أملك الكثير من الوقت كي أتجاذب معه أطراف الحديث وكأنما أحس بهروبي .. فتحول إلى انسان آخر .. أكثر عدوانية .. وقال : لماذا لا ترد .. هيه .. لماذا لا ترد .. في عجلة من أمرى سحبت كيساً بلاستيكياً .. وأخذت أضع فيه ما أريد شراءه من الفواكه والخضروات .. وأحس للمرة الثانية بهروبي منه فقال : أين تعمل ؟ .. لا حول ولا قوة إلا بالله .. تطلع إليّ البائع ولسان حاله يقول دعه .. كرر السؤال مرة أخرى .. وأمام اصراره حددت له جهة العمل .. قال لي بنبرة حادة .. أنت تعرف ابني حمود السلس ؟ ابتسمت .. حمود السلس ؟ ابنه ؟ كيف .. وكأنما قرأ الاستغراب والدهشة المرسوم على صفحة وجهي فقال .. نعم .. حمود السلس ابني .. التزمت الصمت .. فلاجدوى من النقاش والاسترسال في الحديث مع هذا المجنون .. الآن قد تأكدت من جنونه ..

الوقائع تؤكد بُعد الارتباط بين هذا الإنسان وحمود السلس .. من الجائز أن تكون هناك علاقة ما . بين الاثنين .. كأن يعرفه مثلاً أو كان جاراً لأسرته .. أو يرتبط بعلاقة قرابة من بعيد .. ولكن أن يكون حمود السلس ابنه .. فلا يمكن تصور الأمر .. حقيقة العلاقة أولاً . وما داخلي في الموضوع .. قلت لأواصل الحديث .. وقد شدتني نبرته ..

– إذاً أنت ترى أن حمود السلس ابنك ..

– أنا أرى .. ماذا تقول ؟! .. إنني أبوه .. هل تعرف .. أنه من صلبي ..

– ولكن كيف تكون أباه .. "وكأنما قرأ الحيرة في وجهي" .. ثم قلت معلقاً وهل يعترف حمود السلس بأبوتك ..

– هذه القصة طويلة ..

شدني إليه .. الآن أريد أن أسمع القصة .. هل يلعب هذا الإنسان بأعصابي .. ولماذا اختارني دون خلق الله .. تطلعت إليه وكأني أراه للمرة الأولى .. دققت في ملامحه .. فعلاً هناك تشابه .. نفس الملامح تقريباً . نفس الهزال الأبدي وكأنما قد خرجا معاً من مجاعة .. وكأنما قرأ كل شيء فقال : اسمع يا ولدي .. أنا لا أكذب .. وأنت لا تعرفني .. بل تعرف حمود السلس .. تعرفه منذ متى ؟ ومع هذا فلا يمكن لأي مخلوق أن يعرف حمود السلس .. أنه نتاج فريد .. هل لديك القدرة للاستماع .. وضعت الأكياس جانباً .. سحبت كرسياً متهالكاً واقتربت منه .. تنفس وقال .. أنت لا تعرف عني أي شيء .. أما أنا فقد سألت البائع عنك .. فقال لي أنك تعمل مع ابني حمود .. إذاً هذا الإنسان لديه فكرة مسبقة عني .. وهذا ما دعاه إلى الاسترسال .. ولكن ما هو المطلوب مني الآن ثم قلت ماذا ؟ قال : أنت تعرف أولا تعرف ــ وهذا الأمر سيان ــ انني عشت في عدة مناطق .. اشتغلت بحاراً وعاملاً .. تجولت في طول الخليج وعرضه .. هنا وهناك .. في تلك الحقبة لم يكن الإنسان في حاجة ماسة إلى إثبات الهوية .. لم نكن نعرف جوازات السفر ..

قبل أن أعيش هنا عشت في عدة مناطق .. كنت خارج هذه الحدود .. كونت أسرة ورزقني الله بابني حمود السلس وابنتي فاطمة .. فاطمة تزوجت وهي الآن تعيش مع زوجها .. صمت فترة من الزمن .. قلت لعله يريد أن يسترجع شريط الذكريات أو يحاول تأليف حكاية أخرى .. طال صمته .. قمت مرة أخرى وأخذت بعض الأكياس كي أكمل شراء ما أريد شراءه .. ثم قلت هازئاً والآن .. هل حمود السلس يعترف بأبوتك ؟!.

كمارد انطلق من القمقم ثار وانطلق يزبد .. لا تسأل كيف ولماذا .. ترك حتى اسمي واسم أسرتي .. إذاً أنا محق في شكوكي .. اسمع قالها بنبرة حادة .. حمود السلس الآن .. "عود" نعم .. "عود" الآن هو إنسان آخر اتخذ من اسم عائلة زوج أخته اسماً .. وحول اللعبة لصالحه .. الآن ماذا يريد مني .. لا شيء .. وأنا لا أريد منه شيء .. "الحي عايش" .. الآن حمود السلس وصل إلى مبتغاه ..

قلت له .. وهل ترى ابنك .. مثلاً في المناسبات والأعياد .. ضحك للمرة الأولى .. شاهدت خبث ضحكة حمود السلس في العمل .. نفس الملامح .. رد عليّ بحدة .. الآن لا يريدني .. فأنا لا أرتبط به .. اختار اسماً آخر .. ولقباً آخر .. إنني أشكل هاجساً ثقيلاً عليه .. أجلس يا ولدي .. دعني أحدثك .. ذات مرة اتصلت به .. وقلت له .. أنا أبوك يا ولدي .. فأغلق السماعة .. كررت المحاولة ..

فكان الرد كالسكين .. والدي مات وأنا طفل .. صمت قليلاً .. ثم قال .. أنا قد أخرتك كثيراً .. لاتبالِ كثيراً .. ففي الحياة ملايين المآسي ..

لا أدري لماذا رحلت إلى البعيد البعيد .. هل بمقدور أي كاتب أن يخلق شخوصاً كهذه الشخصية .. في الحياة نماذج ونماذج قلما نصادفها .. هل غابت مثل هذه الشخصيات عن خيال الكتاب المبدعين .. ماذا لو كان شكسبير حياً ؟ .. بلا شك فإنه كان سيجسد في أعماله نمطاً آخر من هذه الشخصيات .. إن حمود السلس في تركيبته نمط فريد يجمع بين ياجو .. وشيلوك .. شخص جبان .. وصولي .. لا يطعن إلا في الظلام .. ولكن هل هو خسيس إلى هذه الدرجة .. لماذا ينكر أبوته ؟!.

مر بذاكرتي شريط الذكريات ونحن في العمل .. اكتشفناه منذ سنوات .. شخص صفراوي .. حقود .. حسود .. لص .. يسرق أرغفة الفقراء .. يمارس كل هذا بحقد دفين ولكن هل بمقدور الإنسان أن ينكر أبوة الإنسان .. كان السؤال صعباً .. والإجابة أصعب .. أحس بأنني مشتت الذهن .. فقال يا ولدي لا تشغل ذهنك بهذا الأمر .. فأنا قد نسيت الموضوع .. منذ سنوات .. ولكن هل حقاً ما يقولون .. إن إبني حمود السلس يشغل منصباً كبيراً .. ها هو يلعب بي مرة أخرى ويقول .. ابني .. أردف قائلاً .. هل راتبه كبير .. هل يحصل مثلاً على أكثر من خمسة آلاف في كل شهر .. ضحكت .. يالبساطة هذا الإنسان .. نظر إليّ باستغراب .. قلت له .. يا والدي هذا المبلغ مبلغ تافه .. هذا ما يسرقه من جهد الفقراء .. ثم لا تنسى يا والدي أنه يملك العديد من المحلات .. وأنت أدرى الناس بطبائع ابنك ..

قال بحدة .. لا تقل هذا .. اعتقدت للوهلة الأولى أن سبب ثورته .. أنني قد كشفت خبايا ابنه .. ولكن فيما بعد اتضح أن سبب ثورته شيء آخر .. قال محتداً .. لقد بذرت .. ولكني بذرت في السبخ مع الأسف .. أنه نبت شيطاني ..

سكت قليلاً وكأنما أراح واستراح .. نعم حمود السلس نبت شيطاني .. سنوات وسنوات نعمل معاً .. الانطباع الأول أنه شريف .. مخلص .. أمين .. صادق .. مغلوب على أمره .. ولكن سرعان ما يكتشف الإنسان أنه شخصان .. صورة قاتمة لإنسان غير سوي .. يملك الموهبة والاستعداد .. وفي سبيل مصالحه يدوس على كل المعايير والأخلاق والمثل .. ولا علاقة له بالإنسانية ..

تطلع إليّ ملياً .. وقال يا ولدي .. ليت حمود السلس لم يولد .. ليته مات قبل أن يخلق .. فقام فجأة .. تطلعت إلى البائع وتساءلت في حيرة .. هل حقاً ما رواه هذا الإنسان – قال البائع – نحن من منطقة واحدة ..

وما قاله ــ مع الأسف ــ الحقيقة المرة .. المؤسف أننا أيضاً نرتبط بعلاقة قرابة .. والآن لا يعرفنا .. ولا يريد أن يعرفنا حمود السلس .. نحن أيضاً لا نريد أن نعرفه .. أنت إذاً تعرف حمود السلس جيداً ؟ .. هكذا نطقت .. ضحك معي وهز رأسه .. وكأنما يقول لي .. تأخرت كثيراً .. حمل الأشياء معي إلى السيارة .. ثم قال بهمس .. حقاً أنت لا تعرف أن حمود السلس ابن عمي !! .. حمود السلس ابن عمي !! ..

حصة العوضي – قطر

أمل

قال لها ونظرات اللهفة في عينيه ..

- سأشتاق إليك .. فهل للشوق إلي في قلبك مكان .. !!

كانت صامتة .. تبتسم ابتسامة غامضة .. لم يعرف أهي ابتسامة خوف .. أم فرح .. إنها باردة .. باردة .. هكذا يشعر بها .. منذ أن عرفها وهي تعامله بأسلوب غامض لا يدري كنهه .. هو يتحرق للقائها .. يترقب مجيئها لحظة بلحظة .. يحصي خطواتها على الدرب .. تتسارع دقات قلبه منذ أن تعلن خطواتها دخولها من باب المبنى .. لا بل منذ أن يلمحها من نافذة مكتبه .. وهو يترقب مرورها من أمام مكتبه .. لتقول له في ابتسامتها الوادعة ..

- صباح الخير ..

كم هي ممتعة تلك اللحظات بالنسبة إليه .. رغم إنه يتسمر في مكانه .. أحاسيسه كلها تتجمد .. عروقه تتوقف عن عملها في توصيل الدم إلى أجزاء جسمه .. دقات قلبه تتوقف .. تنفسه .. شهيقه .. زفيره .. كل شيء فيه يصمت في اللحظة التي تطل فيها بطولها الفرع قرب باب عينيه المفتوحتين لها ذلك هو .. ما إن يراها .. حتى تتلبسه حالة من الجمود .. رغم حرارة الشوق إليها .. رغم حالة القلق التي تعتريه قبل وصولها .. رغم الجرح المؤلم في أحد أظافره التي كان يقضمها قبل مجيئها بلحظات .. رغم هذا وذاك .. فإن حالة ما .. تلبسه كرداء من الثلج البارد .. يشعر بالبرودة حتى التجمد .. ولكن ما إن تنتهي تلك اللحظة .. ما إن تعبر من أمام بابه .. حتى يذوب الجليد في داخله .. ويكتسي وجهه .. وجلده بماء غزير يهطل من مساماته الكثيرة ..

غريب أمر هذا اللقاء .. والأعجب منه .. أن لا أحد يشعر به .. لا أحد يتمكن من ملاحظته أو إدراكه .. سواه هو .. هو وحده فقط يشعر بذلك .. هو وحده يعلم كيف تتجمد أوصاله حالما يراها .. لكنه يتمنى لو يعرف لماذا ...!! لماذا ينتقل به الشوق من حال إلى حال .. لماذا يتقوقع لسانه داخل فمه بمجرد أن يلمح طيفها ...!!! ولماذا تتوارى نظراته خلف جفنيه السوداوين ما إن تلتقي بعينيها ..!!

هو الحب .. ولاشك .. هو ذلك الذي يسمونه .. الحب .. إنه رغم سنينه تلك لم يعرف الحب .. ولم يجرب منه لحظة في حياته السابقة .. مع كثرة ما كان يسمع .. ويقرأ ويشاهد من حالات الحب .. وقصصه الكثيرة المتنوعة .. حتى إنه كان يعيشها دون حب .. ودون أن يجد من يحبه .. فقط من أجل أن يكتب قصته الجديدة لصفحته الأسبوعية .. في هذه الجريدة التي يعمل بها محرراً .. من أكثر من خمسة عشر عاماً .. هي عمر هذه الصحيفة .. ولازال كما هو .. محرراً أسبوعياً .. في شئون الأدب والثقافة .. يفهم في الشعر .. ويفقهه .. ويفهم في الأدب ويعيه .. ويكتب عن الحب .. ويرويه .. لكنه لم يعرفه .. إلا منذ سنوات قليلة فقط يحسبها هي كل سنين عمره الماضي ... والآتي أيضاً ..

ترى .. ماذا ستكون حياته بدون (أمل) ...!! إنها الفتاة الوادعة .. التي يخفق لها كيانه كل لحظة .. إنها (أمل) .. وهي حقاً بالنسبة له باتت أملاً كبيراً .. لكن المشكلة هي .. كيف يستطيع أن يصل إليها .. كيف وفي هذا المكان الكثير من العيون التي تستطيع أن تلتقط كل صغيرة وكبيرة .. والكثير من الألسنة التي لا تخرس ..وهي في ذلك الهم تتابع العيون المتحركة .. لتجمع في رصيدها الكثير الكثير .. من القصص والحكايات التي يستمتع بها الموظفون .. والمحررون .. والعمال أيضاً .. خلال ساعات الدوام .. وساعات

الراحة أيضاً .. وهم إن علموا بما يجول في فكره .. وما يعتربه من شوق وحيرة .. لسردوا الرواية تلو الأخرى .. ولنسجوا الحكايات تلو الأخرى .. ولأصبحوا في صنع الإشاعات أبرع منه في صنع القصص والروايات .. ولحامت الظنون بأمل .. ولتعقبتها السياط الجارحة من مكتب إلى آخر .. ولنهشتها المخالب من طابق إلى آخر .. لا .. إنه لن يبوح لها .. ولن يحاول أن يسر إليها بأحواله حتى لا تضار هي .. وحتى لا تحاط بأسوار النميمة والشكوك ..

ولكن .. ماذا إن كانت أمل تحب شخصاً ما ...!! شخص ربما يكون هنا في هذا المكان .. وربما خارجه ...!!

يا إلهي .. كيف إنه لم يحاول مرة واحدة معرفة ذلك .. وخاصة أن صاحبه (عارف) كان يهتم بها في فترة ما .. ترى ...!! هل يحبها عارف ...!! وهل هي أيضاً تبادله نفس الشعور ...!!

ما هذا ...!! ما الذي وضع هذه العلامات الحيرى في داخله ...!! لقد أبدى له (عارف) يوماً ما إعجابه بها .. قال له ذات يوم ...

‑ إن أمل تحمل كل مواصفات الزوجة المثالية ..

فهل فال ذلك لأنه يحبها ويرغب في الزواج منها ..

كيف له أن يعرف وعارف الآن في إجازة دراسية منذ عام كامل .. أي بعد اعترافه هذا .. بقليل .. كان يتهيأ للسفر إلى الخارج ..

ترى هل باح لها بمكنون نفسه .. أم لا .. وإذا كان قد أسر لها بذلك .. هل تبادله هي نفس الشعور .. هل تحمل له في داخلها لهفة وشوقاً .. كطائر غريب يحن إلى إلفه ..!

هل يا ترى يخطر لها أن تتذكره كل لحظة .. وأن تراه في كل وجه أمامها .. وأن تبحث عنه في النجوم علها تجده بينها ..!

يا إلهي .. كم هو أمر رهيب .. لو أن أمل تحب عارف ...!! أقال تحب ...!! كيف يعرف أن كان شعورها نحو عارف هو حب .. أو زمالة ...!! كيف ...!! نظر إلى عينيها .. كانت نظراته لاتزال عالقة بها .. مسمرة في عينيها .. وهي لم تغير من ملامحها .. كل ما في الآمر أنها ارتبكت بعض الشىء .. ثم سحبت كفها مسرعة من بين كفه الذي كان يود لو يستأصلها جسداً وروحاً .. لتطير معه ..

قالت له ..

‑ آمل أن تعود بالسلامة بإذن الله ...!!

أحقاً ترجو له العودة بالسلامة .. لقد رجتها قبل ذلك لعارف .. آه .. تبأ له هذا المخلوق .. ما باله يزاحم لحظاته الجميلة معها .. ما باله يدخل إلى فكره الخاص بها .. بين كل لحظة وأخرى .. هل كتب له أن يفرق بينهما .. بينه وبين أمل ...!! حتى في هذه اللحظة ...!!

قال لها ..

‑ أمل .. أنا ..

لم يستطع الاستمرار .. فصوته اختبأ فجأة كقنفذ مرعوب ..

ابتسمت وهي تقول له ..

‑ ما بك يا حسن .. هل هناك شىء ...!!
‑ أمل .. تعرفين أنني ..

132

قاطعته .. بنظرة حادة .. أحس أنها تخترقه من الأعلى إلى الأسفل .. وفتحت عينيها على مصراعيها .. أكثر .. فأكثر ..

- حسن ...!!

كان هناك شخص جاء مسرعاً عند الباب ..

- هيا يا حسن .. ستتأخر على الطائرة ..

عاد إلى الخلف بضع خطوات .. وصل إلى الباب .. كانت لا تزال واقفة .. تحدق فيه .. هي المرة الأولى التي تخاطبه فيها بعينيها ...

لكن حسن لم يكن يفهم لغة العيون .. إلا أنه الآن يشعر بعينيها تقفزان إليه .. تعانقه .. تقول له ..

- انتظر .. لا تذهب .. وقف أمام الباب مودعاً وهو يقول ..
- إلى اللقاء يا أمل .. مع السلامة ..

كانت لا تزال في مكانها .. لم تنطق .. لم تحاول الكلام .. لكن .. حينما خرج حسن من مكتبها وعيناها معلقتان بها .. قالت له .. وبصوت هامس .. وللمرة الأولى يرى حسن فيها شيئاً غريباً .. لقد رآه في عينيها قبل أن تتفوه به .. فهل حقاً قالت ذلك ...!!

كانت أمل تحدق في حسن .. وهو خارج من مكتبها .. هامسة له ..

- حسن سأنتظرك ...!!

*****

تمت

الدوحة في 1990/01/23 م

وبدأ حديث آخر

ترفع سماعة الهاتف لتجيب بهدوء كالعادة ، فيقابلها الطرف الآخر بسرعة :

آلو .. مريم .. مريم .. انا .. انا بحاجة اليك .. ارجوك .. لابد ان اراك ....

كان متلعثما ، مضطربا ، تتصارع في داخله امواج صاخبة ، قلما عرفتها فيه ...

لم تشأ مريم ان ترده خائبا ، رغم ما يحيط بها من ضيق حانق لا تعرف منه مفرا ...

انصتت له بكل اهتمام ، تتبعت كلماته المبهمة واحدة واحدة ، انها لم تعرف حتى اللحظة سر ذلك الاضطراب العاصف ...

أعادت السماعة إلى مكانها بهدوء بعد ان حددت له موعد اللقاء .. لقد كان في حالة يرثى لها ، لابد ان الامر خطيرا جدا ، فمريم تعرف احمد جيداً ، تعرف انه ليس من النوع الذي يثور ويحطم ما حوله دون وعي ، فأحمد هو الانسان الوحيد الذي تشعر معه بالراحة ، انه في رأيها الانسان المثالي لكل فتاة تحلم بالهدوء والسكينة ولكن ليلى .. هذه الفتاة التي رغم كبرها ، رغم بلوغها العشرين ، ماتزال طفلة في أفعالها ، طفلة في سلوكها ، لا تعي سوى ما تريده هي فقط ، ولاتدري سوى رغباتها الطفولية ، التي كثيرا ما أرهقت احمد واقلقته ، وارهقت معه مريم وأرهقتها ..

انها طفلة مريم المدللة .. الطفلة الكبيرة ...

مريم ليست والدتها ، انها صديقتها الأولى والأخيرة .. صديقتها التي التقت بها في أول يوم دراسي لها ...

انها اول من التقت به ليلى في أيام طفولتها ، تلجأ اليها دائماً .. فعندها يعوض النقص الذي تشعر به ليلى .. حرمانها من الأخوة والأخوات ذلك النقص الذي دفعها لان تتخذ من مريم اختا وأما وصديقة ... ففي ذات يوم التقيتا .. لعبتا معا ... مرحتا معا .. كبرتا معا .. كبرت ليلى يوما بعد يوم .. وكبرت مريم معها .. إلا انه في الحين الذي تكبر فيه ليلى عاماً واحداً .. تكبر مريم عشرة أعوام .

ليلى كبرت كما هي ، بطفولتها ، بمرحها .. بينما غلفت الحياة مريم بسحابة حزن عميقة .. حرمتها من طفولتها ، وأغلقت عليها أبواب نفسها ...

انها لا تعرف طريق المرح .. لان المرح هرب عن حياتها فجأة .. تماماً كغروب الروح عن الجسد لحظة الختام ..

انها تعمل مساء لتساعد والدها المقعد .. ولتعول اخوتها الصغار .. مريم لا تعرف الفرح .. فالفرح غادر روحها الصغيرة برحيل والدتها عن صخب هذه الحياة في لحظة ميلاد ..

لحظة الميلاد تلك كانت لحظة بزوغ أول رضيع جديد .. وكانت لحظة الغروب الأخيرة لنبضات الام ... كانت انفاسها تتقطع .. صوتها يتحشرج .. حتى غاب رويداً رويداً ... ومن الموت يبعث الميلاد ... من الظلام ينجلي الفجر .. اتى لمريم ذلك الفجر الوليد .. لقد افاقت من طفولتها الجميلة مع ليلى .. لتجد نفسها أما لطفلة قد ولدت توا .. لتجد نفسها أما لستة أطفال .. اصبحت أما وهي ابنة الأربعة عشر ربيعاً ..

بالامس كانت تلعب معهم .. بالامس فقط كانت طفلة مثلهم .. بالامس كان ذلك فقط ..واليوم تصبح هي امهم ، الام الجديدة .

كانت رغم طفولتها صلبة .. رغم براءتها قوية .. وحينما اصيب والدها في ذلك الحادث الاليم ولزم فراشه كانت الفولاذ قوة ومتانة ..

ولكن ماذا يدور برأسها الصغير .. لا أحد يعلم ..

انها الان تتحدث بلغة امرأة بالغة النضج .. وتدير البيت كسيدة رشيدة .. وترعى اخوتها كأم روؤم .. وتنظر في العواقب قبل ان تقع .. انها فعلاً تشعر مع ليلى انها أمها الثانية .. رغم ان ليلى تنال نصيبها من التدليل واكثر بكثير مما تستحق .. الا انها لاتطيق صبراً عن امها الصغيرة .. عن مريم .. اذا بكت فإن يد مريم كفيلة بمسح دموعها .. واذا ضحكت فصدر مريم واسع لضحكاتها ..

صغيرتان صديقتان .. أم وابنه ..

ولكن هذه المكالمة التي جاءتها الان من احمد تنذرها بأمر سيء .. ترى ماهو ؟ هل ساءت الامور بينه وبين ليلى .. أم ماذا ؟ ..

خطبة ليلى الى احمد لم تمض عليها الا بضعة شهور ، لكن ليلى بطباعها الطفولية تكاد ان تفقد احمد .. هذا الانسان الذي سعى اليها حبا بها .. املا في تغيير سلوكها .. هذا الانسان الذي رفض الاستماع الى والديه واختار ليلى على قريبته التي اختيرت له ... يكاد ان يجن الآن من سلوك هذه الفتاة ... ترى أهو غضب والديه ... أهو غضب من الله ... ولكن ماذا جنت ليلى لتخسر خطيبها أحمد الذي احبته ...

عشرات من الأسئلة دارت في ذهن مريم ، فعليها الآن ان تنقذ هذا الرباط من الانفراط عليها ان تنقذ صديقتها مما توشك ان تقع فيه بسلوكها وتصرفاتها ...

وبانتظار حضور أحمد اليها في المنزل هذا اليوم عصراً في الرابعة تتمدد مريم على فراشها لتقع عيناها على الصورة المعلقة على الحائط ..

ليلى وأحمد .. انها ليلة الخطبة .. الدفوف والغناء ، الطبل والزمر ، ومريم تدخل منزل ليلى .. العروس الصغيرة .. التي ما ان رأت مريم حتى نهضت من مكانها بسرعة ناسية انها عروس ، وانها يجب ان تلتزم بمقعدها بجانب خطيبها .. لكن ليلى نسيت توجيهات أمها لها ، وأسرعت لتتلقف مريم بالحضان ، مريم التي كانت غائبة في الخارج برفقة والدها المقعد .. وهاهي تعود لتحضر حفل خطبة ليلى .. ويعجب الحضور من هذه الفتاة العروس .. وتحاول مريم تنبيهها للخطا الذي وقعت فيه ، ولكنها لم تكترث ، شدت مريم من يدها بسرعة الى حيث يجلس احمد وهي تقول بلهفة :

أحمد .. انظر .. هذه مريم .. اليست رائعة ..

كانت عينا احمد تلك اللحظة تحاولان القفز بسرعة في عيني مريم المتوهجتين لولا انها اشاحت بوجهها عنه الى عروسه التي استعدت لتلقى التهنئة من مريم والاخرين .. فرغم الشحوب والحزن الذي غلّف حياة مريم إلا انها كانت تلك الليلة تتألق بوهج جميل ساحر .. لفت اليها انظار الجميع .. حتى احمد ..

كانت هذه هي المرة الأولى التي تتعرف فيها مريم على احمد .. ولكنها لم تكن المرة الأخيرة .. فلم تنقطع ليلى وأحمد عن زيارة مريم في بيتها بعد ذلك واصطحابها معهما أحياناً للترفيه عنها ...

فحزن مريم العميق الذي لا يعرفه احد ، تحسه ليلى وتشعر به ، لكنها لاتعرفه مع ذلك كانت تحاول ابعادها عن ذلك الجو الكئيب الى عالمها الخاص المرح ، والمتدفق املا وحياة وطفولة ، عالم مليء بالاحلام الجميلة بربيع دائم ، مخضر الغصان تعيش فيه هي وخطيبها أحمد ، وبيتها الصغير بسوره الممتد المخضر ، حيث يلعب الصغار في حديقته ، صغارهما .. ليلى وأحمد .. حياتهما معاً لاشك ستكون رائعة ..

هكذا تعتقد مريم .. فليلى رغم طفولتها تحب الصغار ... تحب أحمد ... ولا شك أنها ستفعل المستحيل لاسعاده .

وأحمد أيضاً ، رغم عدم رضاه عن بعض تصرفات ليلى ، رغم صمته الدائم فهو يحبها ، يحبها رغم معارضة أهله لزواجهما ، فقد اختارها عليهم جميعاً ، اختارها لانه يحبها .. فلابد اذا انه سيكرس حياته من أجلها ، ومن أجل بيتهما الصغير ..

أما هذه المشكلة المحيرة التي سألها أحمد فيها ، فإنها ولا شك خلاف عابر كما يحدث بينهما دائماً ... وهو يحدث دائماً بين كل اثنين ... سحابة صيف .. ليست أكثر من ذلك ..

136

وعلى ذلك الامل انتظرت مريم أحمد ... ورأته ، بهدوئه .. بصمته ، يقف وجها لوجه امامها .. وقبل
ان يحدثها ، وقبل ان تحدثه ، جذب يدها بقوة .. وحاول شدها إليه .. كانت الامواج تتلاطم خلفهما .. والرعد
يزمجر فوق رأسيهما .. وأحمد يحاول شدها إليه .. الى ذلك البحر الكبير .. وبكل قوتها كانت تحاول التخلص
منه باحتجاج صامت ، والدموع تنهمر من عينيها .. حتى كادت ان تسقط اعياء فصرخت .. ولاول مرة تنطلق
مريم من داخلها .. تنطلق صرخة .. تخفت فجأة على رجفات قلب مريم المتلاحقة وتمتمت مريم :
آه .. ماهذا .. رباه ... هذا فظيع ..
كان حلما رهيبا .. بل كان كابوسا مفزعاً ... هذا الذي رأته لم يكن أحمد .. كان حلما .. وتتنهد ...
حمداً لله .. لقد كان حلماً ..
وتتنفس مريم الصعداء ... فلم يكن ذاك أحمد حقاً ...
هو يشبهه تماماً ... ولكنه ليس أحمد ...
وتتطلع الى الصورة من جديد ، هذا هو احمد .. والطبل والدفوف والغناء .. الا ان جرس الباب يقرع ..
وتهرع هي نحو الساعة .. انها الرابعة وأكثر ، يا الهي ، لقد غفت مريم طويلاً لابد انه احمد ...
وكان هو ، لكنه لم يكن بهدوئه المعتاد .. كان يتفرس في مريم ويرتجف .. يده تطبق على يدها بالتحية
ثم يسحبها سريعاً ... شفتاه تتحركان بصعوبة .. عيناه لا تتركانها لحظة واحدة ..
أحمد ما الأمر .. انك ترعبني ...
كانت مريم خائفة فعلاً .. انها المرة الأولى التي يخرج فيها أحمد من جلده .. يخرج لينفعل .. ويثور ،
ويحطم اعصاب مريم معه ..
وتسأله :
أحمد .. ماذا هناك ..
كان لا يزالان يقفان أمام الباب .. قال لها :
هل ادخل ..
وافسحت له الطريق ، ففي الداخل سيحدثها ، وسيروي لها ما حدث وما جد بينه وبين ليلى ...
لقد اعتادت مريم حضور أحمد اليها كلما تعقدت الامور بينه وبين ليلى ، فهي اكثر من بعرف ليلى ،
وأكثر من يعرف أحمد أيضاً ، بل يفهمه .. انها بالنسبة لهما المرجع الأخير ، هي الوحيدة التي تستطيع
اقناع ليلى بالصواب والخطأ ، فهي أمها الثانية .. الام الصغيرة ..
شيء واحد لم تستطع ان تغرسه فيها رغم محاولاتها الجادة لذلك ، وهو ان تعيش مع احمد افكاره
وطموحاته كامرأة .. امرأة بالغة النضج .. فهل ستتمكن من ذلك مستقبلاً ...
الرياح خارج المنزل هادئة لولا بعض السحب التي تغطي السماء .. هكذا علقت مريم وهي تغلق النافذة
محاولة اخفاء اضطرابها .. ومحاولة سماع ما جاء من اجله أحمد .. الذي يكاد ان يخنق صوته بداخله ..
كان يريد ان يقول شيئاً .. يهم بالحدث .. ثم يتراجع ..
فنجان الشاي يرتعد في يديه ... وتتسارع الافكار الى رأسها .. لماذا لا يتحدث لماذا يضطرب هكذا ..
لماذا يحملق في عينيها هكذا .. ترى ماذا يريد .... هذه الومضة في عينيه تذكرها بليلة الخطبة وهي تكاد
ان تخطفها ممن حولها عجبا له ... ماذا حدث ...
وتسلبها عيناه من أفكارها .. ويدور بينهما حوار صامت .. لاول مرة تصمت مريم لتتحدث بعينيها ..
لاول مرة تتفاهم بعينيها .. وكان الحوار طويلاً . طويلاً .. حتى افاقت منه مريم فزعة ...
لا .. لا .. لا ..
صرخت بأعلى صوتها ثم بدأت تبكي ..

وقف الى جانبها يحاول تهدئتها .. يحاول ايقافها عن البكاء ، كانت عيناه مليئتين بألف معنى ومعنى ..
وكانت يداه فارغتين من كل شيء .. حتى من دبلة الخطبة ... لقد عرفت أخيراً ما يريد .. عرفت كل شيء ..
قرأت في عينيه كل الخبايا ..
قال لها :
مريم ... انا ..
قاطعته بصوتها المخنوق بالبكاء :
ستخرج من هنا قبل ان تقول أي شيء ...
نظر اليها محاولاً استعطافها .. حاول ان يثنيها عن عزمها .. واذ بها تتهاوى على ركبتيها ووجهها
بين يديها ..
أحمد ... أرجوك .. بربك ارفق بي ..
وانخرطت في البكاء من جديد ..
وابتسم احمد .. لقد عرف الجواب اخيراً

حصة يوسف

138

مريم محمد عبد الله ـ قطر

بداية الطريق

في غرفة مظلمة . ومن احدى النوافذ يتسرب ضوء خافت منبعث من اضاءة خارجية إلى إحد اركان الغرفة التي بدت حزينة كئيبة كشبح الفتاة الجالس في هذا الركن المظلم . تجلس القرفصاء .. وتسند راسها الى كفيها الصغيرين متكئة على ركبتيها .

تفكر بصمت دون أن تصل إلى هدف كغريق تائه في عرض محيط ليس له بداية ولا نهاية ، وكمرتحل في صحراء يحاول رسم السراب أمام عينيه ليقنع نفسه بالوصول .

تفكر بدموع اغرورقت بها عيناها .. عينان جميلتان تتلألآن في الظلام لانكسار الضوء الخافت على تلك الدموع النقية .. فتبدوان أكثر جمالاً .. وأكثر فتنة .

وخلال الباب الخشبي لهذه الغرفة تسللت اصوات مهللة فرحة .. وانغام موسيقى عذبة .

ألف مبروك .. عسى أن يتممه الله على خير

اشكرك يا عمتي .. وان شاء الله عن قريب سوف احضر معي "الدبلة" ونتم الفرح باذن الله .

اهلاً بك يا بني .. وارجو ان تبلغ تحياتي إلى الوالد والوالدة ونحن بانتظار زيارتهما لنا.

عن قريب ان شاء الله .. وإلى اللقاء

إلى اللقاء يا بني

ما اقسى هذه الكلمات .. انه الكابوس الجاثم على مصير كل فتاة في هذا المجتمع .. لماذا ؟ لماذا ابن خالي بالذات ؟ انا لا احبه .. ولا ارغب فيه .

صرخت بهذه الكلمات حالما وجدت امها وهي تفتح باب غرفتها واجهشت بالبكاء

ما بك يا ليلى ؟ .. لماذا تبكين يا بنتي ؟

انني لا اريد الزواج يا امي .. لا اريد .. اليس من حقي ؟

انك تعلمين جيداً بأن أوامر أبيك لابد ان تنفذ .. هكذا عاداتنا هكذا تقاليدنا .. ولابد من زواج الفتاة لاحد اقربائها .. ابن عمها ابن خالها ـ ابن عمتها

فلما ترفضين "قاسم" وما الذي ترينه فيه شائناً ؟

لا شيء يا امي .. لا شيء

(وبدا صوتها منخفضاً)

حقا ليس هناك من عيب في "قاسم" انه شاب وسيم ذو قسمات جادة وروح طيبة .. جميل الطلعة بهي المنظر مثقف . وحاصل على ليسانس اداب له طلعة جميلة ورنة جذابة في الحديث يلفت الانظار بعقله ورزانته .

فما العيب الذي تبحث عنه ليلى لتجده فيه .. أو الاصح لتقنع نفسها بأنها لا تحبه لاجل علة فيه ؟

(انها تعلم جيداً ان أية فتاة تتمنى الحديث مع ابن خالها "قاسم" وتحلم بالزواج منه ولكنها ترفضه تماما .. لماذا ؟)

وبدت فاطمة . والدة ليلى وكأنها تحاول اقناع ليلى بالكلام ..

الا ان ليلى تاهت مع شتات نفسها ..وبين طرقات عقلها .. ونبضات قلبها ومكنون ذاتها .. تحدث نفسها محاولة الرد عليها لتصل الى حل يقنع امها .. وتارة تحاول الهرب من نفسها .. ربما لخوفها من مواجهة ذاتها .. ولكن الهرب الى اين .. فلا بد من مواجهة النفس .. والا فأنها تغالط نفسها عندما تفكر أو تحاول اقناع امها بما لم تقتنع به هي نفسها في داخليتها . فالى اين الهروب .. لابد لك من الاجابة .. من المواجهة .

لماذا ترفضين "قاسم" لماذا ؟

(اصرار صوت الذات قوي) فتجيب

انني لا احبه

وهل عرفته جيداً لتحكمي هذا الحكم ؟

انني لا احبه .. لا احبه فقط .. وليس هناك من سبب آخر ..

على أي اساس ترفضين .. وأي مفهوم تتخذين

اريد ان اتزوج شاباً احبه .. اغوص في اعماقه وكأنني اعرفه من سنين طويلة .. انه حلمي المرسوم في عقلي وكياني يسحرني بكل لفتة ولكل همسة له .. افهمت من اريد .. افهت من ارغب فيه

يا له من منطق غريب غريب .. لا اظن ان هناك أحداً في هذا العالم الواسع يفكر بمثل هذا التفكير . اتحطمين مستقبلك من اجل شاب تحلمين به .. تحلمين به .. لمجرد حلم ترفضين .. وعلى هذا الحلم تخططين مستقبلك .

انك حقا فتاة بلهاء .. دون عقل يفكر .. ولا قلب يحس

ترفضين شاباً به جميع الصفات التي تجعله حلم أجمل الفتيات من اجل حلم ليس له أساس .

اليس من حقي ان احلم بما اريد ؟ .. حتى الاحلام بدت مرفوضة

تحلمين .. ولكن ليس على حساب مستقبلك

انه مستقبلي وأنا ادرى به

وامك وأبوك .. وعائلتك .. ومجتمعك

دائماً يحكمون .. ويسيطرون ويفرضون

يجب ان تفكري بمنطق مجتمعك .. وبحدود عاداته وتقاليده

كل شيء حولي أسوار ... وقيود ... اقفال ... و ظلام ... سجناء تحت رحمة جلاد يدعى التقاليد .

عودي لوعيك .. وفكري بأهلك

دائماً هكذا .. أنا .. وأنت .. وهي .. لماذا لا يكونون "هم" ؟

مجتمعك .. وعاداته وتقاليده ..

كرهت نفسي .. كرهتك انت ذاتي .. لم اعد اطيق

يجب ان تحتملي .. وان تفكري

أفكر ـ كيف ؟ .. وكل شيء حولي محرم ..

لن تصلي الى حل بمثل هذا التمرد ..

اصمتي .. لا أريدك ان تكملي .. انك قاسية .. قاسية ..

ان رأسك الصغير هذا لاقسى من حجر الصوان .. فعنادك هذا لن يرسم طريقك في الحياة .. ولن يجعلك تصلين الى هدف كل فتاة .

أي هدف تقصدين .. ان تكون الفتاة اسيرة العادات والتقاليد .. ان تكون سجينة افكار قديمة .. تفرض الأمور عليها فرضاً .. وتقاد كسجينة الى سجن الزواج ..

أي كبرياء يقبل بذلك .. أي كرامة تسمح يه .. أي نفس بشرية ترضى به ..

اذن هو كبرياؤك الذي يجعلك ترفضين .. لمجرد ان هذا الأمر قد فرض عليك فرضاً

ماهو بكبرياء .. انها كرامتي .. كرامتي كانسان يحق لي الرفض والقبول .

انك تغالطين نفسك .. ولكن بأي وجه حق ترفضين .. فلابد أن تكون هناك أسباب تقنع بالرفض .. انك ترهقينني .. انني تعبة .. تعبة جداً .

بل انك تتهربين من نفسك .. تتهربين من الحقيقة التي امامك . تخافين من واقعك

لماذا تصرين على السؤال

انا ذاتك أيتها البلهاء .. فلست بحاجة لاصرار .. وانما انت التي بحاجة الي لاصر ..

لماذا ؟

هل تستطيعين مواجهة ابيك وأمك بحقيقة مشاعرك

انني لا اريد الزواج ..

وهل اقنعك فرضهم عليك بالزواج

بالطبع لا

وكيف تريدينهم ان يقتنعوا بمجرد رغبة لك

لماذا تسدين الطريق في وجهي .. لماذا تجعلين الامل بعيداً عني لماذا تحاولين جعلي خرساء عاجزة عن النطق

انك تعلمين جيداً انه لابد من مواجهة الواقع .. ولابد من حسم الأمور .. وجعل كل احتمال متوقع في الحسبان .. ويجب عليك أن تنظري إلى مدى أوسع وأرحب

انني .. انني ..

مابك ؟ أليس لديك من رد يقنع أهلك بسبب رفضك ؟

ولماذا نغالط انفسنا .. فالسؤال الحقيقي .. أليس لديك من رد يقنع نفسك ؟

يا لك من مرائية بارعة ..

تظنين نفسك كذلك ..

....

أجيبي .. ليس هناك من داع للصمت .. واعلمي ان صمتك في نظر أهلك موافقة ..

اصمتي انت .. ودعيني ارتاح قليلاً .. انني تعبة .. تعبة ..

هل تريدين ان تصمتي صوت ضميرك .. لم اكن بأنك ضعيفة وجبانة

أنا لست بجبانة .. لست بجبانة ـ أنا أقوى مما تتصورين

وأين شجاعتك هذه .. ؟

.... ؟

اجيبيى

ليس هناك من قانون في الوجود كله يجعل الانسان صفرا .. بلا شخصية .. بلا وجود ..

أي فلسفة هذه أيتها الحمقاء .. منذ متى كان الزواج محطة لالغاء شخصية الانسان ووجوده .. بل على العكس .. انه الذي سيجعلك ذات قيمة وكيان في مجتمعك

اليس لي كيان بدون زواج .. اليس لي شخصية بدونه .. اليس هناك من طريق يجعل الفتاة جزءاً من المجتمع سوى الزواج

لا ولكن مجتمعك يفرض ..

وأنا أرفض .. ارفض لا اريد الزواج لكون ابن خالي تقدم لي .. ولكونه من الأقارب أصبح مفروضاً في حياتي .. وسطر مع تاريخ ميلادي .

الم تسمعي عن العلوم الحديثة .. الم تعلمي ان زواج الأقارب غير مرغوب فيه .. فهناك علم يسمى علم الوراثة .. انه علم واسع يبحث في زواج الأقارب ومقدار ما يسببه من مشاكل .. وتوارث الجينات قد يؤدي الى تشوه أطفال المستقبل . وليس العلم الحديث فقط .

بل ان الرسول (صلى الله عليه وسلّم) قد دعا الى الزواج من الأغراب حفاظاً على قوة النسل اذ قال " اغتربوا لاتضووا " أي تضعفوا ..

141

وهدأت نفس ليلى قليلاً .. وكأنها قد وصلت إلى حل قد بقنع أهلها الا ان ذلك غير كاف ..
لا أعتقد بأن أحداً من أهلك سيفهم منطقك هذا .. وربما على العكس سيستخدمون منطقك ضدك ..
وكيف ؟
سيكون رد والدتك ببساطة ان قاسم من نسل طيب .. واصل طيب وابن اخيها .. وزواجك منه شرف
للعائلة ولك ..
ألن يتحقق هذا الشرف الا بالزواج منه ..
انه منطقك الذي تستخدمين .. وهو تفكيرك الذي تصرين عليه دون مبرر له . ودون تفسير منطقي
معقول ..
انك تحاولين تحطيمي ..
بل انني احاول بناءك .. أحاول أن أجعل في داخلك ماهو أقوى من الفولاذ .. اصلد من الالماس ..
أحاول جعل معدنك الداخلي نقياً .. شفافاً .. قادراً على عكس ما بداخلك إلى من يقف أمامك دون ، حاجتك
الى الكلام للاقناع ..
اتعنين انه يمكنني ان أقنع والدتي دون مفهوم أستخدمه .. دون كلام بالطبع ..
وكيف ؟
بمشاعرك .. بقليل من رجاحة عقلك ..
اشكرك لِنصيحتي ..
(ورفعت ليلى رأسها وبدا وجهها مبتسماً وكأنها قد وصلت إلى حل بعد صراع مرير) .
لماذا تبتسمين .. هل هو غرور ..
غرور .. لا .. ليس بغرور ..
اذن لماذا تبتسيمن .. ؟ هل تظنين انك قد وصلت إلى حل نهائي .. هل آمنت حقا بما قلته
نعم .. ولم لا ..
ايتها الغبية .. لماذا تتسرعين قبل انتهاء الأمور .. لماذا لم تنظري إلى نفسك ومشاعرك .. وتفكيرك
هل حقاً تستطيعين أقناع والدتك بهذه البساطة .
الم تقولي بأنني استطيع ..
أنا لم اجزم لك .. وإنما فتحت باباً لك لتحاولي من خلاله الاقناع ..
رسمت خطوطاً عريضة ولكن ينقصها التفصيل والدقة .. وليس القول كالفعل .
هل يعني هذا ان اضع نفسي في متاهة .. وفي دوامة تفكير .. واستمد الأمل من المجهول ..
....
لا أدري .. لا أدري
(وتاهت ليلى مع نفسها .. أو ربما وصلت إلى قمة الصراع مع الذات ..) فلم تحس بصوت والدتها
وهي تنادي ..
ليلى ابنتي .. ما بك ؟ ليلى .. هل من مكروه أصابك ؟ ابنتي .. اجيبي لا ادرى .. لا ادرى ..
مالذي لا تدرينه يا ابنتي ..
(وتنبهت ليلى إلى ان والدتها كانت تقف إلى جانبها طوال تلك الفترة التي أحست وكأنها عام بأكمله ..
ورفعت رأسها الذي بدأ ثقيلاً ربما ربما التقل ما يحمله من أفكار وآمال .. أو من مشكلات وهواجس)
واعتدات ليلى في جلستها
امي
نعم يا ابنتي .. ماذا بك ..

هل تحبينني يا أمي ؟

يا له من سؤال غريب .. هل تسألين أم عن مدى حبها لابنتها .. انك أملي في الحياة يا ابنتي .. ولا اظنني عشت سنين عمري كلها الا لاربيك وأهتم بك واجعلك أسعد فتاة في العالم ..

هل يعني هذا انك تحبينني كثيراً يا أمي

ما بك يا ابنتي .. لماذا تصرين على سؤال كهذا .. أنت تعرفين اجابته جيداً .

أرجوك ان تجيبيني يا أمي .. أرجوك ..

لماذا الاصرار يا ليلى ؟

أرجوك الأجابة يا أمي

حسنا .. احبك

فقط ..؟

ليلى .. بالطبع ان أي أم في العالم كله تحب ابنتها .. وكيف لا .. وهي التي سهرت عليها وربتها .. وعلمتها لتجعلها أملاً للمستقبل .

اذن لماذا .. لماذا تحاولين اتعاسي

اتعاسك !!

وارغامكم لي على الزواج من شخص لا أرغبه .. اليس به تعاسة لحياتي .. "وهل تظنين أن " قاسم " مصدر تعاسة لك في حياتك ..

امي .. ليس بقاسم أي عيب .. ولكني لا افكر في الزواج أبداً ..

وان رغبت في يوم من الأيام – فأنني أريد الانسان الذي أختاره قلبي وعقلي ..

ليس لبنت اختيار .. منذ متى و الفتاة تعارض أهلها في زواجها .. أنا تزوجت أباك .. و .. تقاطعها ليلى) ...

امي أرجوك افهميني ..

اتعنين بأني لا افهم ..

العفو يا أمي .. أرجوك .. اعذريني .. كل ما أرجوه منك ان تسمعيني فقط ان تسمعيني .. ولكن ...

اماه .. الم تقولي بأنك تحبينني .. فليكن صبرك علي وسماعك لي جزءا من محبتك ..

حسناً .. ما الذي تريدين قوله ..

كل ما هنالك .. انني لم ارفض الزواج من قاسم لكونه ابن خالي .. أو لكونكم اخترتموه لي .. غير اني لا اريد الزواج .. أو على الأقل الان وأعدك بأنني لو فكرت في الزواج من شخص فلن اتزوج الا برضاك . وهل تعتقدين يا أمي بأن عصيان الفتاة لاهلها راحة لها .. كلا يا أمي .. بل على العكس .. انه مصدر شقائها .. وتعاستها .. ولن ترضى الام بتعاسة ابنتها .. وكذلك لن ترضى البنت بتعاسة أهلها .. ولولا علمي وثقتي بأنكم تريدون مصلحتي لما رفضته يا أمي ..

؟ ....

(وسادت فترة صمت .. كانت وقفة مع النفس بالنسبة لوالدة ليلى .

فقد كانت العبارات الأخيرة تحمل معاني كثيرة .. الا ان الخواطر التي تجيش في النفس طرحت سؤالاً آخر ..

ولكن يا ليلى هل يعقل ان تبقى هكذا دون زواج

لقد قلت لك يا امي بأنني لو رغبت في الزواج من شخص ما فلن اتزوج الا برضاكم عنه .

ولكن يا ابنتي الا ترين معي بأن "قاسم" شاب ممتاز ورجل ناجح في حياته وانه قادر على أسعاد الفتاة التي سيتزوجها ..

لكلامك وجه من الصحة يا امي .. ولكنني لا اعتقد بأنني سوف أكون سعيدة مع قاسم . وقاسم شخص ناجح الا ان هذا لا يعني ان زواجي منه سيكون ناجحاً أيضاً ..

يجب ان تدركي جيداً بأن الأم لا تريد الا مصلحة ابنتها . ولا تسي ان أباك قد وافق على زواجك .. وهذا يعني انه لابد لك ان تتزوجي "قاسم"

امي .. ارجوك ان تتفهمي موقفي .. لا تجعلي حياتي تعيسة .. انني بين ايديكم .. فلا تقسوا علي ..

(واحتبست الكلمات بين شفتي ليلى .. وارتبكت الاحرف .. ولم تكن هناك قدرة على الكلام بغير الدموع .. دموعها التي انهمرت دون ان تحس بها .. وعبرت عن قول لم يكن له مكان لو قيل .. وتغيرت سحنة وجه والدة ليلى وأصبحت التعابير مختلفة .. وربما أحست بمشاعر لم تدركها من قبل .. فلم تتمالك نفسها من ان تذرف دمعتين كانتا الرد على سؤال ليلى) .

ولكن كيف يصبح موقفنا الان مع بيت خالك .. وماذا نرد على قاسم ؟

والادهى من ذلك كيف اقنع والدك ؟

ان قاسم شاب مثقف وسيدرك الموقف جيداً حينما يعلمه .. وهو كفيل باقناع أبيه ..

أما أبي فليس هناك من يستطيع اقناعه يا أمي فانت الخير وانت البركة .

يالك من فتاة ماكرة ياليلى ..

(تظهر ابتسامة على ثغر ليلى وكأنها فرحة النصر .. وتحس بأن قلبها يكاد يقفز من ضلوعها لفرط سعادتها ..)

أهو حلم أو واقع .. أهو حقيقة أم خيال .. حقا .. كان كابوسا مسيطراً .. وكان الامل فيه بعيداً .. والمستقبل معلق بين الرغبة والتقاليد .. الا ان المشاعر بالحب أقوى من أي فرض في أي مجتمع .. كانت كفيلة بتحريك ذات الانسان الداخلية .. واظهار شفافية الجوهر .. وتغيير كل ما صنع بيد الانسان .. وكل نزوع الانسان للسيطرة .. كلها تلاشت أمام ذات الإنسان أمام مشاعره .. فالتمرد لن يحل مشكلة .. ولا الاصرار والعناد .. والاستسلام يزيد الطين بللا .. ويعقد الأمور تعقيداً .. وان كل الحل ليس جذرياً وشاملا .

(الا ان اصل الشجرة بذرة .. والمشاعر والمحبة بداية الطريق للمستقبل) .

(مريم محمد عبد الله)

ناصر صالح الفضالة ـ قطر

صفاء الروح

جففت صفاء دموعها بيدها ، وودعتني بحزن عميق وقد كست وجهها حمرة الخجل ، وتواريت عنها بأنفاس لاهثه ، لقد بدأت رحلة الفراق ، لم أر من المودعين سوى وجهها ما ان لمحتني أختلس النظر إليها حتى طأطأت رأسها واقتربت مني تتعثر في خطواتها .

"استحلفك بالله ، لاتحنث بالعهد ، لاتنسى ما بيننا"

قاطعني ... تقدم عمي منها وصاح متضاحكاً :

"لاتخافي يا صفاء . انا اكفله ، خالد ولد مؤمن ... لن تغيره أوروبا ولا ملاهيها سيعود لك يا صفاء ... انه أبني أنا احسنت تربيته مثلك تماماً" . لم تستطع ان تمنع دموعها ، لولا الزحام والملامة لاحتضنتها في صدري ، وكدت ان أفقد اتزاني فاتجهت منفعلاً تجاهها ، فما بيننا هو حب طاهر شهدته طفولتنا ، وباركته عائلتنا ، وحمته من العبث اخلاقنا .

"أي خطيئة عمري .. رفيقة قلبي انساك ، وأنا لا املك أنفاسي الا لتبقى على حبك في حياتي ، كيف انساك وأنا دائماً تؤرقني ذكراك حتى معك اشتاق اليك"

لاحظ أخي فرط انفعالي ، فاقترب مني وضمني وابتعد بي بعيداً عنها ، وتداركت نفسي ومسحت دموعي وصحت بأخي :

"صفاء يا صقر ، لاتدعها تشعر بغيابي ، أرسل لي دائماً بأخبارها" قال صقر ضاحكاً :

"لاتجعل بنات أوروبا ينسينك خطيبتك صفاء ، وابنة عمك ، لاتنسي مهمتك المقدسة ، انك ذاهب لتتعلم ، لا لتلهو ، لتصير طبيباً تخدم ابناء وطنك قطر ، لتؤدي رسالة وطنك"

اجبته فيما يشبه الوعد القاطع :

"أعدك يا أخي ، واعدك يا قطر أني سأعود حاملاً شهادتي ، كي ارفع رأس بلادي"

نادى المذيع على المسافرين إلى لندن وتواريت وسط الزحام ، وغابت عني عيناها وان لم يفارقني قط طيفها .

من دفء قطر وحنانها في أيام الشتاء إلى لفحة البرد القارسة في لندن ، اشعرتني برودة الجو وكانني خرجت من ملابسي ، عرياناً وسط زحام لم اعهده من قبل ، الوجوه غير الوجوه ، اللغة غير اللغة ، والنساء لايخجلن من الغير أو من انفسهم يكشفن أكثر مما يخفين .

حملت حقيبتي واتجهت إلى الجامعة لتبدأ دراستي .

في مدرج الجامعة وفي محاضرة اللغة الأنجليزية ، التي لم أكن اتقن منها سوى كلمات بسيطة ، في مدرج الجامعة كنت أجلس منهمكا في متابعة المحاضر ، فقد كنت عاقداً العزم على ان أعود لأهلي , عشيرتي حاملاً شهادتي رافعاً رأسي ورأس أسرتي ، كنت مصمماً ان أعود طبيباً يثلج صدر صفاء ويحقق احلامها .

لم الحظها وهي تبتسم لي ، تتباهى بجمالها ، وعرفت ان امها بريطانية ، اما أبوها فهو اسباني الاصل ، من المؤكد انها تحمل بذورا عربية من دماء صقر قريش حتى قرننا العشرين ، اكسبتها سحر الشرق وجمال الغرب .

ضحكت في نفسي لسخرية الزمان ، كنا نحن العرب قادة العالم ورواده في كل المجالات الادبية والعلمية ، كانت جامعاتنا مصدر النور والعلم ، واصبحنا اليوم نتبع خطواتهم في العلم والادب ، اصبحنا نحن نبحث عن العلم في معاهدهم بعد ان خبت انوار حضارتنا .

145

ابتلعت مرارتي ، ومرت الأيام ...

كانت جانيت تهتم بي دون زملائي ، ترقبني وتعد خطواتي ، كانت دائماً بجانبي اذا احتجت لايضاح في درس استغلق على فهمه ، أو في أمر من أمور الحياة ، كانت تكتب المحاضرات وتعطيني ، أياها ولاتتردد قط في تقديم المساعدة لي .

وفي كل يوم كانت متعتي الحقيقية في اللحظات التي أختلسها في هجمة الليل وتحت الغطاء في غرفتي الدافئة اقرأ خطابات صفاء ، كنت أقرأها لاعيش من خلالها في ربعي وبين عشيرتي اعيش كل سطر من سطور خطابها ، اتذوق كل كلمة ، اضحك مع كل شاردة اذكرها ، وتكاد الدموع تطفر من عيني على كل كلمة تذكرتها منها .

كانت أيام الشتاء قارسة ووحدتي في المنزل قاتلة ، أشعر بالحزن يقتلني أتمنى ان أجد رفيقاً لم يكن يخفف لوعتي سوى ان استعيد ذكرياتي القليلة مع صفاء .

لم يتحمل جسدي النحيل برد لندن ولا صقيعها ، ووجدت نفسي اسعل سعالاً خفيفاً واقعدني المرض في الفراش ، وشعرت لاول مرة بالغربة ومرارتها وبحاجتي الى حنو الأهل وإلى حبهم ، وفي هزيع الليل والوحدة وآلام المرض تحطمت كل محاولة مني للنهوض أو التغلب على روح الكأبة التي انتابتني ، شعرت على غير عادة بطرقات على باب غرفتي ، تحاملت على نفسي وفتحت الباب لارى امامي جانيت .

ما ان رأتني اتحامل على نفسي حتى اسرعت تسندني وتمنعني من الوقوع فقد كان الدوار ينتابني ويكاد يغشى علي من فرط ضعفي ، ارقدتني على سريري واحكمت الغطاء على واستدارت تنظف الغرفة التي اختل نظامها منذ ان سقطت مريضاً ، لم احدثها بشيء وهي لم تعلق على شيء ، وكأن حضورها وبقاؤها في غرفتي أمر تعودنا عليه وليس لدينا ما نقوله .

لم تفارقنى لليالي مرضي ، فقد أهتمت بي طوال أيام مرضي ، لم تقصر قط في ان تعطيني الدواء في ميعاده ، كم من مرة افقت من نومي لاجدها أمامي .

مرت الايام وتماثلت للشفاء ، وشعرت بالعرفان بالجميل ، وان جانيت لها علي دين يطوق عنقي ، لم استطع ان اتهرب منها ، وأصبحت لصيقة بي ، حتى بات اصدقاؤنا في الجامعة لا يتخيلونني بدونها ويتخيلونها بدوني .

كلما امتدت أيام غربتي ، كلما ازددت التصاقاً بجانيت ، وبعد ماكنت اتهرب منها أصبحت اتلمس السبل للقائها ، كانت تعرف كيف تتلاعب بعواطفي ، ترغبني وتصدني ، تتساهل وتتشدد ، كنت كالغريق في بحر هواها لا أقوى على فراقها ، كنت دائماً منجذباً لها تماماً كالفراشة التي أعماها نور المصباح عن ناره ، شعرت بحبها يجرف كياني ، أهملت قراءة خطابات صفاء أو الرد عليها ، ذقت مع جانيت صنوف العادة التي لم أشعر بها من قبل ازددت بها شغفا ، وازدادت صورة صفاء شحوباً ، وبدت وكأنها تتلاشى من مخيلتي .

قارنت بينها وبين صفاء .. جانيت تعرف كيف تتلاعب بمشاعر الرجال ، تبدى محاسنها وتتدلل على حبيبها ، في عيونها يبدو العبث ، واحياناً يبدو الانكسار والخوف والحزن ، خليط من مشاعر قل ان يجدها الانسان في امرأة .

أما صفاء فهي تتعثر في خطواتها وتتلجلج في كلامها ، في عينيها خفر العذارى وعلى شفتيها كلمات حب غير مسموعة ، تفر اذا ما رأتني .. ما أشد الفارق ما بين صفاء وجانيت ... واني في بحر جانيت لغريق .

وشعرت اني غير قادر على ان اتخلى عنها ، ونزعت صورة صفاء من مخيلتي .. وزففت الخبر إلى جانيت ، جانيت العصية التي لم يستطع حتى هذا النبأ أن يذلل تمنعها على ، ولقد حاولت ، وصدتني .. وكم

من مرة انهارت مقاومتي وظننت انني من نيلها قريب الا انها كانت دائماً أقوى مني وتمتاز بثبات أكد لي أنها يمكن ان تكون أكثر قدرة على التحكم في نفسها ربما أكثر من فتيات شرقنا .

أقام أصدقائي حفلاً لنا بمناسبة قراري بالزواج من جانيت .. كنت قد قررت بعد الحفل ان أسافر إلى بلدي لانال موافقة أهلي .. كان الحفل ساهراً وبهيجاً وجانيت ترفل في ثيابها الفاخرة وكأنها عروس تجلت في ليلة من ليالي ألف ليله وليلة ... انساني سحرها كل ما تحليت به من وقار .

واقترب مني أحد أصدقائها .. كان زميلا لنا في الجامعة ، كنت أعلم انه كان يحاول ان يتقرب منها ... وقد حكت لي عنه وصدقتها ...

همس في اذني ضاحكاً ...

"لقد وقعت على كنز .. انها ساحرة .. سوف تريك من صنوف المتعة ماينسيك نفسك وأهلك وحتى دراستك .. في ليال حمراء تجعلك تشعر أنها تملك دلال واغراء كل نساء العالم اجمع"

نظرت له مندهشاً وكأني لم أع ما سمعته فصحت به :

"ماذا تعني ...؟"

"ماذا تعني ... كيف تعرف انها ساحرة في الليالي ؟"

ضحك قائلاً :

"لقد عشت معها أكثر من عامين كزوجين بدون زواج"

لم استطع ان أكتم نفسي وصحت صارخاً ..

"لقد ظننتها عذراء .. لقد تمنعت علي"

وقهقه حتى لفت أنظار الحفل وهمس قائلاً ..

"لقد أخبرتني أنها تمتنع عليك .. لانها تعرف انك عربي ، وأنكم في الشرق لا تقبلون المرأة التي يمسها رجل آخر ، ولذلك فقد منعت نفسها منك ، أما الان فانك تنالها بعد ان تأكدت انك ستتزوجها ."

كدت اسقط من فرط ذهولي ، لم أحرك ساكناً ، لم اعترض ، ماتت على شفتي كل الكلمات وتغيرت نظرتي تماماً لها ...

شعرت في كل نظرة من عينيها نظرة اشتهاء .. وفي كل حركة اغراء .. وكل حديث مع ضيف هو مع عشيق قديم أو عشيق آت .. تحولت أمام عيني إلى خائنة لعوب ... امرأة ليل على نطاق محدود .

بعد ان انتهى الحفل .. حزمت حقائبي .. واتجهت للمطار . كانت جانيت تودعني لم أقل لها ما دار بيني وبين صديقها .

وفي المطار قبلتني وهي تهمس في أذني :

"لاتنسي ان تحضر لي بسرعة .. فأنا متلهفة عليك بعد موافقة أبيك"

نظرت لها ببلاهه

"موافقة أبي على ماذا ؟ .. "

ضحكت متخابثه

"اتداعبني ياشقي .. طبعاً على زواجنا .. الن نتزوج"

كتمت سخريتي قدر طاقتي وقلت لها

"انى عائد إلى قطر .. لا لاحصل على موافقة والدي على زواجك بل لاتزوج صفاء .. وأعود معها لأكمل تعليمي"

لم اعر ذهولها انتباها .. وحولت وجهي صوب المطار ، وقد ارتسمت صورة صفاء بخجل العذارى .. ببسمة الحب البرىء في كل وجه رأيته في المطار .

يا صفاء الروح والقلب اعذريني .. كادت بنات أوروبا ان ينسيني وجهك الضحوك .. يا صفاء الروح
أنا قادم .. قادم كي أجعل من حلم عمرك حقيقة تحميني من أفاعي الغرب ...
وصدق من قال ..
" الشرق شرق .. والغرب غرب يا صفاء .. ولن يلتقيا ياروح عمري أبداً .

(ناصر صالح الفضالة)

يا صفاء الروح والقلب اعذريني .. كادت بنات أوروبا ان ينسيني وجهك الضحوك .. يا صفاء الروح
أنا قادم .. قادم كي أجعل من حلم عمرك حقيقة تحميني من أفاعي الغرب ...
وصدق من قال ..
" الشرق شرق .. والغرب غرب يا صفاء .. ولن يلتقيا ياروح عمري أبداً .

عَروس القمر

(نشرت في مجلة الرائد سنة 1971)

وقفت أمام المرآة تصلح من وضع زينتها ، ثوبها الأزرق المذهب ، تحتضن بحنان مشطا فضى اللون ... هاهى تتركه يسبح وسط شعرها الفاحم الطويل . فيما مضى لم تعرف الطريق الى شعرها سوى المشوط الخشبية ، التى يجلبها التجار من البصرة ... أما هذا المشط الفضى فلقد جلبه والدها من الهند وأهداه لوالدتها ليلة عرسها ، والليلة زفافها ولهذا أصبح المشط من نصيبها .

وجه طفولى لا يخلو من الشقاوة ، عينان سوداوان كبيرتان ، تبحلقان بفضول في وجه العروس الحالمة ، الغارقة فى أفكارها الخاصة جدا ... العينان تتفحصان كل ما يحيط بها من ألوان زاهية ، مثيرة ، تخطف البصر . الطفلة تتململ في مجلسها ، وتحاول أن تتخذ وضعا جديدا ، يسمح لها برؤية أكبر مدموعة من الاشياء المعروضة في الغرفة .

آه كم تستهوينى هذه الكرات البلورية المعلقة على أطراف الروشنة [51] ... لقد كسرت البارحة اثنتين منها ، وكان من نصيبى الضرب ، والشتم ، وحرمت من ثوب جديد ألبسه في حفلة زفاف اختى فاطمة لم يبق لى سوى هذه الخلاخل العزيزة ، ان لها رنينا يذكرنى برنين الجرس المعلق فى رقبة حمار بائع الماء . فكل صباح عندما أستيقظ من نومي ، وأسمع كلمة شوط [52] ... شوط ورنين جرس الحمار . أهرع الى صندوقى الخشبى لاخرج منه خلخالى وأضعهما حول ساقى النحيلتين .

منذ أيام وهناك أشياء غريبة تحدث فى دارنا ... الكل يتحدث هامسا ... غرباء يأتون وغرباء يخرجون .. الصناديق الكبيرة احتلت دارنا ... والدتى تفتحها بين الحين والاخر لتخرج منها أشياء ملونة جميلة وأنا كالبلهاء كلما حاولت أن أفهم ما يدور حولى ، يصرخون فى وجهى قائلين : أنت ما زلت صغيرة وهذه أمور تخص الكبار ... أنا صغيرة ... أنا على أبواب الحادية عشرة صغيرة ... لقد تزوجت والدتى وهى في الحادية عشرة وأنجبت أخى صالحا وهى فى الثالثة عشرة ... لست أدرى لما لم أتزوج حتى الان ...

ان زواج أختى فاطمة هو الذى أحدث انقلابا فى البيت ، عرفت ذلك بالامس عندما كنت أسترق السمع من خلف الباب . سمعت والدتى تحدث جارتنا قائلة : ان ابنتى محظوظة فالخاطبة تقول بأن العريس ثرى وجميل كالقمر — تنبهت فاطمة لوجودى ... ألقت بالمشط جانبا ثم استدارت ناحيتى بوجه بللته الدموع ... تبكى اختى ، تبكى والليلة عرسها ، وعريسها كالقمر !؟

لم البكاء يا أختى فالليلة فرحة العمر وغدا سيكون لك بيت وأطفال ، وخدم .. ستزين أصابعك الخواتم الذهبية ستعيشين كالاميرات ، بل احسن منهن ... فأنت حلوة حلاوة القمر . من قال بأني غير سعيدة ، ولكن صغيرتى هناك ، أمر أخافه . لقد قالت لى سبيكة بنت جارتنا أم محمد ، بأن عريسى جميل كالقمر ... والرجل الجميل سرعان ما يمل زوجته ويشرع فى البحث عن اخرى لا تخافى يأختى ... ان سبيكة غيورة ، فحظها عاثر ... هه المسكين لقد تعنست ، فهى على أبواب العشرين وفى هذه اللحظة دخلت الماشطة ، التى جاءت لتصلح من زينة أختى أما أنا فكان نصيبى الطرد لاننى لازلت أعتبر صغيرة . فى

---

51 الروشنة : تجويف فى الحائط بحجم النافذة يستخدم فى وضع ادوات الزينة عليه ، والتحف ، وهو اشبه برف صغير .

52 شوط : نداء يستخدمه بائع الماء .

المساء خلت بيوتات الحى من ساكنيها ليمتلىء منزلنا بالضيوف ... شعرت بأن جدار بيتنا الطينى سوف ينهار علينا ... اختلطت رائحة البخور برائحة العرق ، واصبح الامر اكثر ازعاجا عندما بدأت المغنيات بالغناء والعزف على دفوفهن ... الذى جعلنى أتحمل كل هذه الازعاجات هى كلمات الاطراء التى وصلت الى مسمعى ... ان وضحة قد كبرت لقد اصبحت عروسة ، انها تفوق فاطمة جمالا ... ان شاء الله نراك في العام المقبل عروسا ...

جاءت فاطمة محمولة على كرسى من الخشب ، مغطاة من رأسها حتى أخمص قدميها بوشاح أخضر ... ومن شدة الزحام لم أتبين وجهه ولكن بعد محاولات شاقة رأيته ... آه يافاطمة آه ياأختى السعيدة ، الخائفة على عريسك الجميل ، ذى الوجه المتغضن كقشرة البطاطة ، المحاط بشعر أسود لم تجف بعد أصباغه .

سليمان الخليفي ـ الكويت

زواج

دخل محسن إلى بيت عمه ليفاجأ بالنسوة يتحركن بإيقاع المناسبات . وكان الوقت عصراً متلألئاً ثرياً بالنور ، إذن فقد التحقت هذه الفتاة بعضوية الأسرة مؤخراً . وانفلتت سلوى تحدثه عنها ... ذكية ... لطيفة ... جميلة ... وتجيد بعض الكلمات الكويتية أحياناً .

وزوجة عمي ؟ كنت أنا الذي أقترح على عَمي مازحا فكرة الزواج من هناك . فرويت له أن رجلاً طاعناً بالسن وثرياً قد لاقى الترحيب وتزوج فتاة جميلة . لم أكن دقيقاً في روايتي . فقد كنت ذلك الرجل ، عدا أنني شاب وليس لدي المال ... ولم ألاق أي ترحيب . وحين قدمتني عَمتي إلى نجيبة قالت محسن ـ وهو الذيّ لم يتزوج ـ لأفاجأ بطريقة التعريف ... ترى كان ذلك رغبة منها ؟ أم إنه المال فعل فعله ... إنها والحق يقال فرص ... فلم يكن عمي على ذلك القدر من الذكاء . ومع ذلك استطاع عبر تقلبه بين زحمة العمل ... في دور الحكومة والعمل الحَر أن يكون ثروة . أجل سيدي ... أفمن الحري بعد ذلك برجل كعمي أن يصدم ، في ذوقة على الاقل ، بالتقليد الذي ساهمت فيه يداه الكريمتان ؟ بل إنه يستطيع وهو يتعامل مع الغاية الآنية أن لا يضطر إلى النظر في جوانبها الأخلاقية الأخرى . لكنه ظل محافظاً على تديّنه ... وذهب عام 1963 إلى الحج وتزوج من هناك . أتراها عرفتني ؟ لكن أن تتزوج من عمي ؟ فليكن ... وتبدو أنحا تحتفل بوقتها كأي عروس تزوجت بطريقة طبيعية . فكيف سلوكها حين يخلو إليها الزوج ؟ ليس مهما أن يبرر الشيطان وجوده بينهما كثالث ، ففي الطريق قبل ذلك ... يحدث أن تلتقي العين بأخرى فيحتد الوعي ، المدارى بالأنا والأنت وخصوصا بالأنت ، وهي تشاكل البلح المسلوق . لكنه لم يستطع وهو يحتقر عمه حتى الحقد إلا أن يراه ... ليس حَراً من القلق . ولكن هل يمكن أن يعني هذا الزواج ، من وجهة نظرها الخاصة أن البقر تتشابه عليها على أية حال ؟ . وأنه عملية تجاوز لأي انطباع غير موهوب عن السلوك الانساني ؟ وبأنها بهذا الزواج تلغي ... حتى ثقتها بقدرتها على التفكير بنفس القدر الفلسفي لمعنى معاناتها ... لمعنى كونها عرضة في كل لحظة لوطء هذه المشاهدة المرهقة لكل تلك المسارات والنسب المذهلة التي في تصوير جسدها ... وهذه الثواني والشهور بنفس الظلال والأصوات وصرير السرير دائماً وعلى ذات الطريقة وشظف العيش .

فأصبحت نجيبة تلبس كثيراً وتضحك كثيراً ... سوى أن محسن وحتى نهاية العام ما كان ليعزو أسباب ضيقه بالمكان حين يكون في بيت عمه إلى ذلك الشعور المتخفي بتوقعاته الغائمة والتي تتحول على رسيمة العلاقة بينه ونجيبة إلى زخم من القلق ... فضلا عما حل في روعه من شعور بأنها تتحفظ كثيراً حينما تكون في حضرته مما جعله يذهب إليهم في القليل النادر إلى أن قالت له ذات مرة ... بنبرة خاصة ... ما تنشاف ؟ فسقط صاحبنا في شعور من السعادة والثقة بالنفس ... وبمرور الأيام حدث لعلاقتهما أن اتخذت شكلاً لها أكثر تحديدا فقرآ وتحدثا وربما افتعلا الشجار أحياناً ، ليمر عام 1964 على هذه الشاكلة تقريباً حتى يوم سفرها فعودتها من السفر ليعرفا معنى أن يرى أحدهما الآخر وهو معنى لا طب فيه .

كان الوقت عصراً .. وقد جلسنا على حافة المدة الجديدة في الليوان ، يتوسطنا الابريق وكنت أقول لها إنها لطيفة . وهو اصطلاح يعني جدّ جميلة ، وتكررت الاصطلاحات بمعان مختلفة حتى غرست اظفرها الطويل بظاهر يدي ... فأردت أن أمعن في إغاظتها ... ولما كنا في حديث الانطباعات ، فقد رحت أصورها بالشكل المناسب كيما تبدو في منتهى الجمال ولكن كطفلة ... وبدون أن أدري وصفت رؤيتى لها ولأول مرة ... قلت إنها يجب أن تمشي في شارع يعطي انطباعاً غير مألوف ... بخلفية قاتمة تميل إلى الرمادى المزرقّ ... كالجبال ، في مدينة مملوءة بالشمس ... وتمشي بلا احتراس الأنوثة ، بركبتين يتردد عليهما ذيل أبيض ... نشط وبلا انتظام . والمجموعة من الاشكال الزهرية بالازرق والبرتقالي تنتثر

على فستانك ... وغديرة سوداء يعبث في مكانها كونك تهرولين وعيناك .. و ... وبهتت وتنبهت أنا على تفكيرها بفستانها وبأني تكشفت عن أخبار جديدة ،، فلم أتمالك لحظة الارتباك . كانت تتصور وبسرعة أشياء حدثت ... وقلت : لا يمكن أن يكون لديك فستان ... وخطر لي أنها ارتعشت ... لكنها استعادت أطرافاً ممزقة مما دار بين أهلها عن شيء ما يخصها ... شاب ... موافقة ... في السوق . فاستطاعت أن تربط بين هذه الأطراف وحكاية الفستان عبر 24 ساعة سبقت ذلك ... وبالذات في السوق وبي شخصياً ... مما دفع بي إلى قمة غيظي .

قالت : ولكنك ... فما شعرت أنني بحاجة إلى الصدق أكثر من تلك اللحظة في حياتي ، وأي شيء يمكن أن تقوله لا كما تشعر به سيكون باهظ التكلفة حتماً ... لكنني شعرت بعباراتها تتخذ مجرى آخر حينما قالت : وطيلة هذه المدة ... فتوقفت وكان المحظور . إذن فأنا وطيلة هذه المدة أغامر على حساب الانتقام من عمي ولست ما كنته بنظرها ... سوى أن ما بها من انفعال سبب اللاتسلسل في عباراتها فجعلها مبتورة ومختلفة كأصوات الغريق في لحظات الظهور على الموج . سمعت هل يكونون ؟ . ولم تكن لتتحدث إلي . لكنها تلفظها هذه المرة بنغمة أطول من تلك الخاصة بالتساؤل . تتعين في لخظة انتباه وإدراك قاسيين . لكنني لم أفهم الكلمة إلى أقصاها ... فقط حس العتاب الذي بدا موجهاً بحدة إلى أهلها وإن كان في الواقع عتاباً أخذ في كليته لون الشتيمة . لهذا اعتقدت بأنها تعطف عليّ في هذه اللحظة . وإذ كنت أتقبل أى شيء فيما عدا العطف ، فقد أحسست أنني وبعملية غبية قد انتهيت إلى حال ليست بمثل ما لدي من فكرة عن نفسي ... حيث أنني وخلال هذه الشهور تشبعت بيقين كملمس الحد القاطع بقيمة علاقتي بنجيبة والتي تتلمذنا على طريقتها في النمو فأحببناها والتي تحاصرني بكل ما يحيط بي وبالكلمات فتتسرب إلى الطعم الذي أذوق وهي أن تصبح على إيلامها خلف ذلك الوضوح والهدوء فيما أفكر وأشعر به هي خلف ما يشذ عنها باستمرار من حس شفيف غامض ... وتقول لي نجيبة أحياناً وهو : كذلك الشيء العجيب ، المتفايض على حافة العبارة تحس به كجرح في قلب الحنين للحياة وأنت ضالع فيها ... فإذا كان هذا الجرح هو النتاج الضروري لمحاولة الابقاء من جانبنا على ما هو غير مكشوف من رغباتنا واحتياجاتنا ، فإن أي محاولة لتحاشي موقف الاختيار ستكون ليست ساذجة فحسب ، بل وأهم من ذلك أنها غير ممكنة ، إذ ليس بميسور الانسان أن يوقف الزمن وأن كان بمقدوره أن ينتحر . فإما أن يظل هذا الجانب من الحاجة والرغبة على ما هو عليه وبهذا الأسلوب الإرادى وإما أن تبلغ بالمطاف نهايته . أما ذلك الفاصل التمثيلي السخيف ... فلا يدل إلا على الشعور والنقص من أمام عمي ، إذ أن الافتقار ألى المادة واستخفافهم بشبابي ، كانا جزءاً واضحاً من معارفي ووسيلة أعتمد عليها في طريقتي في التعبير والحركة . أما أن التفت لأجدهما في أعماق نفسي يستعديانها عليّ ، فلقد أصبحت إذن هدفهم الذي أجادوا إصابته . وإما أنه يعني أن ما تحفظه لي نجيبة من إعجاب غير كاف على تلك الشاكلة ... فلا يلبث هذا الحس الصغير وغير المحترم الذي أرثه عن طبقتي أن يستغل فيّ هذه الوقفات العفوية في خط سلوكي المتواصل من الوعي فيدفعني دفعاً حاسماً إلى استجداء العطف على نفسي . ثم سمعت نجيبة تسأل من جديد عما إذا كنت في البلد عندنا ... كنت مهيأ عندئذ لهذا الشعور العدائي تجاه الجميع . لكنه تترجم على صورة لا مبالاة بليدة . لم يكن ليعنيني التفكير بإمكانية أنها تتألم ... بل لعلني قد حقدت عليها في تلك اللحظة ... خصوصاً انني كففت منذ مدة عن السؤال ، لمَ قبلت الزواج من هذا الشايب ؟ وسمعنا أحد الأبواب يصطفق بقوة ... فقررت على طريقة مذيعي الأخبار أنني كنت هناك ...رأيتها ، وخطبتها ورفضوني ، فقط لا غير . ولم أكن لأتصور ، حينئذ ، وقد وضعت يدها على الأرض ، أن أرى في وجه أي إنسان الصورة المماثلة لعملية الغثيان التي تحدث في داخل الجسد . وسمعنا صرخة ، بعد أن سقط عمي على الأرض المبتلة عند ظهوره من الحمّام ... وشج جبينه ... سبقتها إلى هناك ... وعند توسطي في باب الحجرة إلى الخارج ، كانت تقف هناك تتطلع إلينا ، فلاحظت أثر الصابون الذى أكسب بشرة عمني مرأى كالحاً ... وشعرت فجأة وأنا أحمل هذا الكم من العظام المجلدة ... وهو الرمز الضئيل جدا واللاعقلاني حتى لذلك المبلغ من مئات

الآلاف من الدنانير . ونظرات نجيبة ما زالت بلا معنى ... إنه يمكنني أن ألقي به وبأي شكل كان . كان عمي تعباً جداً ، فلم يستقر في فراشه حتى ذهب في نوم عميف ، وكانت الضمادات تطوق رأسه ومرفقه .

وجاء الشتاء ، وأوشك آذار على الانتصاف ... وأصبح محسن ذات يوم على غيوم خفيفة في السماء ثم انصفت إلى جانبها غيوم أخرى أكثف فأكثف وأخذت زرقة السماء تتناهى والريح تنشط ، وأصبح الصبح لوناً معتماً ، معتماً يوشك على الاغتسال بالمطر ... لم يكن هناك سوى بعض أصوات شرسة لقطط تركض في حوش المطبخ على بعضها البعض وكانت أيضاً نجيبة ... تقف إلى عمود الليوان ... إن الذي يلاحظها هذه الأيام يجد أنها شغلت عن نفسها ، وأن شيئاً ما في وجه نجيبة ... يبدو للوهلة الأولى على أنه ابتسامة ، بينما هو في الحقيقة نوع من الحالة الداخلية لشعور بالتعب من كون القاسم المشترك الأعظم بين محسن وزوجها واحداً تقريباً . أرعدت السماء وشيئاً فشيئاً بدأت الدنيا تبرد ... أما الذي تفكر به فهو الشعور تجاه محسن وكيف أنه يصبح آخر بعد كل تجربة ، وعلى عكس ما تشعر به نحو زوجها خصوصا بعد أن تعرفت على قدراته الزوجية ... مما وفر عليها الشعور بالذنب للمتعة المتصاعدة في نزعتها إلى محسن ... ولكنها لم تتوقع أن تقول له ذلك في يوم من الأيام ... على أنه وذات مرة قبلها بغتة ، فغضبت جدا لكنه لم يكررها أو حتى يعتذر ... وذلك ما وضعها في جحيم من القلق ، بينما استمر يشاكسها عن طريق تلك اللغة المعروفة وكان فيها بعض من التعويض ... كانت حينما يدخل عليهم محسن البيت تفتح عينيها كاليدين مرحبة وتنتصب وهي تثني رجليها من تحتها وكأنها طيلة الوقت تريد أن تنهض ... لكن السماء أرعدت أيضاً ولم تمطر ... حتى كانت حكاية الفستان .. فأرادت أن تلطمه أو يلطمها ، لكن شيئاً من ذلك لم يحدث ... لقد تغير الاثنان في ذلك اليوم . كان زوجها كالجرو الصغير بين يدي بغل كبير ... ولما شعرت برغبة في البكاء ذهبت إلى غرفتها ولم تستطع ، ولم تشعر بألم وقد حطت نفسها بقوة على السرير . كانت تريد أن تشرب الشاى من كأس مثلومة أو تجرح شفتيها أو تحس بالحزام يحزّ خصرها ... كانت تريد للفستان أن يهصرها حتى يتمزق ، أو أن تنشب غديرتها في أكرة الباب فترتد بقوة إلى الوراء ... والعقد يلتف على جيدها يضرب صدرها ... وهي لا تدرك لماذا تتساقط الأشياء هناك في المطبخ وأصوات القطط . لقد تملكها الشعور العظيم بأنها تصرفت بغباء ... فهل من اليسر أن تدرك الآن لماذا استطاع محسن أن يحتل هذا القدر من الحب . لقد هبت ريح قوية ودارت في الحوش كدورة الخائفين من العذاب ، وأظلمت الدنيا أيضاً ... ولأول مرة شعرت أنها لا تستطيع أن تقاوم البرد ، لكنها ظلت في مكانها حينما طيّر الهواء تنورتها فأعادتها بين الركبتين وسقطت نعالها والتقطتها حين رأت إلى جانبها أقدام بشر ... وتابعت المنظر إلى أعلى فرأت محسن وهو يباعد بين جديلتها ووجهه ... لكنه ما كان في الامكان سماع أي شيء تحت قصف ذلك الرعد الشديد ... ولما تواريا وتعذّرت رؤيتهما خلف انغلاقة الباب ... تسرب إلى سمع "بو يوسف" ، وكان في حجرته ... هطول المطر .

ليلى العثمان ــ الكويت

زهرة تدخل الحيّ

دخلت زهرة الحيّ ذات ليلة لا أحد يعرف من هى ! ولا كيف جاءت ! ولماذا جاءت : ومن الذى أستأجر لها البيت الذى تطل شبابيكه على البحر . رغم هذا ، فُتحَ للبيت باب آخر من ناحية البحر . كانت زهرة تشرعه في الليل . تجلس عند بابه . وتسهر . قال جيرانها إن زهرة تعشق البحر . تناجيه مناجاة الخليل للخليل ، تبثة أشواقاً دافئة . تغنى له . يسمعون لها صوتاً حنوناً ، أو صفيرًا ناعمًا ذا موجات كأنها لغة عصافير ضالة .

زهرة امرأة ناضجة فوق الثلاثين . جميلة لها وجه أبيض صاف . مستدير وخدان متوردان يكاد ينفر دمهما . وعينان سوداوان واستعتان يحرسهما حاجبان رقيقان أشبه بسيفين حادين . أما شعرها فينسدل شلّالاً كستنائياً يغطى أطراف كتفيها البضين . وحين تبتسم زهرة تنفرج شفتاها عن صفين من اللؤلؤ الصافي . ويبرز في أقصى فمها طرف سنة ذهبية سرعان ما يختفى حين تغلق الشفتين المكتنزتين .

زهرة جميلة . والحيّ هادئ وديع . بيوته الطينية لا تحمل صدى لأحقاد الناسُ في الحيّ متآلفون . حتى الحمائم على الأسطح تعرف أوكارها . ولا تتوه . ولا تتغرب . وحين دخلت زهرة الحيّ . هلعت قلوب ألنسوة الآمنات . لعب الشك في قلوبهن . ابتدأت السؤالات : هل هى متزوجة ؟؟

إذن ! لماذا تسكن وحدها ؟؟

هل هى أرملة أو مطلقة ؟؟

الخوف يزداد : أم تراها عذراء ستحافظ على نفسها وشبابها ؟

حين عبثت الشكوك والمخاوف في القلوب . لم تعرف النسوة طريقاً لراحتهن إلا بيت " أم محمد " وقلب أم محمد الذى اعتاد أن يحضن هموم الحيّ . ويواسى كل مفجوع . ويبارك لكل فرح . يزغرد لسانه وترقص شفتاه ، قلب أم محمد الذى لا يفرّق ، ولا يعرف الكره أو الحسد .

قالوا لها :

ــ يا أم محمد . زهرة فاتنة بابها مشرع للريح زهرة تحب هواء البحر وأزواجنا فيه يعملون . ونحن نخشى عليهم من الفتنة .

بان الضيق والأسف على وجه العجوز الطيب وعاتبت :

ــ تخافون على أزواجكم . ولا تخافون على بحركم .

ــ البحر للجميع يا أم محمد . زهرة تعشق البحر .

لمعت دمعة في عين أم محمد . طاف حزن كأنه آت من البعيد :

ــ هل تحب زهرة البحر أكثر منا ؟؟ هل تعشق رمله ؟ وريحه ؟؟ وموجه أكثر مما عشقناها ؟؟ هذا البحر بحرنا . هو ذا أمامكم . اسألوه : من عشقه . كم قلباً نهش . وكم قلباً أسعد ! كم أخذ منا ؟؟ وكم أعطانا ؟ عظامُ رجالنا صارت له مجاديف . وأعناقهم صوارى . بحرنا لا أحد يعشقه سوانا . أنتم لاتتأملون .

تململت النسوة . قالت إحداهن :

ــ يا أم محمد جئنا نأخذ منك المشورة . ماذا نفعل مع زهرة ؟ كيف نحمى رجالنا ؟ وأنت هداك الله تتكلمين عن البحر . وكأنك تخشين أن تسرقه زهرة وتترك الرجال .

هزت أم محمد رأسها :

– هذا ما يتأجج في قلبى لكنكم لا تعلمون . اذهبوا إذن إلى زهرة . جُسّوا نبضها . افهموا منها ماذا تريد . ولماذا جاءت ! وتفكَّروا في كل ما تقول .

***

رحبت زهرة بالنسوة ترحيباً فاجأهن . قبّلت كل واحدة منهن وكأنها تعرفها من زمن بعيد . سألت كل واحدة عن أحوالها . تلك عن زوجها المريض . وتلك عن ابنتها التى تعثَّر حظها . وسألت أخرى عن كنّتها التى لا تحبل . وقررت أن تصف لها علاجاً فرفرف الفرح على وجه المرأة . سألت عن "أبو يوسف" النّجار الذى بترت يده وقبع في البيت وعن " شيخوه "(53) التى تبيح نفسها للرجال . وأكدت أن الشرف والفضيلة فوق كل شيء . آخر ماسألت عنه زهرة . وبحرص شديد . سألت عن – أم محمد – وهل مازالوا يلتفون حولها . وتصير شرايين قلبها أذرعاً تضم الجميع ؟ هل مايزالوا يحبونها وبؤمون دارها عند الشدائد والأفراح ؟ فوجئت النسوة بأن زهرة تعرف الشيء الكثير عن الحى ، وأهله .

بادرتها إحداهن :

– إذن هذا سبب اختيارك لحينا . سمعت عن ناسه الطيبين .

رفعت زهرة حاجباً . وبكل الثّقة قالت :

– في كل مكان يوجد أناس طيبون . ليس هذا مقصَدى . سمعت أن الحياة هنا أرحب . جئت أبحث عن وضع أفضل .

قالت أخرى :

أو ربما لأجل البحر .

أو مأت زهرة بكفها :

– بالضبط . هواء بحركم يناسبنى .

– لكنّ الرطوبة عندنا شديدة . تتعب الصدر . وأنت تتركين الباب مشرعاً للريح طوال الليل . ألا تخشين من اللصوص أو الكلاب السائبة ؟؟

ضحكت زهرة باستخفاف :

– لصوص !! كلاب ! أنا لا أخاف . إذا جاء اللص أعرف كيف أتعامل معه . أما الكلاب ! فلها علاج آخر .

– يا زهرة . جئت وحيدة وما تزالين .

فهمت زهرة صيغة السؤال . ابتسمت :

– تركت زوجى .. وأولادى هناك ربما يأتون .

ارتطم الخوف بقلوب النسوة . إذن . لها زوج بعيد وهى جميلة . وأزواجهن لهم عيون فتانة وأيضًا لهم طباع النمل الذى يمشى إلى "رائحة الدسم" .

وزهرة ! يالها من امرأة !

أحست بما فى العيون من رعدات ، فتوذّدت :

---

53 شيخوه : اسم علم لامرأة . وأصله "شيخه"

- أنا لا أحب الخروج . ولا الأسواق . ولا زحام الناس . أفضل أن أبقى هنا . ولكن !!

صمتت . لاح حزن على وجهها . تعاطفت بعض النسوة معها :

- لو بقيت هكذا ستشعرين بالوحدة . أنت غريبة . وصرت جارة نحن مستعدات لكل ما تطلبين . والآ من أين ستعيشين ؟؟

تناغم الحزن فى صوت زهرة :

- هذا ما أفكر فيه . زوجى يتأخر حتى يرسل المال . لهذا أنا بحاجة للعمل . تبادلت النساء النظرات وثارت السؤالات :

- ماذا بإمكانك أن تعملى ؟

- وأى عمل ستقوم به امرأه جميلة مثلك ؟؟

كان فى السؤالات كثير من الفضول . والقلق . والتشوق لمعرفة الجواب .
قالت زهرة :

- أنا أتقن أعمالاً كثيرة . التطريز . الخياطة . عمل الحلوى وبعض الفطائر التى لا أظن أن حيكم يعرفها . وأيضًا أتقن كل ما يهمكن كنساء من أعمال الزينة . "والحفافة" [54] ثم أنا امرأة أتقن لغة جديدة . قد أستطيع تعليمها لمن ترغب .

- ترغبين إذن فى العمل بين البيوت ؟

- هذا ما أريد . أحتاج إلى المال كى أعيش . المال الحلال . وشددت على كلمتها الأخيرة لتبذر الأمان فى قلوب النساء . وتنهدن جميعاً ماسحات على صدورهن :

"المرأة شريفة .. تريد العمل الحلال"

***

عدّلت أم محمد من وضع "ملفعها" [55] الأسود الذى تفوح منه رائحة دهن العود . ومسحت على وجهها .
قالت :

- انتبهن يا نساء يا طيبات الحى .. أيتها العيون التى لا ترى إلاّ الخير . الفتنة تدخل بيوتكن .

***

زهرة دخلت كل البيوت . زهرة الجميلة . أصبحت حديث الحى . سموها "هبّة الريح" لسرعة حركتها وإتقانها كل عمل تنجزه . ارتدت نساء الحى أجمل الثياب . وتزينت "المطارح والمساند" بالتطاريز . وبالترتر الملون . تجملت وجوه النساء بأصباغ . وتفننت زهرة فى تجديل شعورهن الطويلة . صارت كل البيوت تحب زهرة تطلبها وتكرمها . فكل النساء راضيات . زهرة ذكية . تحرص على ألا تحتك بأى رجل . لا من الأزواج . ولا من الأبناء . إذا دخل واحد منهم فجأة دون أن يتنحنح أو يطلب "درباً" تثور زهرة يحتقن وجهها وتسب بكلمات غير مفهومة . تنتصر النساء لها يؤنبن الذى فعل . لا يُرِدْنَ أن تغضب زهرة . وتعاف بيتاً من البيوت . لكن حلم زهرة ظل أن ترى أم محمد .

---

54 الحفافة : إزالة شعر الوجه والحاجبين .
55 ملفعها : غطاء الرأس لكبار السن من النساء ولونه أسود .

سألت إحدى النساء :

- ألا تريد أم محمد أن أخيط لها ثوباً ؟؟

قالت المرأة :

- أم محمد حريصة على ثيابها القديمة لا تستبدلها . ولا تفرط فيها .
- ألا أصنع لها مساند ؟؟ فطائر ؟؟
- مساندها" السدو " (56) أغلى عليها من كل شيء وهى لا تحب الفطائر . تصنع بنفسها "قرص العقيلى" .

ذاب حلم زهرة صارت كل البيوت بيتها . إلا بيت أم محمد . ظل موصداً .

ولم تثر زهرة أية مشكلة فى أى بيت . صارت محبوبة . كوّنت الصداقات . أصبحت الغريبة واحدة من أهل الحى . ونسى الناس الطيبون تساؤلاتهم ، نسى الناس بيت أم محمد . تحدّثوا عن زهرة . صارت هذه الزهرة كالبيت لهم . داخل أوراقها يستريحون . ومن شذاها يتنفسون ومن بريقها يستمدون كل جديد . وحدها أم محمد تمسح كفاً بكف . ترى .. وتصمت .. وتردد :

"لا حول ولا قوّة إلآ بالله . "

***

حين تُطفأ الأنوار . ويغلق الليل عيونه . تشرعُ زهرة الباب . فيأنى هواء البحر منعشا . تحمل رائحته عطراً خاصاً تُلوّح زهرة بيديها الجميلتين . وحدها ساهرة عند الباب .. الناس نيام .. وعيون أم محمد فى الفراش لا تنام .

***

ذلك النهار . لقى الناس فى بيت زهرة صبية جميلة . سألوها فقالت :

- هى أختى .

رحّبوا بها . غريبة جديدة . هى أخت زهرة المحبوبة . والحى الطيب يحب الضيوف . ويكرمهم . بعد أسابيع جاءت غريبة أخرى . استأجرت لها زهرة بيتاً على البحر .

- من هذه يا زهرة ؟؟
- هى ابنة عمى . مات عائلها . جاءت تبحث عن عمل .

وحين دخل البيت شاب جميل . يقف الصقر على زنديه قالت زهرة :

- لا تنزعجوا . إنه زوج أختى . يتقن أعمالاً كثيرة ولكن !

واهتزت قلوب النساء :

- ماذا يا زهرة ؟؟
- يريد بيتاً قريباً منى . ولا أجد .

---

56 السّدو : أعمال اليد البدوية .

لم يدم حزن زهرة أكثر من أسبوع . كان صاحب أحد البيوت يترك بيته ويؤجره .

كثر أقارب زهرة . يأتون . لا أحد يتساءل كيف يأتون . وأى ريح تحملهم . الحى غارق فى طيبته . وفى الترحاب . اليدُ الآتيةُ "تسد العين" تعمل . تنتج . وتبدع . لا تكل ولا تتذمر . لا تكره أن تُؤمر فتطيع . الكل يشكر زهرة التى تكرمت على الحى . فيكرمونها .. أى بيت تختاره زهره يفرغونه . للأنساب . ثم دفعت زهرة مبلغاً كبيراً واشترت البيت . وحذا حذوها كثير من الأقرباء . امتدت بيوتهم على طول الساحل . ولكل "بيت باب بشرع . لأن هواء البحر الذى يناسب زهرة يناسب كل الأقرباء والقريبات . الذين صاروا من أهل الحى . من صلب الحى . وأحبهم كل الحى .

وحدها أم محمد . تضرب كفاً بكف . ويبرعم الخوف فى صدرها تتنهّد :

"لا حول ولا قوة إلاّ بالله . لقد باعوا البيوت".

استيقظ الحى ذات يوم على صدى النواح . كانت النساء الغريبات متشحات بالسواد . سيولاً .. تصب فى بيت زهرة . تساءل الحى ما الخبر ؟؟

جاء الجواب :

– مات لزهرة عزيز

وفى بيت زهرة ولولت النسوة وضربن على صدورهن وخارج بيتها سكن الرجال . وبكوا .

عشرة أيام متتالية والحزن الأسود يعرّش على الحى . حزن له لون خاص . وعطر خاص . تعطل الحى . وقبعت نساؤه فى البيوت فكّرْنَ أن يذهبن لبيت أم محمد استقبلتهن وفى الخاطر عتاب :

– طالت غيبتكن .

– شغلتنا الحياة يا أم محمد .

– بل شغلتكن زهرة .

– نحن نحبك يا أم محمد . ولا نستغنى عنك . ولا عن مشورتك .

– ما الذى يقلقكم ؟

– الحى معطل . الرجال الغرباء على الساحل يبكون ، والنساء فى بيت زهرة يُولولن . لا نعرف معنى لهذا الحزن يا أم محمد .

– لتعرفوا أن لكل حزنه . أحزاننا غير أحزانهم . هذا العزيز الذى مات سيحزنون عليه كل مرة كل عشرة أيام . ونحن ندفن موتانا . نؤمنهم الله . ونترحم عليهم ونكره الحزن . والسواد .

– كل البيوت سوداء يا أم محمد .

– كانت بيوتكم لكنكم بعتموها صارت الآن لهم لا يحق لكم الاعتراض على ألوانها .

وتنهدت أم محمد .

سمعت النسّاء تنهيدتها تشق صدرها . وتقر إليهن . همسات تخرج من أفواه النساء . فيها ندم .. وفيها خوف وفيها تردد فى السؤال :

– ماذا نفعل يا أم محمد ؟؟

ومن قلبها نبعت أذرع حنان . شبكت النساء إلى صدرها . قالت ولغتها أغنية تصدح :

– أنتم أبناء حيَّ . أهلى . وناسى . أعرفكم فكونوا حذرين . اغلقوا البيوت دون كل غريب . واحضنوا البحر الذى من مائه تشربون .

بكت النساء

بكت أم محمد .

اختلط ملح الدموع . صار حبة لؤلؤ تُذكّر بوجه ذلك البحّار القديم الذى صنع السفينة .

***

منذ دخلت زهرة الحى . وعيون أم محمد ساهرة قلقة لكنها الليلة غير كل الليالى . لقد جاءتها نساء الحى . وقد بدأت عصافير الخوف تبنى أعشاشها فى قلوبهن ، وقلوب رجالهن . جئن يفتحن القلب ، والجرح . فتسيل الأحزان وتفتق القلق . أكثر فى عينى أم محمد .

هم ناسى .. وأهل حيى . هم أولادى . يأسفون بعد الخطأ يطلبون مشورتى .. وآه ......
صفقت كفاً بكف :

ما باليد حيلة ياعيالى .

حملها الأرق إلى البحر . هجعت على رملة . خلعت ملفعها وانسدلت ضفائرها الشائبة حبلاً حنونا يَوَدُ لو يضم الشاطئ كله إليه .

امتد بصرها الضعيف إلى البعيد . تذكرت زمنها الراحل . والدها الذى كان يأتى بعد سفر طويل يحمل رائحة البحر ضاحكاً لنصر .. أو عابساً لفشل .

وزوجها الذى تبع أياها وركب البحر . عشقاً ينتقل بالدم . تحس هواه يسرى مع النسمة داخلها . تتنشق روائح " الغاصة " (57) . وتسمع صدى زغريد النسوة وفرحة العودة . المركب البيضاء تلوح أشرعتها وترقص . من هنا كانت تجيء لا من هناك .. والبحر واسع يتلألأ تحت شعاع القمر وعينا أم محمد تعانقانه . وتنزرعان فيه كأنها تصل إلى العمق . لونه تحت الضوء الحانى صافياً .. وهى تتابع موجه تتابعه .. تتابعه .. و .. ماذا هناك ؟

عيناها تصطدمان بأشياء تتحرك .

استقامت أم محمد . لملمت جدائلها الشائبة وغرست النظرة الضعيفة صارت نظرة صقر . مراكب تدنو . ولا تصل ، هى تراها تنزف خيالات متحركة . تتدلق فى الماء . يتطاير الرذاذ . أسماك تلك أم حوريات ! أم تراها شياطين ؟ خفق قلبها . وانهار جسدها الطيب إلى الرمل ثانية . توسدت ذراعها . قالت :

ـ لن أتحرك سأرى ما الذى يجرى فى البحر . أى ريح تأتى وأى شيء تنزفه ؟

الخيالات تتحرك هارعة إلى الشاطئ . ثم خطوطا خطوطاً .. إلى الأبواب المشرعة .

قناديل حمراء تتدلى تعابثها الريح الخفيفة وحين تدلف الخيالات تطفأ القناديل . وتغلق الأبواب .

***

فى الصباح .. وجد الناس باب بيت ام محمد مشرعاً . انهمروا إليه . هم يعرفون أن أم محمد لا تشرع بابها إلآ إذا كان لديها أمر تود الإفصاح عنه .

أعلنت أم محمد عن كل مارأته . وأنبلجت العيون خائفة غير مصدقة . لكن الناس ما اعتادوا منها الكذب . ولا الخداع . هى أمهم الكبيرة . وهى القلب الأليف الذى إليه يهجعون .

كل الآذان أُشرِعَتْ للخبر الكبير . حتى آذان زهرة . والأقرباء .. ثارت .. ثاروا .. صرخت فى الناس :

ـ أم محمد خرّفت .. مجنونة .. تحلم ..

____

57 الغاصة : الغواصين .

160

وصرخت مرة أخرى :

- إنها تتبلّى علىّ وعلى ناسى .

صَدَّ عنها الناس ، حملت جسدها الرائع وثورتها وذهبت إلى بيت أم محمد تبعها الأقرباء الكثيرون ملأوا الشوارع بالهياج .. وبالصياح .

وقعت عينا زهرة على بيت أم محمد .

هى المرة الأولى !

خرجت أم محمد هادئة . واثقة . مبتسمة . شعاع منير ينبع من كل الوجه الذى اعتاد الطيبة . وعاش فى سلام . رفعت ذراعها لتوقف السيل . فتدلى كُمّ ثوبها المشغول " بالزّرى " (58) التمعت عليه أشعة الشمس أثار وهجاً نقاطاً ذهبية شعت فى المكان . وعلى الوجوه الحاقدة كسرت الأشعة العيون . لكنها لم تكسر اللسان . صرخت زهرة فى وجه العجوز بكلمات فاسقة . فوجىء أهل الحى . كأن الصرخة لطمت كل الوجوه ، تجمعوا حول أم محمد . حول جدران البيت الطينى التصقوا يحمونه . وبعضهم وقف سدًّا .

كانوا قلة كانت زهرة والغرباء أكثر . لكنهم وقفوا ، هيأوا الأذرع لتدافع عن أمهم .. وجدار البيت .

شتمت زهرة . عيرت أم محمد بعجزها . عيرت أهل الحى الذين استكانوا وتعالوا .. عيرتهم بسواعد الأقرباء التى تعمل .. عيّرتهم بكل جديد جاءت به إليهم . عيّرتهم بأنها بأموالها غيّرت .. وبدلت فى الحى . وفى البيوت .. لم تأت أم محمد بحركة .

لم تبك .

لم تلطم خديها .

لم ترد على السباب ... ولا التجريح . كل ما يحدث أمامها .. وما يقال . كانت تعلم أنه سيحدث . لكنها لم تستطع أن تقنع الناس به .

النساء باهتة وجوههن ، والرجال كاظمين الغيظ ولكن ! حين صرخت زهرة مهددة :

- سأطردكم من هذا الحى .

اشتعلت الثورة فى النفوس . صرخوا بصوت واحد :

- سنطردك يازهرة .

هزت ضحكتها المكان .

تطلع الناس إلى وجه أم محمد الباكى بصمت .. تابعوا نظرتها الحزينة . كانت تعد البيوت الممتدة على الساحل .. وتابعت كل العيون .... كل البيوت .. كلها .. ليست لهم .... وهزّت أم محمد رأسها .

____

58 الزَّرى : خيوط القصب المذهبة التى تزين ملابس النساء .

ليلى محمد صالح – الكويت

جراح في العيون

وسط الاصوات والهمهمات

كان صامتا ينظر الى الثريا المدلاة من سقف الغرفة ، الثريا تفرش دائرة عريضة من الضوء على الجالسين بينما يموت النور في الاركان .

كانت اصواتهم وهمهماتهم تدور حول الرهائن وارتفاع الذهب ، وهبوط الاسهم وركود البورصة .. ثم تتحول الى ارقام يجمعونها ويطرحونها ..

همس في نفسه كيف يتظاهر الناس بالذكاء .. في اذنه تطايرت كلماتهم كالشظايا المتناثرة .. آراؤهم مختلفة ومع هذا فقد لاحت له جميعاً متساوية في الخواء .. انها تحمل زيفا من النوع الذي لا يعالج لأنه لا شعوري ..

بدأت امعاؤه تتقلص .. احس بأنه سوف يلفظ شيئاً ما في داخله ورغما عن انفه . ضاق بالاشياء وحديث الذهب والاسهم وحرب ايران والعراق .. سحب نفسا عميقا ثم تطلع الى ظلال الناس وهي تتحرك على الجدران ..

اغمض عينيه .. شعر برغبة عارمة في ان يتعرف على العالم بشكل اكثر صدقا من خلال قياس علمي دقيق .. امامه مرت ضاحكة فبانت اسنانها بيضاء مصفوفة بدقة ، تعكر وجهه .. فماتت الضحكة على شفتيها .. بللت شفتها السفلى وهي تحكها بصف اسنانها العلوي .. تذكر خصلة شعرها الرائعة وهي تتدلى فتحجب نصف عينها اليسرى ، انحسرت الآن داخل (اشارب) لا يفارق رأسها ابدا .

لم يعد يهمها كيف كان يغرم بشعرها الاسود الفاحم المنسكب وراء ظهرها .. لقد تناست اشواقها القديمة .. خطاباتها .. تعلقها الشديد .. وذهبت الى رجل اخر عاشت معه .. استيقظ الجوع عنده وعربد في ارجاء المعدة ..

ابتسم لجوعه ثم تمتم : ليت الماضي يضغط على الحاضر لتعود اصالة الانسان اليه .

***

في الطريق كان الصمت يعانق سواد الليل في هدأه مريبة ، رفع رأسه الى السماء الرمادية فأحس لأول مرة .. ان الجو بارد وليس معه (جاكيت) ، والجوع مازال يعربد .

واصل سيره الى مطاعم (شرق) ..

بدا الطريق امامه طويلا .. فراح يتذكر اخر مرة سار فيه ، لم يبقى شيء كما هو الا السماء والهواء فهما كما كان في الايام الخوالي حين كان طالبا في مدرسة الصباح يفيض قلبه بالاحلام العديدة .. الشارع يمتد في رحابه ، والبيوت تسبح في السكون والظلام ، حتى البنايات التي كان يعرفها بدت مكتئبة .. ساكنة .. لا ترغب مطلقا في مبادلته الود .

شعر بحزن داخلي .. الحزن يسير ببطء كلما تقدم في احياء (شرق) القديمة .. الحزن يتخلل خلايا جسده .. دمعت عيناه وهو يتذكر امه التي ماتت في بيتهم القديم وعينيه .. من يومها وهو يخاف من الفراق .. والغربة .. والوداع بالعين .. اقترب من المقبرة القديمة .. المقبرة مسكونة بالخوف .. والظلام يوحي له بمعنى الموت .. احس بالدماء تندفع حارة في عروقه حين رأي النجمة البراقة التي كان يتفاءل بها تتلألأ الآن في السماء السوداء ..

***

انثنى في عطفة جانبية ، ظله يمتد امامه طويلا عملاقا .. ومن بعيد لاحت له انوار مطعمه المفضل .

اقترب من المدخل محاولا ان يرى من بالداخل .. ولكن الدخان العابق والزجاج المشروخ حجبا عنه الرؤية ..

دفع الباب ودخل .. كل شيء على حاله كما تركه منذ سنين .. المقاعد .. صاحب المطعم .. اللوحات على الجدران .. واعلان باهت اللون لزيت (المازولا) ..

فقط تغيرت وجوه الزبائن فلم يتعرف على واحد منهم . جلس الى طاوله قرب الجدار الى جانب طاوله ثانية يشغلها خمسة شباب صمغ النيكوتين اصابعهم .

تناول الطعام بعجل .. ضايقه الدخان الكثيف العابق في المطعم .. فاثار سعاله العنيف ..

قذف نفسه الى الخارج وركب سيارته نحو البحر المتأجج الغاضب .. رأى الابراج تتطاول بعد ان انغرست قمتها المخروطية في بطن السحاب ، ايقن ان شوط النهاية قد بدأ وأن عليه قبل ان يصل الى القاعدة ان يركز جميع حواسه وخبرته .

***

في طريقه الى الاجتماع رأى بائع الجرائد الصغير يشق طريقه بين السيارات في قلق وتوتر رافعا صوته بنغمة متقطعة متكررة .. وعيناه مفتوحتان على الجمع الغفير وكأنهما مفتوحتان على صدر غيب مجهول لا يعرف طالعه ..

أبتسم بمرارة للعناوين الساخنة والى البائع الصغير الذي التمع وجهه بقطرات مطر لامسته برفق ..

- ضع شيئا على رأسك ألم يعطوك مظله وملابس للمطر ؟
- تنهد البائع وهو ضحك .. قل لهم .. قل لهم .. المطر يزداد والبائع يتنهد و يضحك ..

حينها ادرك معنى التنهيدات .. معنى ان يجد الانسان نفسه ازاء احساس لا يستطيع التعبير عنه سوى بالتنهيد .

***

المكرفونات .. الاوراق .. صحون السجائر .. كؤوس الماء .. بعد انتظار ، دخل المدير وتبعه مجموعة من بطانته وحاشيته الذين يلتفون حوله وينفذون مشاريعه الخاصة .. المدير يحمل وجها بلا ملامح ..

بعد فترة صمت اخرج من جيبه ورقة مطوية اخذ يقرأ منها : اسمحوا لى ايها السادة ان اشكركم على حضور هذا الاجتماع الذي سنتحدث فيه عن موضوع هام هو موضوع مباني المؤسسة ال .....

وبعد الديباجة .. والاسهاب الممل قال : (أرجو أن نخرج بتوصيات ومقررات تنفذ في الحال ، وانا واثق من أن النتيجة ستكون لصالح الجميع ، المهم أن نحدد العمل .. وان لا نختلف على الهدف) الاعضاء ينظر بعضهم الى بعض ..

والمدير يتكلم .. ويتكلم .. ويكرر ما يقول .. ومن خلف سحب الدخان التي ترسم علامات استفهام كان يبحث بين كل العيون عين عينيه ...

خشى عينيه الواثقتين اللتين تشعان بجو الجد .. في نهاية الاجتماع اردف المدير قائلا : كل شيء تمام ؟؟ وافقه الجميع ثم اقفلوا محضر الجلسة ..

164

فجأة احس بشعور حزين ثائر .. يتسلل اليه كالحلم .. ويتساقط داخله كالمخدر .. يتموج .. يثور .. يعلو .. يحترق .. يتمدد .. يطفو .. يغور .. حتى ليكاد يحس مذاقه الحارق يلسع لسانه كالجمر .. ويفجر في نفسه بركانا عاصفا .. هذا الشعور هو الذي دفعه الى ان يتخذ قراره ..

جار ملف الاجتماع بين الحاضرين ..

وصل اليه .. صرخ .. لن اوقع عليه .. اعطوه لأحد غيري .. كذابون .. لصوص .. وجوهكم محملة بالزيف .. واعماقكم قاحلة فارغة .. صرخ المدير فيه .. انت مجنون . سئمنا السكوت وآن لنا ان نقول كلمتنا ..

- اخرج يامجنون ..
- لأني لا اجيد التزييف .. والتزوير .. كما يجيده اخواني المجتمعون .. ضرب المدير بيده في عنف على مكتبه ثم كتب في ورقة امامه يحول الى مستشفى الامراض العقلية ..

اخذوا يصرخون ..

مجنون .. مجنون .. مجنون ..

تصلبت اصابع يده .. وتحجرت عيناه ..

انكفأ على وجهه . أجل .. أجل ....

ما لا يستطيع العقل ان يحله قد يحله الجنون .. كي نطلق الايمان .. ويصبح التعساء سعداء .. والسعداء تعساء .. حتى تعرف الحقيقة .. صوت المدير يتردد في أذنه كالغضب الاحمر .. رفع وجهه .. التفت .. تطلع الى كل شيء في المكان .. ثم صاح مكررا بأعلى صوته ..

طاردوا اللصوص .. اريد دمارهم .. المزيفون .. اغرسوا اصابع الاتهام في عيونهم بتكرار الكلام استطاعت ان تميز صوته .

بكت .. وبكت .. وبكت ..

شريط قديم قصير أخذ يدور على وجهها الراكد في جدران الذاكرة الشريط عمره ثلاث سنوات فقط . هو عمرها مع الرجل الاخر ..

تذكر .. وتذكر .. وتذكر ..

في خوف مكتوم همست في اذنه :

لقد أخرج الرجل الآخر صورتي من مخيلته واطلقني حره .. كان وجهها يقطر صفاء ومودة .. ورغم الايشارب والرداء الاسود تراءت له .. ودودة ، خضراء ، متألقة .. عيناها الوادعتان ترسمان له طريق الرجوع الاخير ..

اغمض عينيه على صمت الجراح .. وراح من جديد يحلم بعطر شعرها المبخر .. وبأبتسامتها المدهشة .. وبعذوبة اللحظات التي كانت تمنحها له من قبل بلا تحفظ ...

***

165

منى الشافعي ـ الكويت

اسطورة(59)

قالت صديقتي بدهشة واستغراب ...

- أحقاً يحبك .. ؟! غريبة أن يحب هذا الإنسان !!

- نعم يحبني !

- كيف ؟!!

- يقول .. إنني الوحيدة التي أبتسم .. وأن ابتسامتي سحرته .. وأنه تعلق بي .. فهل تصدقين ؟! هل حقاً أنا الوحيدة التي أبتسم ؟!!

نظرتْ إليّ صديقتي بغير النظرة وقالت ..

- أسطورة أنت !!

شاركتني أمي هذا الحوار الجاف المختزل فرددت ..

- تزوجيه يا ابنتي !! فالحب معدوم هذه الأيام .. وفرصة ثمينة حتى تحصلي على الـ ..... !!

وأنا ما زلت أسير على شطآن أرضي أمارس حبي للرمال فيحرقني التراب .. وتلسعني الأرض بسياط الرفض .. التي تلهبني عذاباً وتحرقني يأساً .. وأنا ما زلت أسير .. أحب التمرغ في ترابها المشتعل ظلماً وهي ما زالت ترفض بشدة خطواتي .. يؤلمني الرفض .. فأبكي !!

أمي تقول .. "تزوجيه .. حتى تحصلي على .." وصديقتي تقول .. "غريبة أن يحب هذا الإنسان" وأنا الوحيدة التي تبتسم في عالم الرفض .

***

ما زلت أسير .. الشاطىء طويل وصوت أمي يأتيني عبر فراغ الروح .. يخترق صداه أذني ..

- ابنة جارتي التي تصغرك بأعوام .. ستتزوج يوم الخميس ... الفرحة مرسومة على وجهها .. ألا تغارين منها ؟! تزوجيه يا ابنتي .. حتى تحصلي ....

ويخترق أذني حواري وجارتي ...

- هل تحبينه ؟ إنه لا يبتسم !

- له رائحة رجل !!

- فرحتك معتمة !!

وأنا ما زلت أسير على تراب أرضي التي ما زالت تلسعني .. فتحرق قدميَّ فتتورمان .. وتقول أمي "تزوجيه .. الحب معدوم .. "ويقول هو " أحب ابتسامتك وأعشق ضحكاتك وسط السكون "وتقول جارتي "له رائحة رجل .. "وأنا أسير على التراب .. وأرضي تلسعني .. بل تطردني تمارس الظلم على قدميَّ

---

59 إهداء إلى الصديقة الشاعرة سعدية مفرح .

الصغيرتين فأتمرد أنا وأقرر .. سأهرب من هنا .. من أرضي .. منه .. من أمي .. من صديقتي .. من جارتي التي تعيش عتمتها بداخلها لكنها لن ترفض فله رائحة رجل .. !!
وأنا أسير .. الشاطىء ممتد .. سألني ..

- أحقاً حبيبتي .. تنوين الرحيل ؟!!
- نعم !!
- وتموت الابتسامة في داخلي .. وتختفي ضحكاتك خلف السكون ؟
- أجل !!
- .. وسيقترب الموت أكثر من هنا .. وستزكمني الرائحة .. وأعيش غريباً في أرضي !!!

وطأطأ رأسه ينظر إلى أسفل .. إلى أرضه .. إلى ترابه .. وشممت رائحة التراب .. تأتيني من تحت عينيه وردد بصوت مختنق ...

- هل ستعودين يا حبيبتي ؟

بإصرار وعناد ...

- لن أعود !!

وهل أهون عليك ؟! حبيبتي أنا من دونك صمت وسكون !!

- كما هنت أنا على أرضي التي ترفضني ابنة .. لماذا ترفضني أرضي ؟!
- ولكنك ستصبحين زوجة لابن هذه الأرض !!

***

وما زلت أسير .. يأسرني الدرب .. أعشق تراب الأرض التي ترفضني .. تقول أمي " تزوجيه حتى تحصلي على .. ؟ " ويقول هو " ستصبحين زوجة لابن هذه الأرض .. " وتقول جارتي " له رائحة رجل " وتقول صديقتي " أسطورة أنت .. "
... وأضحك أنا وأقول " تعبت من الالتصاق دوماً بغيري ! أنا كيان .. يجب أن أمارس حقي من خلال ذاتي المملوءة بعلامات التعجب والسؤال !؟! .. متى يحق لي أن أنتمي لنفسي .. متى ستسبقني الأنا .. !؟! متى ستهبني هذه الأرض السر لذاتي بلا وسيط ؟! ما زالت تلسعني .. فأتعذب .. واحترق كشمعة .. ما زالت تتجاهلني .. فأبتسم كستار ..
الوحيدة أنا التي تبتسم في عتمة الأيام !!
ما زلت أسير .. والشاطىء يمتد أكثر .. وصوت الأمواج يرتطم تحت قدميَّ العاريتين احتراقاً ... تدغدغني موجة .. فأبتسم .. وتلسعني أرضي فأنتبه .. وما زلت أسير .. وحيدة .. غريبة .. يطويني الطريق ويطويني الزمن ويرفضني المكان .. لماذا ترفضني أرضي ؟! وأمي تقول " تزوجيه .. " وجارتي تقول " له رائحة رجل " وهو يقول " ستكونين زوجة لابن هذه الأرض .. " وصديقتي تقول " أسطورة أنت .. " .
وما زلت أسير .. وما زال التراب يلسعني حرارة ومرارة ... وما زالت الأرض ترفضني ... لماذا ترفضني أرضي ؟!!!

وليد الرجيب – الكويت

نجوم أقل .. نجوم أكثر

(مشهد أول)

غرفة الرئاسة – الأركان العامة :

تحية عسكرية من نجوم قليلة .

مثلها (بحماس أقل) من نجوم أكثر .

نجوم أكثر : نعم .. (تصحبها ابتسامة) .

نجوم أكثر أقل خطوة منتظمة . يمد يده . ورقة .

نجوم أكثر (بعدما فرغ من قراءتها) : أهذا كل شيء ؟

نجوم أقل : نعم سيدي .

نجوم أكثر : منذ متى تعرفان بعضكما ؟

نجوم أقل : منذ الطفولة يا سيدي .

نجوم أكثر : ومخطوبان ؟

نجوم أقل : (سعادة) منذ سنتين يا سيدي .

نجوم أكثر : همم .. ثم يستطرد وهو يقلب الورقة :

هل كتبت ميولها الثقافية ؟

نجوم أقل : نعم يا سيدي .

نجوم أكثر : و ماذا عن صديقاتها ؟

نجوم أقل : (بإستفهام) نعم سيدي ؟!

نجوم أكثر : (يسند ظهره على كرسيه قبل أن يقول) :

أقصد .. هل لديها الكثير من الصديقات ؟

نجوم أقل : (براحة) لا يا سيدي .. هي تحب الوحدة .

نجوم أكثر : (يضغط مفتاح الجرس خلف ظهره وهو يقول) : هل كتبت أسماء جميع أقاربها ؟

نجوم أقل : نعم سيدي .

الفرّاش يدخل ويقدم الشاي للنجوم الكثيرة .

نجوم أكثر : هل تربطك بها صلة قرابة ؟

نجوم أقل : لا يا سيدي .

نجوم أكثر : (وعيناه على الورقة) أظنك تحبها كثيراً .

نجوم أقل : (يبتسم) نعم يا سيدي .

نجوم أكثر : (يبتسم ابتسامة ود ثم يتناول الشاي) حسناً .. بعد شهر نكون قد أعددنا الأمر بإذن الله ..

تحية عسكرية من نجوم أقل .

مثلها (بحماس أقل) من نجوم أكثر .

***

(مشهد ثان)

منزل الخطيبة :

هي والنجوم الأقل يجلسان في منزلها .. انفرجت شفتاها بابتسامة وهي تقول :

هل تعتقد أنهم سيمنحونك التصريح بالزواج ؟

نجوم أقل : طبعاً .. ماذا يمنع عن ذلك ؟

هي (تمسك بيده) :ونعيش معا ؟

نجوم أقل : نعم (بدون سيدي) .

هي (بتساؤل) : إذن لماذا كل هذه الأسئلة ؟

نجوم أقل : (ينظر في عينيها) : ليتأكد أننا نناسب بعضنا .

هي : ...

نجوم أقل يعبث بخصلات شعرها . وبصوت خافت : سألني إذا كنت أحبك .

هي (خافضة عينيها) : لا بد أنه رجل طيب .

نجوم أقل (يقطب جبينه) : ولكن لماذا سألني عن صديقاتك ؟!

هي : لا أدري .. ربما أراد التأكد من سلامة علاقاتي .

نجوم أقل (يمسك بيديها ثم يقول بجدية) : أريد أن اسألك سؤالاً .

هي : ماذا ؟

نجوم أقل : هل .. تحبين الحكومة ؟

خفضت رأسها قبل أن تقول : لا أكرهها .

نجوم أقل (برجاء ملح) : هل تحبينها ؟

هي : ما دمت لا أكرهها .. إذن أنا أحبها .

نجوم أقل : وتعملين لصالح الوطن ؟

هي (باستغراب) : بالطبع .. ولكن لماذا ؟!

نجوم أقل : (مستبشراً) : إذن تأكدي أننا سنتزوج بعد شهر .

هي (بفرحة وأمل) : "يا ليت"..

هي والنجوم الأقل يضمان بعضهما

**

(مشهد ثالث)

بعد شهر في غرفة الرئاسة :

تحية عسكرية من نجوم أقل .

مثلها (بحماس أقل) من نجوم أكثر .

نجوم اكثر ينهض من وراء مكتبه . يشعل غليونه قبل أن يقول : أنت ضابط مخلص ونشيط .

نجوم أقل (مع ابتسامة صغيرة) : شكراً يا سيدي .

نجوم أكثر (نافثاً دخانه) : هل تحب عملك ؟

نجوم أقل : نعم سيدي .

نجوم أكثر يذرع الغرفة وإحدى يديه خلف ظهره ، يقول وهو يشير بغليونه :

أنت مستعد أن تضحي بكل شيء من أجل وطنك كما أقسمت يوم تخرجك .

نجوم أقل : بكل تأكيد يا سيدي .

نجوم أكثر يقف . يضع الغليون في فمه :

إذن .. حاول أن تتمالك نفسك وأنت تسمع هذا الخبر .

نجوم أقل : يرخي من وضعه ويشير بيده :

تقصد ...

نجوم أكثر (يقاطعه بحدة) : إنتباه يا حضرة الضابط .

ثم يستطرد بعد ثوانٍ بلهجة مختلفة :

بعد البحث .. اكتشفنا أن أبا الفتاة التي ترغب بالزواج منها كان ضد الحكومة .

نجوم أقل (بدهشة) : لم أفهم يا سيدي !

نجوم أكثر يجلس خلف مكتبه :

عرفنا أن أباها كان أحد زعماء المعارضة .

نجوم أقل يفغر فاه دهشة ويتطلع الى وجه النجوم الأكثر بتوقع مؤلم .

نجوم أكثر : ولا أظنك تجهل المصير الذي انتهى اليه ذلك الأب .

(لحظات صمت) .

نجوم أكثر : وأنت تعلم أن سلامة الوطن والحفاظ عليه فوق رغباتنا .

نجوم أقل يقف بانتباه .

نجوم أكثر يبحث بين الأوراق . يمد ورقة للنجوم الأقل :

جاء الأمر بعدم الموافقة على زواجك منها .

نجوم أقل يقف بانتباه .

نجوم أكثر : على العموم عليك أن تختار بين البزة العسكرية .. وبينها .

ثم ينهض ويجمع الورق وهو يقول :

عفواً .. لدي اجتماع بالوزارة بعد نصف ساعة ..

تحية عسكرية من النجوم الأقل .

مثلها (بحماس أقل) من نجوم أكثر .

آذار 1976 م

المحتويات

174

www.ingramcontent.com/pod-product-compliance
Lightning Source LLC
Chambersburg PA
CBHW071521100726
47908CB00004B/1243